CODENAME: GHOUL

OPERATION JUDAS BOOK 1

MAVIS KEMO

DIMENSIONAL WALKERS PUBLISHING

CODENAME: GHOUL

OPERATION JUDAS BOOK 1

Book Cover Art by Anonymous Artist

Book Cover design by LazyHunnyBee

Illustrations, and Back Cover Art by Diana Mooney

Header Art by S. Huntley

Editors: Torrie Harjes and Karlee Renkoski

Formatting: Refine and Format

First edition 2025

Published by Dimensional Walkers Publishing LLC

Paperback ISBN: 978-1-969199-00-4

Ebook ISBN: 978-1-969199-01-1

*This book is dedicated to the good people
of the Masktok and Call of Duty cosplayer communities.*

*Without the inspiration from your Taco Tuesdays, Thirsty Thursdays,
and Feral Fridays*

(How could I forget the Thirst Traps?), this story would not be what it is.

THANK YOU!

*Lastly, to my biggest supporter and my own personal masked man, Kemo.
This book is for you baby.*

To My Readers

Diversity Statement

This book series is inspired by our diverse world. These characters are robust and dynamic, each with their own struggles and trauma they must overcome. They are born from a variety of unique and queer backgrounds. Each character, regardless of where they come from, has an important role to play. I desired to create a story based on the world I see around me.

I hope you enjoy reading *Codename Ghoul*. Buckle up!

Trigger Warning

This story is a dark military thriller romance and contains adult content. Out of respect to you, the trigger warnings cover both book one and book two because, together, they make up one story.
Some of these trigger warnings do not appear in book one and are specific to book two. I want you to be fully aware of what the story contains before you read.

A detailed list of triggers is on the next page.

Trigger Warnings

Open-door love scenes, including masturbation and sexting, (on page, and past). Mentions of cheating.

Brief captivity and restraints, attempted rape, sexual assault. Verbal sexual threats against a minor (past). Mentions of a man with an underage girl.

Past and present abuse. Child abuse and abandonment (past). Domestic violence (past and brief scene on page). Toxic parental relationships.

Moments of PTSD. Eating disorders. Attempted suicide (on page).

Drug and alcohol usage (past and on page). Parents who are drug and alcohol addicts (past).

Violence, death, and torture. Gangs, a drug cartel, and mentions of human trafficking.

Adult language.

Chapter One
Swiss Cheese is Nasty

Yasmine sits uncomfortably with a splitting headache and her muscles screaming in pain. She has no memory of how she got here. Wherever here is? All she sees around her is a filthy room, long abandoned, with refuse and shards of broken mirrors littering the concrete flooring. Her eyes land on an old stained ballerina slipper and a pair of tattered tights.

The only light source is the sun coming through the skylight overhead. The dusty clock on the wall in front of her is frozen in time, and she finds the likeness between the clock and herself disconcerting. She doesn't know how long she's been handcuffed to the pipe protruding from the wall behind her.

The last thing she remembers is Marshall walking her home to her apartment a few blocks from the university. She had finished her classes for the day and needed to get home to work on her final research paper before winter break. Which is why, when he had asked if she wanted to stop for coffee, she declined. Then there is nothing. Her memory turns black.

Once more, Yasmine takes in her surroundings, hoping to glean something useful, but the graffiti and mysterious stains on the walls keep their secrets. The only information she can extract is the kidnapper is holding her in some kind of storage room. She lays her head against the wall and closes her eyes, running through her memories again to try to put the puzzle pieces together. She has nothing better to do, and this distracts her momentarily from the physical discomfort.

The one missing piece to the puzzle is she doesn't know why her father assigned her a bodyguard in the first place — a lot of good it did. Obviously, he knew she was in danger and suspected she'd be abducted if he sent Marshall to protect her. But the least that narcissistic asshole could have done is warn her!

She curses herself at the same time for not pressing her father about it, like a normal person would, and questioning why she needed a bodyguard. All she got from her father was a text a week ago stating she'd have a security detail until further notice, and she learned a long time ago you don't question General Charles Pennington's authority. Period.

When she had opened her door to leave for class the next morning, Marshall was leaning against the railing, waiting for her with a cup of coffee and a charming smile. At first, Yasmine only offered a cold shoulder, but Marshall's easygoing personality quickly made her warm up to him. She found herself liking the guy by the time he had walked her home that evening.

The days Yasmine worked as a substitute teacher, Marshall drove her, dropping her off before school and picking her up afterward. When she had classes, he stayed close like a shadow. She didn't know where he went after he returned her home, and she didn't ask.

There was no physical attraction to him at first, but after a few days together, her feelings toward him began to shift. It felt like there was a spark between them and he possibly could be into her. But her father was paying him, and Marshall would leave once her father called him off.

Refocusing her thoughts to her current predicament, Yasmine shifts her weight, trying to ease some of the physical strain, and fails. There is no relief. The handcuffs make a metal-on-metal sound when she tries to take the pressure off her bruised wrists. She shivers from the cold concrete underneath her, which feels like a block of ice, prompting her to pull her legs closer to her chest to conserve what little warmth she has.

Her grey woolen peacoat does nothing to protect her from the chill setting in.

Not wanting to dwell on her situation, her thoughts return to Marshall. She hopes he's okay. She knows it's an unhealthy coping mechanism to put others before her, but knowing it doesn't stop the automatic defense from firing. A sharp pain runs through her hip, interrupting her thoughts. It radiates down the leg and into her back, and she tries once more to find the smallest amount of relief.

With nothing but time on her hands, she starts checking off more things she knows. She's been kidnapped, and she's being worn down physically and mentally. Which is probably what the kidnapper wants when he comes in with his threats and grabby.

She pulls against the pipe she's handcuffed to, testing it once more for a weakness, but there is none. Her gaze takes in the room again, but she gives up. It's not like she can escape or defend herself while handcuffed. Hopelessness smothers her until it's hard to breathe.

The French asshole can try and break me, but if HE hasn't broken my mind in twenty-eight years, then this French asshat won't be able to either. If only I could get my hands free, I'd go full Rambo on him with that shard of mirror and kick him in the balls. She gives herself a little mental pep talk, but she's not fooling anyone. She's pathetic. And weak.

The drug he pumped her with still runs in her system and, mixed with the stress she's under, her body wants to shut down and sleep. Maybe it can temporarily take her away from this real-life nightmare she can't escape. Just before Yasmine loses consciousness, the last thought running through her mind is that for once in her life, she's going to be a smartass and talk back. She's already in trouble, so how's it gonna get any worse? If she's going to die, she's not staying silent.

"Keep looking at me with those defiant eyes of yours," the kidnapper hisses, sinking his grip deeper into her cheeks and painfully forcing their faces together. "The next time I come in here, I will have no other choice than to break you, Ms. Pennington."

During the first encounter with him, she learned to hold her breath against his Swiss cheese and stale cigarette exhale. She had almost gagged when he shoved his face into hers.

Some would consider him handsome with his European physique, strong jawline, and French accent. But the guy is a predator, and everything about him is foul. His pale green eyes are dead like the cold steel blue eyes she grew up with. The menacing smile on his face sends a shiver of fear coursing through her body, triggering that sixth sense of warning women get when they know a man is dangerous.

He leans distressingly close to her, inhaling her scent. Her skin prickles, but she can't recoil. The handcuffs and pipe hold her in place. Even though she's wearing clothing, she might as well be naked with how vulnerable he makes her feel. Yasmine's eyes close — the only means she has of distancing herself. Her plan to talk back is forgotten.

He pulls away with a sinister sneer on his lips. Seeing her trembling makes his dick strain against his pants. She's not weak enough yet for him, but soon she will be and then he'll take her.

He releases his hold by shoving her hard into the wall. Yasmine sees a flash of light across her vision, and a new throbbing pain is in the back of her skull. She feels the welt forming with each throb. Her entire being is in pain, and she swallows the cry that's desperate to escape, refusing to give this asshole the satisfaction.

As he turns at the door, his eyes creepily devour her, envisioning how he'll take her body during his next visit. He licks his lips, looking her over once more before leaving. He closes the door behind him but doesn't bother locking her in. She's not escaping.

His footsteps fade in the distance, and Yasmine lets out the breath she was holding before silently cursing herself for not showing any real defiance. In the stillness of the room, she breathes through the pain in her head and tries to calm the festering fear. She wishes she could be like the strong female characters from the books she reads. But real life is different than fiction. Fear is a natural reaction, and it keeps most humans alive because they can't override the lizard part of their brain.

And right now, the lizard part of her brain is making it hard to keep breathing.

The nausea festering in her core makes her stomach clench. She turns, daring to gaze at her reflection in the half-broken mirror leaning against the far wall. Since regaining consciousness, she's ignored her reflection, afraid of what she'll see.

A ghost of herself is staring back at her. Her normally bright hazel eyes are glazed over and red. The dark circles make her look like a raccoon. Her brown hair is tangled and matted where it sticks out of her braid. Her naturally tan complexion has a zombie-like shade of green to it, and her face is etched with worry lines. Just a few visits from the asshole and his threats have made her look older than she is.

Everything about her screams weak and pathetic. Just what the asshole wants.

No matter how much she's been telling herself how strong-willed and strong-minded she is, she's not. She's been weak her entire life — never speaking her mind or having the courage to stand up for herself — because *he* made sure of that. And now Yasmine is painfully aware she's a woman who's going to get assaulted in the worst possible way. So she shuts down, succumbing to the emotional numbness like she always does.

She tries to find a comfortable position again, but every time she moves, the pain worsens. Stray tears escape, and she quickly buries her face into the space where her aching shoulder and sleeping arm meet to muffle the sob.

No one is coming to save her. That thought alone renews the terror clawing at her chest.

The light streaming in above takes on a rust orange hue as the sun begins to make its descent over the horizon. The door bursts open in a flurry, startling Yasmine awake. She blinks to clear the fog from her vision, and once it's gone, she sees Frenchie sauntering toward her. He's leering like she's nothing more than a piece of meat to be consumed, and to him, she is.

She forces herself to yawn at the same time she chokes on her apprehension. She can see it on his face. He's here for her and his own selfish gratification. If she's going to be assaulted, she's going to be defiant, not just with her eyes but her words too.

"These accommodations are five-star." She keeps her tone unimpressed and laden with heavy sarcasm. "Are you here to take my order for room service? I'll have a cheeseburger, extra pickles, hold the tomatoes, and a side of fries."

Frenchie's sneer turns into a smooth grin as he unbuckles his expensive leather belt, which is out of place with the rest of his attire of unkempt faded jeans, a sweat-stained white T-shirt, and a dark blue hoodie. He holds her gaze while he opens his fly.

Her mind goes blank, and her fight, flight, freeze, or fawn response surges, paralyzing her. She expected this, but it doesn't make it any less terrifying. This guy's been planning to use her for his own sick pleasure, even copping a feel on one of his previous visits.

His eyes rove over her body as he pulls himself free of his pants. He's already hard, but he strokes himself while walking slowly toward her for further intimidation. He stops in front of her.

Yasmine turns away, but he lashes out, slamming her head against the wall. She can't stifle the yelp because her head hits the same spot as the last time, causing stars to explode across her vision. When she can refocus, his nasty dick is inches from her face. He pins her head back and rubs the tip over her lips, and she reflexively clamps them shut. Using his thumb, he pries them apart, forcing her mouth open.

"I was told not to touch you but you have such a disrespectful mouth on you. I will show you what happens when you speak that way to me." One hand pins her forehead to the wall, his other pries her jaw open. He leans in close to her ear; his hot, cigarette-cheese breath makes her body shake. "Do not blame me for this. You brought this on yourself."

Her legs are numb from the cold, and her muscles refuse to work, so she can't even try to kick him. And biting his dick off isn't possible with his hand clamped onto her chin to force her mouth open.

"Is that what you tell your mommy?" Her words are distorted but he understands her.

He releases her only to backhand across the face.

The blow does more than just sting. It sends her back to all the times her father hit her. She learned to slip away from those unpleasant experiences by allowing her mind to drift free of her body, and this is the first time she's thankful for that protective ability. Is it healthy? No. But if she goes to the place in her mind where no one can harm her, it doesn't matter what happens to her body because her mind will be safe.

Yasmine finds herself at a cabin covered with moss and vines. The tall aspen and oak grove around it provides shelter and safety. The beautifully overgrown herb garden she so carefully nurtured has all kinds of flying insects; many of them buzz around as they move from flower to flower. A small brook bubbles next to the front porch, where she lazily lies in a hammock nestled between the support beams. Her favorite romance author's new book is in hand. A bowl of homemade kettle corn drizzled in dark chocolate rests at her side. The tumbler covered in dragons, which she paid way too much for, is tucked against her other side. The raspberry iced tea inside is perfect for the warm day.

Here, in this serene place she created long ago, nothing can touch her. She's peacefully detached from anything unpleasant. Yasmine settles herself deeper within her mind because, with everything she's survived, she'll survive this.

The tiny stream loses its trickling sound and becomes gasps of choking gurgles. That's not how her peaceful brook sounds ... And something is tugging on her arms. The pain in her shoulder breaks through into her safe place as something or, rather, someone is invading, forcing her mind back into her body.

Her eyes snap open as she comes back to the horrors of reality. But she doesn't expect to see the man who was about to rape her lying on the floor and bleeding out from his throat. His head is bent at a grotesque angle where it pulls away from the neck. She stares at him, blinking in confusion until the gurgling stops and his body stills. With great effort, she scoots her legs away from the pool of blood spreading toward her.

It takes a moment to comprehend what's happening. She doesn't understand how Frenchie is dead on the floor. The clanking sounds of handcuffs bring her attention back to the rest of her body, and she realizes her arms are free. Sharp pain radiates from her shoulders now that the muscles can finally move into a different position. She can't hold back the groan of pain.

Her gaze shifts to something large and black blocking her view. Hands in black fingerless gloves wrap around her wrist with the handcuff still attached to it, freeing her from the restraint.

"Come on," a low, deep male voice says. He holds his hand out to her.

She remains frozen, keeping her butt planted firmly on the concrete, and she also doesn't take the offered hand because all she sees is the fresh blood on the outstretched fingers. She stares at it in horror. The hand quickly wipes the blood on a pant leg and is back in front of her.

"Get up," the man barks.

Blinking, she gazes up, searching for a face, but there isn't one. Only a black mask with a skeletal jawline. The white of the skull is faded and frayed with stains; the newest one is Frenchie's blood splatter when this mystery man sliced open his throat. Yasmine recoils, but there's no place for her to go.

The masked figure squats, bringing his dark gaze level with hers.

"I'm not going to hurt you, but get your ass moving." His tone is commanding.

He pulls his hood up, casting his limited features into further shadow and making his presence more intimidating. He claims he's not going to hurt her, but the wicked-looking knife handle sheathed into the tactical vest under his coat says otherwise.

So much has happened in the span of a few moments Yasmine is struggling to catch up, and she's still dazed from the backhand to the face. She was about to be raped, and now she's being saved?

"If you don't move, then I'll pick you up and carry you out. Your choice. Move your ass, or I will move it for you." His tone becomes more urgent, but there's something else she can't quite place ... Concern maybe?

The light is fading, and the only visible feature is his eyes since the rest of his face is hidden under the mask. He looks like that one guy in the popular video game, Call of ... something. She knows a guy like this will make good on his threat, so she nods in agreement. As fast as her protesting muscles can allow, she takes his hand.

Once he has her hand grasped in his own, he helps her stand.

"Take it slow," he tells her, pulling her up.

She whimpers the whole way to her feet, and he doesn't release his hold. Rather, he hooks his arm around hers for support. She tests her legs to make sure they can carry her. The moment she puts weight on one of them, a sharp pain runs from her hip to her knee, causing it to buckle. If he wasn't there supporting her, she'd fall straight back on her ass to the concrete. His body heat soaks into her, making her want to curl up into his side.

"Move slowly and shake it out. Try bearing your weight again." He instructs, and she listens.

It still hurts, but the pain begins to ease as her stiff muscles start to wake up. She's going to be sore for a long time after this ... if she doesn't end up dead.

"Take a few steps." He keeps hold of her.

Yasmine moves tentatively with his assistance. She chances a glance at him as he hovers over her like a concerned parent watching their child walk for the first time. She hopes to get a glimpse of who this guy is, but he's like a mysterious shadow. He's wearing a black coat, which resembles a thickly lined hoodie, and black cargo pants with combat boots. Her eyes dart quickly to the knife once more like it's about to jump from his vest to attack her.

When she's steady on her feet, the masked man grabs her hand in his, pulling her behind. He leads her out of the back room and down a narrow hallway. Her legs move awkwardly as feeling comes back to them. From her right hip down to her toes, the icy sting of needles is prickling as blood circulation returns. She grits her teeth against the painful sensation because this guy doesn't seem like the type who would allow her to stop and let it pass.

They reach the main room, which is an abandoned dance studio. It's just as messy, filthy, and covered in gang graffiti as the storage area. With the last remaining bits of twilight casting shadows from the skylights, her eyes land on another corpse lying on the floor next to a toppled metal folding chair. The man's throat is slit open, and he's lying in a pool of stagnant blood.

She gasps when she recognizes the cheap grey suit and blond hair. The once handsome "boy next door" face that smiled at her so easily every morning is now devoid of life. She digs her heels in, trying to rip her hand free of the stranger's grasp, but his only response is to hold on tighter. She's staring at the vacant blue eyes of Marshall.

"Oh my god. You killed him!" She yells her accusation, still trying to pull herself free of his hold, but he has a death grip on her.

Alarm bells sound in her head, and she tries more forcefully to jerk away. Her plan is to make a run for it. It's one thing to kill the would-be rapist, but this was Marshall. He was her bodyguard, and this masked asshat killed him!

The man's eyes flare, and he jerks her hard toward him, not letting her go until both of his hands are roughly holding each side of her face. He understands her shock, but there is no time to go into a detailed explanation.

"Yasmine," he barks, getting her attention. "He was in on the kidnapping and was never there to protect you."

His words hit her like a punch to the gut. She stops struggling and turns her gaze to Marshall's body. He was? How could she not have seen it? She was even starting to have feelings for him! If this is true, he was going to let her be assaulted.

Suddenly, the stranger flings her over his shoulder, fireman-style, like she weighs nothing. Yasmine tries to struggle free, but his grip is too strong, and she's too exhausted to put up any kind of real fight. Her eyes are locked on her supposed bodyguard as the masked man carries her from the building through a side door and out into the cold night.

Taking the stranger at his word because of his authoritative demeanor, Yasmine directs her anger at herself for not suspecting Marshall. Then it dawns on her ... how does this guy know her name?

Her head hurts from the swirling thoughts. She spent so much time with Marshall, and he was working with the kidnappers? How? Why? Did her father know? Did he make a mistake when he vetted Marshall? She runs through countless questions, but no answers come. She's trying to make sense of everything that's happening but then is jostled when the man breaks into a jog despite her added weight, which interrupts her confused thoughts. He takes her to a white van parked on the side of the building away from any prying eyes on the street.

He squats and slides her off his shoulder, setting her gently on her feet.

She doesn't know why, but something tells her to trust the masked stranger, which is why, when he opens the door and shoves her inside the van, she doesn't put up any resistance.

Running around to the driver's seat, he pulls out a set of keys from his pockets. There's blood on them — Marshall's. He made sure to take the keys after he sliced his throat.

The engine roars to life; at the same time, the masked man buckles himself in.

"Seat belt," he commands, adjusting the mirrors.

She complies as he pulls out onto the darkened street into traffic. Yasmine breathes a sigh of relief that she's leaving the horrors of the dance studio behind her. She also realizes, for the first time in her life, she's been saved. Even though it does feel like she's being kidnapped again.

At least, this time, she's awake for it.

Chapter Two
Cardboard, It's Delicious

Yasmine leans her head on the van window and pulls her peacoat tightly around her. She can't tell if she's shivering from the cold or if her body is responding to the trauma of her kidnapping and attempting to purge itself of the built-up adrenaline.

She's pretty sure this is the same vehicle that was used to take her hostage because it's giving off kidnapper vibes. The lessons in "stranger danger" when she was younger come to mind, but a lot of good it did when it was her own damned bodyguard who abducted her. Even so, she can't help eyeing the glovebox and wondering if there's candy in it to lure little kids?

Glancing at the dark figure behind the wheel, Yasmine doubts he's the type to drive a van. This can't be his. She resumes staring vacantly out the window, watching the city lights and cars blur across her vision.

She's cold and thirsty. Her throat feels like she ate a bowl of sawdust. She wants nothing more than a hot shower to rid herself of Frenchie's lingering touch, some food, and sleep — in that exact order. But only after she gets some water and warms up. She has questions, but they are fleeting. Part of her mind is running behind the van, trying to catch up. The questions will come, but for now, she's too exhausted to ask them.

They ride in silence, and he keeps his eyes focused on the road. Only he knows where they're going, and soon, they leave the city lights behind. She sees the town names on the road signs, but the letters are an undecipherable blur.

He catches movement out of the corner of his eye when she pulls her coat tighter around her again. She's pressing herself into the door to stay as far away from him as she can without exiting the vehicle. He can't do anything to bring her relief except turn up the heat and adjust the vents to blow on her.

She's refusing to look at him, and he can't blame her. Every so often, she wipes tears from her cheek. She was kidnapped, almost raped, and now she's in a van with a stranger covered in blood, the same man who killed in front of her without batting an eye. He's not going to push her.

After an hour, he pulls off the highway and takes a two-lane back road. The warmth from the heater and the rhythmic sound of the road are lulling Yasmine's exhausted body to sleep. She should stay awake because she doesn't know who this guy is, but she can't fight it. She's tired of struggling and surrenders to the exhaustion. Maybe when she wakes up, she'll find this was all just some terrible "end of the semester, finals are approaching, stress-induced" nightmare. She'll wake up passed out on one of her textbooks and have to wipe the drool from her mouth.

He watches from the corner of his eye and catches the moment her body slumps against the door. Within seconds, her breathing deepens, and then she's softly snoring. He can do something to reassure her she's safe with him soon, but his priority is to dump the van.

His eyes keep shifting between the road and her. Even in her tousled state, she's more beautiful up close than he realized. He forces his eyes back on the empty two-lane road. His gloved fingers are gripping the steering wheel tightly, and he takes some deep breaths.

He wasn't supposed to engage. His orders were to observe from a distance and report in when she was taken. This is the first time he's blatantly disobeyed orders, but he couldn't stand by and let her get raped. He'll gladly accept the punishment awaiting him if it means he protected her.

She startles awake when her door opens. If it weren't for the seat belt holding her in place, she would have crashed to the ground.

"We're switching vehicles," he tells her while holding the door open and waiting for her to get out.

She's groggy from her brief nap, so she doesn't move right away. He reaches around her and hits the seat belt latch, freeing her from it. She catches a whiff of sweat and the masculine scent of deodorant, with a hint of a metallic tang from the blood, and her nose crinkles.

She slowly starts untangling herself from the seat belt. If she moves too quickly, her muscles and joints scream in protest. She casts a quick, worried expression at him, but instead of impatience or the condemnation she expects, he looks at her with concern when she grimaces. Connecting with the ground causes another grunt of pain to escape from the back of her throat.

"I imagine you're sore," he comments, stating the obvious. He's not sure what to say, but this silence is making him restless.

"How do you know my name?" Her voice box is barely able to produce the words because of the sawdust coating her mouth and throat.

"Huh?"

"When I saw Marshall dead, you called me by name. How do you know me?" Her tone is demanding, and her eyes narrow on him, expecting an answer.

He sighs, trying to focus on anything other than her. The only thing around is the dark forest where he hid his personal vehicle away from prying eyes.

Shit. She's observant. He doesn't want to make up a lie and then have to remember what he told her. He opts for partial truth because it's how he prefers to operate.

"I've been keeping an eye on you." He keeps his answer simple and direct.

He starts walking to his older 4Runner once he's sure she can move on her own. When he doesn't hear footfalls following behind him, he stops and glances back at where she remains rooted in place.

"What?" he demands. He suspects she's about to bombard him with questions or freak out and hurl accusations. Depending on the questions, he may not answer.

"You stalking me?" The look she gives him is unreadable.

He lets out a huffing chuckle and turns his back to her again before pulling his keys from a pocket of his cargo pants. He's dismayed at her challenging the image he's built of her in his mind since he became her shadow. Her behavior and comments are not what he expects, and she's even harder to predict in person.

"No. I'm not stalking you." He unlocks the 4Runner and then motions with a jerk of his head. "Come on. We need to keep moving."

The urgency from before, when he saved her, has turned down a notch with the increased distance from the dance studio, but he doesn't know if the van has GPS tracking or not. He highly doubts it, but he's not going to chance it.

He moves to the back of his vehicle, opens the rear door and grabs a stack of protein bars and bottles of water from his emergency supplies. She hasn't had anything to eat or drink all day, so he figures she's dehydrated and famished.

Watching his movements closely, Yasmine notices that something about his presence and how he carries himself screams military because he moves with purpose and confidence. She's been around enough service members to recognize them. It also explains how he knows her name.

Does he have ties to her father? Did her father send him? Unlikely. That doesn't feel right. Her father doesn't care, but then why did he send a bodyguard? Nothing about this makes any sense. Then the next question prodding her mind is, why would the military send someone to watch her?

"Did my father send you?" She's still not moving from her spot next to the van.

Something is going on with her father, and the military must know about it if they sent someone to follow her. She's the innocent bystander caught in the middle of a dangerous game she doesn't know how to play. Nor did anyone ask if she wanted to play.

He doesn't answer.

She closes the van door, coming to a decision because, so far, he's yet to do anything to harm her. Not that she trusts him, but she'd rather take her chances with him than Frenchie any day.

"You don't seem like the stalker type." Yasmine walks to the passenger side of the 4Runner and sorely climbs in. She belts herself in as he walks up, and she flashes him a tired grimace.

"Then again, you could be a serial killer leading me to some abandoned summer camp in the woods." She takes the offered bottle of water. "If you're going to chase me through the woods in that scary mask of yours, you need to know you won't get much fun out of it. I don't like running. So, just save us both some time and kill me now."

She uses humor to deflect her fear and hides behind it; it's how she keeps herself sane. She flicks the cap off the water bottle and downs a third of it in one go.

He stares at her, dumbfounded. "Man, you really do have a mouth on you."

When he jumps into the driver's seat, he throws two protein bars onto her lap, shakes his head, and shuts the door.

"You need to eat." He motions to the bars with a nod.

She picks up the bar, eyeing it suspiciously, while he starts the engine. He smoothly shifts the vehicle into first gear, pulling out of the hiding spot and heading back the way they came.

She opens the wrapper and takes a bite. Her stomach begins convulsing at the taste of food on her tongue; it threatens to puke up the water she just drank, which happens often when her anxiety and nerves are like this. The next bite she takes is much smaller. She's starving and, at the same time, doesn't want to eat, but she forces herself to slowly finish the bar.

The man steers with his knee as he grasps one of the water bottles and lifts the bottom of his mask to take a drink.

"Where *are* you taking me?" Yasmine finally asks after downing the rest of her water. Life is slowly returning to her.

"An abandoned summer camp. I thought I'd chase you through the woods with a knife." His tone is deadpan.

"How unoriginal." She opens the second bottle of water and takes another big gulp. Her headache is slowly receding. "So, you're a stalker and serial killer. Got it." She matches his expressionless response.

He glances sideways, not understanding how she can be so nonchalant with him when she went through something so terrifying. He notes her pulling the sides of her coat around her again, prompting him to turn the heat up in the 4Runner and adjust the vents toward her shaking body, even though he's roasting.

Using his knee to keep the vehicle straight, he unbuckles and tears his coat off, throwing it in the back seat. He thought about giving it to her, but it smells of sweat and blood. Next, he unzips the combat vest under the coat and tosses it in the back.

When both hands are back on the wheel and he's buckled in, he continues casting quick glances at her. He's pleased to see the color is returning to her cheeks.

"You should be terrified right now, and you're cracking jokes." He can't help but comment.

"What can I say? I think the last of my fucks died with Marshall." She shrugs and then sighs. "God, I'm stupid. I never suspected him. I can't believe I thought he was a good guy." She makes a spitting sound in disgust, running a shaking hand over her face before turning to face him. "I have a theory. I think you're military, or at least were military."

Her comment startles him, and, once again, his assessment of her is confirmed: she's too damned smart.

When he remains silent, neither confirming nor denying her assumption, she goes back to resting her head on the window. The cold from outside seeps through the glass and cools her forehead, which helps ease the headache but also makes her shiver.

"Don't blame yourself for not suspecting your bodyguard. You were under the impression he was there to protect you and not be part of it," he says after a few moments.

"I still don't even know why I needed a bodyguard in the first place. It's not like my father cares about my well-being. Something's going on, and that bastard knows about it," she scoffs, more to herself than to him.

He's taken aback at the blunt comment about her father. He wants to probe her more with questions, but he keeps his mouth shut. She's been through enough already, and he has time to question her later.

"Are you kidnapping me?" she blurts, her eyes still closed.

"No," he responds without hesitation.

She should be terrified and suspicious as well as trying to think of how to get away from this guy. Instead, his short response makes her relax. For now, she accepts his answer and gives him a small level of trust. He did save her after all.

Chapter Three
Summer Camp or A Creepy Cabin?

The masked man's next priority, after dumping the van, is to get Yasmine somewhere safe. That part of the plan is in progress. Next, he needs to report in, wait for his orders, and then get an ass reaming because he fucked up.

He nearly choked on nothing when she guessed his military background. He realized too late, with a career officer for a father, she must have spent a lot of time around members of the armed forces and could easily identify them.

His thoughts return to the moment he freed her. He expected her to put up more of a fight or try to run away. Even when he picked her up and threw her over his shoulder after seeing her dead bodyguard, she accepted it. In his experience, she's either too trusting or she has some strong survival instincts. He decides it's the latter.

She shifts in her seat, trying to get comfortable, and the movement draws his attention. He can't help taking in every detail of her body. She's undernourished, which he hates to see on anyone, but especially a woman. He pushes out the images of his drugged-out mom wasting away on the couch from his mind.

Watching Yasmine over the past few weeks had piqued his curiosity. Although some might see a mundane daily life, he recognized much more. There are questions he wants to ask to learn who this woman is. He caught moments when shadows clouded her face, and when they appeared, he wanted to know what caused them. What pain was she reliving? He saw it because he recognized himself in her.

The main tell is the eyes. And hers reflect depths of pain he wants to dive into and understand. A part of him wishes to give her a little bit of reassurance. Something he certainly never had.

Then there's his male side, the part of him he long thought dead, that is physically drawn to her. She's oblivious to the stares of the men around her. She rarely wears makeup, which only enhances her natural beauty. The way the sunlight hits her milk chocolate hair creates streaks of caramel highlights that flash like a light beckoning a soldier to safety. He enjoys watching her.

Shit! Maybe he's closer to a stalker like she said? He shifts himself in his pants because of the chub he's given himself from thinking of her. It's not good fantasizing with her right there, but he can't help it.

He's intrigued with her different expressions, and over the past three weeks tailing her, he passed the boredom trying to decipher them. The one he's most curious about is the one when she looks like she's hiding a secret — the one when she bites her bottom lip. That smile sends his heart racing, just like the day at the coffee shop.

The pavement ending startles Yasmine from her dreamless sleep. She jumps, trying to remember where she is. She blinks against the headlights reflecting off the compacted snow. Snow?

She glances at the man, but his attention is focused on the road.

"Why are you still wearing the mask?" she asks, reaching for another bottle of water.

"To hide my face." He keeps his tone even.

"Wow, so insightful." Yasmine tilts the bottle back with an eyeroll. Then she peers through the window; pine trees line the road.

"Creepy woods. I guess my death is inevitable at this point. No hope of escape."

Truth be told, with a little rest, impending doom grips at her chest. She's with a strange man, and he volunteers no information about where he's taking her.

"You did mention a summer camp. Don't worry, I won't chase you, at least not too far." He's smirking under the mask.

"Great. I hate running." She throws her hands up, exasperated. "Will you let me pee first? Cuz I really need to."

She's leaning into the joke. He might not win any comedy awards, but he's running with her earlier wisecrack. So far, she's not sensing any ill intentions from him. On cue, like he has read her mind, he speaks.

"I have no intention of harming you. I need to keep you out of sight and safe until I report in." He looks at her. "And until I figure out what to do with you."

She purses her lips together, nodding. She doesn't trust her instincts because she's questioning her ability to read men after Marshall, but so far, this guy's been taking care of her basic needs, giving her water and food. If those nasty dry bars can be called food.

He's like one of those masked men characters from the dark romance book covers she sees at the bookstore or the ones from social media with their thirst traps. She peeks at him from the corner of her eye. He pulls the look and vibe off well. Not to mention, he's been stalking her, so maybe he's the morally grey masked man type? Not that she knows much about it because she refuses to read books with trigger warnings around her own experiences, but she does hear people talk.

She shakes her head and bites her lip, trying to hide the smile. Those damned intrusive thoughts always come at the worst time. She focuses on the road ahead to keep them at bay.

This is real life, not a potential start to a romance book. She glances at him again, and his fingerless gloved hand grips the steering wheel. Damn, he certainly has a strong masculine presence about him, and his deep honeyed voice is nice too. Trying once more, she pushes the intrusive thoughts from her mind.

He catches her biting her lip and then sees the coy smile, the one he wants to ask about, but he keeps silent. This is not the time. But, fuck, does he want to know what she was just thinking about.

The headlights fall on a small log cabin hidden among the tall pines. The four-wheel drive 4Runner easily plows through the fresh snow until he parks it and turns the ignition off.

"Yeah, a creepy cabin in the woods is SOOO much better than a summer camp," she quips sarcastically. "So, do I start pretending to run now or later?"

She opens the door, untangling her limbs and stretching after the long drive.

"But really, can I pee first? Maybe get real food in me instead of the cardboard you gave me?" she whines.

"Sure, you can pee before I start chasing you. I don't want to be called an inconsiderate stalker. Let's get you some heels and a long dress so you can trip for me," he responds, closing the door.

She chuckles at his comeback, and her worries turn down another notch. He has a sense of humor at least.

He goes to the back of the 4Runner and pulls out two duffel bags. Carrying both in one hand, he trudges through the ankle-deep snow toward the cabin.

The moon reflecting off the white powder provides enough illumination for him to pull the screen open and unlock the door. She takes a hesitant step onto the cabin's front porch.

He opens the door, flicks the light on, and then moves aside, beckoning her in first.

She takes a deep breath and walks over the threshold, not knowing if this guy truly has no intention of harming her or if he meant what he said about protecting her. She can't run now, so she takes a few more steps into the isolated cabin.

Chapter Four
Cold, in More Ways Than One

Yasmine gives the interior of the cabin a courtesy glance. She shoves her hands deeper into her pockets — it feels colder inside than outside — and hovers at the entrance, not sure where to go.

His shoulder brushes past her on his way to set his bags on an old loveseat that has seen better days, and then he moves to the woodstove. It's a few feet away from the door on the same outer wall.

Shifting nervously, Yasmine takes a few tentative steps further into the single room. It has a small motel-type kitchenette on the far side. She stands next to the loveseat and keeps a keen eye on the masked man as he gets a fire going.

On closer inspection, she realizes he's wearing typical street clothes and not fatigues. It makes sense because he would have needed to blend in while he followed her, but she knows he wouldn't have been wearing the mask. Maybe that's why he's keeping it on? He doesn't want her to be able to identify him.

"If you're still cold, come stand near the fire," he offers, breaking through her thoughts.

He pushes off his knees to stand. As soon as his eyes connect with hers, she looks away quickly. But as he walks into her space, instead of cowering, she holds her ground. In her calmer state, she realizes he must hover around the six-foot mark. He doesn't tower over her, but he still has to look down at her. His shoulders are of a medium build, and when he moves, his muscles press against his clothing, hugging his frame. She imagines he has the typical military regulation haircut under the mask.

"I need to get the water turned on, but then you can take a shower and get cleaned up." He points down a short narrow hallway off the main room. "The bedroom and bathroom are that way. There are spare clothes in the closet and dresser. You should be able to find something to wear since your clothes are filthy and you smell."

Rude! But, he's not wrong. She needs to clean herself of Frenchie's foul touch.

He heads to a door off the kitchen, unlocks it, and walks down into what she assumes is the basement, disappearing.

She lets out a long breath, dragging herself over to the fire and planting herself on the floor to soak in some of the heat. The urge to pee is forgotten when she starts to relax, and the exhaustion sets in further. She hugs her knees to her chest, resting her head on her arms, and stares at the flames. The tears will come in due time. They always do after something traumatic, but she has to feel safe.

Her whole life has been nothing but trauma. She's been in therapy for years to deal with her past nightmares. This recent PTSD-triggering event brings with it an unfamiliar response. The closest word she can find to express the feeling is *exposed*. She is, for the moment, physically safe, but some part of her feels she isn't.

Her fingers brush her cheek where the goon backhanded her. The ache is like an old familiar friend. This wasn't the first time, and probably won't be the last. However, this was the first time she was close to being sexually assaulted. Emotion floods her chest, threatening to choke her. If it wasn't for her masked savior, she would have been.

She scoots closer to the fire, wishing the flames could burn away the pain in her stomach. Instead, all they can do is warm her from a distance as a few silent tears escape, streaking down her dirty face. The real and violent emotional release remains locked away.

Yasmine is lost in her misery, and the sound of water sputtering through the kitchen faucet does nothing to break her out of her trance.

When he comes up the stairs and shuts the kitchen faucet off, she makes no indication or acknowledgment of his presence. He moves closer, allowing himself a moment to watch her like he has been doing.

In the weeks he was her shadow, he never saw her make the face she has on now. A fire deep inside him ignites. He wants to gather her in his arms and kiss those tears and sorrowful expression away.

The sensation of wanting to plant his lips on hers, trailing kisses across her face until she smiles again, hits him unexpectedly. He's had no desire to be with anyone since he caught his fiancé, Jessica, with another man. Since then and the messy breakup, there's been no one he's wanted to share himself with. Her betrayal broke him. He hasn't wanted to be with someone — until now. And with her? He doesn't even really know her.

He clears his throat to announce his presence. She lifts her head, simultaneously slipping her own kind of mask on. He understands why she's keeping her guard up, and he can't blame her. Not after what she's been through.

"The water's back on." He moves to the woodstove and throws another log on. "I'm sure you'd like to clean up. And didn't you need to pee?"

"Yeah, right." She unfolds her legs and stiffly gets to her feet. "Bedroom?" she asks, pointing in its direction.

He nods.

Pursing her lips together, she moves to the bedroom, leaving tiny puddles of melted snow from her boots. He needs to clean up too; the smell of sweat and blood is strong. But she deserves to go first. When it's his turn, it's going to take him a while to scrub off the blood.

Chapter Five
Does He Have A Fetish?

"He expects me to wear this?" Yasmine holds up a revealing sexy maid costume. "Like hell, I will!"

She hangs the costume back in the closet and flips through the next several outfits. A nurse's uniform, a sexy ninja ... When she gets to the belly dancer costume and realizes the rest of the outfits in the closet are much the same, she gives up.

Is he the type of person with a kink and likes to dress up in women's clothing? She decides it's unlikely because his build is too big for the outfits.

Does he have a girlfriend, and these are hers? She glances around the tiny bedroom.

There's a queen-size bed, one dresser, and a nightstand with a lamp. The only other furniture is a tall old bookcase with books haphazardly shoved into any free nook and cranny on the shelves. There are no pictures or art hanging from the wood paneling. She eyes the bedspread on her search for clues, but the faded green color gives her nothing. There's not even a rug covering the hardwood floor. There's no indication of there ever being a woman's touch in the room — definitely a bachelor's pad.

She slides the mirrored closet door closed and heads to the dresser in hopes of finding something nonsexy to wear. She's alone with a strange man hiding behind a mask, and the last thing she wants is to look sexy. The feeling of Frenchie pinning her and forcing her mouth open lingers along with his repulsive touch. She wants something big and baggy to cover herself and her feminine features with; there won't be any flaunting.

The dresser is a different story from the closet. It's filled with men's clothing. She easily finds something she can hide her body in.

When he hears the door close, followed by the lock clicking into place and the shower turning on, he steps away from the fire and slips down into the basement.

He's not concerned about her leaving. He has the only set of keys, and there's no way she will be walking ten miles to the main road and then another five miles to the nearest little town. Especially in the dead of night in winter.

He collapses into a metal folding chair and lifts his mask, exposing his skin to fresh air for the first time since he donned it just before saving her. The water is running through the pipes overhead, so he's not worried about her storming into the basement.

Staring at the dried blood under his fingernails, he's reminded how much he needs to scrub himself clean when it's his turn. It's not the first, nor will it be the last time he's had another person's blood on him. With every kill, regardless of whether the person deserves it or not, he feels a twinge of remorse afterward. Except the two he killed tonight. He feels nothing and briefly wonders if this means he's finally lost all his humanity?

Needing a few moments to himself, he throws his cell phone on the card table in front of him, putting off the call. It's already past the time he was supposed to check in, so what's a few more minutes?

Grabbing a protein bar from one of his pockets, he tears it open with his teeth and takes a bite. He can't remember the last time he ate a proper meal. He's been surviving on protein bars, MREs, and fast food since volunteering to tail Pennington's daughter.

His orders were simple. Keep an eye on her and gather any intel as to why a French bioweapon dealer has a connection to her father and why there's a plot to kidnap her. He expected the abduction, and he had a gut feeling the bodyguard was part of it. Something about the guy seemed off, and he didn't like him one bit.

Simple. Easy. Except nothing in life ever goes as planned, because when the would-be rapist went into the room to harm her, he threw his orders out the window. Her being kidnapped is one thing, but he couldn't stand by and let her be brutalized.

His commanding officer won't be happy about it, but he doesn't give a shit. He's going to hell anyway, so what's a pissed off CO? In any case, he made the call to pull her out, and he almost didn't make it.

The tip-off about her abduction means she potentially has intel on her father, so she could be an asset to him and the unit. At least, that's how he'll present it when he calls in to report. He's not looking forward to telling his commanding officer he fucked up and disobeyed orders.

Letting out a long breath, he picks up his cell phone.

It takes some extra steps to make a secure call, so he has a few more moments before getting ripped a new one.

His CO picks up after the first ring.

"About fucking time, Ghoul. Care to explain why Auclair's men showed up to the dance studio to find his men dead?" General Forrester is not exactly yelling, but he's yelling.

Ghoul holds the phone away from his ear to protect his eardrum.

"And why have you been radio silent?" Forrester finally stops speaking and waits.

"I brought her to my cabin. We've been driving since I pulled her out," he reports. "They believe she has information on her father. I believe so too. I made the call to pull her out before an innocent woman was raped. I refused to sit back and allow it to happen. I'll accept whatever punishment is deemed necessary for disobeying orders."

"Shit," Forester swears.

No one knows of his personal connection to the Penningtons or that Yasmine grew up with his kids when they were neighbors living on a joint base. He understands why Ghoul did it, and he can't fault the man. Forrester would have done the same if confronted with the decision. He sighs at having to be the hard-ass.

"I understand why you disobeyed orders, but expect to deal with the consequences." Forrester's volume drops to normal.

"Yes, sir. I understand." Ghoul isn't worried. His service record is near pristine.

"Have you learned anything else?" Forrester asks.

"Yes. They planned to use her to lure out her father. They wanted him out in the open, but I didn't learn why. The bodyguard her father hired was working with the kidnapper, but I suspect he might not have been the real bodyguard."

Forrester levels indiscernible curses on the other end of the line, and then he goes silent.

"What about the girl? Your orders?" Ghoul really wants to move this along.

"For now, stay put and find out if she knows anything. We're checking other leads and expanding our investigation. You'll have your orders when we know the next move." Forrester's voice takes on a trace of empathy. "If you can get intel from her, that will help your case when it comes to any disciplinary action."

Then the line goes dead. Forrester is never one for goodbyes.

The past three weeks and events of the past twenty-four hours are catching up to Ghoul. He pulls the mask down so only his eyes show. His lids are growing weary.

"Fuck." He closes his eyes and rubs his head.

It's hard enough trying to keep his thoughts focused with her in such close proximity. Now he's going to be stuck with her until he hears otherwise. The images running through his mind of her in the shower are not helping, and on top of that, he needs to find out if she knows anything about what her father is involved with.

Ghoul needs to rest before he starts questioning her. In his current state of fatigue, he's not sure if he can muster the cold steel wall between them or if it'll hold. He can't get her eyes out of his head. The fear she had when the goon came in ... She was powerless to stop him. The moment the guy touched her, she mentally checked out, like someone who's been through shit.

God help him. Ghoul enjoyed those kills the most, knowing he saved her. But Marshall's death when he snuck up from behind ... He wishes he could have taken his time to make him suffer more. Both men needed to suffer more before he ended their miserable existence, but time was not on his side.

His thoughts of violence are interrupted by the image of her eyes snapping open. They were fearful, but then quickly turned trusting on the way to the cabin. He's not sure if he can see hate directed at him in those beautiful eyes. Those eyes with streaks of steel blue mixed with the shades of brown. He doubts she will look at him with trust, especially if he has to push her about her father.

It won't be tonight. She's been through enough for one day, and they both need rest.

Chapter Six
Baggy Clothes Aren't Sexy

A crash from above startles Ghoul awake from his unexpected catnap. He didn't realize he had dozed off. Footsteps sound overhead, and he can hear her rummaging around in the kitchen. No doubt she's on the hunt for food. He tries to roll the kink out of his shoulder and neck. The knot first formed when she was taken and only got tighter the longer she was in the kidnapper's hands. He checks the time and sees he slept a little over twenty minutes.

The single lightbulb reflects off the tools on the workbench in the corner. The various past and modern torture instruments he's made over the years are hanging on the basement wall. His knife collection, likewise on display, consists of those he's crafted and the ones he has collected as trophies over the years on the battlefield.

The back wall of the basement has one of those carnival spinning wheels; the type on which someone is strapped and knives are being thrown at them. He uses it in his downtime to keep his knife-throwing skills sharp. The basement is his work area, but he's seeing it through her eyes. He concludes she really shouldn't come down here until he's gained more of her trust. She'll freak out if she sees it now.

He pulls out a stack of folders from his bag. They're the files on her, her father, and Auclair, the one who ordered the kidnapping according to their man they've got on the inside. He drops the stack on the card table with a flop. He stares at the main file, *OPERATION JUDAS*, with the red *CLASSIFIED* stamp across it. They're just not sure *who* exactly in the government is the traitorous Judas working with terrorists.

He sighs. He can easily and quickly extract the information from her through unpleasant means — namely, torture. He's well versed at it, but he has other nonviolent ways of getting the intel. It's just going to take time, and he'll need to gain her trust. He won't harm her physically, but mentally is another story.

This is the part of the job he hates the most. Luring someone in, gaining their trust, letting them feel safe, and then utterly destroying them when they realize you've used them. He doesn't prefer that route, and instead, he's going to see what he can learn from her organically.

It's been a long time since he tried to relate to anyone, especially a woman, but if he wants to see what she knows, he's going to have to try and connect with her.

The army green T-shirt she found in the dresser hangs off her frame. She pulls her wet hair out from under the shirt and uses the towel to wrap it. The hot shower finally warmed her, and she doesn't want to get cold again. She puts on the grey sweats and thick socks she found. Everything she's wearing is baggy on her and covers her body well.

Good. She has made herself as unattractive as possible.

While in the shower, she thought about stealing the man's keys, but she never learned how to drive a manual transmission, so she threw out the idea immediately. The other idea she had was to just leave, but she wouldn't know where to go, and from what she saw on the drive in, they're in the middle of freaking nowhere.

Toward the end of the shower, her thoughts turned to the stranger. The man in the half-skull mask did save her from the kidnapper and took care of her basic needs on the drive, although she's not counting the nasty protein bars. When she fell asleep, he did nothing to her when he could have. Still, she doesn't know anything about him, not even his name.

What she does know is he's well trained, easily killed two men, and he's been stalking her. He dryly joked with her about chasing her like those old corny slasher movies, so he has a sense of humor. She'd like to think he was trying to help ease her apprehension.

Using her hand to wipe the condensation from the medicine cabinet mirror, she looks at her reflection before it fogs over again. A black eye and a face full of exhaustion stare back at her. She pulls in a breath, and her body responds by buckling her knees, sending her to the bathroom floor. Her stomach threatens to empty the sparse contents on the floor because she's yet to purge the pent-up anxiety and adrenaline. Thankfully, the bathroom is tiny, and she only needs to turn and lift the toilet lid if she needs to vomit.

Can she trust her safety with the masked man? Shit! Her stomach clenches again. No, she can't. The tears are threatening to spill out, but she can't afford to lose her shit now, and she needs to stay alert. As much as her body demands to release the scream she's suppressing, she can't allow herself to break. Not when she's stuck in a cabin with a known killer.

She should have tried to escape. Yeah, those lessons in school on stranger danger were bullshit!

Chapter Seven
Baggy Clothing is Sexy

Stepping out of the bathroom, Yasmine turns toward the main room. It's empty, but the door to the basement remains cracked open. Like hell will she go down there to check. It's probably some creepy sex dungeon or torture room, and she wants nothing to do with it.

She takes a more detailed look around the cabin, and there's nothing in the way of personal effects here either. The furniture is mismatched, likely from thrift stores. The worn, extra-long loveseat sits next to a funky 70s orange chair that doesn't look cushy at all. The fire is roaring behind the protective mesh screen to keep the woodstove open so heat can flow easily into the cabin. There's still a chill in the air, but it is starting to warm. The kitchen has a sink, a small refrigerator, and counter space roughly the size of a large cutting board. There's an island that doubles as a tabletop with two unmatched stools. One with a back and the other without.

She pads to the kitchen and starts pulling open the two cupboards on the hunt for food. She finds plates, cups, and bowls in one and canned vegetables, beans, and a stack of MREs in the other. The cupboard under the island holds the cooking pans.

No way in hell will she eat MREs. She's had more than enough of them in her lifetime. But, it's another clue leading her to think he's *definitely* military. Who else would eat nasty MREs?

On the hunt for something appetizing, Yasmine turns to the small refrigerator and freezer. The inside of the fridge is completely bare, and the only thing she finds in the freezer is two packages of hot dogs. Nothing appetizing at all. Her nose wrinkles as she pulls out a package. She despises hot dogs, but she doesn't have much of a choice, and they are better than MREs, though not by much. But she's hungry, so she's going to choke them down. She hopes he'll be willing to run and get them real food in the morning ... if he doesn't kill her while she sleeps.

She shoves the thought aside and instead lets the thought of choking down MREs to survive replace it. She'd rather starve than eat food that tastes like toilet paper.

She glares at the cracked-open basement door, shakes her head, and then pulls the cans of beans from the cupboard. She loses her grip on the two cans stacked on top of each other. Both crash to the wood floor and roll away. The clatter in a quiet space makes her jump. She braces herself against the counter, her head hanging, and places a hand over her heart to calm it. The towel comes undone, leaving her long hair to drape down past her shoulders.

"Shit." She throws the wet towel over the back of the stool and bends down to scoop up the cans once her heart stops threatening to pound out of her chest.

Still shaking, Yasmine places the cans on the counter. She heavily plops her arms down, resting her head on them, and attempts to take controlled breaths. She's a mess. A few tears leak out, and she pulls the bottom hem of the T-shirt up to wipe them away.

Swallowing, she tips her head back and stares at the wooden support beams, willing her mask to come back. The last thing she needs is to lose it right now. Crying makes her look weak, and men take advantage of weakness. Never let a man see you cry — men hurt women who do. If she wasn't so hungry, she'd go straight to the bedroom, lock herself in there, and hide under the covers.

Yasmine focuses on finding the can opener and begins moving around the utensils, so she doesn't hear him come up from the basement, nor does she notice him staring at her from the doorway. When she eventually becomes aware of his presence, she jumps, sending the can opener flying.

Frozen like a deer caught in the headlights, Yasmine suddenly locks her eyes onto his, matching his stare. Her heart is pounding because she can see how truly intimidating his presence is. Especially with the blood splatter on the white part of his mask. Getting a better look at him in the light, she's growing more anxious because she depends on being able to read people's expressions to know how to safely interact with them. With him hiding behind the mask, she has no expressions to read.

The can opener that skidded across the floor has stopped at his feet. He breaks eye contact with her when he picks it up and then moves slowly toward her. To her credit, she doesn't cower when he invades her personal space. The wetness leaking from her eyes draws him in.

Without thinking, he moves his hand toward her. She slams her eyes shut, preparing for the blow. But instead, he gently wipes the tear away with the back of his hand. His touch brazenly lingers as he brushes along her black eye. When she no longer feels his touch, her eyes open, and she sees him holding the can opener out to her.

Startled with this guy's nerve to touch her — and so gently too — she takes the can opener from him, blinking away her reaction, and returns to the task of opening the cans of beans.

He turns to lock the basement door but also to squash the anger at her flinching. The reaction was a reflex, the kind someone does when they've been hit. He wants to know if someone other than the kidnapper hurt her. No woman should have to flinch away from a man.

While she struggles with the can opener, he allows his eyes to study every curve teasingly peeking through his old clothing she wears. Her wet hair is clinging to her shoulders, and he averts his gaze when arousal grows, pushing against his pants. He never expected to be in her presence and talk to her like this. He thought he would stay in her shadow.

"Why are you wearing my clothes?" He doesn't mean to sound gruff, but the growing stiffness is making his vocal cords strain. "There are women's clothes in the closet."

She spits out a laugh. "If you think I am going to wear those thin, revealing costumes, you're dumber than you look," she counters, not bothering to look at him. "I'd freeze to death in them. The other women you bring here to your creepy sex cabin might do that for you, but I will not."

Her defiance could stand against an army, and win, but at the same time, he catches the slight hitch in her voice, revealing her apprehension. He sees right through the fake bravado act she's putting on.

His eyes rove over her body again, and he does nothing to hide it. His old shirt is hugging her small breasts perfectly, leaving nothing to the imagination since she's not wearing a bra. She catches his lingering stare, but unlike Frenchie's foul gaze, this guy makes her feel a different kind of exposed.

She clears her throat and then swallows. "If we're going to be staying here, we need food."

Stepping closer, he ignores the request for provisions.

"For your information, those clothes do nothing to cover your body." As he brushes past her, he pauses, leaning in closer and dropping his tone. "I can see everything."

He keeps walking until he's standing outside the bathroom and turns back to face her. "So you know, I'm not like that guy. I'm not going to touch or harm you."

She doesn't know how to take his remark because it makes her stomach lurch, but in a different way than when she was in danger. Food is a safer subject, and that's where she's going to put her focus. She'll just ignore his comment.

"Unless you have food down in your sex dungeon" — she points at the locked door and throws her shoulders back — "there's not much here. If you think I'm hard to handle now, just wait until you see me hangry."

He's glad the mask covers his face and he can hold dead eyes as long as he needs to because, if not, she would see the smirk playing at the corner of his lips.

"Hangry?" He moves closer until she has to tilt her head back to look up at him. "What are you, five?"

Most people cower before him when he takes this intimidating pose, but instead, she smiles up at him. His eyes drop to her lips. He wonders what she tastes like and how soft those lips would feel on his.

He shouldn't have been the one to volunteer to stalk — no — trail her.

Ghoul's out of practice with the whole man-woman thing, and it's going to be harder than he expected to get information from her. He's going to need to rethink his plan because being this close to her only brings up one thought in his mind: how much he wants her.

She shrugs a shoulder, turning away from him and grabbing the knife before pulling out a hot dog. Her fingers wrap around it, and he can't help imagining them wrapped around his dick. Ghoul swallows. He desperately needs a cold shower. He's glad her back is to him, or else she would see the full bulge in his pants. It's been so long since he was attracted to a woman, and his long-lost urges are coming back with a vengeance.

"You can believe me or not. I don't care. But just know I do know how to handle firearms and knives, and I'm not above cannibalism if I don't get food," she says in a snotty tone.

I'd like for her to cannibalize me. The intrusive thought comes out of nowhere. *Stop! She was just kidnapped and almost raped. Don't be a dick!*

To make her point on her knife skills, she brings the knife down quick and hard, expertly cutting the tip of the partially frozen hot dog off. The movement kills his pulsating desire because his dick starts to turtle up with the implied threat. She throws the pile of sliced hot dogs into the pan, causing steam to billow as it sizzles, and cuts up the second one.

He turns away. "Make a list of what supplies you want, and I'll get them in the morning." The ache between his legs is stuck in a weird state of arousal and fear of her knife. "We should only be here a few days. If I have to endure a hangry, childish brat for that length of time, you can do the cooking."

The sound of her obnoxious cackling echoes as he grabs the second duffle bag and enters the bathroom.

Alone, he rips the mask off and leans his back against the door. His dark, bloodshot eyes fall to her soiled clothing on the floor. He shakes his head at the disorder but then stares at her bra and panties lying on top of the pile.

He reaches down and picks up her bra by the strap. It's a simple grey cotton bra, nothing sexy about it. It doesn't match the pink polka dot panties. Her modest choice of undergarments fits with his observations while stalking her.

Damn woman! He wasn't stalking her; he was doing his fucking job, and she implanted the idea in his mind.

The irritation triggers an errant impulse. Bringing her bra to his nose, he inhales her natural musk of sweat and body odor. It's strong, but nothing like a group of sweaty Marines crammed into a troop transport. He throws the bra back onto the pile, disgusted with himself for doing something creepy and how it sent a pulse of arousal straight to his dick.

"I'm not a stalker. I was doing my job, dammit!" he mutters under his breath.

He strips and throws his clothing on top of her pile. He turns the shower on to warm the water while he takes in his reflection.

He looks like shit. His amber eyes are glazed over, and the golden highlights streaking his dirty blonde hair are muted and plastered to his forehead from the excess oil. He desperately needs rest. He hasn't gotten much since he started tailing her. He grasps his chin, moving his head side to side. The growth on his strong jawline is beginning to itch after three weeks of not shaving. He's not used to having facial hair.

The woman's too smart! She pegged him as military right away.

He shakes his head, stands to his full height, and grabs the can of shaving cream from the medicine cabinet. He quickly shaves and hops into the shower, letting the warm water cascade down his tired, aching body.

His muscles are toned and well used from years of training and hard labor from his time in the Marines. He's littered with scars and tattoos across his body. Bracing himself on the shower wall, his head hangs between his arms, allowing the water to run down his back.

The throbbing in his dick isn't going away, and smelling her bra only made it worse. Opening his eyes, they land on one of her long hairs stuck to the side of the shower wall. Closing his eyes again, he can see her fully in his mind, and he wants to rip his clothing from her body and show her not all men are assholes. There are men who can be gentle regardless of what they have done. Yet, he's acting like one of "those" men with this desire for her.

The past three weeks stalking her have left him with an overstimulated imagination. He shifts his weight, bracing one arm on the shower wall. The other curls around his dick. Rubbing one out will take the edge off. His breathing becomes labored as his pleasure builds. He stifles the groan, but part of it slips out like a low growl.

He imagines pinning her against the shower wall with his hand wrapping around her neck, pressing her against the tile before his lips take over hers. His tongue plunges into her mouth to taste her moans. She wraps her arms around his neck, pulling him closer to her. Her tongue teases and caresses him back, her body moving in time with his. The need, and longing, is palpable between them. They're both breathless when they pull apart. He runs his fingers across her face and then, fisting her hair, he pulls her head back, trailing kisses along her neck. She's pulling him tighter to her body until suddenly she pulls away, going to her knees. She looks up at him and smiles. He wants nothing more than to surrender and become lost in those dangerous eyes.

Holding his gaze, she opens her mouth, waiting for him. He brings his length to her, brushing the tip along her lips.

She wraps around him with a moan. Her head bobs on his head, and the noise she makes is between a whimper and a moan. Her tongue slides along his length. She takes him to the back of her throat to the point of gagging.

He comes hard, and much quicker than he expects.

He keeps rubbing to the point he needs to brace both hands on the shower and release his cum on the wall. The release barely takes the edge off, but it's all he can do.

Taking a deep breath, he turns the water to cold and scrubs himself clean. He's not only cleaning the blood physically and mentally from him but also trying to purge the thoughts he just had of Yasmine. Guilt tears him up. He saw what almost happened to her at the hands of the kidnapper, and now he's imagining doing the same fucking thing!

At least in his fantasy, he didn't force her. She willingly went down on him. It helps ease some of the guilt, and the cold water calms his dick down. He needs a calm dick because, as much as he wants her and wishes he could live out the fantasy he just had, he's not touching her.

Chapter Eight
MREs and Hot Dogs Are Not Food

She's scooping beanie weenies onto their plates when he comes out of the bathroom carrying their clothing in his arms. He's dressed in a long-sleeved pullover and heather grey cardigan with black pants. His blood-stained mask has been replaced with a solid black one.

"You left your dirty clothes on the floor," he remarks with a scolding tone.

He opens the slatted double doors off the kitchen, revealing a stacked washer and dryer. He shoves all the clothes in, pours in the laundry soap, and gets the machine going. He turns, and his eyes land on the wet towel draped over the stool. He quickly grabs it and throws it in the wash before closing the slatted doors.

She glances at him from the corner of her eye while she finishes serving them, attempting to establish if he's upset about the dirty clothes. His tone is gruff, but she's not sensing hostility. Returning to her task, she shakes her head at how ridiculous he looks still wearing the mask.

Who's really being the childish one here? She keeps the thought safely in her head.

"I was going to go back and pick them up," she counters, keeping her tone neutral. "Food was the higher priority on my list than doing laundry."

She sets his plate down opposite her on the island top.

Ghoul sees the plate of food waiting for him. His stomach growls despite the protein bar he ate earlier. He looks at both plates and sees the pathetic serving size on hers.

Before taking his seat, he slides the more comfortable stool, the one with the back support, over to her spot. He's used to eating on the ground, or wherever, so a stool without a back is a luxury. He pulls the other chair underneath him and looks down at the offering she left of beanie weenies. He glances at her and then back at the plate.

"What?" she snaps.

"You didn't poison it, did you?" He picks up the fork. Even if she did, he'd still eat it.

She chuckles and takes a seat. "Considering it's hot dogs, yeah, it's poison."

Yasmine stares at the plate, convincing herself to take a bite. Without tasting it, she chews the chunk of hot dog and beans twice before swallowing.

The look of disgust at her own cooking leaves him curious. Being in front of her, he can ask her about all those faces he caught her making over the past few weeks.

"I take it you don't care for hot dogs?"

She shoves another bite of food into her mouth, chews a few times, then swallows. "They're disgusting."

He scoffs, pulling the mask away from his lips enough to shove a spoonful into his mouth. It's the best thing he's tasted.

After swallowing, he shrugs. "It's not that bad."

"What the hell have you been eating if you think this is good?" Her tone is judgmental.

"Protein bars, MREs, and fast food." He pulls the mask away to take another bite.

She wrinkles her nose in disgust and bobs her head side to side, contemplating.

"Hot dogs and beans are at least a step up from MREs. Not by much, though." She takes another bite, not sure how much more she can choke down. There's a growing pile of hot dog chunks on the side of her plate; she's only eating the beans.

His head cocks to the side in disbelief. "You've eaten MREs? I find that highly unlikely."

As he stalked — watched her — he saw her as the type of person who likes bougie drinks, sweets, and junk food. Apparently, he made a wrong inference.

She glares at him because his assumption irritates the crap out of her. He might have been stalking her, but he knows nothing about her.

"Every summer, two weeks of my vacation were spent in survival training with my father. All he would bring were MREs. I've had them." Her tone is flippant.

He catches a dark shadow creeping along the edge of her face.

"If I couldn't capture, hunt, or forage for my own food, he would give me an MRE when I was getting too weak to continue with our 'father-daughter time.'" She says the last part with heavy sarcasm.

She's not sure if it's the food or talking about her father turning her stomach sour, but she can't eat anymore. She pushes the plate away.

His amber eyes try to penetrate her expression, looking for any holes in her story. She has none of the tells of lying, but instead, he sees pain and sadness as she props her head up with a fist, supporting her chin. She stares off into space in the direction of the fire across the room. She clearly is somewhere else.

Silence falls, and he hungrily devours the food on his plate. When he finishes, he eyes her discarded leftovers.

"Are you going to finish that?" He points to her plate.

She snaps back to the present, shaking her head and pushing the plate closer to him. "Go for it."

"You should eat more than that. I know they didn't feed you."

She shakes her head and leans back in her chair. "I can't eat anymore. How long was I ... How long did they have me?" She can't keep the hesitation from her voice.

"You were unconscious for a few hours, and it was only half a day," he answers.

She nods, and the tip of her tongue nervously pushes into her cheek to self-soothe. Such a short time? It felt like days.

"And you were where, exactly?" she presses.

He stops shoveling the food into his mouth and sits up. "On the roof listening in."

Which, he forgot to grab his equipment off the roof before they left, and he's probably going to have to pay for it out of his paycheck.

She scratches the top of her head, her lips pursing together in thought, and nods in acceptance.

"How long have you been stalking me?"

He debates how much to divulge, but he needs to gain her trust. He decides to answer her questions as long as it doesn't compromise him.

"I've been *trailing* you for three weeks."

He watched her every move and followed her and the fake bodyguard around campus. He trailed her on the days she worked, parking down the street from the school. He watched her front window until she closed the curtains. He waited outside when she stayed late at the library working on her research paper. The more he thinks about it, the more he does sound like a stalker.

And you did just jerk off to thoughts of her in the shower. Which is exactly what a stalker would do. So there's that. The damn voice in his head is getting annoying.

He expects her to continue to bombard him with questions, demanding to know why he was sent to tail her. Like before, she completely breaks through those expectations.

"Ah." There's understanding in the simple sound. "So, you weren't there to save me then?"

"No." He does nothing to spare her feelings. "I was only to observe, not engage."

She doesn't know what's worse: Marshall being part of a kidnapping scheme or that she had a stalker and never knew it. Either she doesn't pay enough attention to her surroundings, or the man shoveling beanie weenies into his mouth with a mask on is that skilled at going unnoticed. Yasmine wonders how many times she may have passed him on the street or if he was sitting at the table next to her when she went to the coffee shop?

A chill runs up her spine thinking about it. Her father would be so proud of how pathetic his daughter is and how none of his "special" training worked. She had a stalker and had gotten herself kidnapped. She takes a small amount of solace in the fact the man sitting across from her could have killed her but didn't. She decides to give him a tiny bit of trust, until he does something to revoke it.

She sits up taller, her voice turning deep and mocking.

"Expectations are the death of a soldier. Plan, but always be prepared for that plan to go to shit, and be prepared to act to survive and get the job done. Sometimes when things go to shit, you have to go with your gut to get you out of the situation and deal with the consequences later." Her diction and elocution become someone else's, and then her voice returns. "I was the part of the plan that went to shit. And now you have to deal with the consequences?"

"You're not wrong." He shrugs, scraping the bean juice on his plate into a pile and scooping the last of it into his mouth.

Yup, military dog, she notes, and imagines he would lick the plate if it weren't for the mask.

"You're military. Or, you could be working for one of the three-letter agencies. CIA, DOJ ... But I don't think that's the case." She sighs heavily, feeling sleep wanting to overtake her. "I'm caught up in some serious shit and have no clue why. I'm going out on a limb here, but considering I had a bodyguard forced on me, and I'm a nobody college student, this must have something to do with my father?"

Holding his gaze, she works something out in her mind and visibly comes to a decision.

"That means you're undercover, and that's why you're not showing your face. Leave no witnesses, or make sure no one can identify you. If I ask for your name, you'll refuse to tell me. So, what about a call sign or a made-up name I can use?" She grins sarcastically. "I'd rather not call you 'creepy masked stalker.' It's cumbersome to say. Or, do you prefer 'stalker?'"

God, this woman and her mouth!

He realizes he's going to need to be careful around her. She's beautiful, smart, and has a smart-ass mouth. She'll probably figure things out she has no business knowing. Likewise, he needs to be careful or he'll find himself falling for her more than he already has.

"You can call me Ghoul," his gravelly voice sounds from behind the mask.

She slaps her hand on the top of the island countertop with a burst of laughter. "Ghoul? God, that's lame."

The desire to reach across and clamp his lips to hers to shut her up hits like a punch to the chest. She's taunting him, and goddam it, it's making him turn into a horny teenager because she's being fucking adorable. It's hot.

"God forbid you tell me your first name. Okay." She's nodding emphatically in acceptance, snorting in her failed attempt to hold in the laughter. "You got this whole dark and mysterious masked man vibe. I can respect that. You probably have one of the common boring names like John."

"Ghoul it is then." Cocking her head to the side, she smirks at the daggers he's throwing at her with his eyes. She waves them away. "Oh, don't look so scary."

Then her face drops, and a cloud of fear causes shadows to form. All the joking leaves her instantly. Her demeanor is changing so quickly, he can't follow her switchback mood swings.

"Are you going to kill me? You know, cleaning up loose ends and all. If you are, I'd rather know now than retain hope I'll survive this." She's staring at the hands in her lap, unable to look at him.

One moment she's insulting his name, and the next she's asking if he's going to kill her. She is exhausting, and he just needs to go to sleep.

"If I'm ordered to, yes," he tells her truthfully, before getting up from his seat and throwing both their plates in the sink.

Thick silence settles between them. He turns on the faucet and rolls up his sleeves with his back to her, but she catches a glimpse of his suntan forearm and the swirling ink of a tattoo.

He doesn't want to kill her, and it'll eat him up inside if the order comes. But, while he washes the dishes, his inner voice reminds him he did go against orders already because of her. Realistically, if the order came to end her life, he'd disobey.

"There will be no order issued for your death," he offers in reassurance. "I can't guarantee someone else won't try to kill you, though."

He cleans up all the dishes in record time and turns toward her. The silence builds between them, and he decides to have some fun with her, hoping to ease some of the tension brewing.

"And, I can't promise I won't ring your neck because of your smart-ass tongue." He leans against the sink, bracing his arms against it.

She raises an eyebrow at him and gives him a crooked grin. She notes the smirk under the mask because his eyes are no longer emotionless. God, help her, she believes him.

"You take the bed." His tone leaves no room to protest.

He takes himself to the loveseat and sprawls out the best he can, his legs dangling over the side of the armrest. Immediately, his snores start to fill the cabin.

Yasmine sighs and slides her tired, aching body off the stool. She searches through the kitchen drawers until she finds a notepad and pencil. She makes a simple grocery list as his rhythmic snores fill the room. When done, she checks over it until satisfied and then leaves it on the island.

Yasmine drags her tired ass to the bed in the next room, making sure the bedroom door's locked before she collapses. Exhaustion overtakes her to the point her sleep is blissfully dreamless.

Chapter Nine
Cracks Form on Day One

Sunlight streams in through the window and falls across Yasmine's half-dead form on the bed. It reflects off the fresh dusting of snow that came down overnight, sending a blinding light across the tiny bedroom.

She rolls to her side, covering her head with the green quilted blanket to shade her eyes. She doesn't want to get up because the room is cold. Before drifting off to sleep, she wasn't thinking about the heat of the fire finding its way through her locked door. Why did she think a locked door would keep a guy like him out? He could easily break into the room if he wanted. All she ended up with is a cold-ass room.

The simple movement of turning over makes her entire body scream in protest. No matter how she positions or contorts herself, she can't get comfortable. A spring from the old lumpy mattress is poking her in the ribs, right when she realizes her bladder is about to burst. She throws the blanket off in a flurry of movement, swinging her feet off the bed to the cold floor. A shiver wracks her body, which only adds to the pain of her muscles pulling in protest.

She's disoriented when she stands, and it takes a moment for her body to remember how to move. Then the memories come flooding back: the dance studio, Marshall not being a real bodyguard, the van, the remote cabin, the stranger in the mask, and that same masked man stalking her for weeks.

Close to pissing herself, Yasmine scurries to the bathroom as fast as her sore muscles will carry her. When done, she leans over the chipped sink and splashes cold water on her face to help her wake up. It makes her shiver, leaving her to take stock of the gnawing irritation from all her pains. She gives up instantly, determining her body is one giant sore. She breathes out a sigh of relief that Ghoul didn't do anything to harm her while she slept. Maybe he is trustworthy ...

Inspecting herself in the mirror, she turns her face side to side. She has dark bags under her eyes from stress and the lack of sleep. Thanks to Frenchie, there's a large bruise on her cheek and a black eye. Using the sink for support, she lets her head hang, allowing her shoulders to relax. She survived, and for the most part, is unharmed.

As horrible as her kidnapping was, it wasn't the worst thing she'd ever experienced. Her father had made sure of that. And yet, her body still hasn't purged the adrenaline and terror that has been festering since yesterday.

Her apprehension with Ghoul is lessening, but she's not ready to drop her guard with him completely. Although he says he won't hurt her, she'd be stupid to believe him without seeing proof through his actions.

She catches a wild grin from her reflection. Her smart mouth is one way she can retain a little bit of control. Speaking her mind and letting the intrusive thoughts be voiced is a way to gauge his trustworthiness.

It's hard to look at him and not be drawn to him. This is why her classmates tell her not to read smutty romance books — they set unrealistic expectations. But, for her, she can't help comparing her current situation to the scenarios in the romance books she reads. It's not just that, though. The main reason she's drawn to him is because he saved her when no one else ever has. And that is damn appealing!

For the first time, she wonders if he's handsome under the mask? It's a good thing he's keeping it on because if he's handsome to boot, she'd turn into a giggling, incoherent mess. She cannot handle handsome men without looking foolish.

She shakes her head to clear the thoughts. No! She's a strong, independent woman! Her brain is doing everything it can to jump her thoughts around — switching from the dark ones to the distracting ones about him faster than she can keep up — to protect itself from the trauma.

Feeling snoopy, she opens the medicine cabinet behind the mirror. She finds several new toothbrushes still in their packaging, along with a tube of toothpaste, shaving cream, and a razor. She grabs the turquoise toothbrush and rips the packaging open before slathering on the toothpaste.

While she brushes her teeth, she zones out thinking about Ghoul. He's confidently arrogant and carries himself as such. She runs through the things she knows, adding the new ones since her mind has had a night's rest. He doesn't talk much, he's guarded, but he has a deep sexy voice like the actor who played Geralt of Rivia, one of Yasmine's book boyfriends from the *Witcher* series.

These damn intrusive thoughts are not helping! She's a pawn to him in whatever game she's caught up in. But, he did rush into the dance studio to save her when he was given orders not to engage, so that must count for something? He has a grumpy disposition, but he's keeping her safe. He fills out his clothing just right and he's got a fine ass too.

Allowing one more errant thought, she acknowledges he's hot and then spits in the sink. He was dirty and covered in blood when he saved her, and she still couldn't help but feel attracted to the protector-type energy he exuded. Especially when he offered her a hand up. His eyes were full of rage, but they softened when he told her not to worry.

Heat engulfs her body clear up to her cheeks. Her knees weaken and tremble as she thinks about how *else* he can take care of her. His hands running across the length of her body, feeling his touch on her skin. Him wiping the tear away the night before — his touch was so gentle, and she's already craving more.

"I bet he'd be gentle," she whispers to her reflection.

Cursing her body and mind for the hijacking, she slaps her cheeks with both hands to clear those thoughts from her mind and winces. She forgot about the bruise. She can't let her imagination run wild. He was stalking her for fuck's sake! Well, not really stalking. He was doing his job, but it makes it sound more exciting to call him a stalker.

Shaking her head at the crazy conversation she's having with herself, Yasmine walks into the living room to find it empty. The door to the basement remains locked, so he's not down there.

"Ghoul?"

He's not hiding anywhere else. The cabin is a three-room space, and she came from the bedroom and bathroom.

She walks to the front window and pulls the yellow curtain aside to see the 4Runner is gone. Tire tracks in the fresh snow lead out of the driveway. She lets the curtain fall back into place and walks to the counter where she left the grocery list. It's missing.

She crosses her arms and heaves a sigh. Her hollow stomach demands food because she didn't eat enough the night before, but she can't do anything except wait.

A chill runs through her body. The air inside the cabin has lost its warmth, which reminds her to put another log on the fire to rekindle the flames. She opens the door to the woodstove and sees a pile of smoldering coals; he's been gone for a while. She throws another log on, using the long metal tube to blow on the embers to heat them until it catches fire.

With nothing to do, she heads back to the bedroom to look over the bookcase she had spied the night before. Maybe there's something worth reading to kill the time until he gets back.

She runs her finger over the spines of the books on the shelf. Tom Clancy, Robert Ludlum, Vince Flynn, and even Ian Fleming are some of the names she recognizes. The other names, she doesn't. The only books on the shelves she's read are *the Hunt for Red October* and a few of the old James Bond novels when she was going through a phase. Yasmine looks through the books until something catches her interest.

Chapter Ten
Waiting in Ambush

Pulling up to the cabin, the snow crunches under the off-road tires of Ghoul's late 90s 4Runner. The vehicle appears to be an unassuming shitbox. It's easier to blend in because people don't give it a second glance. Just what he wants, to be easily forgotten. Under the faded paint job, a mix of colors and repaired rust spots, the internal workings of his SUV are well maintained, with upgrades to make it a powerhouse.

Ghoul doesn't indulge himself in much, but this SUV is his baby. He drives it any chance he gets when in the States, which really hasn't happened much over the past several years. He's modified the vehicle in his quest to restore it, but the main mod is the bulletproofing and turning the engine into a workhorse, which includes a V8 engine swap, two one-ton axles, and two transfer cases for "fun," going off-road.

The snow around the cabin remains undisturbed. He lets out a sigh of relief to see only his footprints in the snow. Smoke billows from the chimney. He's glad she kept the fire going and didn't try to take off.

Good. Maybe she's not such a pain and can be good and listen. The thought rolls through his mind.

Today will be better because he won't allow her to get under his skin and cause those feelings of desire to well up. He can keep himself professional with her and maintain his bearing.

He steps out of the SUV, opens the back door, and grabs all the grocery bags from the backseat in one go. His snow-covered boot kicks the door closed. When he gets to the cabin's front door, his fingers awkwardly grip the handle at the same moment the door opens.

"I will never understand men and their incessant need to carry all the grocery bags at once," she quips, rolling her eyes and stepping aside for him to enter. "I would have come out to help bring them in, but no, the big tough Marine doesn't need any help."

Calling him a Marine instantly gets under his skin because there's no way she could have figured it out. He has given her nothing, and there's nothing in the cabin, except what is safely locked in the basement, to give him away. He sets the bags down on the floor and turns on her.

His professionalism quickly dissolves as soon as he takes in her long hair cascading down her shoulders. It stops at the swell of her breasts, where his gaze lingers. Prying away from her feminine attributes, he looks at her face and sees life has returned from a night of sleep.

He's an idiot, but he can't help it. She's right there looking so tantalizing, and he wants to taste those lips that are pressed into a thin line below her expectant stare. The way her fists are jammed on her hips ... she looks so bratty, and he wants to wipe the look right off her face.

After closing the door, Yasmine turns around with the intent to bring the groceries into the kitchen. But the next thing she knows, Ghoul is sauntering into her space. The piercing, indecent glint in his expression makes his brown eyes seem darker. She finds herself retreating from his advancement until her back is pressing against the door. Her hands come up and press into his chest to stop him. She involuntarily holds her breath and swallows when his arms cage her in. He leans into her space until his masked face is inches from hers.

"I don't like to make extra trips." His tone turns smoky.

He's taking this too far, and probably scaring the shit out of her considering what happened the day before, but he can't control himself. He's never been pulled this strongly to anyone, not even his ex. But with

Yasmine ... from day one, she has had some kind of power that can summon this part of him.

When he stops his advancement, Yasmine realizes he's not actually touching her, but she is the one touching him. She's not in any immediate danger, so she relaxes, remembering how to breathe. Her legs nearly melt from under her from his musky, masculine scent and the faint hint of soap.

She had fantasized about experiencing a door lean since she first read about it in a book, so even though she should be scared, his closeness shuts her brain off. She stares into his eyes. For the first time, she sees various shades of brown streaking through his irises behind his thick lashes. His eyes remind her of amber or tiger's eye. There's something primal in them, which sends a wave of heat crashing through her. Her stomach lurches and does *the thing* from his close staring.

She mindfully reminds herself to keep her hands on his chest to maintain space between them. But she desperately wants to wrap herself around him; there's an overwhelming urge to seek comfort from this man's touch. Instead, she gives him a teasing smile.

Pressing into her was a huge mistake, and Ghoul quickly leans back, standing to his full height, but his arms continue to cage her in. With her inviting smile and his old shirt slipping off her shoulder, he doesn't know how he's going to keep his hands off her. What did him in was her palms resting on his chest, and her heat instantly flowing into him. He never should have volunteered for this job. This woman is chipping away at his resolve to stay professional, destroying his finely honed bearing, and it hasn't even been twenty-four hours yet.

Goddammit, this is going to be harder than he originally thought.

Her smile turns into a smirk. "If this is your way to start grooming me for Stockholm syndrome, you're going to have to do better."

Inwardly, she's cursing the heat quickly building in her core and flushing her cheeks. This is not the kind of situation to be feeling that! She playfully taps her hand on his chest and ducks under his arm toward the kitchen. She should not have touched his chest in such a familiar way because she can still feel it, and his muscles under his shirt.

He grabs her arm, making her stay put, and then his fingers are pressing into her cheeks. He's definitely losing it. She just had the

French asshole do this to her, and here he is doing the same thing! The only difference is he isn't doing this to physically hurt or scare her.

His forwardness startles Yasmine, causing her body to surge with adrenaline because he's pressing into the bruise on her face. The other guy touched her like this, so she is in a weird state of fight and arousal; she doesn't know how to handle it. Her expression glazes over like a soldier at attention because it's what she's been conditioned to do, but her fists grasp his shirt.

Ghoul lets loose a string of curses in his mind; his body moves on its own. Everything he's doing is backfiring on him.

"Are you ever not a fucking brat?" His words come out breathy. Then he notes the wince of pain on her face, and her bruising is the visual reminder. *Fuck*. He hurt her without thinking. He loosens his hold on her cheeks until her grimace disappears.

She shifts her weight, planting her feet firmly in case she needs to knee him in the balls. If he tries anything more than this, she's going to defend herself. But oddly enough, she's not feeling threatened. His touch started hard but turned gentle. She tries to smile, but with his hand still on her cheeks, the best she can do is pucker her lips.

He holds back a laugh because she looks adorable.

"No." The word comes out distorted. "It's an unhealthy coping mechanism I developed, and there are some things even years of therapy can't fix."

He releases her and steps away. Most people tend to hide those painful parts of themselves. He wants to ask what she experienced, but instead, he shoves his hands deep into his pockets.

Awkward silence follows, so Yasmine picks up a few bags of groceries and takes them to the kitchen. Ghoul shakes their encounter off, picks up the rest of the bags, and follows her.

She takes stock of the groceries with a puzzled expression.

"No milk?" She stares up at him in question.

"I left it in the truck." He lets out an exasperated sigh.

She's proud of herself for not laughing or pointing out the obvious because he has to make another trip to get the milk. He storms out of the cabin to retrieve it.

Thankful to have a few extra moments alone, she sorts out what just happened between them. All the other times she's been roughly manhandled, she never had THAT kind of reaction. He crossed some space boundaries for sure, but he didn't touch her, except her face. Which was kind of sweet?

She begins putting groceries away while her mind sorts itself out. She pulls out a big green leafy bundle she doesn't recognize. She looks at the tag: "Collard greens." Not her favorite, but she'd rather eat them over MREs any day.

"He must like these."

Continuing to go through the groceries, she leaves the eggs and pancake mix out because she's starving and plans to pack away the pancakes. The bottle of red wine is a surprise. Not knowing what to do with it, she leaves it on the island.

"Huh. He must have gotten it for himself."

Another bag reveals a box of tea meant for stress relief.

She chuckles. "He certainly can use this."

She sets the tea next to the bottle of wine and dives back into the bag to find a stack of chocolate bars from white to dark. He even bought the good kind of chocolate. She sets those next to the wine and tea, not thinking anything of it. Reaching back into the bag, she finds some mixed nuts and a box of cheese crackers, the kind she likes to snack on.

"I don't know whether to find this endearing or creepy?"

She decides it can be both because although he was stalking her, it was also sweet he got her snacks. The next item she pulls from the bag is a box of assorted tampons, and this makes her forehead wrinkle.

"What a considerate stalker you are, Mr. Ghoul."

She makes a *humph* sound in the back of her throat because how dare he think to grab feminine hygiene products and be considerate. She feels more of her apprehension of him melting away. He can't be a bad guy if he got her snacks and tampons, right?

She doesn't use tampons, but it's getting close to her time, and she might need them. On her way to the bathroom to put them and the toilet paper away, she pauses mid-stride. Has he somehow figured out her cycle from following her? She shakes her head. There's no way he could. She dismisses the thought.

The last bag of perishables contains the meat, and she notices there are steaks on top.

"I guess he wants steak. I'll cook these tonight." She shoves all the meat into the fridge.

Yasmine frowns because it's taking him too long to get the milk. He should have been back by now. While she prepares their breakfast, she expects him to come stomping through the door at any moment. He doesn't.

Yasmine makes up her mind to go check on him. Maybe a bear ate him? She heads to the door and is slipping her second boot on when the door hits her in the shoulder with a thud. She loses her balance and falls backward on her ass.

"Ow." She's rubbing her shoulder, trying to ignore the pain coursing through her body from the jolt.

Ghoul stares down at her with wide eyes. "Are you alright?"

She gets to her knees, rubbing her backside where she landed. It's added another layer of soreness.

"I think you broke my ass," she whines.

"You were the one hiding in ambush," he retorts with a hint of amusement. "Not my fault if your ass is broken."

He can't stop the low chuckle from rumbling in his chest as he shuts the door behind him. Taking a few extra moments outside to calm his dick down helped. He had also come to accept the fact that his balls are going to be hurting until they can go their separate ways.

She gives him the meanest look she can muster. "I was not hiding. I decided to come out to get the milk. You were taking too long."

If he did not have the mask on, she'd see the smirk playing at the corners of his mouth. He offers her a hand up. She reluctantly accepts it, and he easily pulls her up. She kicks her boots off and then reaches for the milk, which he lets her take.

"A brat, and you're impatient. Noted." He doesn't release her hand.

Instead, he brushes the back of his other hand over the bruise on her face before looking away in remorse. "I'm sorry if I hurt you earlier."

Dropping his hands, he moves toward the kitchen.

She holds back her retort and instead swallows down her emotions at his simple touch and apology. She takes her broken ass, and the milk, into the kitchen too.

He sits at the island and watches her. She does her best to ignore his staring while she starts making breakfast, but she's hyper aware of him tracking her every move. It's hard to miss when all she can see are his eyes. They are moving in time to her movements, and it's making her self-conscious.

"Thank you for getting the groceries," she mumbles while adding the milk to the pancake batter.

"I'd hate to see you turn into a cannibal," he replies dryly and shrugs.

"How do you want your eggs?" She pours some batter into the pan.

"I don't care."

"Oh, okay, raw it is. Saves me time," she says sarcastically.

He jabs his fist under his chin, resting his elbow on the island's top.

"Fried, over easy." He's proud of not rolling his eyes at her bratty comeback.

After flipping the first pancake, she turns and flashes him a patronizing smile.

"Now, was that so hard? God forbid I figure out your true identity by knowing how you like your eggs. It's not like you're Bruce Wayne." She can't stop herself from making a wisecrack. "I'm going to cook up the steaks for dinner. How do you like your potatoes? Baked or mashed with gravy?"

He's too tired to try and keep up with her. What does it matter if she knows some of this trivial stuff about him? Hopefully, she will be out of his life in a few days.

"Mashed with gravy."

"Okay," she intones. "As you wish."

Chapter Eleven
A Stalker Can Be a Good Thing?

Ghoul comes up from the basement as Yasmine is sliding the pan of steaks into the oven after searing them in butter. She tracks his movements in her peripheral vision, noticing he's still rolling his shoulder on his way back to the couch to read.

Yasmine had been sleeping most of the day, curled up in the orange chair next to the fire with a blanket wrapped around her. Her body and mind needed the time to reset itself. Unknown to her, instead of Ghoul reading his book from his spot on the couch, he sat watching her sleep. But when he stirred to go to the basement for his daily check-in, he woke her, and she got herself up to cook dinner.

Part of her is curious about what he does down there, but the other part doesn't want to know. She would rather stay blissfully clueless about anything nefarious he might be doing. The logical part of her brain says he's probably doing military stuff like her father used to do when he locked himself in his study. She liked those times because it meant he wasn't yelling or "training" her.

She stares at the back of his mask-covered head; her lips purse, and her brows furrow. "Any word yet on when I can go home?"

Despite the kidnapping, she still has the semester of grad school to finish and doesn't want any more delays in her graduation. But it's not like she can change her situation. The stress begins to pile on, making her chest clench with anxiety, when she realizes this aspect of the situation. She should have already finished school, but there were semesters when she couldn't go full time.

"Not yet." Ghoul doesn't bother to look up from his book.

His daily check-in was a whole lot of nothing, and his orders remain: hold position. Aka, babysit her, until they know what to do with her.

He's looking after her, but he also desperately needs a break. He hasn't taken leave since Jessica, and after that whole mess, he threw himself into work because there was no one waiting for him. Tracking down and disrupting the arms dealer trade doesn't leave much time for vacation. So, he's taking advantage of this forced downtime to relax and rest, even if it's only for a few days.

After she gets the potatoes going, there's nothing more to do, so she returns to the book she's been slowly trudging through. She doesn't notice his eyes lift from his page when she bends over in front of him to pick up the book. He stares at her ass and thighs. Even on the scrawny side, she's a sight to behold.

He refocuses on his book and shifts himself inside his pants because of the growing discomfort.

"Dinner," she calls, setting their plates on the island.

She might not be able to do much to show her appreciation for him saving her, and for keeping his hands to himself, but a nice meal is doable. It's the safest.

The door lean thing ... She decides to let it go and not bring it up because she had always wanted someone to try it with her to see what all the hype was about, which she now gets. It was pretty hot and is now ranked as the top hottest moment of her life, even if he only touched her cheek. What she doesn't understand is why he did it, and then backed off immediately?

Her body is going to be treacherous with her touch deprivation because, if he does touch her, she's not sure if she can tell him no. Her mask fetish is rearing its ugly little head, which she doesn't need right now. It's hard to keep her unwanted arousal in check.

Turning toward the couch, she sees he hasn't moved from where he lies, so she moves around it, her hands on her hips, to get his attention. She sees his eyes are closed, and he is breathing heavily, sound asleep. He has dozed off with his book lying open across his chest.

Standing over him, she takes her time examining the small patch of skin through the eye slit. His eyebrows and lashes are a dirty blond color. She tries to imagine what he looks like under the mask, but the image is not forming. He must be handsome — he has to be. You can't have those eyes and not be handsome. A curious smile takes shape after seeing how peaceful he is in his sleep. The poor guy must be exhausted from watching her every move for three weeks.

The small patch of skin peeking out between his shirt and the bottom of the mask is tempting her. She knows she should keep her hands to herself, but can she stop herself? No. She brushes the back of her fingers delicately on his exposed skin. His neck is soft and warm. She wants to brush her lips over the spot too but holds herself back because THAT would be asking for trouble.

She jumps with a yelp when his hand springs up and roughly grasps her wrist, holding her in place. His eyes fling open and bore into her, not really seeing her.

Doing her best to calm her racing heart, she smiles.

"I wasn't trying to take your mask off. I needed to wake you up in a way that wouldn't get my throat cut," she jokes poorly. "Dinner's ready."

He stares at her as he comes back to reality. Her wrist feels frail with his fingers wrapped around it. Just a little pressure, and he can easily snap it if he wanted, but instead, he's holding onto her.

"Sorry," he mumbles groggily and sits up.

"It's okay." She shrugs like it's no big deal, even though he scared the shit out of her. He still hasn't released her. "I'm gonna need that hand back if we're going to eat."

He releases her and gets up, and then his eyes widen at the spread she has waiting for him. The aroma of food seeps through the mask, making his mouth water. He sits at the island without a word, hovering over the plate, lifting the bottom of the mask away, and inhaling deeply.

"It smells good," he exhales.

He had planned to make the steaks himself, but this is way better. It's been years since he had a home-cooked steak dinner. He grabs the steak knife and cuts into it without waiting.

She takes her seat opposite him, but instead of going straight for the steak, her first bite is of the mashed potatoes and gravy.

"Wouldn't it be easier to eat if you took the mask off?" Her brows are raised in question.

"I'm not taking it off," he tells her after he chews and swallows the next bite. Then his tone softens. "This is really good."

She nods, not understanding why the quick offhand compliment sent her heart into feeling all kinds of things.

"I'm glad you like it." She looks down and plays with her potatoes.

He must be enjoying the meal because he's shoveling it in. She stares again because she has never seen someone eat so fast. She wonders if he's even enjoying it, let alone tasting it. But with each piece of steak he puts in his mouth, his shoulders fall and his eyes roll until they close. So, he very much is enjoying the meal, and that makes her ... what? Glad?

"Are you hoping if you stare long enough, you'll catch a glimpse of my face?" he asks, not bothering to look up.

His comment snaps her back to the present as she realizes she's been rudely staring.

"No." She speaks through a mouthful of potatoes. "Just wondering if you're tasting the food with how fast you're wolfing it down."

He stops eating to look up. There's none of the darkness in her features he saw before. Instead, she's staring at him with a bemused expression, like watching a train wreck and not being able to turn away.

"With the way you don't eat, I thought you didn't know how to cook." He points to his plate. "This is damn good."

His backhanded praise causes a subtle smile to form. She decides to see if he'll answer some more of her questions.

"If you choke because you're eating too fast, don't blame me." She pauses, wondering if she is truly ready to ask these questions. "Exactly how close did you get to me when you were … stalking me?"

"The closest I got to you was at the coffee shop two weeks ago when it was raining. I went into the shop to get out of the rain and to warm up. I was two tables over from you," he tells her truthfully.

She nods, considering his confession. "Seeing I don't remember spotting anyone in a mask, I assume you didn't have one on."

"I'd stand out like a sore thumb if I wore this in public." He taps his forehead with his fork to indicate the mask.

"When did you know Marshall was working with the kidnappers?" She *is* in a place emotionally to ask these harder questions.

"I didn't like the guy from the moment he showed up at your door." His thin expression narrows with spite. "When he was with you, he put on an act, but as soon as your back was turned, he couldn't hide his true nature. I suspected his intentions were not those of a bodyguard. He's the one who knocked you out with drugs, and then his asshole partner drove up and tossed you in the back of the van."

Her dinner threatens to come back up at learning this information. So, Marshall was the one to do it. She closes her eyes tightly to hold back her bitter emotion. When she opens them, warm amber is staring at her, and she can see his concern in the way the little exposed part of skin between his eyebrows is wrinkling.

If not for him, who knows where she'd be now? She shoves the thought aside.

"I guess it's a good thing I had a stalker then." She offers a tiny smile of gratitude.

She finishes her potatoes and the greens, but half of her steak remains. She slides the plate over to him.

"Here, you can have the rest."

He looks from the plate to her. "You're sure you had enough? You barely ate anything."

She nods and then watches him dig into her steak. She's been trying to remember all she did while having a stalker. Thank God she's boring and only goes to school, work, and the grocery store.

"Did you follow me everywhere?" she asks, but she's already guessing the answer.

"I did." He gives up the information because it'll help gain her trust. "Everywhere, except for the bathroom, and IN your apartment."

She notes the emphasis. "Were you watching me through my window?"

She's suddenly feeling self-conscious about what he might have seen. God, she hopes she didn't do anything embarrassing like leave the drapes open while she undressed. The thought causes blood to flow to her cheeks.

"Why are you turning red?" he demands because whatever thought went through her mind turns her face the darkest shade of crimson he's seen so far.

"I didn't do anything embarrassing, did I?" She does her best to ignore his question.

Leaning back and gripping the island, Ghoul stretches his lower back, which triggers the knot in his shoulder to pull. He presses into the muscle with his fist and, at the same time, rolls the shoulder.

"Embarrassing how? Like when you fell asleep at the library and were drooling out of the corner of your mouth? Or the times when your lunch consisted of chocolate and coffee? He leans toward her. "Or when you went to watch that kids' movie, and I had to sit next to a mom who kept staring at me like I was some creep after her children?"

Yasmine bursts out in laughter, and her hand darts to stifle it, but she fails. She quickly gets herself under control and screws on a serious expression, but the smile remains under the surface.

Ghoul sees the moment and glimpses the light radiating from her, but then her guard comes back up. He wants and craves to see more of the real her.

"I'm sorry," she apologizes, dropping her hands to her lap. She's looking at him differently. "I'd feel sorry for you, but you were stalking me. Are you a Peeping Tom too?"

"No." He keeps his tone casual. "I didn't cross any of those personal boundaries. I kept my distance. You didn't know I was there, so that tells you how good I am at my job."

Staring at her hands in her lap, she's considering what she's learned. When she looks up, their gazes meet, and she comes to a decision.

"Well, the way I see it is, if you were going to hurt me or do unspeakable things to me, you had more than enough chances to do it. So, I'm going to trust you, Mr. Ghoul, for now."

A yawn escapes, and she gathers their plates, taking them to the sink.

"You made dinner. I'll clean up," he says, moving to crowd her out of the way while pushing up his sleeves.

She's not going to argue, so she heads to the orange chair.

The warmth from the fire, a full belly, and the cozy blanket force her body to sleep. The years of working her tail off in school and to support herself haven't left her with much downtime, and their talk over dinner helped her with the decision to trust him. He easily could have done something but didn't. That counts for something, right?

Chapter Twelve
When You Can't Play Strip Poker

"How can you read this?" she bellows.

She's peeking at him through her lashes and hiding the rest of her face behind the pages of a military thriller. After breakfast the next morning, she had labored her way through the first chapter and then succumbed to sleep. When she awoke, she tried again. At least she wasn't sleeping the entire day away like she did the day before.

Ghoul slowly lifts his gaze from the page of his book. "I read it just fine."

He keeps his expression blank, so he gives nothing away about how cute she looks curled up on the chair next to the fire. When she fell asleep, he watched her the whole time again, forgetting his book altogether until she woke up.

Slamming the book shut, she sets it aside on the armrest. She glowers at him but remains quiet while he goes back to his book.

It's her turn to stare at him. His eyes slowly move across the page. Her gaze pierces through him, and he resists the urge to look at her because he's been staring at her too damned much. He blames his job because he's in the habit of watching. He thought having her at a distance was hard, but being in her presence, where her scent mixes with his shampoo, is downright unbearable.

After a few moments, he can't stand it. He drops the book to his lap and stares back at her.

"What?" His tone carries with it the exhaustion of keeping his thoughts in check.

"I'm bored." She pouts.

"Okay, go do something."

If she's bored, there are several positions I'd like to try on her... Shit! Those intrusive thoughts are back.

"Go do something?" She's unimpressed with the suggestion. "Do what? You kidnap me and bring me to the middle of nowhere. I don't have my phone, there's no TV, certainly no romance books." She taps the book on the armrest. "All you have are these depressing stories. Hell, I'm so bored, I'm even considering asking you to chase me through the woods with a knife just to see if you can catch me."

Sounds intriguing. I wonder if she's up for that? he wonders.

It's a good thing the mask hides his face, or else she would see how willing he is to chase her. When he catches her, he'd stab her, just not with a knife. He shuts down the fantasy of pinning her against a tree before it starts to play out fully.

"Oh, I'd catch you." His tone is promising. "You wouldn't get away from me."

Heat flushes her cheeks, and her legs squeeze together because his words, and those eyes of his, are promising something else entirely. She's not used to men flirting with her, so she can't tell if he's flirting or not.

Swallowing, she clears her throat and nods with a shrug. "Yeah, you're right. I don't like to run. Knowing me, I'd trip over nothing. And I'd put up a fight, but with your size and extra weight, you'd stab me to death."

"You'd like how I'd stab you." Fuck! He did not just say that out loud.

His instant regret is short-lived when he sees how wide her eyes open and her cheeks turn an even brighter shade of crimson from understanding his innuendo.

She has no idea what the hell's up with this guy and how he can so easily make a comment like that and then act as if nothing happened? She doesn't know whether to be on guard because he is a man or give it right back to him?

Folding the corner of the page down, he sets the book aside and gets to his feet. She tracks his movement, cautiously, all the way to the island where he withdraws a deck of cards from the drawer.

"Get your ass over here. If you're bored, we'll play some cards." He's already shuffling.

Taking a deep breath to calm the nervousness from his demand, she does what he says.

"Have you played poker before?" He deals the cards because, whether she has experience or not, they're playing.

"I have, but I'm not very good at it," she tells him truthfully, taking a seat. "You know I don't have money on me, so what do we use for bets? Pinecones? Snow?"

He tilts his head, his eyes roving slowly over her body. "There's always strip poker?"

He deliberately offers the suggestion to see her blush again, and she doesn't disappoint. Yasmine grunts and glares at him in challenge.

"Not. Happening." She musters as much authority as she can, even jabbing a finger at him to make her boundary crystal clear.

He shrugs nonchalantly, picking up his hand. "The only currency I see you having to offer is information."

This could work. A way to get information about her father and to gain more of her trust. He might be letting her sleep, but he hasn't forgotten he needs to gather what intel she might have on the target.

"Information?" Her face scrunches. "What kind of information?"

"Basic."

He's already making decisions about his hand and strategizing on how he'll win because he always wins. He doesn't think she'll be much of a challenge, so he's going to do something he rarely does: have fun.

She still hasn't picked up her hand because something tells her if she does, she'll be locked into more than a friendly game of poker. So, she keeps her hands relaxed on each side of her cards, glaring at him from across the island.

"Basic? Meaning you want to know my favorite color? Or my

favorite cookie?" She's not going to agree to anything until she knows the ground rules.

She notes the glint in his eyes changes and knows he's smirking under the mask.

"Something like that." He gives away nothing. When she doesn't answer, he quickly adds. "It depends on how you bet."

Her chin juts out and she levels a stern look at him. "What are you willing to bet?"

He rolls his shoulder again because the muscle is still refusing to relax. From the look on her face, he knows she's suspicious, and he's going to dangle a juicy carrot in front of her.

"If you can win one game against me, I'll take the mask off."

She doesn't know it, but the game has already started, and he's playing her. His offer to unmask is the biggest tell on her face — her curiosity is piqued.

"You'd take it off and show me your face, for real?" she confirms.

The smug smirk is engulfing the slit she can see of him, and it's annoying her.

"*IF* you can win against me." He knows the second he has her.

Scooping up the cards, she starts organizing her hand, accepting his challenge.

"Deal," she agrees. "Be prepared to show me that face of yours."

"Alright, pay up. Answer the three questions you bet," he demands after he dominated her in the last hand.

She hasn't learned how to keep her face blank, and he reads her like a children's book.

"Fine," she growls, throwing her cards down. "Favorite color is turquoise, and I take my coffee with half-and-half."

"No sugar?"

When she shakes her head, he follows up with a comment. "I thought you went for sweet drinks."

"I don't really like sweet drinks." She thought she had him with her hand, but he still beat her. "And, my favorite cookie is oatmeal craisin."

"Oatmeal? That's a grandma cookie," he chides.

"Screw you!" She glares at him. "You probably eat Oreos dipped in the tears of the women you've chased through the woods before you ..." Her thumb slashes her throat, making a slicing sound in the back of her throat.

"What can I say?" He shrugs. "You're wrong, though. There's another kind of fluid I prefer to eat from a woman." His tone turns sultry, and then he chuckles at the range of expressions she goes through before settling on an unimpressed one. But she can't hide the blush.

"Gross. Your pick-up lines need improving." She rolls her eyes at him before looking at her next hand.

"I like a good old classic chocolate chip cookie." He gives her a freebie since she looks like she's about to hyperventilate from his previous comment.

"Come on, you need to offer up something more substantial if you want to see my face."

Ghoul almost feels sorry for how easily he's playing her. Almost. She makes it damn easy to read her tells. She gives it away instantly when she has a decent hand, and he has nothing. Except, the skill to bluff, and he's willing to bluff to learn more about her.

"I don't know, what else do you want to know? I'm boring," she laments.

He breathes a laugh. "You're anything but boring."

He sets his cards down as he starts pressing a fist into his tight trap muscle.

"Let's start with an easy one. You tell me who would win in a fight, Darth Vader or Predator?"

A slow smile spreads to each corner of her mouth. "Okay. I accept the bet."

Ghoul keeps his expression blank, but inside, he can't wait to hear what she'll say.

"I'm starting to feel like this isn't fair to me." Her words interrupt his thoughts of the coming conversation after he takes this hand too. "I know you're betting your face reveal, but you should throw in a question I can ask too."

"Don't worry, when I feel your bet exceeds what I offer, I'll raise."

His arrogant reply makes her blood boil, and she desperately wants to win this hand, so she pictures how dumb he'll look with a face full of shame because he lost. She does have a decent hand, but she can't read anything on him. The mask gives him an unfair advantage.

"What other information will you add to the pot?" he presses.

"I don't know." She's terrible at thinking of herself or what she's willing to share. "Just ask me what you want to know, and I'll agree to answer or not answer."

"Why don't you run?" He adds to the pot.

The question makes her freeze. How do you tell a stranger something so personal, and painful? Her hesitation doesn't go unnoticed, and he's not sure if she'll agree to answer. Her face goes through a range of emotions, but the one he focuses on is the dark cloud casting a shadow. He saw that face many times while stalking her.

"Fine," she agrees. His question unsettles her, but she's confident in her hand. "I raise you. What's your most embarrassing moment?"

He accepts her question and adds another to the pot. "What did you cherish the most as a kid?"

"What's your deepest darkest fear?" She's feeling tense from his prying questions, so that's why she's asking some of her own.

She rarely shares this information because people can't handle the truth of her life. So, in her way, adding her questions to his, she's making it fair. Her questions are more than he's willing to share, so he's upping the ante.

"Last question, and I call. What's your top sexual fantasy?" He hides the shit-eating grin when he visibly sees her stop breathing.

She tosses her cards down in a huff. "Fold! I'm not answering that."

He picks up her cards to check her hand. He tosses the three of a kind with eights face up and then reveals his hand of garbage. Her mouth flies open, and she gasps in anger.

"You son of a bitch! You were bluffing," she accuses.

He allows the smile to form so she can see it in his eyes. He gathers up the cards and then shuffles. "Bluffing is all part of the game, darlin."

He knows to hold his laughter in with the daggers she's throwing at him. So he deals out the next hand, deciding to keep the previous questions on the table instead of collecting them, but he does have another one he wants to add to his "winnings."

"What's one thing in your past you'd change if you could?"

He's confident in the hand, and he knows he's taking this hand too because, when she looks at her cards, her face drops.

"Fine. Call."

Yasmine's stewing in her seat, but she does have a chance at winning this hand because she has a pair of kings, and he gives nothing away. He lays his cards down, showing his two pair, with queens high.

"Shit!" She throws her cards on the table and glowers at him. "I'll answer the questions, but we're done playing because you're a freaking cheater."

He makes a helpless gesture. "I didn't cheat. You can't bluff."

"Ask your stupid questions." She doesn't remember them all, and she's hoping he won't either.

"Who would win in a fight, Darth Vader or Predator?"

"Does the Predator have the Force in this matchup?"

He's taken aback at her question because he might get a good response from her.

"No Force powers."

"Darth Vader, hands down." Her tone reflects her confidence in her decision.

"Explain why," he prompts.

She stares at him like he asked the most ridiculous question on the planet. She brings her hand up in front of her then mimes choking someone.

"Force choke, enough said. Even if Predator somehow escaped out of the choke and went invisible, Vader can use the Force to sense the

Predator's location. Vader might toy with Predator for a bit, but in the end, Vader wins."

Even some of his squadmates can't give that level of explanation, yet she just did. Smart, beautiful, with a touch of nerd. She is a deadly combination.

"Most impressive. I agree," he praises. "Why don't you run?"

She groans in her head because he didn't forget. She clasps her hands together in front of her, staring at them.

"Being screamed at and then forced to get up at four in the morning to run has a way of leaving its mark." She takes a deep breath, and her eyes close against her stomach being crushed. "Being forced to run to the point of puking your guts out, being depleted of energy, and then being expected to go to school and not fall asleep in class ..."

The rest is too painful. "I don't like to run."

Ghoul's furious. When Yasmine looks at him, she quickly looks away anxiously because of the murderous intent in his eyes.

"Your father?" he asks, but he knows the answer.

"Next question?" She ignores him because she wants to get this over with and doesn't want to talk about her father.

"What did you cherish the most as a kid?" he asks after a few heart-beats to calm his anger.

She takes a slow breath in and then lets it out. She looks to the side, and her expression glazes over as she stares off into the distance to her past.

"That'd be Sammy, my one and only friend." Her eyes blink rapidly as she comes back to the present. "Until he wasn't. Was that all of them?"

She's not sure if she can answer any more.

"What's the one thing in your past you'd change if you could?" He's doing nothing to mask the emotion in his voice.

He sees the dark storm clouds darkening her normally bright face.

She stares right through him, blankly. "If I could change one thing, I'd want my mom to take me with her instead of leaving me with my father."

Her lips become a thin line, and her chin puckers as she attempts to hold back the overwhelming emotion. Sliding off the stool, she returns to the orange chair and does a quick swipe of her palm to wipe the stray tears away. She curls herself into a tight ball and wraps the blanket around her. She stares into the dancing flames in the woodstove through the metal grate. Her eyes become heavy, and sleep takes over.

From his spot in the kitchen, Ghoul has the realization that the dark expression she gets is when she's reliving something soul-crushing from her past. At least he's solved the mystery.

He rolls his shoulder because it has somehow tightened further with the poker game and the personal details he learned about her. A knot forms in his gut when he gets a clearer picture of the kind of man her father is. He already wants to kill the man because she clearly suffered more than she's letting on.

Chapter Thirteen
Hot Tea Fixes Everything

Yasmine is back in the dance studio, handcuffed like before, but this time she's naked and her body is numb from the cold. There's nothing she can do to protect herself from Frenchie running his hands over her, touching her most sensitive and private areas. Where he touches, her flesh burns.

A shadow appears behind him, and he pauses his assault to look at the newcomer. She focuses on the figure and finds she's staring into familiar steel blue eyes. She hates those eyes and the soulless man behind them.

"You stupid girl. I trained you better than this." The man with soulless eyes is sneering at her over Frenchie's shoulder. "You are a disappointment. You deserve what's coming to you."

A new shadow takes shape on Frenchie's other side. This figure is dressed all in black and is wearing a ghost mask with blood dripping from it. He folds his arms across his chest and sits back to watch Frenchie take her body for his own selfish pleasure.

Something's wrong. Instead of the steady sleep-state rhythm, her breath is erratic, and her body is twitching. Whatever nightmare she's in, it's not pleasant. He sets his book aside, deciding it's better he wake her than let her stay in it. Kneeling next to the orange chair, he gently touches her shoulder.

"Yasmine." She doesn't stir, so he squeezes her shoulder, shaking her.

"Yasmine," he calls louder.

Her eyes fly open, and she comes out of her dream fighting. She shoves his hand from her shoulder, trying to free herself from the blanket.

"Stay the fuck away from me!" she screams.

Tears fall, and Ghoul backs off, putting his hands up. He knows this reaction is because of the nightmare.

"You're fine, you're safe here. I'm not going to touch you. You were dreaming."

She's gasping for air, unable to pull in enough.

"Take some deep breaths."

He guides her, taking long, slow inhales and exhales. She follows in time with his breathing, but she's still shaking. The overwhelming urge to pull her into his arms and reassure her she's safe overtakes him. But, in her current state, he dare not touch her. Eventually, her shoulders relax, and then her body slumps into the chair.

"I'm sorry." She shoves her palm to her eyes to wipe away the tears.

She feels like a complete fool for her behavior and the fact he saw her have a nightmare. Worse yet, are the tears falling without her permission in front of him. Men hurt women when they cry — the thought remains on repeat in her head.

"I'm going to make you a cup of tea."

She keeps a weary eye on him in the kitchen while he fills a pot with water and puts it on the stove. Suspicion of him from her nightmare is lingering, putting her on edge. She's so drained, she wants to go back to sleep, but now she's afraid to. Instead, she stares once more into the fire, allowing the dancing flames to lull her into nothingness. Existing is easier when you are nothing.

A cup of steaming tea appears in front of her vision, bringing her focus back to reality. The pleasant hint of lavender and chamomile tingles her senses. She accepts the offered coffee mug.

"Thank you." Her words are barely audible because of the shame.

She's no stranger to bad dreams, but this is the first time someone has seen her wake from one. She doesn't like feeling vulnerable.

His hand rests on the top of her head gently. "I have nightmares too."

He gently pats the top of her head in reassurance then takes a seat back on the couch to give her space. He's not sure what to tell her, but he can at least let her know she's not alone in whatever nightmare she found herself in. He's no stranger to them.

They sit in silence while she slowly sips the tea he made her and he pretends to read his book. He's not liking the expression on her face because she's trying to hide the pain.

The thought of someone hurting her ... The look on her face is from something old she's carried for a very long time. He wants to demand who did it, but he knows who it was: her father. He wants the confirmation so he can go on a murderous rampage.

She doesn't deserve this.

Chapter Fourteen
Never Challenge a Stalker

Yasmine slams the book closed, letting out a growl of irritation. Time loses all meaning with the days blending together and because she's been sleeping so much.

"I'm so bored with this book. How can you read things like this?" She groans.

"You already asked that." He looks up from his book, eying her. "If you're bored, care for another game of poker?"

She gives him a dirty look. "No. Because you cheat."

He lets the chuckle come. "I don't cheat. You just don't know how to bluff," he counters. "We could play a friendly game like rummy or bridge, or something easy like war?"

She sighs, rolling her eyes. "Maybe later, but stop distracting me." She slaps the book. "I'm getting lost in all the technical jargon. I've read the same three sentences five times and keep zoning out. Page after page, it's just describing all the ins and outs of the gear he's carrying."

She gets to her feet and begins to pace in front of the fire.

"This is why I like fantasy and romance. Better yet, give me a smutty romantasy with world-building. *Mmmm....* These stories, based on the real world, are too close to real life, which is depressing enough as it is."

She stops her pacing and presses her fists into her hips in challenge, staring at him. "How is this fun to read?"

He looks up at her, not knowing how to respond. So, he shrugs, returning to his book. He's reading one of the stories she's complaining about.

When he doesn't respond, she clenches her fists at her side. He's totally ignoring her. Frustrated, she walks to the door and pulls her boots on.

"Where are you going?" he demands without looking up from the page.

"I need some air. I'm going stir-crazy being stuck inside. I've literally had my nose in textbooks or research papers going on six years, and the thought of missing my finals this semester is giving me a headache."

She puts the spare jacket and gloves on that he loaned her. She can't put her own on, not yet anyways — the memories are still too fresh from the kidnapping. She turns away to hide the embarrassment at letting her worries about school slip out. The main underlying reason why she needs some space is she's feeling claustrophobic.

"Don't worry, I'm not going to run away. I wouldn't make it a mile before freezing to death." She pauses with her hand on the doorknob and looks at him. "Unless you want to come out with me? You can scowl at me from the porch, or we can play in the snow? You do know how to play, don't you?"

She can tell from the lines appearing around his eyes he's glaring. She knows there's no point in trying to convince him. She leaves him to his book and heads outside.

Breathing in deeply, Yasmine feels the cold bite at her lungs, waking up her senses. It helps clear away some of the tension she's been holding onto.

It was dark and snowing when they arrived at the cabin. How long ago was that? Two, three days? Now, in the daylight hours, she has a better view of the log cabin and surrounding area. Tall pine, oak, and aspen trees surround the cabin. And snow. Not much else to see at all.

From the front porch, she starts walking, with difficulty because of the pain in her hip. Her trailing footprints move in a spiral, disrupting the layer of fresh snow. The only sound is the crunch under her boots.

The snow is too perfect, and she hates pristine things. Perfection makes her cringe because it's a reminder of how broken she is. Seeing the virgin snow demands she mess it up. When she reaches the center of her spiral, she sticks her arms out and falls backwards. She moves her arms and legs, making a snow angel. She stops moving and stares up at the cloudy sky. Moisture is tickling her nose, telling her it's going to snow again.

Satisfied there's a snow angel under her, she stops moving and carefully gets to her feet so as to not disturb her artwork. The cold has seeped through her clothing to her back, making her frigid in a short amount of time. She steps away from the angel to admire her creation.

She smiles at the simple childish figure but quickly frowns when tears involuntarily spring up. Her chest is tightening, wanting to release all she's held inside since her kidnapping. But it goes deeper than that. The dream is still fresh in her mind from the previous day, and she can't shake the anxiety clinging to her. The dream is a reminder of who she's going to face when she leaves the cabin ... her father.

The kidnapping feels like it happened a lifetime ago and like it happened to someone else. Ghoul has admirably kept his promise not to hurt her. She's caught in a weird state of trusting him, which allows her to relax for what seems like the first time in her life, and not trusting him because he's a man and hiding behind a mask.

"Shit. Not right now. Now's not the time to have an emotional breakdown."

She wipes the moisture from her eyes with the coat sleeve.

He's been considerate, mostly, but he's also an arrogant prick who likes teasing her, and she knows he's deliberately making her blush. But there is another side of him she hasn't seen, and she doesn't know what he'll do if he sees her cry. She stares off into space from the old memory flooding her mind.

When her mother left, she was rightfully upset. She couldn't understand why her mom didn't take her only child with her. At eight, she could take care of herself and wouldn't have been any trouble for her mom. She was forced to mature at a young age because of the one-sided fights and her father screaming at her mother. She learned how to behave properly and to stay quiet and unseen so she wouldn't get hit

when her father lost his temper. Not that she didn't suffer his wrath —
she certainly did. Sometimes, no matter what, he would erupt.

When she was a teenager, Yasmine went through a hard time
because of a school bully, and one day, it all boiled over. She snapped,
lashing out at her father. In the process, her emotions about her mother's abandonment came out. She screamed at him.

A normal father would comfort their child, but what did he do? He
backhanded her so hard across the face her lip split and her eye soon
blackened. She couldn't go to school because it would bring attention to
him, so he locked her in her room for a week. She was only allowed to
use the computer to do her homework. When she returned to school,
the evidence of what had happened was healed.

Yasmine's hand is cradling her face where Frenchie hit her. The
black eye is fading, but the area is still tender from the blow. Why do
men have to hit women? It makes no sense.

Part of the reason why she needs to get out of the cabin for some
fresh air is that she hates feeling trapped and anything reminding her of
when her father kept her locked in her room. She wasn't able to leave,
not even to use the bathroom, until he came home, sometimes late at
night. She had to hide bottles to pee in and snacks in her room for those
times.

Ever since her emotions erupted in front of him, she hasn't allowed
herself to show anyone how she's feeling. No wonder she's such a mess.
A low wild cackle escapes from her chest. This is why therapy only
worked to a point. She couldn't talk about the really painful parts of her
life with the therapist. She doesn't feel safe enough to let out her inner
turmoil, even to a professional.

"Yasmine!" Ghoul's hand wraps around her arm and gently shakes
her, pulling her back to the present.

She blinks rapidly and realizes she's hugging herself tightly. She
brushes the tears away quickly, screwing on a fake smile, and then points
at the snow angel.

"Isn't it the most beautiful snow angel ever? My best work yet." Her
voice is cracking. She didn't realize she got dragged to the painful place
in her memories. It happened so quickly.

He glances at the snow angel and back to her. She keeps her face turned away, but she's still wiping away the tears. He comes around to stand in front of her, but she backs away and puts distance between them.

Ghoul looks down at the snow angel again to give her space. He saw this expression on his own face when he was younger, trying to hide his pain from others. He's done terrible things since then, so he's numb to his feelings now. Except when he looks at her, his chest tightens. He sees a woman trying to keep herself together and her past buried, but it's harming her more than anything.

Squatting down, Yasmine quickly makes two snowballs. She doesn't think she can hit him, but she needs something to distract herself from the heaviness weighing her down, and laughter is the quickest way she can mask the pain threatening to escape through a scream.

With a snowball in each hand, she stands up, locking eyes on her target. He remains staring at the snow angel, lost in thought. She moves into his blind spot; she needs just the right distance if she expects to hit him.

"Ghoul!"

Her arm is locked and loaded, waiting for the right moment. She refuses to shoot a man in the back. He turns, and she fires.

The snowball erupts into a cloud of powder when it lands on target — the middle of his face. He brushes the snow away from around the eye slit of his mask. Before he can move or react, though, she launches her second attack. He barely catches it before it hits him in the face. He hurls it back at her, and the snowball clips her thigh.

Yasmine grins wickedly as she hurriedly bends down to make another snowball. When her focus returns to him, he's coming at her. Retribution plain as day in his eyes. He has his own snowball in hand; his arm is cocked, ready to fire.

She takes off for the truck, needing cover and when she rounds the front of it, she almost loses her footing in the process. But when Yasmine looks back to where he was, he isn't there. She turns to check the back of the 4Runner when a snowball hits her on the side of the head. She throws her snowball in a blind panic, completely missing him.

She begins pulling snow from the hood at the same time he squats to gather more ammo. When their eyes lock, they're each waiting for the other to make the first move. A giggle escapes through her lips. He looks so intimidating, but she can't help but laugh.

"Ghoul uses a mean look to trap his opponent." Her tone takes on the quality of a sports commentator before changing to one of mock fright. "Oh no, I can't escape!" She's struggling to keep a straight face.

"Are you seriously likening me to a Pokémon?" This woman is adorably irresistible.

"She throws snow attack!" she yells, aiming for his chest. But it ends up hitting the side of his face, causing the snow to land inside the slit once more.

She takes advantage of him removing the snow so he can see and takes off running, gathering the last of the snow from the hood of his vehicle, not really knowing where to go.

"And where do you think you're going, brat?" he taunts in a playfully evil tone.

She's fast for someone who doesn't run, but he knows he's faster. His legs are longer, and he is in shape.

A rush of excitement and impending doom hits her, knowing there's no way to outrun him nor any place to hide. She hears him coming up fast behind her, so she decides to face off with him. She has one snowball in hand, so she squares her shoulders back. He's loaded with a snowball, but he's waiting for her to lock eyes with him. She giggles, biting her lower lip. God, she's dead when he catches her.

"Glad to see you're not going to try and run. I'd catch you anyways because ... *Someone. Doesn't. Run,*" he heckles.

"Just remember who the trainer is, pocket monster!" Her lips curl in a mocking grin.

His eyes take on the appearance of a predator eying its prey as his gaze lingers on her curves. She holds a defensive position with a challenging smirk. He desperately wants to take chase, so he can pin her to the ground and claim those lips until he makes her breathless, wiping the grin off her face.

"I'll make you a deal. If you can make it to the bottom step of the stairs, I won't take my revenge on you and end your life." He tosses the snowball threateningly in the air and catches it without looking. "If I catch you before you can touch the stairs, you're dead."

She throws her last snowball, and it goes flying wildly at him. He easily steps to the side, avoiding it. But Yasmine has no idea if it hit him or not because she's sprinting to the porch.

He knows the snowball is a distraction, and she's using it to make a run for it. He's prepared and takes off; he's going to catch her one way or another.

She can see the porch stairs. They're right there! She only needs to touch the bottom one. He's gaining on her from the sound of his boots crunching in the snow, but she knows better than to look behind her and risk losing her balance or speed. She pumps her legs as fast as they'll move, which isn't much considering they still hurt.

She can't believe he got her to run. The asshole! Running from him is causing whatever stirred earlier to pool heat in her core, flooding her lower extremities and making her legs turn to jelly. An annoying urge comes up — she wants him to catch her — but she shoves it down and pumps her legs faster. She's going to make it. Her hand reaches out, and just when she thinks her fingers are going to connect with the bottom step, arms wrap around her waist.

With his arms fully around her, he digs his heels into the snow, pulling her into his chest. She's fighting like a hellcat to get out of his hold, and they lose their balance, crashing to the snow. He positions himself so his body cushions her fall.

Still, she struggles to get away from him, but his damned arms are locked around her like a vice. No matter how she pushes, pulls, or wiggles, she can't break free! She's gasping from the exertion.

"I surrender." Yasmine gives up. Her body goes limp on top of him, but it's mostly because she wants to melt into his embrace.

She lays her head back on his chest, panting from the run. His hold remains firm. She's never been held from behind, or ever for that matter. She takes a moment to imagine what it would feel like if he hugged her from behind for real, instead of this awkward position in the snow. One arm releases her, but his palm lies across her stomach, holding her in place. A clump of snow hits the side of her face. The clump disintegrates into her hair; some even makes it into her mouth.

"I don't take prisoners. You've been executed." His tone's devilish.

Her childlike laughter echoes through the open space around the cabin. He releases her, and she slides between his legs, which are caging her in from the sides.

She spits the snow from her mouth, but the sound changes into fake coughing as she starts, badly, acting out her big dramatic death scene.

He rests his arms on his knees, unable to look away from the terrible performance. She pounds her gloved fist into the snow in her final throws of death. Her scene ends with some fake gurgling. He doesn't realize he's grinning like a fool, watching her overdramatized death.

When she finishes, her deep belly laughter rings out, and her eyes are sparkling.

"Careful, stalker. That might be the beginning of a smile I see in your grumpy eyes." She lets out a breathy chuckle, brushing chunks of snow from his mask. "You need more training, I'm afraid. It's the gym for you!"

He rolls his eyes at her comment. "Please, who needs training at the gym? I'm the one who caught you, even without using my balls." He playfully brushes a finger on her nose, *booping* it, and then he turns serious.

"Are you alright?" He does nothing to mask the concern in his tone.

His gaze never wavers when he brings his gloved hand to her knee; his other starts brushing chunks of snow out of her hair. He runs the back of his gloved hand down her jaw to her chin. They're locked in silence, staring into each other's eyes, his hand lingering on her face.

She looks away quickly. "I'm fine." She's breathing heavily, but it's not from the run. "You jerk! I hate running."

She moves to get to her feet, but he holds onto her arm, stopping her. "You're lying. You're not fine."

"No. I'm not fine, but what can I do? Nothing. So, I bury that shit, and I'll deal with it another time." She pulls her arm free, getting to her feet.

She brushes the snow off herself and then offers him a hand up, which he accepts. Her words are echoing through his mind like a gunshot. She sounds just like him when he's dealing with his feelings, when they're too much to handle.

Heading up the steps, he follows behind, taking in how her hips sway in time to her movements. He hopes his plan later with the wine works to loosen her tongue and get her talking. Maybe if it works, he can ask her what goes through her head when she makes that heart-wrenching face like the one she had when he came to check on her before their snowball fight.

He's beginning to understand the two of them aren't so different. Both are weighted down with dark pasts. Maybe that's why he's drawn to her. Despite the darkness she lives with, she hasn't been fully consumed by it. Unlike him, who became the darkness.

Chapter Fifteen
When Mask Meets Book

Back inside the warm cabin, Yasmine pulls the orange chair closer to the fire. It really should be sent to the landfill and put out of its misery. It's not the most comfortable chair she's ever sat in, but it beats the floor or the worn couch. The chair's become a place of security for her.

She tucks her legs under her and wraps the blanket around herself to warm up. With nothing else better to do, or read, she trudges her way through the spy thriller.

Ghoul takes his spot on the couch and goes back to his own book. He steals glances at her from time to time, especially when she makes cute vocalizations about the book. He hides his shock at how quickly she's blowing through it. She reads much faster than he does.

"How are you reading so fast?" He needs to know.

Her eyes lift from the page. "Huh?"

"How do you read so fast?"

She's peeking at him over the top of the book, hiding the lower part of her face. "It's a secret."

He scowls through the slit of his mask.

"You're a fucking brat, you know that?" *Why the hell did he get a hard-on?* "Why don't you tell me?"

Her eyes return to the page, her chin sticking out defiantly.

"I'm mad at you," she states flatly, pretending to ignore him now.

"Why the hell are you mad at me?" he's in true disbelief.

She musters everything she has to level a glare at him. "I'm mad because you made me run." Her tone could turn glass molten.

Her words sink in, and he bursts out laughing. The deep-from-your-gut kind of laugh. Once it quiets, he looks at her and almost loses it again with the adorable glare directed toward him.

"You can command an army with that look."

Her expression falters ever so slightly, losing some of its bitter sting.

"I don't know why you don't run. You're fast as hell." His voice turns that special, deep kind of sexy. "You almost made it, but I told you, I'd catch you. I always catch what I hunt."

Her mouth gapes open. Is he flirting? And why is the little bit of praise at her running speed making her insides turn to jelly?

She swallows, refocusing on the page. "I'm skipping a lot of the useless information."

"You're skipping!" He's not hiding his judgmental tone. "You're going to miss something important."

She gives him a half smirk. "I'll take my chances."

Before she goes back to her book, she catches him shaking his head.

"Is this book based on a true story?" She breaks the silence, startling him.

"Yes. The author used to be with special forces before he retired," he explains.

A nod is the only reaction he gets from her before she turns her attention back to the page. "God, this stuff is seriously fucked up. I can already tell the ending is going to suck."

He knows the ending of the book is indeed tragic because real life is tragic.

The main character ends up killing the girl he has feelings for because she's a spy. People like the character in the book, and Ghoul, live with suffering and misery. If they somehow make it out alive, they're left with PTSD and gaping wounds. No one understands the suffering people like him endure to keep others safe. He's a killing machine sent to stop the monsters of the world.

Speaking of monsters ... He checks his watch. It's time for his daily check-in. He folds the corner of the book down to mark his spot.

"Oh. My. God!" she blurts in horror. "You did not just do that?"

He grimaces. "Do what?"

"That's why they invented bookmarks, to stop the abuse of books!"

He has no idea what she's talking about.

"So?" He sets the book aside, getting to his feet.

"So? You dog-eared the pages!"

She holds the book in her hand up and points out the folded corner of the pages. She wanted to mention this when she first noticed it, but now she's caught him in the act, so it's the perfect opportunity to call him out.

"Being in backwater parts of the world, you don't always have something to use as a bookmark." He turns away from her, heading for the basement. He's not going to tell her he never once thought about using a bookmark.

"*Tsk, tsk, tsk.*" She clicks her tongue. "You abuse books. I'm not sure if I can ever trust you again," she calls after him with mock hurt.

Returning to the book with a grin on her face, she knows she should stop bugging him, but their snowball fight from earlier left her with a warmth in her chest. She wants to know a little bit more about him.

The end of the chapter comes. Regardless of her teasing him about folding the page corner down, she does the same thing. His book's already dog-eared, so what's a few more creases?

She throws the blanket off, stretching her limbs, and then stretches again once on her feet. The pain in her joints and muscles, no matter how much she stretches or tries to rub them, refuses to calm down.

Moving to the window, Yasmine pulls the drapes back to find it's turned dark and gloomy. There's a light snowfall. The indentation of their earlier tussle already has a light layer of snow covering it. She can't remember the last time she did anything remotely close to playing like a kid. It had to be middle school with Sammy. She'd be at his house as much as she could, once her mother took off. Her heart turns heavy, letting the drapes fall into place.

"What have you learned?" General Forrester says in a way of greeting after two rings.

"Not much," Ghoul reports. "She's only made comments here and there about her father. From what I've gathered, she and her father aren't close, and he's a real piece of shit. Which tracks with what we know. She might not know anything valuable."

"Is there anything else?"

"She's difficult." Ghoul's tone carries a hint of irritation.

"Difficult, how?"

He breathes out through his nose. "She pegged me square in the face with a snowball. She has damn good aim."

The other end of the line goes still, and he wonders if their call got intercepted or the signal dropped.

"Sir?"

"Did you say a twenty-eight-year-old civilian pegged one of my best Marines in the face with a snowball?" The general keeps his tone dead, expertly holding back his laughter. "If that's the case, then maybe you should start thinking about retirement."

Ghoul holds back the retort he wants to make because he's already in enough trouble. Instead, he ignores Forrester's comment.

"Getting back to it, sir, what have you found out about the group who kidnapped her?"

He's asking because he's not sure how much longer he can stay cooped up with her, especially with how at ease they're becoming with each other. After a few days of rest, she is loosening up more around him.

"We're still working on it. Auclair is involved, but we can't see how he and Pennington are connected. There's a piece missing. The orders remain. See what information you can get from her until we know our next move."

"Understood." The call disconnects.

Ghoul throws the phone onto the plastic card table. His eyes drift upward upon hearing her padded footsteps. The mask is bunched at the top of his head to give his face a chance to breathe. He rubs a hand over his face, pressing hard into his eyes. A half smile breaks through the frown.

He replays the snowball fight like it's a movie. She ran from him until he got closer, then she slowed. He wonders if she ran out of steam or if she wanted him to catch her?

In his long, lonely, and dark existence, he never had a moment of fun like he did with her. It was childish to have a snowball fight, but for one brief second, he felt human. Like his heart was shocked back to life.

There's no hope for him ever having a life, not with his current line of work. But, having a taste of what life could be like with someone like her, it leaves him craving more. Nothing will become of them, but it's all right if they have more moments like that while they are stuck together.

He groans, forcing all the pointless thoughts from his mind. They are only distractions, and she's the biggest distraction on the planet. He rubs a hand over his face again and then pulls the mask into place.

When he told Forrester she was difficult, what he left unspoken was, *it's* difficult for *him*. He's finding it hard to keep it professional and his inner thoughts to himself.

"She's not a lost little puppy that needs rescuing," he grumbles under his breath.

Her footfalls draw his attention once more, and he looks up like he can see her through the wood flooring. She's falling in time with him. For the past several nights, she had begun making dinner while he was down in the basement doing his daily check-in. It's starting to feel like a home with a good woman.

It's been so long since he had a taste of home. The last time was when he escaped to his grandparents on summer break; it was the only time he could relax and be a kid.

Ghoul lets out a heavy sigh. He's not sure what's going to happen when he sees if he can get her drunk. He's not sure if he can handle hearing what else she's been through, especially knowing her father has a thing for young girls.

Chapter Sixteen
Good Girls, Head Pats and Hand Necklaces... WTF?

Yasmine puts the boiled carrots and potatoes to the side while the chicken finishes cooking in the pan. When Ghoul comes up from the basement this time, he doesn't lock the door behind him. Either he trusts her not to go down there, or his mind is elsewhere.

The space between his eyebrows is creviced with wrinkles trying to merge into one. From his grumpy scowl in the tiny window of the mask, she knows something's troubling him. She shoves the surge of anxiety away that makes her want to retreat and hide.

"Everything alright?" She keeps her voice timid.

"Yeah, fine." He barely registers her question as he goes to the cupboard and pulls down a white yet heavily stained coffee mug.

She clears her throat. "If you're fine, then why are your caterpillar eyebrows trying to escape your face?" she cautiously teases.

Uncorking the bottle of wine, he fills the coffee mug to the top. He sets the mug down harder than he means to because he's lost in thought, and it makes her flinch, which knocks him out of his head.

"I don't have caterpillar eyebrows. They're proportional to the rest of my face. Here, I poured you some wine."

She stares at the offered wine because she never drinks and doesn't care for the taste of alcohol. Hence, she usually declines when someone invites her out for a drink. She takes the offered mug because he did buy it, and maybe it'll help her relax. She sips it tentatively and makes a face at the bitterness.

"Do you not like wine?" Looking back, Ghoul realizes he never once saw her drink or buy alcohol.

She takes another sip, but this time she holds the sour face back.

Yasmine shakes her head. "I rarely drink."

The chicken is sizzling in the pan, and with nothing for her to do while the meat cooks, she leans on the counter, eying him distrustfully.

"Aren't you having any?" She brings the mug to her lips, taking another sip, determined to finish it.

He shakes his head. "Not while on duty."

One eyebrow raises in question. "Are you on duty now?"

There it is. The warmth from the wine is spreading to her limbs, and her cheeks are flushing.

"I am." His eyes drift to her ass when she turns her back to him to check the chicken.

"If you're on duty, then why buy the wine?" She sets the chicken on their plates.

He doesn't answer until she turns around with both plates in her hand and sits down across from him. She forgot her wine on the counter, so he reaches for the mug then sets it in front of her.

"I bought it for you."

She's only had a few sips, and she's already starting to feel the signs of a buzz.

He digs into the simple meal of chicken with potatoes and carrots, but he's not complaining. A beautiful woman is cooking him a hot meal. Even if the chicken is overcooked, it's better than some of the things he's had to eat in his life. A guy could get used to this.

"I don't understand." Her voice and furrowed expression show her confusion as she takes another sip. "If this is your cabin, and we're in no immediate danger, why are you still on duty?"

He pauses with his fork full of chicken halfway to his mouth. "I'm still on duty because I'm looking after you. You might not be in imme-diate danger, but after the front door—"

He's not going to talk about the fact he was about to pin her against the door and kiss her the first day.

Keeping his eyes on her, he pulls the mask away to take a bite, hoping she'll drop it. Yasmine's flushed cheeks turn a brighter shade of red. Her breath hitches, and she might have stopped breathing, but he can't tell. Instead of looking at him, she's intently staring at the mass of mushed carrots and potatoes she's creating.

"Yeah." She's struggling to find her voice. "What was the thing with the door lean?"

She can't bring herself to look at him, but the wine gives her enough courage to ask the question that's been rolling around her head.

He lets out a long controlled breath. "A failed attempt."

"What does that even mean?" Her nose crinkles with derision.

She downs more wine to hide her jitters since she's not sure if she can handle his answer.

"Nothing. Don't worry about it."

Nothing? Don't worry about it. What kind of jackass answer is that? Instead she says, "That's the lamest copout I've ever heard."

His nonchalant shrug for a response annoys her. Awkward silence descends on them while they eat, and the wine makes her relax. When she downs the last of it in the mug, she's proud of herself because it's a first for her. But then he's refilling the mug to the brim once more.

Shit! She already feels lightheaded, and she doesn't want to tell him no since he got the wine for her. She feels obligated to drink it.

"Are you ever going to take the mask off?" The wine loosening her tongue makes her tone obnoxious.

"No." The response is brisk.

He can never take the mask off at this point; the fabric barrier is the only thing holding him in check.

Her expression cycles through a wide range of looks. She starts talking with food in her mouth but keeps her voice low like she's mumbling to herself, allowing her inner voice to come out.

"He must be really ugly under the mask. He could have a scar he's ashamed of. I bet he's like that guy from the movies. Hideously disfigured in some freak accident with burns over his entire body, and now he's immortal. Maybe he has mutant superpowers? Maybe he's like

Spider-Man? No, he's more the Deadpool type." She takes a larger sip of wine to wash the chicken down. Yeah, she totally overcooked it.

He's trying his best to ignore her external monologue.

"I doubt it's anything cool like that. He's probably too shy to talk to girls, and he has to keep his face covered to hide his embarrassment," she continues, letting her thoughts flow off her tongue. "Yeah, he's a shy guy, and sensitive."

At the last comment, he slaps his hand on the counter. Not in anger, but he's trying not to choke on his chow. Shy? Sensitive? He's anything but those things. He's torn between laughing his ass off and showing her how shy he is not! She can't see how much he's holding back his lust for her.

When his hand hits the table, she holds her breath, waiting to see if she pushed too far. His eyes slam shut when his body starts to shake from holding back his laugh. She lets out the breath she was holding and smirks.

"I'm sorry," She's biting her lip to hold a giggle back. "I thought I was still in my head. You weren't meant to hear those comments."

Her arms fold in front of her, and her head crashes on top of them as she laughs hysterically. One arm comes up and moves like she's swatting a fly away.

"I'm sorry," she croaks. "I'll be quiet now. I'm not usually like this."

Once she reins in the laughter, she gulps down more wine and resumes eating her dinner. But this time, Yasmine stays silent, purposefully not making eye contact. Her movements are sluggish and uncoordinated from the wine, so cutting a piece of chicken is a struggle.

The silence wears on her, and she feels his piercing gaze. She chances a quick peek at him. He's staring at her in disbelief, and it's more than she can handle. She falls over again in another fit of laughter. His fork flies to her plate, aiming for her chicken. She quickly grabs her plate and slides it away from his invading fork.

"Back off! You don't get to touch my meat." She glowers at him, then there's a quirk in her expression. "At least warm a girl up first! Tell her she's a good girl and pat her on the head. Maybe even throw in a hand necklace. Have you never learned how to properly woo a girl?"

She freezes after it slips out.

"I'm sorry." She breathes through her cackle. "I don't know what's wrong with me."

He shakes his head. Good girl? Head pat? Hand necklace? Is she telling him her kinks? He files those comments into his memory.

"You really don't drink much, do you?" he asks instead of pressing her to explain.

"I told you I didn't, and no, not after I went out with a classmate for my first drink at twenty-one. My one and only time. I swear." She raises her right hand like she's swearing before a judge; her left covers her heart. "I only drank half of a margarita, and then I was in the bathroom puking my guts out. I usually just take a sip of someone else's drink if I go out, which you would know if you were a good stalker."

"You haven't gone out since I started stalking you. Damn it! Watching you." That doesn't make it sound any better, so he stops trying. "I never would have pegged you as a lightweight."

Despite the chicken trying to choke him to death, he's enjoying dinner with her because she's finally letting out more of her unfiltered inner thoughts.

"I don't think I've ever had a full glass of anything." She takes another sip.

He's kept an eye on how much wine she's consumed, and it's only been a mug and a half. She's barely touched her meat, which he's noticed has been a pattern with her. She gets up on wobbly legs to go for another serving of potatoes and carrots. Once seated, she cuts one last chunk of chicken off and pops it in her mouth.

The conversation comes to a natural lull, and then they eat in silence, not needing to fill the void with unnecessary conversation.

"Do you want the rest of this?" she asks eventually, pointing to the chicken jerky.

"Now you'll let me touch your meat?" His tone is dangerously flirtatious. "You don't want any more?"

She slides the last of her chicken onto his plate; it takes a great effort with her heavy limbs.

"All yours. But you forgot to call me a good girl." She giggles. "So, the book boyfriend persona will need some work if you wanna get the ladies."

"Book boyfriend?" He speaks the two words slowly and deliberately. She's speaking English, but he has no idea what she just said.

She scrapes the last of the potatoes and carrots into her mouth.

"Book boyfriends are the best. And you already have the mysterious masked man character vibe going." She inspects him like one would a purebred at one of those pretentious dog shows. "Yup, I've decided to whip you into shape to be the perfect book boyfriend."

The wine is making her all giggly. She raises her finger in the air.

"Lesson one, tell her she's a good girl, add in a head pat and forehead kiss. Like this." She slides off the stool, stands on shaky legs, and presses into his space.

"That was a good boy for saving the girl from the bad guy." She pats his head and then leans in, kissing his forehead through the mask.

The look in his wide eyes makes her laugh to the point she has to use the island to hold herself upright. She takes a deep breath, holding two fingers up.

"Lesson two. Grab her by the chin or neck."

First, she starts taking hold of his chin in hers, and then her hands slide down his neck, her fingers wrap around his throat. She can't get a good grip because his neck is much larger than her hand.

Ghoul grabs her wrist, pulling her hand away from his neck, and his fingers wrap around her throat. The wine dulls her senses, so she doesn't react, but it also helps that he's not actually hurting her.

"Yes! Just like that, perfect!" she praises, patting his arm.

She's not reading the room and is clueless about the desperate hunger in his eyes.

He holds her in place for a moment while she speaks; it would be so easy to kiss her to smother her words, but instead, he breathes heavily through his nose and lets her go. She's still so oblivious to how men around her react. He shifts himself to make his sudden erection from her grabbing him by the throat more comfortable.

"Calling her a good girl needs to be sincere if you want to get any action from her. See, if it's patronizing or mocking, it will have the opposite effect, and she'll punch you in the dick!" She continues in her lessons as if nothing happened.

"And who is this mystery woman you speak of?" he asks as she walks back to her stool, clearly drunk off her ass.

She waves him off dismissively. "Silly, if you ever date someone who reads romance. Hell, I think this would work on most women. The girls go weak in the knees at that kind of thing."

She's certainly been having intrusive thoughts about him, and his grabbing her by the throat made her go weak at the knees, but she's not going to tell him. She sits and then sees her plate; she needs to take it to the sink. Standing carefully on wobbly legs once more, Yasmine doesn't think she can make the two steps it takes to get there. She quickly plants her butt back in the seat before the room spins her ass to the floor.

"The room is spinning." She carefully sets her plate down with great effort.

"Leave it. I'll take care of it." He stabs her last piece of chicken on his fork and looks at it. "You don't really like meat, do you?"

A dark cloud passes over her face. "It's not that. I have issues with food sometimes."

"Is that why you're so scrawny?"

"Rude! And excuse me?" Her tone is incredulous. "Stressed-out grad student." She points a finger at herself as if it explains everything. "I get hyperfocused on homework or studying and forget to eat. Or I'm too tired to eat."

He shifts his weight on the stool. She's drunk enough, so he's going to start with the questions.

"You said you have issues with food. Does that mean food allergies?"

She shakes her head, which makes the room spin. She lays her head down on the top of the island. How much did she drink? The last sip of wine in her mug is taunting her, so she downs it, making a face at the taste.

"No food allergies." She never shared the painful truth with her therapist, so why him? "It doesn't matter. It's something I have to deal with."

"No, you can't leave it at that." He pushes.

"Don't worry about it." She throws his words from before back at him in the same tone he used on her.

He doesn't like his words coming back to bite him, but he understands she has her reasons for hiding the unpleasant things of her past. He holds his fork out to her with the last of the chicken.

"Here, do you think you can be a good girl and take this last bite for me?" He deepens his voice, adding extra gruffness to his tone.

He was listening, and he's trying the words she taught him to see if they work on her. Yasmine's eyes widen, and she blushes before looking away. If he asks anything of her with a *good girl* thrown in, she's not going to be able to say no.

She quickly recovers, her eyes lighting up.

"See! There you go! Book boyfriend material!" She covers her mouth to hold back the snort, but it still slips out.

He keeps the fork in position, waiting for her laughter to settle. She looks so adorable trying to cover the blush. He rather likes her blushing and snorting; he doesn't think it would ever get old. It almost makes him feel human.

She leans in with her mouth open. He brings his fork closer, and her lips wrap around the chicken, pulling it from the fork. The simple movement causes heat to surge through his body. He imagines those smooth lips wrapped around his cock. This is why he needs to keep the mask on, or else she would see his face turn hot with desire.

She struggles to chew. "Mmm, chicken jerky, it's the best. What did you ask me? I forgot."

She tries to remember the previous question, but the *good girl* comment made her brain short-circuit.

"You answered my question and then distracted yourself." *And me,* he adds to himself while he stacks their plates and silverware together. "Your father seems like a real bastard," he tempts.

She answers with a gagging sound in the back of her throat. "You have no idea. I'm sure his records at DoD are pristine as ever, though. He can do no wrong!"

I wouldn't be so sure, Ghoul thinks to himself, wishing he could say something in reassurance. There are some high up in the government who know some of the things her father's involved with.

"I take it you two aren't close?" He rests his elbows on the island top, interlaces his fingers together, and rests his chin on them.

She shakes her head vigorously and then winces. "No, don't do that.

I just made myself dizzy ... No, we're not close. I'm trying to figure out how to cut contact with him, but I don't think I'll ever be free of the monster."

"Monster is harsh," he prods, but internally, Ghoul winces because he's a monster too.

She throws her hands up in frustration. "Yeah, he's a hero and fucking father of the year. I've learned to keep my goddamn mouth shut because no one ever fucking listens. He's great, he's perfect, a real asset to our country."

Her unfiltered anger breaks free so quickly it startles him.

Testing her balance, she slides off the stool, holding onto the counter so she doesn't fall to the floor.

"Alright, legs, just get my ass to the couch, and I won't ask for anything else from you for the rest of the night. 'Kay?"

Thankfully, they agree to her terms because she wobbles over to the couch without incident. Deciding to give her a break, Ghoul starts on the dishes. He debates on seeing if she'll drink more wine but decides against it — she's had enough. He puts the cork into the bottle, sticks it in the fridge, and then fills her mug with water.

He ponders the comments she made about her father while he cleans up the kitchen. There's no love lost between them, which is crystal clear.

Chapter Seventeen
Monsters Can Get the Girl

When the dishes are done and left to dry, Ghoul grabs the mug of water and the stack of chocolate bars. From stalking her, he knows she likes chocolate, but he never got close enough to see what kind, so he bought one of each.

His seating options are limited: either the orange chair or next to her on the loveseat. He builds a wall of steel around his desire to run his hands over her curves and takes the seat next to her. The wall of steel melts instantly from her body heat penetrating him. She's testing his resolve, and she's clueless about it.

Yasmine is slouching with her legs outstretched in front of her. Her eyes are closed, and he wonders if she passed out already, but then she opens one eye when he takes the seat next to her.

"You must really like chocolate."

"These are for you. I know you like chocolate from ... stalking you." Time to lean into the teasing to make this easier. "You do eat a lot of chocolate."

He fans the bars in front of her like a deck of cards.

She smirks. "What a considerate stalker you are."

Her hand shoots out to the darkest chocolate in the stack before sliding her thumbnail along the fold to open the cardboard surrounding it. After pulling the rose gold colored foil away, she bites straight into the bar. Her eyes roll back, and a moan of pleasure emanates from the back of her throat.

"It's good." She holds the bar out for him. "You want a bite?"

He leans in, lifting his mask away enough to take a bite of the offered chocolate. The mask hides his bitter grimace; it's similar to the face she made with the wine.

"You like chocolate from the void. How can you eat this?"

"Fine, I won't share any more with you." She protectively hugs the bar close to her chest. There's a pause before she murmurs. "I appreciate this. Sometimes chocolate is all I eat for dinner."

He clicks his tongue. "I know, and that's not dinner! You really need healthier eating habits."

He takes the bar of white chocolate from the stack.

Yasmine turns sideways and takes another bite of chocolate. She stares at Ghoul when he takes a bite, catching a glimpse of his full lips. She squashes the urge to lean over and taste them. Instead, she makes a weird face at him.

"What?" Her looks are becoming exasperating.

"White chocolate is not real chocolate, you know? It's basically cream and sugar posing as chocolate."

He glares. "I don't care, I like it."

"Okay," she mocks, bobbing her head side to side. "I would have pegged you for at least a milk chocolate kind of guy. Not someone with a sweet tooth."

Yasmine takes one last bite of chocolate and wraps the foil around the uneaten portion. She sets it on the armrest next to her then returns to staring at him.

"You know, your eyes are really pretty. They're like amber."

Her random comment catches him off guard. He's not sure how to respond, so he ignores the compliment, but his mouth softens under the mask. If he's not careful, she's going to distract him, which she has a habit of doing without even trying.

"What are you going to school for?" He takes his last bite of chocolate and sets it aside.

The turning movement causes the spicy muscle in his shoulder to pull. He jams a fist into the shoulder, rolling it.

"Teaching." She's staring at him working on his shoulder. "Next semester would have been my last, but with this situation ..." Her arms raise to motion around her at the cabin, and then to him. "I have no idea what's going to happen. I don't even know how many days I've missed, and hell, I probably already missed my finals. Who knows, since I have top grades and extenuating circumstances, maybe they will let me make it up? That is, if I don't end up dead."

"That's why I'm babysitting you. To make sure you don't end up dead." He pats the side of her calf, then jerks his hand away. He touched her without thinking.

She sits up straighter from the touch because his heat permeated into her skin, sending a surge of electricity, nearly short-circuiting her synapses. She's going to ignore it like she has been doing. It's worked for her so far.

"See." She points an accusing finger and then jabs it into his chest, just to be able to touch him back. "I don't think that's the case. I know all too well even civilians are expendable if it's in defense of the nation. My father's a general for Christ's sake! None of this is making any sense to me, and I know you're not telling me all of it. Which I get. 'Need to know,' and I don't need to know. All I'm saying is, something's fishy."

He turns his body to face her, his back to the armrest and his leg bent at an angle in front of him.

"Despite what you may think, we don't know much either."

He rests his arm on the back of the couch, his hand dangerously close to her shoulder. He only needs to move a few inches, and he could touch her hair.

"Why become a teacher?"

"I'm not sure if I want to tell you." Her chin juts out in defiance.

He grasps it since she's practically asking for it and he needs to test his theory that she was telling him earlier how to woo her. He holds a firm grip, noting the blush creeping up her face along with her widening eyes.

"Come on, be a good girl and tell me."

Her breath hitches in her chest at his touch and words. Damn him.

This touch is softer than before when he crowded her at the door. His gentleness causes her shoulders to relax.

Unable to meet his gaze, she looks away. Her choice of career was another part of her life she was unable to speak about with her therapist.

Her father's expectation was that she join the Army then transfer to military intelligence. He conveniently ignored the fact she failed boot camp and got kicked out. When she decided to go to college to become a teacher, it was the one time she didn't cave into his demands or buckle under his authority — he couldn't control this. She hasn't told anyone the true reason why she wants to become a teacher.

It must be the wine loosening her lips because she takes a deep breath.

"Mr. Barlowe and Ms. Johns. Those two got me through some really hard times. They were the adult role models I desperately needed. They knew I had trouble at home, which is putting it mildly. Freshman year was rough. I mean, it's always rough, but the fact that I didn't have anyone to support me made it much worse. My father was ... absent. And my mom was gone. Those two teachers never pried into my personal life, but if it wasn't for them, who knows where I'd have ended up. I know I'm not the only kid to go through some fucked up shit. Some kids have it better, some worse, but I want to be the adult who helps those kids."

She continues. "The ones who are homeless, the ones who don't have a safe place to be themselves." A lump forms in her throat. "The kids who are abused but can't tell anyone. The kids whose parents are drug addicts or alcoholics. I want to be the kind of teacher the kids know they can go to for help with anything, even if it's for food because they don't have it at home. Maybe, I could be the one to help that one kid stay off the streets." She finally turns to look at him. "You know?"

The eyes staring back are not what she expects. She expects scorn, derision, or even contempt. Instead, she sees pain and years of suffering behind those eyes, along with gathering moisture. Something she said touched close to home with him. Her heart aches for the man who's hiding behind the mask.

"I believe every kid and every person deserves a chance. Life makes it so hard sometimes." She blinks away the pooling tears in response to seeing his.

Hands grasp each side of her face as his thumbs brush away her tears.

"Mr. Lamb was the teacher who helped me get my life sorted out. He's a Marine and went into teaching when he got out. I ended up dropping out of high school, but he encouraged me to enlist when I turned seventeen. Which I did." He stares into her eyes. "You're going to be a great teacher."

He wants nothing more than to pull her into his arms and hold her, but it's not the entire truth. He wants her to hold him. He's never voiced any of his sad backstory, not even to Jessica. He's kept it bottled up inside. No one ever listens to men when they are dealing with shit.

There's more to her story, the same as him. He sees himself reflected in her, yet she remains kind. She's going to help kids, unlike him, a hardened, heartless killer who's done terrible things. He's been conditioned his entire life to be a monster, which is why he's sent to rid the world of some of the vilest of monsters. He justifies his actions because he believes he keeps good people, like her, safe.

Showing her attention, buying the wine, all of it is a way to get her to trust him, to get information on her father, and he hates himself for it. The internal conflict inside him boils over into anger because he doesn't want to see her drunk, not after his childhood. Even him wiping her tears away is calculated and selfish because he wants any excuse to touch her.

"The file I read on you said nothing about a mother, but I didn't know she left." He reluctantly releases her face, his arm returning to its spot on the back of the couch.

"She abandoned me with him." Yasmine's tone is full of disgust; she's hugging her legs tighter to her chest. "He hit her a lot. But he made sure never to do it where others could see."

Her eyes close against the memories as she lays her head on her knees. She had begged her mom to take her while she hurriedly packed a bag after her father left for work.

Yasmine opens her eyes before the memory of the past overtakes her.

"It was the summer after I turned eight. She packed a bag and left. Left me with him. I haven't seen her since. Twenty years, and I have no idea where she is. But I haven't exactly bothered looking either. Do you want to know the really messed-up part?" She's caressing her arm to self-sooth. "I understand why she left. I don't blame her, and I don't even hate her for it. At least she got out."

His hand moves with a mind of its own, resting on the side of her calf, his thumb making tiny circles through the fabric of her sweats.

"I drank too much." She laughs and pinches her shirt, using it to fan herself. "I'm really warm."

The flush she feels is not only from the alcohol but also him so casually laying a hand on her. She shifts in her seat, and it's his turn for his eyes to widen before he quickly looks away. She raises her butt off the couch, pulling the sweatpants off, her bare legs on full display to him.

"That's better." She resumes fanning herself with her shirt. "You made it too hot in here." She points at the fire. She'd rather not tell Ghoul she's overheating because of him.

His eyes can't stay respectful. It's not long before his gaze is devouring her and focusing on the dark space between her legs. There's not much left to the imagination at this juncture with her. She's only in his shirt and panties.

"I'm glad you had a teacher who helped you." She turns the conversation back to him. "Teaching is such a thankless job. Most of the time they never know how they impact lives, but you and I are both living proof of their efforts. I try to remember that when I have those days, when I feel like giving up and nothing I do matters."

Ghoul is trying to remember how to breathe. All the questions he was ready to ask are forgotten. His entire plan is shot to hell because of those bare thighs. She sinks lower into the couch, stretching her legs out onto his lap.

Goddamn her.

Her relaxed and familiar pose sends his mind into a tidal wave of intrusive thoughts, the kind of thoughts he doesn't need right now with her so close, and bare.

He turns away, closing his eyes and resisting the urge to run his hands over those legs. She's drunk, and her defenses are down, showing her vulnerable side, so he can't blame her for crossing any boundaries. He will not be THAT guy who takes advantage of her in this state.

But, he does lose some of his self-control. His arm begins to slide from the back of the couch to her thigh when the damned shoulder pulls, making him wince. His fist pounds into the stubborn muscle.

"Alright, that's it," she blurts, pulling her legs off him and getting on her knees. "Turn around. I'll rub your shoulder."

Ghoul pauses at the stern teacher's voice, and damn it, if it isn't sexy as hell! He finds himself doing what she says and turning to put his back to her. She immediately digs into his shoulder, making him groan.

"Sorry." She lightens her touch when she feels the mass of rocks in his shoulder. "Are you going to stay doing ... whatever this is? Or do you have other plans? Goals? I'm tired of being the only one talking."

She's barely putting any pressure on him, but the pain is radiating up into his head.

"I plan to keep doing this until I die. Or I can't anymore. And then I'll end it." He lets loose another round of groans when she digs deeper into the knots.

She stops rubbing and makes an ugly face he can't see. "No. Unacceptable. That sounds like you're just waiting to die. You have to want something?"

She's definitely going to make a good teacher with her lecturing tone.

"Men like me don't get to have a life or a chance at happiness."

"No. I don't accept that," she repeats.

His words cause her to dig into him more than she means to, making him grit his teeth.

"You should read a monster romance then. The monster always gets the girl and has a happy ending. But I'm not saying you're a monster." She frowns to herself as she starts to work on the other shoulder. "A monster wouldn't think to get tampons or chocolate. I grew up with a real monster. I know what they look like, and I don't see one sitting in front of me now."

She gives his shoulder a reassuring squeeze before her elbow jabs into the stubborn muscle, causing him to hiss through his teeth.

Her words are challenging his belief and self-image. He never allows himself to dream of a life other than the one he lives. Not that what he does is considered living. Always in danger, never getting truly close to anyone. Ever.

"You don't think I'm a monster?" His words turn somberly dark. "You know nothing about me or what I've done. How many I've killed."

She stops and leans around him. "Have you ever given someone a thousand papercuts then doused them with apple cider vinegar mixed with cayenne pepper juice? No? Then you're not a monster. Just because someone does horrific things doesn't mean the person's evil."

His mind is reeling at her absurd torture example, but he can't counter her argument because her fingers are gently massaging the tight muscles in his neck under his mask. A whimper escapes, and he's leaning his head back into her, with his eyes closed. The shoulder rub was torturous pain, but now it feels so damn good to have her rub away the tightness.

"I get you think you're unredeemable. And yeah, sure, you've done some seriously messed up shit and will probably do more fucked up shit that will make you question who you are. You can see yourself that way, but that's not how I see you."

"There must be something wrong with you if you can't see I'm a fucking red flag," he grumbles and then sucks in a hard breath when her elbow goes back to torturing his shoulder.

"There's something wrong with me, huh?" she challenges, then snickers. "What's wrong with me is I read too many smutty romance novels, and I don't get out much."

The giggling causes her to lose her balance and fall into his back. Her breasts are pressing into him. He stops breathing to savor the feeling.

"As messed up as this situation is, it would make a good plot for a romance." She pauses, glaring at his shoulder. "God, what did you do? This muscle is like cement," she complains, making a disgusted sound in the back of her throat. "I'm doing all the talking. Your turn."

"You're not serious, are you? There's nothing about this situation screaming romance."

"I'm serious." She swats his shoulder, her tone turning bratty. "Have you ever read a romance?"

He turns at the waist, so she can see the deadpan eyes. "Do I look like the type?"

"Fair point. You're too grumpy for romance. You should, though." She pokes his side playfully. "You could learn a few things if you did, although you do have the brooding masked man vibe down."

She's distracting him, like she always does, but he's enjoying seeing this side of her. She's coming out of her shell like the most precious of pearls.

"I doubt I'd learn anything from reading romance, AND, I don't brood." The last part he says a little too defensively.

She pats his shoulder in encouragement. "This can totally work for you. You have the whole," her tone goes deep, mimicking him, "'I'm a monster, I live in the shadows, but touch my woman and you're dead!' vibe going for you." She's laughing at her terrible impersonation of him. "The ladies would eat this up! You could totally pull it off. And I'll coach you."

He's curious if her coaching him, on whatever she's talking about, if it would work on her? Is she subconsciously spilling the beans on how someone can get her?

"We just need to work on your grumpy side." She's still squeezing his shoulder. "But your door lean was, chef's kiss." She makes the gesture, and he hears the kiss sound.

"What about this situation makes you think it's a romance?" He grunts as her elbow pinches something in his shoulder, causing him to see stars.

"Sorry."

She tenderly rubs the spot she hurt, easing away more of the tension. She gently kneads into both shoulders, which makes him lean back into her again. He doesn't care if his dick is stirring from her touch because it's been so long since anyone rubbed his shoulders. She rests her chin on the top of his head, making the moment more intimate.

"I'm not answering that because I'm not drunk enough." Her laugh is huffy.

His hand covers hers on his shoulder, holding her squeeze in place.

"Come on, be a good girl and tell me. How would this situation be a good romance?"

She really should not have told him the magic words because he's totally using them against her.

"You really want to know?"

"You're a teacher, so teach me."

Damn his deep sultry tone. Her legs almost give out; she is now hyperaware she's leaning into him for support. Then his warmth is seeping into her, making her want to wrap herself in his body heat. He has this way of making her not feel so lonely, despite only knowing him a few days.

She clears her throat and those thoughts from her mind. Her voice takes on a storytelling quality.

"A beautiful young college student gets kidnapped." She immediately interrupts her story. "Although I'm not young or pretty enough to be the main lead for a romance." She resumes her narrator voice. "But, she gets kidnapped by the mafia." She's interrupting herself, again. "What I would change is that she's someone really important, like the president's daughter, and they use her to get to her father." The narrator's voice returns, becoming more dramatic. "She's saved by this hot, grumpy, mysterious masked stranger and gets whisked away to a remote cabin. Danger lurks in the shadows, and he has to figure out how to save her from the villains, while not falling for her."

Her tone returns to normal. "Since time isn't a thing, there's tons of sexual tension building. They have to deal with a bunch of shit, but there's a moment when something finally clicks. Bow-chick-a-wow-wow, it's amazing. More conflict, the issue with the villains gets resolved, and they have their happily ever after."

If Ghoul didn't have his mask on, she'd see his mouth gaping open. "Ridiculous! That kind of shit doesn't happen in real life."

She punches him in the shoulder. "That's the point! Real life's depressing enough with no happy endings."

Her grip becomes harder, and then she's pounding her tiny fists into his upper back muscles.

"What's wrong with wanting to be lost in a story where the characters have to deal with crap, but they figure it out somehow and then can be together? You've never read romance, so who are you to judge?"

"And you don't judge?" He huffs, shaking his head. "You keep talking smack about the books I read."

She meets his comment with a scoffing laugh. "The difference is, I'm actually reading one of your books, and I'm just sharing my impressions as I go."

"Alright, I'll give you that. Is there more to this story of yours?"

She grins shyly, but he can't see it. "I glossed over the most important part of the romances: the spice." She provocatively says spice in a way to draw him in.

"Spice?" He's dumbfounded because she's using the word differently than how he understands it.

She giggles as both hands lazily rest on his shoulder, and she leans closer to his ear, lowering her tone.

"It means they fuck a lot in vivid detail," she whispers into his ear, then chuckles, going back to the shoulder rub. "Unlike the sex scene in your lame ass book, which was so disappointing. It was wham bam thank you ma'am, done. There was nothing to show any emotional connection or desire between the characters."

Her tone turns mocking. "Oh baby, you're so hot, fuck me. It was JUST about the sex. Don't get me wrong, I like a hot feral sex scene. But it gets boring to read if it's always just that." She bites her lower lip. "But, *mmmm*, give me details on the touches, the desire, how it makes the characters rabid for each other." She moans in the back of her throat.

"So, you read porn?" he questions.

"No, no, no," she protests like a child, and with each "no," she pounds her fist into his shoulder for emphasis. "See! This is what men always do. They try to put down women for reading smutty things, but if a man writes smut like that Game of whatever show with dragons, it's hailed as a masterpiece. Is it arousing? Yes, of course, it is. But, unlike porn, the romance I read has emotional connections. Like I said, they almost always end up together at the end. It's *romance*. It has a happy ever after." She snickers until she snorts. "Yeah, this information will totally help you in your dangerous monster work in the future. I can see it now."

She pats him on the shoulder and sits back, done with rubbing him. He rolls both shoulders, testing out the muscles. He's going to be sore, but the pain is gone. He's never had a shoulder rub as good as what she just gave him.

He turns to face her and deepens his tone. "I'll read a romance. Just tell me which one."

She stares at him in disbelief. "Um. Let's see ..."

She brings a finger to her lips in thought, but the alcohol is making her brain work extra hard, and she's struggling to stay awake.

"There are so many to choose from. Do you want paranormal, like vampires and lots of blood? Or fantasy?" She yawns.

"You choose."

"Uh, for paranormal ..." Her words come out with great effort. "Try *A Throne of Blood*. For fantasy, try *Court of Tears*. Mavis Kemo is the author. She's one of my favorites, and those are the first books in each of their series."

"Alright. It's only fair that I read one since you're reading one of my books." He leans down to pick up the mug of water off the floor and offers it to her. "Drink. It'll help so you don't have a hangover in the morning."

Both her hands come up and grasp the mug to avoid spilling. She gulps the water down in one go.

Blaming the wine, she can't stop herself from staring at the man across from her, who is looking at her intently. She might not know what he looks like, but she sees the kind of person he is. This is the first time she's felt safe enough to open herself up to anyone.

Sure, he has his flaws, but everyone does. He might have this negative image of himself, but he disobeyed orders to save her.

When this is over, he'll go back to working in the shadows, probably dying in some remote part of the world where no one will ever know the sacrifices he made. The thought nearly drives her mad. A kind, considerate man like him deserves better.

The damn wine is summoning an impulse she has no willpower to squash. Yes, it's the wine's fault; she's clumsily leaning closer to him, struggling to keep her balance while on her knees. She's probably going to regret this, but he deserves to know there's at least one person who doesn't think he's an irredeemable monster.

Her gaze drops to where his lips are under the mask. She brings her cheek to his, wishing she could feel his skin on hers instead of the coarse fabric.

Ghoul holds his breath when she hooks her thumb under the bottom of the mask, slowly pulling it up. His hand grasps her wrist harder than he means to. He pulls her hand away, causing her to lose her precarious balance; she falls forward into his chest. He's looking down at her as she looks up at him. She knows she went too far.

"I wasn't going to take your mask off," she whispers.

He sits, unmoving, not even daring to breathe. She's too close, and the only thing holding his control in check is the thin mask. If she kisses him, he's done for.

Abandoning her original idea, another thought forms, something not as intimate as a kiss. She pushes off him, going back onto her knees. She rests her palm on the top of his head. Using her thumb, she lifts the top of his mask away from his forehead to expose the small patch of skin between his eyes. It's furrowed together in confusion.

There's a war raging inside him. Shove her away, or see what she does?

Her smooth lips press into the spot on his forehead. She kisses it three times because, yes, he's counting. She holds her lips to him then pulls away. The small intimate gesture causes his chest to tighten. He wants to hold her to ease the sensation.

She moves the mask back, and he loses himself in those beautiful hazel eyes of hers. She gives him the same smile she did the first time she looked at him at the coffee shop. He can stay lost in those eyes for all eternity, and it would never be enough.

Losing the battle to support herself, her body falls forward into him again. Her arms wrap around his core, awkwardly hugging him, with her head resting on his chest and her backside sticking up in the air.

"I never thanked you." Her words are coming slowly and with great effort. "I never thanked you for saving me."

"I wasn't there to save you." He wasn't, not really, and the dark truth is reflected in his tone.

"I know," she mumbles into his shirt, losing the fight against sleep. "You could have left me there to be raped, but you didn't. Regardless of why you were there, thank you, Ghoul."

Deep breaths of sleep sound from her passing out on top of him.

"Yasmine?"

His hand rests on the small of her back, gently shaking her. There's no response other than she relaxes and becomes heavier. She's lying peacefully on his chest at a weird angle. She hugs him tighter in her sleep.

He pulls the mask away from his lips and presses them to her forehead.

"You're such a brat," he whispers.

He wraps his arms around her, holding her tightly to him. He kisses her forehead again and then tucks her under his chin. Resting his cheek against her, he closes his eyes, breathing in her scent. It's been so long since he's held anyone, and it's easier to keep his desire for her under control with her like this. Since she passed out on top of him, he's going to stay like this with her for a little while.

Chapter Eighteen
Discipline? What Discipline?

Yasmine wakes the next morning sprawled on her back and taking up most of the queen-sized bed. The blanket has been pushed to her feet, and her sweats are back on. The shirt is bunched up, exposing her midriff.

Blinking at the wooden support beams of the ceiling makes her head pound. The last thing she remembers is talking with Ghoul about romance books. Then everything is hazy, and there's no memory of how she got to bed.

Slowly, she pulls herself to a seated position and takes stock of her body. Other than a splitting headache and wanting to hide under the blanket from the light streaming in through the window, she feels fine. The tension and worry she's carried inside since the kidnapping have eased, but her hip still feels like a sword is piercing her, sending sharp pains down her leg.

Heat rises to her face the more her brain wakes up, wondering if she did or said anything embarrassing in front of him. She has a lingering feeling of wanting to kiss him but doesn't understand why. Why would she want to kiss him?

Groaning from the effort, she swings her legs over the side of the bed. Turning her head, the stained white mug is waiting for her, filled with water, and so are two white pills on the nightstand. A quirk plays at the corner of her mouth as she reaches for the painkillers and downs all the water. At the same time, she vows to never drink again. It's not worth it.

Ghoul sits at the island, lost in thought while drinking a cup of instant coffee. He finished breakfast a while ago and now waits for her to get up. He can't bring himself to wake her. He checked on her to make sure she was breathing when he woke up and left her with water and painkillers.

The pain in his shoulder is all but gone when he rolls it to get the muscles moving. Even in her inebriated state, she gave him the best shoulder rub. The woman also finally dropped her guard and opened her inner world to him. She's so full of life when she's not hiding away to protect herself. Ghoul easily could have been "that guy" and taken advantage of her, and yes, he was desperate to feel more of their skin touch, caressing each other until they join together. But instead, the urge to protect her replaced the lustful desires.

Something last night shifted inside him. He still desires her, but there's more to it now because instead of the heat going to his "little head," it's now warming the space around his heart to the point it's difficult to breathe. It happened when he put her to bed after getting the sweats on. He had sat on the edge of the bed, brushing the hair away from her face with the back of his hand, and stroked her cheek while watching her snore before he left.

He gets up and is at the sink washing his dishes when the quiet flutter of movement reaches his ears. The bathroom door opens and closes, and then a minute later, the shower turns on.

A smile plays on his lips. She's up.

After she passed out on top of him, he had held her to his chest, trying to remember a time when he was this drawn to a woman. He's only had experience with a few others, and they don't come close to what he felt last night. He never just cuddled with anyone, and it not be just about sex.

Could this be him? Not the monster he was molded into because of childhood trauma and the operant conditioning of the Marine Corps, but the human part of him, who wants to feel her and the connection? When this is over, the thought of letting her go leaves a hollow space in his chest.

It doesn't matter what he wants; he has a job to do, and the thought leaves bitter ash in his mouth. Tonight, after dinner, he's taking her into the basement for questions. Down there, he can focus and get down to business and find out what she knows about her father.

When he's done with her, she'll return to fearing and might even hate him. She'll see what kind of person he is with his imposing presence. His chest tightens, not liking the idea one bit. She told him the night before she doesn't see him as a monster, but she doesn't know why he earned the nickname Ghoul.

The shower, painkillers, and brushing her teeth help clear Yasmine's head. She's slowly feeling more human. The only thing she needs now is food, and her stomach growls in agreement. For once, she feels hungry in the morning.

Wrapping the towel around herself, she gathers up the dirty clothes, peeks out the door to see if the coast is clear, and pads to the bedroom, closing the door behind her.

She tosses the clothing onto the bed on the way to the closet. Maybe there's something in there she missed. She already picked through the clothes from the dresser and knows there's nothing else in there she can wear. She just needs something to put on until she can wash the other ones. After a few days, they need a good washing. She tries to count how many days it's been, but they're blurring together.

Her clothes from the day of the kidnapping are folded neatly on the floor next to the bed. She could wear them, but instead, she makes a face. She's not ready to put them on. It doesn't matter if they're clean; they're a reminder of what she went through.

She starts flipping through the costumes, bypassing the ones she saw the first night. The further she goes, the more revealing the clothing becomes.

He must have some kink with women's clothing? Maybe a fetish? The thought comes and goes.

A growl of frustration sounds from the back of her throat when she pulls out a piece of black faux leather lingerie with all the naughty bits exposed. There are holes where the nipples go! Heat flushes her cheeks before she shoves it back in the closet, shaking her head.

She's losing hope she'll ever find something acceptable to wear among the women's clothing. She glances at the shirt and sweats she's been wearing that she tossed on the bed. She can probably wear them another day; they don't stink too badly.

The next outfit she pulls is a sexy maid costume, and while the skirt is too short, it's the only one with the most fabric she's found. She holds the clothing to her body and takes a step, leaning to the side to peek at herself in the mirror attached to the closet door. The thought of dressing like a maid in front of Ghoul ... Showing skin in this outfit is not something she thinks she can do.

"I did take my sweats off in front of him last night, so he's seen my legs," she reminds herself. But then she's shaking her head. "No way!"

She aggressively shoves the maid's outfit back into the closet, deciding she'll have to wear his clothes because it's what she feels safe in. Before turning away, though, a piece of black cloth at the very back catches her eye. She reaches for the hanger and pulls out a black dress. It's reminiscent of something Morticia Addams would wear. A long flowing skirt with a slit to the thigh and long bell-shaped sleeves. Lace spiderwebs cover the plunging neckline. It would be form fitting on her if it wasn't two sizes too big, but it will cover her up.

She only needs to wear it until she washes the other clothes, and then she can change.

Resisting the urge to look in the mirror after putting the dress on, she gathers up the dirty clothes and wet towel and then heads out to get them going in the washing machine.

Ghoul is standing at the stove with his back to her, cooking eggs.

"Morning," she mumbles because it hurts her brain to speak.

He doesn't bother to look at her when she blows past him to open the slatted doors and shoves the clothes into the washer.

"Morning," he responds coolly, flipping the scrambled eggs on a plate next to two pieces of buttered toast. Since she didn't eat much the night before, he knows she must be hungry, and it's late morning. "How's the hangover?"

Yasmine's rethinking her choice in clothing the second she stares at his shoulders. She should have worn his clothes another day, but it's too late. She's committed to wearing the dress because everything else is now wet. There's no turning back.

"It's not too bad," she tells him, stepping to her claimed spot at the island. Her hands rest shakily on the back of the stool. "Thanks for the Tylenol."

He turns and nearly drops the plate of food. His eyes widen. His gaze slowly travels up and down the length of her body and lingers at the slit at her thigh and then at the plunging neckline where her skin under the lace is teasing his eyes. She hasn't been wearing a bra this entire time, but now seeing her without one, in THAT dress, it sends a surge of heat straight to his dick. He sees every one of her curves through the fabric. Her wet hair is clinging to her shoulders, leaving him speechless at the goddess in human form standing before him. Her chest is rising and falling rapidly in nervousness at his gawking.

He doesn't care if she sees him ogling her. But she looks away quickly; his intense staring is more than she can handle. She's tempted to hide in the bedroom until the clothes are done with the way he's looking at her. He's causing heat to pool in places she'd rather not get hot right now. Yasmine shoves down the feelings his stalking gaze elicits. As much as she wants to hide, he's already seen her, and it'd be more awkward for her to do it now.

"I'm only going to wear this until the clothes are done. I didn't ..."

She hedges. "I-I'm uncomfortable wearing my own clothes at the moment. Because of what happened, you know?"

She fumbles over her words, and she doesn't know where to put her hands or where to look. His silence, and unblinking stare, unnerves her, and she can't look at him or she'll spontaneously combust.

"You seriously have some weird clothing fetish." She attempts to deflect from her feeling of being exposed with some joshing. Yeah, it's not working.

"You can wear the dress as long as you want." He finally breaks his silence, regaining a measure of composure with great effort, and sets the plate down. "You should eat."

He leans against the counter, shoving his hands in his pockets.

Discipline, discipline, he repeats like a mantra, but he can't waste this opportunity of seeing a goddess in real life.

She moves into her seat, looking down at the plate of food. "You made this for me?"

"Uh huh." He nods, keeping his distance. His years of learning and maintaining discipline are being fully tested.

Her fingers curl around the fork, and then she's digging in. His incessant staring is making her more self-conscious by the minute. So, she does what she always does when she's nervous and distracts herself.

"I'm wondering," she asks after devouring a slice of toast, "what DO you do with all the provocative clothing in your closet? Are they your clothes? Your girlfriend's, maybe? Do you cosplay in your free time?"

Her eyes wander over his masculine frame, lingering like his gaze does. If he can do it, then so can she!

"That would fit, especially with the mask look you have going."

They're locked into a staring contest with each other. She takes a bite of egg without breaking eye contact with him. She stubbornly doesn't want to be the one to look away first this time, despite being barely able to keep her heart from pounding out of her chest. In her way, she's trying to take control and is tired of being the one always blushing. She'll see how long this can last before she loses her composure.

He kicks away from the counter and takes the seat opposite her. He needed time to remember all the tactics he's learned about maintaining discipline in the face of an enemy. She's not an enemy, but he can use the same techniques to keep his damn cock caged in his pants.

"That's not something I'm going to tell you." He keeps his tone nonchalant. "It's need to know."

No way in hell will he tell her; it's too cringey to share. He's burning the image of her into his memory banks because seeing her in the dress plays into WHY he has the clothing.

She feels like she's burning up. She caught him a few times checking her out, but this is the first time he's not trying to hide it.

"Fair enough. I'll just make up my own story then." She clears her throat, smirking.

"Oh god." He groans. "Please, don't."

Grinning mischievously, she doesn't listen.

"It's been established you're a stalker. Meaning, you're the kind of stalker who steals women's dirty underwear to sniff." She points an accusing finger at him. "First point in your training, Ghoul: EW, that's gross. Don't be a creep."

She gasps, clutching her chest. "That's why you keep going in the basement! Your panty stash is down there!"

"What the fuck?" He face-palms himself, shaking his head.

She makes herself laugh at her creative story she's making up on the fly. It takes a bit for her girlish giggling to stop.

"The clothes are too small for you. I mean this dress ..."

She holds her arms out and looks down at her chest then studies his frame and muscular build. He does have a nice build, just the right amount of muscle tone but not overly bulky like a gym bro.

"You're much larger than I am." She taps her finger to her chin in thought. "I'm going to go with what I said when you brought me here. This is a secret sex cabin you bring women to when you're on leave. And! You have some seriously weird kinks and fetishes. I mean the ninja outfit barely covers the naughty bits."

"Naughty bits?" he murmurs under his breath.

"That black faux leather—" Her eyes widen. "Never mind, I'm not going there."

"Oh no, please continue," he urges because of the instant embarrassment crossing her face. "I assume you're talking about the one with the nipple holes and crotchless panties. What about it?"

His tone turns teasing, and he wants to see her blush deepen. He's a man after all, and he knows she would look great in the piece. He would utterly destroy her until her legs shook so badly she couldn't stand or walk. Her fork clanks loudly on the plate when she hides her face behind both hands.

"Did I find the brat's weakness?" he teases, deepening his voice. "You can read smutty books and tease me about kinks and fetishes." He leans forward and grasps her chin. "Look at me," he commands.

One eye peeks out from between her fingers.

"But in real life, this makes you nervous and embarrassed. Why?"

"That's need to know," she croaks out with great difficulty.

She keeps her left hand up, shielding her eyes from him like he is glare from the sun, and focuses on finishing her breakfast.

This woman is such a brat. Why does she have to be so cute? He's learned what makes her tick, and God is she adorable when she's bashful.

Ghoul's laughing makes her head snap up, not sure if she's hearing right. Sure enough, the laugh reaches his eyes. She's heard low chuckles and low rumblings before, but not this. He's honest to God laughing, and it's causing an unintended reaction in her body — it's trembling. A laugh has never once turned her on.

Silence settles over them while Ghoul watches her eat. All she can do is focus on her breakfast and tell her lady parts to calm down. When the silence becomes too much, she can't handle it.

"Did I do or say anything weird last night?" she asks apprehensively.

"Do you mean weird like collapsing on me and I had to carry you to bed, or do you mean your loud snoring?"

"I don't snore!"

He gives her a yeah-right-you're-not-fooling-anyone look. "Sure, you don't, angel."

Her mouth flies open to protest, but she thinks better of it because his random nickname causes her mouth to snap shut.

"Did you do anything to me?"

"No. But when I carried your ass to bed, I did see part of a tattoo on your hip. What is it?"

She shoves eggs into her mouth. If he's asking about the tattoo, then maybe he didn't do anything with her in a passed-out state.

"You saw that?" she questions through a mouthful of eggs.

"I saw some color on the top of your hip." He easily could have lifted her shirt to see, but he didn't. As much as he wanted to, he wasn't going to touch her while unconscious.

"It's a phoenix." No one else knows about it except her and the tattoo artist.

He briefly wonders if he asked to see the tattoo, if she'd show him? He likes tattoos, especially on women. The artwork enhances a woman's natural beauty, being a work of art herself.

After a long pause, Yasmine tries again. "I really didn't do anything weird or embarrassing?"

"If you did, what does it matter?" he answers with a shrug.

She sits, munching on the last bit of toast, and contemplates the question. Why does it matter? She was drunk, and her inhibitions crumbled along with the walls she hides behind. For the first time, she let go of all restraints. She allowed her authentic self to come out with someone she barely knows. This is a new one for her, to feel a connection to someone who hasn't even shown his face.

"I guess it doesn't matter," she agrees.

Yasmine continues to eat, and the entire time, he stares. She's had enough.

"Is there a reason why you're watching me eat?"

"Stalker, remember? What else do I have to watch? I have nothing better to do, and I'm making sure you eat."

After she puts the last of the toast in her mouth, he stands and takes her plate.

"That's a good girl, eating all your food." He's hungry to see how she reacts when he uses the words she taught him, and she doesn't disappoint.

Blinking rapidly, a cute girlish smile forms across her lips. What he knows of her father from the file, and the information she's shared about the man, he sees she's probably never been praised — much like himself. The thought crosses his mind of her calling him a "good boy," but he shakes it off.

Her stomach flip-flops, doing what she calls *the thing*. His tone is genuine, but she wonders if she really is a good girl for eating?

"Why are you so concerned about my eating habits?" Does he actually care about her well-being?

"As long as you're under my protection, I'm going to make sure you eat enough," he answers with his back to her. Ghoul washes the dishes and leaves them in the rack to dry. She hops off the stool, the fabric of the dress cascading to the floor. She leans her back against the island, folding her arms across her chest.

"You didn't answer the question."

When done, he turns to face her. The view is gorgeous, and he's ravaging her with his careful inspection, like she's at attention just for him.

"With your build and height, especially being a female, your BMI is too low." His hand comes up to graze her cheek, but he pulls away before touching her. "You have a haunted gauntness in your face because you don't eat enough."

He shoves his hands in his pockets, pressing his hips into the counter opposite her. His hands need to be restrained, or he's going to lose control ... again.

"Is it society's unrealistic beauty standards or something else?" he asks and then jumps right to the point. "Did a guy make a comment?"

She glares at him, but it's because he reached for her face and then pulled back. She wants to feel his touch on her face again. It's sweet and addicting.

One little almost touch, and I'm ready to break. She scolds herself.

Yasmine purses her lips together and blows her breath out through her nose.

"First off, guys are never interested in me," she states matter-of-factly.

Her words punch him in the gut. Can she not see how much he's attracted to her? He can't take his fucking eyes off her!

"Second, society's beauty standards. I don't know any woman who doesn't feel the pressure from time to time, even if we know deep down it's bullshit and unrealistic expectations placed on us."

The truth of her struggling with eating doesn't stem from society's unrealistic expectations of women. The real source springs from someone else. The sting of acid tears burns her eyes. One silently runs down her cheek.

He pushes off the counter, slowly reaching for her. He gives her a chance to move away, but instead, she waits for the touch. Her arms wrap around his core, and she buries her head in his chest without thinking, desperate to feel the slightest amount of his protective warmth.

So much for keeping his hands to himself. His arms protectively cradle her, rubbing his hand down the length of her back. She's so frail and breakable in his arms. He pulls back to wipe the tears away.

"Please tell me," he coaxes.

Between his closeness and her own emotions threatening to break through the wall she hides behind, she has to take a deep, steadying breath. She's surprised at how easily she's relaxing into his embrace.

Unfortunately, he's probably playing with her just like the guys in the past, just leading her along in some twisted mind game to get her body. But damn if being in his arms doesn't make her feel safe.

"Take your time, but you're not going anywhere until you tell me." His thumb makes slow circles on her cheek.

What he's asking for is something she never told her therapist because she couldn't find the words to start. His eyes are full of concern, and his strong, secure hold he has her in is slamming into her walls, making them crack and crumble. She holds him tighter, laying her head on his chest to ground and prepare herself to finally say it. She believes what he says about not letting her leave until she tells him.

"My father wasn't exactly loving," she begins with a self-deprecating laugh. "When I was younger, if I refused to eat anything on my plate, he'd force me to. Even if I wasn't hungry or if something about the food grossed me out, he'd force-feed me. He'd grab me by the throat and choke me until I ate it. But if I ate something I wanted, like sweets, he'd fat shame me. I could never win and was damned either way. That fucks with a developing mind. I've dealt with an eating disorder ever since.

Mom did what she could to protect me from him. She'd make my plates how I liked them and cook foods I could eat, but it got worse when she left."

The words spill out. The shame and disgust in her quivering voice causes him to pull her tighter to him. The fury is settling in his gut at what she just revealed about her upbringing.

"The more time I spend away from him, the more it's slowly getting better." Her voice is muffled by his chest. "I'm getting better at seeking out foods I enjoy instead of forcing myself to eat something I hate. But years of abuse don't exactly go away overnight. Sometimes, it's hard to eat much of anything."

Her shoulders rise and fall with her breath. "Then add the stress of life and grad school on top of everything ... I'm the type who doesn't like eating when they're stressed, so it makes for an exciting combination."

She buries her face in his embrace, prepared for him to laugh, or worse, yell. She waits for the reactions, but they don't come. Instead, his grip becomes almost crushing with how tightly he's holding onto her.

Anger flares, consuming him in a fiery blaze. All his hate is solely directed at her father. He's going to kill the man, but not before he thinks of all the ways he'd torture her father, slowly drawing out as much pain as he can inflict before wiping the man's existence from the face of the earth. This tiny woman, whose forehead barely makes it to his chin, who's shaking from her emotion, deserves to live in safety.

Keeping one arm around her waist, his finger brushes along her cheek and comes to rest under her chin, guiding her to look at him. It's inconceivable to have a father choking his own daughter to make her eat.

"Any man who harms a child or woman doesn't deserve to remain breathing." His words are filled with violence.

The initial reaction she has at his touch and the anger in his tone is to flinch away because of all the times she's been hit. But his touch is different; it's so gentle. She breathes through her fright and relaxes her shoulders, and then the tears are blurring her vision.

"I'm sorry," she chokes, wiping the tears away with her palm. In so many ways, she's still such a child.

"I'm sorry," she repeats, not knowing why she's saying it.

His hand cups the back of her head, pulling her forehead to his lips. He holds her there. The fabric of his mask is rough on her skin, but she doesn't mind.

"Don't you be sorry for what someone did to you. You have no reason to be sorry." His hot breath warms her forehead.

His lips pressing into her causes more of her walls to fall away because he didn't get angry or yell at her. She can't hold back the feelings she's been suppressing all these years. She shared something painful about her experience with another person. It's like he's given her permission to unleash the tears she tries so desperately to hold back.

Tucking her under his chin, he holds on to her while she quietly sobs into his chest, giving her the time she needs.

The tears eventually dry up, and she pulls away to see the large wet spot on his shirt.

"I'm sorry. Your shirt is full of snot." Unthinking, she tries in vain to wipe it away.

He grabs her hands, holding them flat to his chest. He brushes a stray strand of hair from her face, tucking it behind her ear.

"Never say sorry to me." His voice is reassuring. "Even if it takes years, do me a favor, and be a good girl and eat."

All she can do is nod in a silent promise.

"Can I ask you something?" she says hesitantly.

"Yes."

"You still haven't answered the question. Why are you concerned with how much I eat? No one has ever cared before." She's all too aware they're still holding onto each other.

He crushes her to his chest because, if he's holding her, maybe he can share his pain with her like she did with him. He's never been vulnerable enough to tell anyone. His other relationships never got close to this level of trust, not even with his fiancé.

"My parents were drug addicts. Pop's drugs of choice were alcohol and coke. Meth was my mom's. It made her waste away. Having two deadbeat parents who can barely work meant I went to bed hungry a lot of times. I was the kid in school the teachers always brought extra food for. If it wasn't for the free breakfasts and lunches, plus whatever my teachers brought me ..."

He chuckles sadly. "You can say I don't like to see someone malnourished because it reminds me of growing up and having a drugged-out mom." Her arms squeeze around him a little tighter. "You still have life in you, and I don't want to see you wasting away."

He tightens his hold of her in return when she starts shaking in his arms with quick inhales of breath, and then the sniffling begins anew. She's crying, but this time, she's crying for him.

No one's ever cried for him. Not even himself.

Chapter Nineteen
A Man Chopping Wood is Damn Sexy

Ghoul braves the cold to gather more firewood from the stack outside. The snow has stopped for now, but the clouds remain. Rage and frustration continue to fester in his chest. The familiar sensation of bloodlust is boiling. He's going to kill her father, whether it's sanctioned or not. Accidents happen on the battlefield all the time.

His need for blood triggered when he realized she was going to be assaulted, and it's only been stewing the more she's revealed about her relationship with her father. This overwhelming urge is not what he needs right now. She can't see this side of him, a bloodthirsty killing machine. She's only now coming out of her shell and allowing herself to be vulnerable with him. He's conflicted. He wants to murder anyone who hurts her but also wants to hold and keep her safe while she cries.

He pulls the tarp back, taking out dry wood and stacking it in his arms. He tries to recall a time when he was comforted. His fiancé certainly never did, and now he doubts if he truly had a connection with her. He's feeling things toward Yasmine he never felt toward any girl because, while they held each other in the kitchen, her compassion wrapped around him like a protective blanket.

Stacking the logs in a pile next to the woodstove, he steals glances at her. She's sitting on the couch. The spy thriller is propped on her lap, but she's staring blankly at the same page. He doesn't know what he can do for her. He's used to "solving" problems, but what she's dealing with is a problem he can't solve. This is why his focus turns to General Pennington; he's part of the problem Ghoul can take care of ....

When Ghoul finishes stacking the wood, he throws another log on the fire and heads back outside to chop more. Not that the wood needs chopping, but he needs to channel this anger into something physical.

With each swing of the axe, he imagines slamming it into Pennington's head. He becomes creative in how he will torture him, drawing out as much pain as possible until the brink of death. He even imagines using her torture method of papercuts and pouring something acidic on her father. Ghoul's no stranger to dishing out torture. In his youth in the gangs, he found a knack for it, and then in the Marines, he refined his techniques. No matter what punishments he comes up with, it's not good enough to make the motherfucker pay for what he did to his daughter.

No wonder Yasmine has issues with food. All the weird habits he's noticed since they've been at the cabin and while he stalked her make sense now, and he's barely scratched the surface.

He doesn't know it, but he has a Peeping Tom. Hazel eyes are peeking out from the bottom of the drapes at the bedroom window. She hopes he'll take the mask off since he's working up a sweat, but he's still stubbornly wearing it. After he held her during her breakdown and shared a part of his past, she wants to see his face now more than ever.

He pulls his coat off, throwing it on top of the woodpile, and pushes up his sleeves, showing off the tattoos covering both arms. The next swing of the ax comes down, and his muscles strain against his skin from the impact. The ax lands with precision, slicing through both logs.

Her breath hitches, and butterflies form in her stomach, sending a wave of heat to the space between her thighs.

When he begins stacking the chopped wood on the pile, she realizes he's done and slips back into the living room.

He hangs his coat next to hers on the line of hooks on the wall. Before heading into the basement, he glances at her. She's on the couch nibbling on a square of dark chocolate; her eyes are moving across the page. The box of cheese crackers he got for her is open and leaning against her thigh. The same one with the slit, which draws forth a deep longing from him.

Good. She's reading and eating something, and even seems to be more into the book. He pushes the desire to sit next to her aside. His internal conflict and anger need to be controlled. If she doesn't know anything about her father, he's going to cause her more pain. The last thing he wants is to add to what she's already carrying, but duty calls, no matter how strong she's pulling him to her.

In the basement, he takes off the mask and shirt. Chopping wood barely took the edge off his anger and thoughts of revenge. He pulls the dust cloth off the weight set he keeps in the corner. When he gets like this, he needs to move to get the anger out, so he begins a series of calisthenics, resistance, and strength exercises. He grounds himself, working his body to the point of exhaustion.

Sweat pours from his brow as he does the last few burpees and pushups. His muscles burn, but the rage has been subdued, for now. To cool down, he does a series of yoga stretches. As he holds his final plank, beads of sweat drip from his toned, suntanned skin to the floor. His shoulder is loose enough to move without causing him pain since she gave him the blissfully painful shoulder rub.

Once done, and with a calmer mind, he sits on the metal folding chair and leans forward, elbows to knees. His head hangs as he focuses on some slow, deep breaths to aid in recovering from his workout. He takes a drink of water from the plastic bottle but he remains lost in thought.

Somehow, it's become personal. How? And when did it happen? The last thing someone like him needs is to be emotionally involved with someone in their charge. He's witnessed firsthand when a squadmate from his unit went through something similar, not long ago. Ghoul saw how it tore up his subordinate, and it made Hill an even bigger asshole than he was before.

This is the first time it's happened to him. He always stays emotionless and detached. It's what makes him so good at what he does. But

Yasmine, her father, all of it. It's way too personal, and he doesn't know how to manage these mysterious feelings.

Before leaving the basement, he meticulously wipes down the free weights and other equipment he used during his workout and then covers them with the dust cloth.

Throwing the towel over his head, he doesn't bother putting his shirt or mask on when he climbs the stairs. He doesn't even bother locking the basement door because she's going to find out soon enough what kind of man he really is, so what does it matter? She needs to stop looking at him with those trusting eyes of hers.

Stopping on the way to the shower, he checks on her. She's leaning on the armrest of the couch, using her arm as a pillow. She doesn't stir from her sleeping position when he comes behind her, takes the book from her hands, and marks the page she's on.

Clothed in black cargo pants and a black Henley, he heads into the bedroom, closing and locking the door behind him. He needs a break from the mask because his hair needs to dry.

Sitting on the edge of the bed, he pulls out his cell phone. His daily check-ins have been unhelpful, with the same order: hold position. The one part of the job that gets under his skin is the boredom of waiting. He hasn't been bored because of her, but he's antsy for things to start moving. Subconsciously he knows he needs to get away from her ASAP before he grows more attached.

He pulls up the app where he buys his books and types in the names of the books she recommended. He reads through both descriptions and decides to buy both. Neither is his type of read, and never in a million years would he willingly read either, but he promised her.

Here he is, a battle-hardened Marine, and he's going to read a chick story. A smirk causes the corner of his mouth to lift.

Once his hair is dry enough, he slips his old mask on, the same one he wore when he saved her, only now there's a new bloodstain. This has been his go-to mask for years, and it certainly has seen a lot of action. It's time he throws it out and gets a new one.

He finds Yasmine hasn't moved, except her mouth is slightly open and she's drooling. The poor girl has been sleeping most of the time since he brought her here. He puts his soiled clothes in the wash and then checks her clothes in the dryer.

Since she's the type to prefer comfortable clothing and not a dress, he folds her clothes and leaves them on the bed for her when she wakes. Then he heads into the kitchen to make a cup of instant coffee before settling himself into his book. He eyes the orange chair and the seat next to her on the couch. Her soft snores fill the space, prompting him to make his decision.

Taking a deep breath, he opts for the couch, easing into the seat next to her and being careful not to disturb her. He crosses an ankle over a knee and glances at her sideways. She's in a calmer state of being. His desire remains, wanting her to give him control of her body for a time, to devour her and bite those thighs. But there's something else present; he doesn't have the words for it because he's never experienced these feelings.

A kink in Yasmine's neck and hip stirs her awake. She sits up, rubbing the spot where it hurts in her neck, but gives up on her hip. She wipes the drool from the corner of her mouth, realizing there's a large wet spot on her arm. She unfolds her legs from under the blanket and stretches her arm out, smacking right into Ghoul's chest with a thud.

"Sorry, I didn't know you were there." She pulls her arm back.

She's questioning her survival instincts because she didn't stir awake when he sat next to her. How long has he been sitting so close while she slept? Embarrassment hits when she realizes the drool is clinging to her face, and he must see it.

"Sorry. I'll wash the dress." Using the back of her hand, she wipes the remaining wetness from her mouth.

"It's just spit." He takes a sip of coffee, pretending to read his book.

She throws the blanket off her, revealing the slit riding up high on her thigh, which causes his attention to divert to her exposed skin.

"My clothes are probably done." She's still groggy from her unexpected nap.

She moves to get up when he holds an arm out to stop her.

"They are. I put them on the bed for you."

"Thanks. I should change." She moves to get up again, but his arm is blocking her once more.

"There's no rush," he insists. "I saved your place. You're getting close to the climax."

He holds the book out to her, and she notices the folded corner marking the page she was on when she passed out. She eyes him and the book.

"That good, huh?" She takes the offered book.

For the third time, she moves to stand, and his arm blocks her. She glares, about to demand what his problem is, but he speaks first.

"Why are you in such a hurry to move away from me?" He closes his book, turning to examine her expression. "You were sitting next to me last night with no problem."

She only has a vague recollection of the night before.

"I was drunk," she retorts defensively. "And now, I'm not."

"You're right, you were drunk." His gaze challenges her, holding her in place. "You're not scared of me, are you?" His voice turns dangerously flirtatious. "You left yourself WIDE open last night. I could have done whatever I wanted to you, and I didn't. So, stop being a brat, and stay next to me while we read."

God help her, he's using a deep commanding voice. She finds herself lying back on the couch. It's unnerving how easily his words make her want to do what he says.

"I didn't get a chance to say it before you passed out, but thanks for the shoulder rub." He returns to his book.

She nods and opens hers to the page he folded over.

"No problem, it's the least I can do," she mutters, pulling the blanket up to cover herself.

Nervousness is overwhelming her senses because of how close she is to him, so she uses the blanket as a barrier. Her mind's screaming at her to move to the chair to put some space between them, but she can't help wanting to stay close to him. She turns her attention back to the book; she's going to ignore the conflict brewing inside her.

He didn't touch her last night when he could have, so it's fine now, right?

An hour later, she's sniffling, and he pauses his book to find moisture gathering in her eyes.

"You alright?" His hand is moving with a mind of its own again, rubbing the top of her shoulders in reassurance.

"Yeah. It's just sad." She's shaking the book. "Jack just killed her, and he had feelings for her."

"You're crying over a fictitious character in a story?" he asks in disbelief.

Her response is to elbow him in the side with a *shh*. The simple sound carries a threat he takes seriously.

He shakes his head. Why does she have to be such a brat and cute at the same time?

Later, when she finishes the book, she closes it and wipes the tears from her eyes.

"Poor Jack. I hope he finds someone."

"You do realize he's not real? And Clare was the villain, right? He had no other choice?" Surely, she can see this.

"I get it, but it was obvious before Jack found out she was the villain that he had feelings for her. Even after he killed her, it hurt him. What's he supposed to do? Just pretend like nothing happened? God, that's so fucked up." She plants her feet on the floor and pulls the blanket off. "See, this is why I don't read stories like this. It's too much like real life. No happy endings."

She stretches her arms over her head at the same time she stretches her legs out in front of her. Her tight muscles protest. She decides if she ever makes it home, she's going to the massage school for a nice massage. She needs it desperately.

"But," she cocks her head, "regardless of the sad ending and all the unnecessary details, I liked the story." She gets to her feet and then folds in half, her fingertips touching the floor. "I don't know if my heart can take another one."

The sound of a slap echoes through the cabin, and the force of his hand slapping her ass pushes Yasmine forward, making her catch herself. She freezes, startled at the fading stinging sensation. She turns to stare at him in shock. He sits motionless with his eyes moving back and forth across a page in his book, but his smirk is reflected in his eyes. She's throwing daggers at him because he knows what he did. She wants to be angry, but her heart's pounding.

Once again, he was in motion before he could stop it. Her ass was right there, and in his face! How could he not smack it? Her eyes are wide under the fiery stare she levels at him. One eye twitches as her hand comes up and flips him the middle finger. Then she turns on him and storms to the bedroom.

He throws his head back, doing his best to stifle his laughter.

Pressing her back into the bedroom door, Yasmine rubs her face viciously with both hands.

What the actual fuck? Her mind reels. *He smacks my ass and then sits back and pretends like nothing happened?*

Peeling the black dress off, she puts it on the hanger and throws it back in the closet. She's not going to feel guilty about getting snot on the dress now, let alone go out of her way to clean it. He can do it himself!

She's staying in the T-shirt and sweats, even if they start smelling again. She'll wear them until she leaves the cabin.

After changing, she's still flustered and sits on the edge of the bed, holding her head and trying to convince herself this is real life and not one of her romance novels. They've been stuck together for ... how many days has it been? He's relaxed around her now and just being a typical dude.

She pulls her hands away from her face and stares at them. No way he's into her. It would be impossible, right? She thinks back to all their interactions, and she's not so sure.

Shaking her head to clear it, she starts doing her hair in a French braid, allowing her thoughts to wander back to him. Sure, she rubbed his shoulder to help him. He held her while she cried in the kitchen, but he was only giving her a safe place to do it.

That's all it was, right?

Even if he's into her, it'll never work between them. They come from two very different worlds. But, would it be terrible to allow herself to get wrapped up in whatever this is with him?

Before her thoughts can implode on her, she finds her hair tie and secures the end of her braid from unraveling. She takes a few moments to compose herself. She's going to be keeping a closer eye on him, and his intentions.

Chapter Twenty
Wait, What The...?

Returning to the main room, Yasmine finds Ghoul immersed in his book like he did nothing. Two can play this game. If he can pretend, then so can she!

She sits on the floor next to the fire with her legs in front of her. Folding herself in half, she tries to stretch out the sore muscles in her back and hips. She takes herself through various yoga positions. No matter how she moves, though, she can't get enough of a stretch to alleviate the protesting muscles.

He attempts to focus on the book, but she's distracting him again. The view before him is sexier than any woman at a strip club. Not that he frequents strip clubs; they're not his vibe. But this private showing is causing him to tent his pants. He's embracing what he's done for weeks — watching her — but now he's leaning into a voyeuristic persona, and he doesn't care. The sight before him is beautiful.

"Careful, stalker, I can hear your heavy breathing." Her voice breaks the silence, snapping him out of the trance.

Is she a goddamn mind reader? He wonders how she knew he was looking.

Her eyes are closed, and she hasn't so much as looked at him since she came out of the bedroom. The little grunts she makes cause him to take notice of her physical pain.

"Is it your back?" he asks.

She stays in child's pose, not bothering to look at him.

"Yeah, since I had to sit on the cold concrete in that awkward position. It's getting spicier, and I can't seem to work it out."

"You want some help?" He puts both feet on the floor and leans forward.

She helped him with his shoulder, so it's only fair he helps her.

She eyes him suspiciously, trying to judge if he has some ulterior motive or not.

"Keep your hands away from my ass," she warns.

He chuckles, getting on the floor with her.

"No ass slapping," he promises. "But, you did leave yourself wide open." He's on his knees, sitting on his haunches in front of her. "Show me where it hurts?"

She likewise gets on her knees. Her hand moves from her lower back to her hip and buttocks.

"On your back," he orders, pointing to the floor. "Do a bridge."

She keeps a suspicious eye on him the whole time until she's on her back. "How do you know about yoga poses?"

She pushes her heels and shoulders into the floor, lifting her hips in the air as high as she can.

"Can I touch your waist to lift you higher?" he asks.

Her hips fall back to the floor, and she stares up at him with a flippant expression.

"Now you ask if you can touch me?" Her tone is condescending.

The smile under the mask makes it to his eyes.

"You're right," he agrees and slides his hands under the small of her back, lifting her hips and pelvis. "I'm going to touch your back."

A groan sounds from her throat from the stretch. Her inhale and exhale come in deep, controlled breaths.

"I'm going to slowly move you side to side, so relax," he instructs.

He begins rocking her pelvis slowly and gently. He carefully sets her down, which triggers her to let out another groan. Her face grimaces when she rolls to the side and jabs her fist into the angry muscles.

"Keep your leg out straight." He hooks his hand behind the other leg, bringing her knee over the bottom leg.

Her groans are accompanied by heavy breathing. It takes every ounce of discipline he has to focus his thoughts on relieving her pain instead of the precarious position he's balancing with his hands intimately touching her body. He takes some deep breaths, the same ones drilled into him when he's about to snipe someone.

"I'll rub your hip." He shoos her out of his way.

Using the heel of his palm, he pushes into her hip and thigh, urging the muscle fibers to untangle themselves. He makes sure to keep his fist closed because she's trusting him, and he doesn't want to cop a feel. Even though he absolutely wants to run his hands over her thigh to the curve of her ass.

When he digs in deeper, she bites her lip, slams her eyes shut, and whimpers from the sharp pain radiating down her leg.

"Sorry." He lightens his touch.

"It's fine." She's gritting her teeth, breathing through the pain. "It just hurts."

"If you want me to stop, I will," he tells her. Ghoul massages down her leg, following the trail of tight muscle fibers, to give her a reprieve before he goes back to working on the stubborn knot in her hip.

"It feels good." She moans out in blessed relief but also because his touch feels so damn good.

Shoving his desire down, he looks anywhere else except at her. Her moans sound like when a woman is in the throes of pleasure; it's taking all his years of training to not think of sex right now.

Once he finishes rubbing both sides and feels the muscles have loosened, Ghoul sits back on his heels, resting his hands loosely on his thighs.

"How's that?

She moves her leg around, testing it. The shooting pain is gone.

"Much better!" She smiles and gives him a thumbs-up.

Pointing her toes straight and her fingers in the opposite direction, she fully stretches and then relaxes back to the floor.

"Yup, better." She's grateful for his help.

His hand lands on her chest, pushing her back to the floor. He interrupts her attempt to protest.

"You're not done!" He's leaving no room for argument. "You still need to stretch, so bring your knees to your chest."

She's not going to say no to having his hands on her again. He pushes on her knees, moving them further into her chest, deepening the stretch.

"Good." He guides her feet back to the floor. "Put the bottoms of your feet together and drop your knees."

She stares at him with protesting eyes. Opening her legs in front of him does not sound like a good idea, and the bastard's smirking. He rubs the outside of her thigh in encouragement.

"Come on, be a good girl and drop your knees for me." He deliberately makes his voice rumble in his chest with his coaxing.

She closes her eyes, so she doesn't have to see his damn infuriating grin reflected in his eyes. When her knees drop, he's pressing on them, deepening the stretch. Her mouth opens, and the air escapes both from pain and relief.

"Open those legs wider for me." His tone is dangerously enticing with his teasing.

His words might be seductive, but he respectfully keeps his hands on her knees despite wanting to explore the space between her thighs.

"And you call me a brat?" A scoffing laugh meets his comments. She's unable to keep her thoughts to herself. "What was I thinking teaching you how to be a book boyfriend? I think I just betrayed all of womankind by telling you the secret."

She'd never admit it, especially to him, but she's enjoying this. She's never been genuinely praised before. Her whole life has only been her failures thrown or screamed in her face.

"You are a brat," he insists. "But you can be good, if you want to."

Just like he thought the night she was teaching him, a little praise and she puts up no resistance. She's more than happy to follow his instructions because he used those words genuinely. He doesn't care about her betraying womankind's secret. He's only using the secret on one woman. Her.

"You enjoy picking on me, don't you?" she accuses.

He slowly releases the pressure on her legs, allowing her to bring her knees together.

"Who's picking?" he asks innocently while sitting back on his haunches. "I'm helping someone in my care stretch her sore muscles."

She sits up quickly, coming face to mask with him, and juts her chin out. "You know exactly what you're doing."

"If you don't want my help, I'll go back to my book." He wants to grab her chin so badly to wipe the defiance from her.

Touching her how he did left him sweating and in a desperate need to throw his mask off and stick both of his heads in the snowbank to cool down.

He's resting on his knees in front of her with the stupid eye grin of his. She holds no hope it'll work, and he'll probably just call her a brat again, but she feels the need to make a point.

Regardless of the outcome, she feels like retribution is on the menu for the ass smack. She wraps her legs around his middle and uses her body weight to twist, throwing him off balance.

She doesn't know if he let her or if she truly caught him off guard, but suddenly he's on his back and she's straddling his hips. His eyes are staring up at her in amusement, and his hands are fully grasping the sweet spot of her hips.

He accepts her challenge with great effort because the heat from between her legs is enveloping him. Her little stunt is overwhelming his already slipping resolve. He's losing control, and he must take it back in this situation before he does something he'll regret.

"Don't threaten me with a good time." He locks his arms around her legs, holding her in place. "Just remember, you brought this on yourself."

The moves he uses on her happen in a blur. It's so quick, she can't keep up. Now she's on her back with him straddling her hips. He uses one hand to easily pin both arms above her head; the other is tickling her side.

She's thrashing, squealing, and shrieking between gasps of laughter. Her legs are flailing, trying and failing to get him off, but it's like a boulder is pinning her down. He's much heavier than he looks.

He stops tickling, and it takes her a few more laughs to realize it before her thrashing stops.

Breathless, she yowls, "You asshole."

He holds his hand up, making it look like a claw, and tauntingly brings it back to her side. He hovers, wiggling his fingers threateningly.

"What was that? What did you call me?"

She tries to get away from the clawed hand, but she has nowhere to go with him pinning her. She makes an ugly face at him.

"You heard me."

Her eyes go wild with the impending threat, and his fingers resume wiggling at her side. Her eyes clamp shut, and she grits her teeth in preparation, making small whimpers of anticipation but refusing to scream or laugh. He's using her own expectation against her in torture. Then his fingers are lightly dancing at her side and pressing into her flesh. Her focus is on the hand tickling her side, so she doesn't even notice her arms are free to move. Nor does she catch that he's supporting her head.

Questioning lips brush over hers, waiting for her response. Her eyes fling open and meet his at the same moment he presses his lips to hers. Then he draws back enough to speak.

"Be good and keep your eyes closed for me." His hot breath fills her mouth, making her insides turn molten.

She should shove him off. That'd be the smart thing to do, but her body's not listening. Her eyes close, and his body weight presses into her. His tongue brushes across her lips, asking for permission, and she obliges.

Surrendering to his tongue's invasion, Yasmine wraps herself around his neck, pulling him into her. Apparently she's not going to listen to the warning bells telling her this is dangerous. Instead, she's listening to her traitorous pussy throbbing in desire and returning the kiss because — damn — this is hot.

He should take it slow, but being stuck in the cabin with her for five days, he no longer has the will to fight. He hungrily devours her mouth for himself, finally able to taste and feel her body pressing into him. His kiss is strong and commanding, showing her how much he craves and wants her.

Every fantasy he has had of her since the first morning he hid in the shadows outside her apartment, to when she smiled at him in the coffee shop and then turned away blushing, to her drunken state in nothing but panties and a T-shirt ... nothing compares to the real woman he can hold.

His free hand feels along the fleshy part of her thigh he's dreamed of touching. Working his way down, he relishes in her softness. He grasps her knee, guiding her leg to wrap around him.

Following his cue, she brings the other up, hooking both legs onto him and making him sink deeper into her. His body moves without his consent. Dry humping her sends a surge of electricity coursing through his body, lighting up all his nerve endings. His tongue plunges into her mouth, exploring every inch, and she's so willingly inviting him in, but it's not enough — he needs more of her.

She's had enough of his mouth, and his plump lip is calling her to bite into it, which she does, and then she licks where she bit. His fingers are cupping her ass, pulling her tighter to him while pushing his hardness into her.

There's little room for her hands to explore with how tight of a hold he has on her, but she finally pries a hand free. She starts at his wrists, feeling his muscles through his clothing, and works her way up his arms and then his shoulders until she can get her fingers in his hair. She curses the mask because it's covering most of it. When her fingers cautiously slide under the mask, she starts alternating between caressing his neck and playing with the short hair along his hairline.

Breaking their kiss, he takes his time to savor the feel of his lips and tongue trailing hot kisses and licks down the length of her neck. Her head tilts to the side, giving him full access. When he reaches the sweet spot where the neck meets the shoulder, he bites. Her fingers turn into talons clutching his neck. Her limbs constrict around him.

Her hands find their way under his shirt; her short nails rake across his back. His answering moan causes his hips to thrust into her, needing her to see and feel how hard he is for her.

Tiny fingers slip between his waistband and skin, teasingly brushing along his waist. She grasps onto him, pulling him at the same time she pushes her pelvis into him.

Warning bells signal a red alert. He has to stop this. NOW. What the hell is he doing? He royally fucked up. Again. They never should have done this.

He quickly pulls the mask into place and then creates distance between them by getting to his feet. If he doesn't stop, he won't be able to, and he refuses to use sex to manipulate her, and that's what this would be, manipulation.

Her eyes open, and she stares at him in confusion. Her clothing is crumpled, and the way her legs are laid open is so inviting. He could so easily take her, and she wouldn't put up a fight. He felt how eager her body responded to his touch.

He turns his back to her, grabs his book, and heads to the basement without saying a word, inadvertently slamming the door behind him. He needs to cool down and get some distance from her.

Yasmine's still on her back as she listens to his footsteps fade down the stairs. She stares at the ceiling, not sure what just happened. Then the self-doubt takes over. She wonders what she did wrong.

Chapter Twenty-One
Hiding Like a Bitch

For the rest of the afternoon, Ghoul stays in the basement, and several times Yasmine stops herself from storming down there and demanding what the fuck his problem is. Anger gives her a small amount of strength. The alternative is to break down crying. Both routes aren't good. Something stops her from going to him. Maybe it's the creepy basement or knowing she should leave him alone like she does with her father.

She attempts to start another one of his books to distract herself, but she can't shake the lingering feeling of him pressing into her or the kiss, so she finds herself at the bottom of the page not retaining any of the words. Her body remains in a state of arousal, to the point it's uncomfortable. Slamming the book closed, she gives up, throwing it on the couch. She needs air and to get out of the cabin. She hopes a walk in the cold will help clear her mind and get this throbbing sensation out from between her legs.

Bundled up against the cold, she starts making circles again in the snow. The spot where her snow angel used to be has been covered over. Everything is blanketed in a fresh heavy snow, muffling the sounds from the forest. All she can hear is her breathing and the snow compacting under her footsteps. The cold bites at her nose and cheeks.

She's walking down the short tree-lined drive to the road. She's not going far, but she needs to do something, anything, to get the feel of him off her. Her gloved fingers brush her lips; they remain swollen from the kiss.

That was hot. The thought sends a fresh wave of heat to her core, making it hard to support her weight and walk.

Her mind keeps replaying the moments leading up to the kiss and how quickly she succumbed to him. She's never done that with anyone. She slaps both cheeks to take her mind off him and how hard he was each time his hips thrusted into her. She's trying to calm down, not stay hot and bothered.

She kicks at the snow in frustration and stomps down the road, pissed off at him for making her lose her mind. She's mad at herself, but it comes down to the fact she doesn't have experience with men besides kissing and light petting. In fact, she has zero experience when it comes to dealing with men like him who cause these kinds of feelings to ignite. The stupid masked man with those beautiful eyes of his! Why did it have to be him to give her her first real, passionate adult kiss?

Her first kiss was with her friend Sammy. He wanted to know what was wrong with him and why he wasn't attracted to girls but liked boys instead. She suggested he try kissing a girl to see if he felt anything. He asked if she'd be willing because they were friends. They were each other's first. Sammy made an ugly face once their innocent childhood kiss ended, pretending to gag, and she punched him. Their friendship soon fell apart because of her father, and then a few months later, Sammy moved.

She smiles, remembering her friend. From time to time, she tries to look for him on social media but never has any luck. He was such a gamer geek he's probably doing something in the tech field now. He was bullied in school because he was gay, but that's why they were good friends, because they were both outcasts. Wherever he is, she hopes he's happy.

The other kiss was a boy in high school, but it doesn't count because he lost a bet. He had to kiss the sad, depressing girl. She certainly didn't kiss him back and ended up kneeing him, which got them hauled into the principal's office and her father called in for a meeting. Thankfully, the one benefit of having a controlling father was when she told him what happened and it was self-defense, he turned it back on the school, and the boy got suspended for two days.

She dated only a few guys once she became an adult, but when they kissed, she didn't feel anything.

Kissing *HIM* was a different story. She's not even sure what she's feeling. Her first real, toe-curling, arousing kiss left her speechless and wanting. No. NEEDING more. But why did it have to be him, a man who was stalking her and whom she knows nothing about? Not to mention, he's infuriating. Most of the time, it feels like he's playing some game with her, but then he turns around and is kind, caring, even sweet.

She rubs her gloved hands over her face and sighs heavily, her frozen breath dissipating in front of her. A frustrated growl escapes from the back of her throat.

"Fuck him!" she yells at the trees, kicking another clump of snow and making it explode into powder.

Her eyes land on tire tracks disturbing the freshly fallen snow from the previous night. She has walked to a T in the road and realizes from the fresh tire tracks there are people around.

Briefly, she contemplates walking until someone picks her up. She can use their cell phone to call her father, and he'll send someone to get her. She dismisses the thought because she's confident the kidnapping is connected to him. He did assign a bodyguard after all. But, Marshall was working with the kidnappers, so is her father involved in the kidnapping too? He probably isn't involved directly. He's a lot of things, but that's out of character, even for him. She's never really trusted her father, but now the tiny sliver of trust she did have is gone.

If she keeps walking, she can get some help and maybe salvage the last few days of her semester, if she hasn't already missed finals. She doesn't want to repeat the whole semester. But worry grips her chest, stopping her at the crossroad. She was kidnapped, and they could show up again. Fear of the unknown causes the worry to fall lower until her stomach is clenching.

Turning, she heads back to the safety of the cabin. The cold is seeping through her clothing, and her toes are getting cold. The cabin will be warm, but he's there. How can she handle herself around him after the toe-curling kiss? The jerk's probably going to pretend like it never happened if he stays true to character.

On the walk back to the cabin, she notes her lower back and hips are better. The assisted stretches and him rubbing her helped to work out the tight muscles. She's even more irritated with him. How dare he help her and be considerate!

"The asshole thinks he can just kiss me and run away?"

She's glaring at the cabin when it comes into view. It's closer to the road than she thought.

She storms up the porch steps and kicks the snow off her boots on the support post of the handrail. She thought there was a connection forming between them, but him running away after *HE* kissed her is bullshit!

Yasmine opens the front door to the tangy smell of tomato sauce and hamburger cooking. She kicks her boots off and hangs her coat while shooting daggers at the back of his mask.

She loudly stomps to the orange chair and pulls it closer to the fire before holding her frozen fingers and toes out to warm them.

The sound of her barging into the cabin and stomping tells him enough. She's pissed. He thinks it peculiar he can already pick up on her moods, considering the short amount of time they've spent together. Despite her being pissed, he breathes a sigh of relief. *She came back.*

His intention was to help, like she did with him the night before, but he lost control being so close and touching her. He's furious with himself. Not only is she a distraction, but she's dangerous with how easily his control slips when he's around her.

This brings back the pain of his childhood. He was out of control when he watched his parents succumb to their addiction. That drove him to fights at school and then, eventually, into the gang. The gang was when he was most out of control. He didn't care what he did or who he hurt or tortured for fun. It was the only way he could deal with the pain. When he took his first life at fourteen, he barely felt any guilt.

When he enlisted in the Marines, he learned discipline to rein in the rage. He vowed never to lose control again. Then there was her, smiling at him, not knowing he was her shadow when he slipped the tiny tracking device into her bag as she looked away, blushing. She makes him lose his damned mind.

Despite his failed attempts at trying to get the information out of her about her father, he's out of time. He must question her tonight.

General Forrester at the daily check-in was tight-lipped about what changed on their end, but he assured Ghoul he would receive new orders tomorrow when two members of his unit show up to take her.

She's returning to her life, and they're going their separate ways. He's never going to see her again, and it's leaving a sour aftertaste. He knew this was coming, but he selfishly wants a little more time.

Chapter Twenty-Two
Two Can Play This Game

Tonight is his last night with her. He's partially relieved, and at the same time, he's turned surly. Ghoul considered his options, but none of them sat well with him, so he puts his emotions aside, turning stoic. He doesn't get a say in what he wants. He once more repeats the reasons why he doesn't deserve someone like her while he dishes up plates of spaghetti.

Setting her plate at her spot, he chances a quick look at her.

She's back in the orange chair, staring into the fire. She's hugging herself tightly, her head resting on her knees. Even with the pissed off expression on her face, she's beautiful. He turns away, burying the tightness in his chest.

Turning from her does nothing to ease whatever it is that constricts him. He's invaded her world, and he doesn't want to leave. She's the light to his darkness, and being around her shows him he hasn't lost all his humanity yet. She's experienced darkness, but her light still shines brightly.

A stinging sensation creeps into his eyes; it's one he hasn't felt in years. He doesn't want her to leave. He wants to stay with her to ... what? Have a life with her?

Fuck. This isn't good. He quickly wipes away the stray tear gathering.

Despite his best efforts, he formed a connection with her, but it doesn't matter because he can't have a life with her. She deserves to be with someone who makes her happy. Someone who can cherish life and not coldly take it. Someone who doesn't hide behind a fucking mask.

After the kiss, he can't take the mask off, ever. It's better for them if she doesn't have a face; this way, she can easily forget him. He sighs, trying once more to shove away the gnawing ache in his chest. He needs to focus.

"Chow time," he calls and winces at how thick his voice sounds. He settles himself at the island.

She unfolds herself from the chair without a word, not bothering to look at him, and takes her seat. He wishes she'd look at him, but this is for the best because he crossed a line.

"Thank you for dinner." She keeps her tone polite as she jabs her fork into the spaghetti and twists the noodles around it. "The stretching and rubbing my hips helped. The shooting pain is gone."

She shoves the fork full of spaghetti into her mouth, finally fixing her irritation on him with her hazel eyes. They're laced with coldness.

"You're welcome." God, this is awkward, and it's his fault.

Yasmine loves spaghetti, so her first bite triggers a groan of satisfaction, and it slips from the back of her throat. She doesn't care about the sauce now staining her face; she's going to savor the meal he cooked for her. The longer she chews, the more her irritation at him for running off is fading.

The moan makes him pause, a forkful of food halfway to his mouth, and all he can do is stare. She's making the cutest face while she rocks happily and ever so slightly in her seat. His brain forgot how to send the signal to his lungs to breathe. He files this image of her in his memories. She never made any noises when she ate her cooking, nor did she make any adorable faces. She's devouring the meal he made for her, and it makes him ... happy.

"You like it?" he asks when he remembers how to breathe.

The tightness in his chest from earlier lessens with each cute moan of delight from her. He takes a careful bite to not get sauce on his mask since his other is still drying. It's difficult and slow going for him to eat.

She grins, her annoyance at him temporarily forgotten. "I love spaghetti. It's one of my favorites. This and Chinese are my main go-tos. Not too smart to make spaghetti when you refuse to take the mask off," she chides without remorse because, well, he deserves it.

She pauses, with her fork halfway to her mouth, and watches him struggle to eat spaghetti in his mask. She sets the fork down with a clank.

"Oh my god." She grabs her plate in both hands. "I'll go eat in the bedroom so you can take your mask off."

His hand is on her wrist in an instant, preventing her departure. "No. I'm fine. Stay." He's not going to waste their last meal together.

She levels a threatening glare at him. "God, you're a stubborn one."

She looks at her plate and mourns what little she has left.

For once, she wolfed her food down. She tilts the plate to her mouth and shovels the last of the food in, staining her mouth with sauce. Her cheeks puff out like a chipmunk while she chews.

The laugh that comes from him breaks the silence and surprises them both.

"You look like a child. You have sauce all over your face." His tone is light.

She swallows and then takes her plate to the sink. While there, she turns the water on, washing the sauce away, and then dries herself with a dish towel before turning back to face him.

"So, you *can* laugh?" She has an incredulous scowl. "I thought I was hallucinating before."

She slides into the stool, her hands covering her eyes like a child would to stop themselves from peeking.

"Take your freaking mask off so you can eat. I won't look." Her smile turns naughty. "Promise."

"If you peek, I'll have to kill you," he threatens, but there is no real bite behind it. He pulls the mask off.

"Why kill me when there are better and, shall we say, more pleasurable things you can do to me?"

She's never spoken something so brazen before to anyone. It's a good thing she's covering her face with her hands because, if not, he'd see how she triggered herself to blush. She hears him shift in his seat and clear his throat. She resists the urge to peek, but she hopes she got to him. If he thinks he can kiss her and then pretend like nothing happened, he has another thing coming to him! Finding her confidence, a plan slowly takes shape in her mind. She's going to use the weapons at her disposal. Namely, smutty romance books.

"I've read A LOT of smutty romance, so I know things. Maybe even more than you," she brags. "I doubt with your surly personality and the 'I'm a monster' complex, you know the finer points of wooing."

He doesn't even bother trying to ignore her because this woman makes it impossible. She's sitting there, looking even more adorable covering her eyes and making threats. He cannot wait to see what crazy shit she comes up with.

Her original idea turns wicked, and her lips rise upward to match. She doesn't need to pull from the romances she's read. She can make up her own story, and what better than to use a real-life example.

"That little stunt of yours this afternoon ... You kiss me and run away like a little bitch. I'm going to tell you a story on how it really ends." Her tone is arrogantly confident.

He finishes eating, and the mask goes back on, but now he's going to enjoy the show she's putting on. Her boisterous confidence has him curious about what she's going to make up. She is right, though; he did run away like a bitch.

The fire from the kiss reignites, sending heat straight to the traitor between her legs, who can't keep herself from reacting to him. She refuses to squeeze her legs together and is going to endure the fire to see if she can torture him for once.

Because she's oblivious, she doesn't realize how much she's been torturing him this whole time with her presence alone.

"You say you'll kill me if I peek? Nay-nay, Mr. Ghoul. It'd be more fun to finish what YOU started."

While one hand continues covering her eyes, the other is pointing an accusatory finger in his general direction. The feel of his skin under her touch and how her fingers curled into the space between his waistband come to the forefront of her mind.

"I'd start with undoing your belt and pants. Of course, you're already hard, so I pull your cock out and wrap my fingers" — she pauses to mime the action — "around you and start pumping. Up. And. Down. The moment you make a sound, I go down on you. I keep working your cock until you want more and my mouth isn't enough."

She really wishes she could see his eyes right now. She bets they're wide, and the jerk deserves it after the heat she's had to endure since the kiss.

"You flip me on my back, forcing my legs wide open. You can't hold back any longer, so you shove into me as hard as you can. I cry out as you pound into me."

Her visual storytelling makes it exceptionally difficult for him to not reach over the island and take her. Goddamn it, does he want her. Since the first fucking day he saw her, he wanted to take her. In the time they've spent together, it changed from being purely sexual to something else. Now he wants to take his time making love to her. If she were to walk around the island, she'd see him straining against his pants.

"After you come, it still isn't enough. What do you do? I'll tell you what you do."

Her mouth is in gear telling the story, but she's distracting herself with the visuals she's creating in her mind, and the traitor still wants him, sending more heat to her core. Meaning, she doesn't hear him moving.

"You flip me on my stomach and spread my ass cheeks wide as you—"

Suddenly he's pulling her hands away from her face. He is way too close, only inches apart, but he's holding her in place by her chin. All she sees when she stares into his amber eyes is wild desire. He looks longingly at her lips and then meets her gaze.

Ghoul's tone is low, and he speaks slowly. "See, this is the difference between your smutty romance stories and real life. The first thing I'd do to you is tell you to be a good girl and keep your mouth shut as I lick every inch of your pussy inside and out."

Yasmine's mind shuts off to the point of forgetting how to breathe.

"I'd consume you, until you are screaming for me to stop. Only then would you be hot and wet enough to take my cock."

He squeezes her chin and then lets go. He turns his back on her, satisfied with taking the upper hand and leaving her breathless. He doesn't bother looking because he knows she's beet red.

After her brain finishes its reboot, and he steps away, she realizes how much she fucked up in that stunt and how he turned it against her. Once again, he's the one making her stomach do the thing, but this time, before he turned away, she got a side profile of how much his dick was pushing against his pants.

She hops off the stool, testing her legs to make sure they can support her after his comment. The arousal coursing through her is on a whole other level than what she's experienced reading a book. She takes a deep breath and grabs the dish towel, moving to his side.

"You wash. I'll rinse and dry." She chuckles tensely. "I have done my job! I've turned you into the perfect book boyfriend."

He sighs. "Are you ever not a brat?"

The bantering is helping calm them both.

"Actually, yes. I think it's a new unhealthy coping mechanism I've acquired since we met. It's just you who brings out my inner brat with this" — she waves her hand at him as water droplets fly around them — "dark vibe thing going on. I can't help myself."

"You need to learn some better coping mechanisms." He throws the silverware into the second half of the sink for her.

"I know. That'll be the next thing I work on when I start therapy again." She becomes serious for a moment as she wipes the silverware dry and puts it back in the drawer. "Most of the time I'm quiet and keep to myself. Which you *should* know since you're my stalker. I don't even talk like this with my friends, not that I really have any. It's your grumpy ass making me want to annoy you."

She turns toward him, leaning an elbow on the counter and waiting for him to finish cleaning the pot.

He eyes her sideways. "So, you're deliberately being a brat to me?"

She grins and slaps him on the back. "Yup!"

They fall into easy conversation about movies and music while they finish up the dishes together. They're not talking about anything important, but each of them is sharing the lighter parts of themselves and what they enjoy. Ghoul remains partially guarded, allowing her to do most of the talking and not sharing much with her. This is the last few moments he has with her, and he's savoring it like a vintage wine.

On the other hand, Yasmine's completely unguarded with him, making her own perverted jokes and highly sexual innuendos. She can't help but laugh at his strained reactions. He's enjoying the time of freedom in her company and realizes this is why he's drawn to her physically. It's not about the sex, it's companionship. Since he's never had anyone like this in his life, he mistook his desire for her as some men do. He wants someone to talk to and have fun with. He craves touch and connection.

They continue talking about their tastes in music and discover they follow similar bands. This is why he hated Marshall from the beginning: because he could easily pull her out of her shell and make her laugh. He was jealous because he didn't know what made her laugh, but now, here she is, laughing while they talk about meaningless things.

A relaxed smile is glued to his face the whole time they talk.

"So, you do other things than read smutty books? Here, I thought you were only a raging pervert," he teases.

"Rude! But, I can see you're more than a stalker." Her voice settles. "Look at us, the pervert and the stalker."

Just like that, the moment passes. This is it. There are no more relaxed conversations or playful banter.

"Are you okay?"

She senses his mood shift from the darkness overtaking his eyes. It leaves her frightened at the sudden change. It reminds her of her father.

The concerned look she gives him makes him angry. He doesn't deserve her concern. Yet, here she is, freely giving it to him. Worst of all, she saw when the man disappeared and the hardened soldier came out of hiding.

"I want you to come down to the basement with me." His words and tone leave no room for argument.

He can't lead her on anymore. His selfishness in playing house with her is only going to make it more painful when he breaks her trust and they separate.

Taking her hand, he pulls her from her seat. Her warmth flows into him when she grasps his hand tightly and follows without question as he leads her to the basement.

Yasmine's not sure what brought on the sudden change in demeanor. Descending the stairs, worry grips her chest because a dark presence flooded his eyes.

Maybe he is a serial killer, and getting her to drop her guard to the point of trusting him is what gets him off. Of course, her mind picks right now to start playing out the worst-case scenarios. To counter the thoughts of him being a serial killer, she reminds the scared part of her mind about the kiss and all the kind things he's done for her. But then she remembers he *is* a killer, though he killed those two men to save her. She doesn't need the ping pong ball of thoughts right now.

"Oh, you're finally taking me down to your sex dungeon? Okay." She laughs, trying to be playful, but she's not convincing anyone.

Chapter Twenty-Three
Being Used Sucks

Yasmine follows without a word. She stares at his back while he leads her into the dimly lit basement. There's one lightbulb hanging from the support beams; it casts the outside edges of the basement into deep shadow. Two metal folding chairs have been placed at a grimy card table, interview-style. A stack of folders sits on top of the table with CLASSIFIED: *OPERATION JUDAS* stamped across the front. Her eyes land on the knife sitting on the table at the corner. The same knife he used to slit the kidnappers' throats.

Prying her eyes from the knife, she focuses on Ghoul, who is taking the seat on the other side of the table. He pulls the chair out, flips it, and straddles it, resting his arms on the back.

She screws up her face with pursed lips, but remains standing.

"Take a seat." He motions to the chair across from him with a head nod.

Her eyes are beginning to adjust to the dim lighting, and she wishes they didn't. Nausea causes her stomach to drop, and she sits down before her legs give out.

Behind him, hanging on the wall, are metal instruments. Some she recognizes as common household tools. Others she's only seen pictures of in history books but knows they are used to torture and cause grueling, unbearable pain while keeping the person alive. She's not sure how she's managing to keep dinner down.

"This certainly is a different kind of sex dungeon." Her words retain their playfulness, but the growing apprehension makes her tongue heavy.

She stares at her lap, where she's wringing her hands. She can't bring herself to look at him. She thought he was a good guy, but she was wrong about Marshall. She's probably wrong about the man who's hiding his face. The door lean, the concern, and the kiss were all a game to use her — she's just another tool for him to use and manipulate. The same terror she had when she awoke in the dance studio is washing over her. She swallows back the rising bile.

"Are you going to torture me?" she whispers.

He cocks his head to the side. Of course, she sees the instruments behind him. The color draining from her face confirms it.

"No. Not unless that's one of your kinks? But, dare I say, I have other, more pleasurable things in mind we could do." He uses her words from before to hopefully reassure her. He has no intention of harming her.

"If you're concerned about my tools ..." He gestures behind him at the wall, chuckling darkly. "You saw firsthand how easily I can kill. I'm not a good person. I didn't hide that fact from you. I'm experienced in the art of torture, drawing it out and prolonging it as long as possible before ending it. Those tools behind me are ones I've made. Call it a sick hobby of mine. I've never used those on anyone." He stares down at the folder in front of him, wanting to get this over with. "Yasmine, I promise I'm not going to hurt you. I do, however, have some questions for you about your father."

She sighs loudly and then pulls in a full breath.

"Well, shit. Why did you have to bring me down here for that?" She laughs without humor as she pulls her braid over her shoulder and starts to fidget with the ends.

"When I'm here, I like to keep the upstairs free from work. Down here's a different story. I wanted up there" — he motions above — "to be a space where you could feel safe. I didn't want to bring you down here, but you're too much of a distraction for me." He shrugs both shoulders at his confession. "I apologize for bringing you down here, but my superiors and I think you know something about your father that could help us."

Understanding dawns on her, and her shoulders visibly relax. "That's why you have been coming down here! You're working."

He motions to the workout equipment in the far back corner with his thumb. "I come down here to work out, too. And, other things."

"What other things?"

He refuses to let her distract him, and he's not going to confess all the times he's had to jerk off because of her.

"I see. Need to know, and I don't need to know." She fixes a stern gaze on him, examining what little she can see. "Let's get this over with then. Whatcha want to know about him?"

She wants to get this over with as soon as possible because the old, nasty feelings are resurfacing. This time, however, there's a different feeling welling up with the old one she can't put a name to ... apprehension? Her vision clouds, making Ghoul blurry. Whatever the unknown sensation is, it has to do with him.

"What do you know of his business dealings?" He starts with a simple question.

"Business? He has no business that I'm aware of." Her eyebrows turn downward, and she frowns. "He's a decorated general with an impeccable service record but a real shitty father."

"You're unaware of his business dealings outside of his military service?" he presses.

She shrugs. "This is the first I'm hearing of it. We don't exactly sit down to a family dinner where we talk about our day. I don't see him much anymore since I started college. Usually only birthdays and holidays or when he demands I see him. Other than that, I don't reach out to him, and I keep my distance the best I can. It's safer that way."

He pulls the folder closer to him. He believes her, but he has to push further because something small and meaningless can be the last puzzle piece to see the completed picture. He needs to be sure there's nothing she unconsciously knows. He hates what he's about to show her, especially if this is the first she's learning of her father's indiscretions.

He pulls the first photo out and slides it to her across the table. She picks it up and examines the photo of a pile of U.S. cruise missiles, the American flag on them, stacked in a warehouse.

"U.S armaments," she says, putting the picture back on the table. Her expression narrows. "What's this about?" A sinking sensation hits her in the gut.

He pulls another photo out and lays it on top of the first one. "Those missiles were used here."

The next photo is of a devastated desert city, probably somewhere in the Middle East. Without waiting, he drops another photo. This one makes her stomach churn. It's a close-up of the bodies. When she makes out the remains of a child, she looks away, slamming her eyes shut. Bile rises to the back of her throat.

"Someone has been stealing and selling U.S. missiles to arms dealers across the globe, and they're being used on innocent civilians." He motions to the photo.

"You believe my father is involved?" She forces her gaze back to the masked man across from her.

Gone are the kind eyes she's seen for days. The ones staring back at her belong to a soldier with a duty to carry out.

He nods, reaching for another photo.

"We suspect, but the problem is we can't find any real connection to him or any of the arms dealers involved. Either we're wrong, or he's covered his tracks incredibly well. Then, there's the matter of your kidnapping. Do you know anything? Have you seen or heard anything suspicious?"

She's looking everywhere except at him, searching through the recesses of her memory banks for anything to give him, but she's drawing a blank.

"I-I don't know," she tells him truthfully.

He places another photo on the table. This time, it's adults and children in cages.

"Not only do we suspect he's involved in selling U.S. armaments, but we uncovered possible ties to human trafficking." He allows her a moment to take in the photo. "They're weak connections, but we're missing the main tie. We know who's behind your kidnapping, but how is your father tied to him?"

He reaches across the table to take her hand, but she recoils before he can touch her. He should have anticipated the reaction, but he's losing his resolve the more he sees her shutting down and retreating from him.

"We can put a stop to this." He waves his hands over the photos. "If you know anything ..."

Her lips purse together in a thin line. Her father's a real bastard, but learning this about him enrages her. He abused her and harmed her in more ways than one, but seeing how his cruelty goes beyond what she's aware of makes her insides boil.

Yasmine wants to give him anything to help, but her emotions are hijacking her mind, making her unable to think clearly.

"I don't know," she mutters weakly before turning her head away from the photos, unable to stomach them anymore. Cracks are forming in the dam she's created to keep out any feelings she has about her father, but now those emotions are threatening to drown her.

Ghoul knows the last picture will break her because she has a heart, unlike her father. He sees her putting up her walls already. She's learning about a whole new terrible side of her father.

He takes a deep breath, turning callous, and drops the last picture on the table. "Do you know about this?"

Yasmine focuses her gaze on the photo long enough to register it, but then the little bit of color she has retained during his questioning completely drains from her face. Her stomach clenches, and her chest constricts around her heart. She desperately tries to shove everything behind the dam, but part of the wall is already crumbling. She's going to be sick.

The photo of her father shows him in a provocative situation with an underage girl. It's too much for her to bear.

"No." She barely chokes out the one-word answer.

"You are his daughter, and you know nothing about any of this?" He gestures over the photos. His voice is unsympathetic and impersonal. He has to be, or else he's going to break along with her.

She turns her head away from him and the photos. Her bottom lip is quivering from holding back the emotions boiling inside. It's becoming harder to breathe. She bites down on her lip until she feels the sharp sting of pain.

"I don't know anything," she spits out through clenched teeth. Her fists clench and unclench in her lap. The sting of tears assaults her eyes.

Everything her father has done to hurt her comes flooding back. Everything he put her through. For fuck's sake, she was kidnapped by that French dude, and Ghoul confirmed her father's involved. French? A memory tries to resurface, but the emotional tidal waves wash it away before she can recall.

She refuses to look again at the photos in front of her and wants them as far away from her as possible. She shoves them back to him.

"Here's the thing ..." His voice is like ice. There's no feeling in his words, not like before. "I think you do."

He doubts she's protecting her father. He sees how she despises the man. Hell, what she's revealed about her father triggers murderous rage inside him.

Her hand slams onto the table when she jumps to her feet, knocking the metal folding chair over.

"You think I give a shit about that motherfucker? You think I'm hiding something?" she screams. "He beat my mother in front of me for no fucking reason. I watched for years as she became a shell of a person. No kid should ever have to fucking see that! When I misbehaved or did anything out of line, he'd lock me in the fucking closet or my room for days at a time. Throw me in 'the brig,' he told me. It was 'for my own good,' to teach me to fall in line and to respect his authority. If I looked a certain way, he'd hit me. If teachers suspected anything, he would charm them. If they didn't buy it, he'd intimidate and threaten them until they let it go."

Her words come spilling out; her face is turning a deeper shade of red with each confession. "Poor Sammy, my one and only friend up until middle school, my father scared him so badly he refused to talk to me even at school after that. I don't know what he did, but that monster completely isolated me from everyone."

The back of her throat is raw from the yelling, but she keeps going.

"He'd make me strip in front of him to do 'an inspection' and have me spin around to make sure I was developing properly. If I told him no, he'd hit me. And what did my mother do? She fucking hid in the bathroom. When she finally left him, she didn't take me. And you think I'm protecting him?"

She's never said these words out loud, and there's so much more she could tell him. She has too many stories, and it would take years to let everything out, but what does it matter? It fixes nothing. She'll remain a broken woman, undeserving of love, and never have someone care for her.

Uncontrollable tears are falling down her cheeks.

She stares at the man who's coldly staring up at her. Betrayal slams into her, and she can't bear to look at him.

"You used me, didn't you? That's what the kiss was, right?" she accuses, and those words hurt the most.

She pounds her fist on the table one last time, squeezing her eyes closed, holding in her rage and the building scream, but she can't. Everything she's kept buried surrounding her abuse and the sense of treachery from Ghoul threatens to erupt.

Metal scrapes against the concrete, the noise breaking through her emotional torment. He's getting to his feet and moving toward her. It's all too much. She bolts for the stairs.

Chapter Twenty-Four
The Hellcat Awakens

Yasmine runs up the stairs and stops in the kitchen. She thought it'd be enough distance for her to shove everything down and bury it once more — the years of abuse, the new trauma of the kidnapping. Worst of all is the realization that, once again, she trusted a man, and he used her. Just like they all do. No one has ever been there for her; she's had to do everything alone.

Like a volcano once it starts erupting, nothing can stop the emotions from coming. She bends over, trying to take deep breaths, but the more she breathes, the more suffocated she feels. The walls of the cabin are closing in on her. The only escape she has is out.

She bolts for the front door and flings it open, running out into the cold darkness.

Ghoul stands in a daze in the still basement. Her raw emotion soaked into every fiber of his being. He can't fathom the sort of abuse she's endured. The "inspections" are particularly horrifying.

Fuck. He runs a hand over the back of his neck. Her accusation of him using her was a kick-to-the-balls kind of pain. He never wanted her to think he used her, but despite his best efforts, she does.

Her footfalls stop at the top of the stairs, then the sound of her gasping for air reaches him. He wants to run after her, but what right does he have when he's the one who caused this?

He hears more footfalls and then a slamming door, which snaps him out of his thoughts of self-loathing. There's no way she had time to get her boots or coat on. He runs up the stairs after her, taking two steps at a time.

She runs into the cold night; another light snowfall greets her. The cold bites sharply into her feet. Her socks do nothing to insulate them, but she doesn't care. She makes it five yards from the cabin when she collapses to her knees. She rears her head back, her face points skyward. A scream erupts from her chest, cutting through the serene silence of the woods.

She screams like a wounded animal. And continues until she has no air left, and her body forces her to breathe. Then her howl turns into a mix of wailing and sobbing. The tears leave frozen streaks down her face. She collapses forward on her hands and knees, faceplanting into the snow. Her wails continue as she pounds her fist into the snow. Her stomach no longer wants to purge its contents because her heart has finally taken over to purge the stored trauma.

Hands wrap around her waist, pulling her up. She lashes out. Hitting, flailing, slapping, and even kicking at Ghoul, who is struggling to get her onto her feet. *He's the one who caused this!* She wants to disappear into nothingness and to not be touched, least of all, comforted by someone who used her and fucked with her emotions.

He holds on tight, refusing to let go, not until he gets her on her feet and back in the cabin. She's not going to last long in the cold dressed the way she is. He tries wrapping his arms around her from behind, but she shoves him off. In the process, she loses her balance and falls backward into the snow.

He's never cared about the pain he's caused others. He's always remained perfectly detached. So why now? Why does he care about her? Her screams and sobs wound him deeply, like a knife to the heart. Her visceral scream will haunt him for the rest of his life, especially knowing he's the one who triggered it.

She continues to cry and is unable to pull herself up. He reaches for her again, knowing she'll lash out, but he can't leave her here.

The worst part of this that leaves him with a bitter taste in his mouth is he lost her trust. Her accusatory words hurt him more than he thought they would. Once trust is lost, you can't regain it, and the thought causes him to already miss the tiny bit of affection she's given him.

He pulls her up, and she fights him the whole way, but he manages to get her standing.

"Don't fucking touch me!" she screams.

Yasmine manages to jerk one arm away. She balls her fist, rears back, and lands a punch to his jaw. There's fury behind the blow, but when it lands, it weakly grazes him. If she was focused, the punch would have sent him reeling.

He roughly gets her arms pinned to her side and uses his arms to wrap around her in restraint. She's stronger than she looks, but she's running out of the will to fight, and she can't get enough leverage to break away from his fierce hold.

This is it. He's going to hit her because that's what men do. Her sobbing begins anew, but this time it's the kind of pathetic crying she'd do in secret after her father was done with her.

Escape is impossible. His hold is too strong, and the cold is zapping her strength. She's shivering, but more from the emotional purge taking place. Her whole life, she's never been able to escape, and now is no different. Tears of defeat flow along with the painful sobs of the child long forgotten.

When she stops thrashing and surrenders, Ghoul's hand goes to the back of her head. He gently pushes it to his chest, tucking her in under his chin.

"I'm sorry, Yasmine." He's stroking her braid.

She's shuddering violently, and his touch makes her sob harder because she's waiting for the blow. Yasmine's vaguely aware of him scooping her up in his arms. He cradles her close and carries her inside. She curls in on herself, trying to make herself as small as possible. The more she tries to stop crying, the more she does.

He sets her in the orange chair next to the fire and first strips off the wet socks before rubbing her ice cold feet between his hands. He peels the wet sweatpants off next and is thankful she's not putting up a fight.

His hands move over her cold skin, rubbing warmth back into her. He's more concerned about her condition than taking note of where he's rubbing.

Yasmine no longer has the strength to fight and gives up. He can do whatever he wants. She doesn't care; the dam has crumbled. All she can do now is let the flood of emotions run its course until the landscape of her being has been transformed. She doesn't know who she'll be once the flood passes.

He wraps the blanket around her after he throws the sweats in front of the fire to dry. He needs to get the shirt off, but he suspects she'll start fighting him again if he tries to take it. Instead, he tightens the blanket around her shoulders and head but keeps her legs uncovered facing the fire.

Before he leaves to make her a cup of tea, he leans down, putting his hand on the back of her neck and smashing their foreheads together in an intimate gesture.

"You stay here. Cry as much as you need." His tone is hushed. "I'm going to be right here, but I'm going to get you something hot to drink to warm you. You promise to stay here and get warm and not run back outside?"

Her lips are pursed together, and her eyes are closed tightly, but she gives him a tiny nod. He pats her head lightly then gets to his feet.

Why is she trusting him? He used her. But he did run after her, and he's handling her with a level of gentleness she's never experienced.

Using the blanket to wipe her tears away, she shakes it off her shoulders. She's already exposed emotionally, so what if he sees her boobs? She pulls the wet shirt off and tosses it in front of the fire next to the sweatpants. Her wet panties come off too. She places the blanket back around her shoulders and uses it to hold herself together.

The hysterical sobs have stopped, but she keeps having to wipe tears away with the back of her hand or the blanket.

Suddenly, Ghoul is holding a cup of tea in front of her face, waiting patiently for her to take it. He notes the shirt and panties on the floor. Instead of raging desire, all he feels is shame, an emotion he hasn't experienced in a long time.

A shaking hand sneaks out from under the blanket and grasps the handle. He goes to his knees in front of her. While she continues to cry, he inspects her feet for signs of frostbite. They're ice cold but look like they'll be okay. He rubs her toes between his hands to warm them.

"Drink," he tells her as he moves to the next foot. "It'll warm you."

She stops crying long enough to take a tiny sip and tastes the hint of lavender and chamomile. His warm hands feel like fire to the point it kind of hurts from the temperature difference. But he doesn't stop at her feet and moves up, massaging her calves. His touch is warming her quicker than the fire or the tea; it's something she shouldn't be feeling, which shows how messed up in the head she is.

At some point, he gets her a roll of toilet paper from the bathroom so she can wipe her tears and snot away. She blows her nose, but it instantly clogs. He doesn't speak because he feels like he has no right to say anything, nor does he know what to say. He focuses on taking care of her physical needs.

After some time passes, and she calms herself to the point where she can speak, the memory that had tried to resurface from before in the basement comes back. She might know something about her father, but she's not sure if it's what Ghoul's looking for.

"My ..." Her throat is raw. She takes a sip of tea, hoping it'll help her find her voice.

"My father took me to a fancy restaurant for my birthday. Toward the end of dinner, he left to use the restroom. This French guy in an expensive suit took his seat. He wished me a happy birthday and gave me a velvet jewelry box. When I took it, I heard something thick rolling around inside, but it didn't sound like jewelry. When my father came back, he was livid when he saw the man. Since we were in a restaurant, he couldn't cause a scene. I don't remember much because when my father gets angry, I shut down. It didn't make sense at the time, but looking back, I think they were speaking about business-related stuff."

She continues. "The French guy mentioned something about being a backer? And they were going to be business partners, but my father owed the guy money. My father was upset because the guy wasn't following through on his end of the agreement. I don't remember, but something in their business deal went sour, and they were blaming each other for it. The guy took my hand, kissed it, said something in French, then left. My father took the jewelry box. When he saw whatever was inside it, he slammed it shut and got so angry we left. He was unusually quiet on the drive home."

Ghoul's hands are on each of her knees; he's staring up at her.

"Do you think you can recognize him from a picture?" he hurriedly asks.

She gives him a minuscule nod.

He pulls his cell phone from his pocket and moves his fingers over the screen. When he finds the picture, he turns his phone around to show her.

"Was this him?"

She studies the picture and recognizes the man almost immediately. The face with the hard edges and hooked nose, the same expensive suit, and those dead eyes.

"Yeah, that's him."

"This is the guy who met with your father, and they were discussing business?" He wants to make absolutely sure.

"Yes," she confirms for a second time.

He cups the sides of her face, his thumb brushing her cheek lightly, and kisses the tip of her nose through the mask.

"That helps us more than you will ever know. This is exactly what I've needed. He and your father are in business together."

His fingers fly over the screen, quickly typing out a secure message confirming her father's connection to the bioweapons dealer. It's time to put an end to this terrorist ring. When the message is sent, he throws his phone away from him onto the couch. His duty's done, and he can turn his full attention to her.

She's staring at the dancing flames, aware of the void inside her. She pulls the blanket tighter around her shoulders. She's exhausted and depleted, but surprisingly lighter. She wants to sleep and yet metaphorically dance in the sunshine.

"Yasmine," Ghoul says softly, getting her attention.

"Huh." She remains transfixed on the fire.

He leans into her, touching her lower jaw and gently pulling her face to look at him, but she refuses.

"Please, look at me." His tone is begging, but he doesn't care.

Her expression is blank, but at least she's looking at him now. He cups each of her cheeks, holding her in place so she can't look away. The moment their eyes lock, the tears well up and fall again, and he's right there wiping them away with his thumb.

"I can't do anything to take away what he did to you."

He knows all about inspections, but it's one thing for him to be subjected to them. He signed up for it, and he was clothed. For her, it must have been humiliating and degrading to be subjected to that in her developing years. Fury consumes him. How could a father do any of these things to his own child? The force-feeding, hitting, and now the inspections? Yasmine is such a kind and loving person, not to mention gentle, she didn't deserve any of the abuse she's suffered. Ghoul's not counting her punching him — that wasn't so gentle — but she was in fight mode. Then he realizes their upbringing was similar. His own parents were abusive to him too.

He brings their foreheads together in shared understanding.

"I'm supposed to stay detached, but you're telling me what he made you do and what you've suffered ... staying impersonal and detached is no longer an option for me. This has become personal. Your father is a dead man. I won't rest until I hunt him down and end him. Once I'm on the hunt, I always get my prey, no matter how long it takes." His grip pushes her cheeks together. "I'm going to rip his fucking throat out, but I'll make sure he suffers for what he's done."

She lets out a strained, raspy chuckle, but there's no humor in it. "How scary. I guess that's why you're called Ghoul, huh?"

Silence settles between them. He releases her face and sits on the floor at her feet. A hand withdraws from her protective cocoon blanket and grabs a fistful of his shirt. She follows him to the floor, rests her head on his shoulder, and buries her face in his neck, needing to take in his masculine scent. He quickly adjusts to support her between his legs.

Throwing all caution out the window, she collapses into his arms, needing to feel safe with his touch. Her head slides down from his neck and rests on the center of his chest. The steady rhythm of his heartbeat sounds strong; it makes her close her eyes. His body heat seeps into her.

His arms wrap around her, and his cheek rests on top of her head. He got what he needed from her at a cost, so the least he can do is hold her. He doesn't understand how she can hold him back or why she's giving him comfort.

She pushes off his chest, getting herself to a kneeling position. She makes sure to keep hold of the blanket to cover herself since she's naked. One hand comes out and brushes along his jawline.

"Is this where I hit you?" Remorse floods her expression.

"Who would have thought you could throw a punch like that." His tone is serious.

He grasps her wrist and places her hand to his chest. He's not worthy of her touch.

"You might not believe me, but the kiss wasn't to manipulate you. I kissed you because I lost my self-control."

Her piercing gaze is making him uneasy. Her thumb slides under the mask, caressing his stubbled chin. She shuts her eyes and pulls the mask up until his jaw is exposed. She softly kisses where she thinks her punch landed.

"I'm sorry for hitting you." She breathes, leaving a trail of kisses in the area.

Her lips continue brushing along his jawline until she's tenderly pressing her lips to his.

A tingling sensation runs through his body at the simple apology. His hold tightens, pulling her closer to him. He doesn't deserve this, but he can't push her away either. He forgets how to breathe when her tongue is brushing over his lips, asking for entrance, and he can't deny her.

It's so warm and inviting. He returns the kiss.

This kiss doesn't have the raw passion from earlier in the day. Instead, it's two people seeking refuge and sharing an understanding. It's slow and lingering.

Ghoul, like before, is the first to break the kiss because he's not going to take advantage of her in her emotional state. He's an asshole, but not that kind of asshole. Kissing and holding her was all right since she came to him, he justifies.

When he backs away, she keeps her eyes closed until she pulls his mask into place. Then she gazes at him and the compassion reflected in his eyes.

"I'm ashamed to share half his DNA, but after seeing what he's done ... He's not my father, and he doesn't deserve to live." Her voice breaks, and she swallows the disgust of seeing him with an underage girl.

Fingertips brush down her cheek to her chin and then continue to her neck.

"And he won't live, I promise. Or, I'll die trying." He'll kill her father no matter what.

"I'd rather you not die." Her fingers lace through his and squeeze. Her thumb traces circles on the back of his hand.

Yasmine's head tilts down. She can't bring herself to look at him. And she's not entirely sure if he *did* manipulate her, but he came for her, and most of all, he let her cry without telling her to be quiet or silencing her with a blow. She hasn't completely lost all trust in him.

"I get you have to do bad things, but I don't see you that way. You do what you need to do to keep people safe. So, please, don't place so little value on your life. You deserve a chance at life just as much as anyone"

"And, what about your father? Does he deserve a chance at life? I'm going to kill him. Doesn't that revoke my chances?"

He's never voiced questions like this, but they have remained in the back of his mind, plaguing him for as long as he can remember.

She shakes her head and squeezes his hand. "Do what needs to be done, and then give yourself a chance at life. Something tells me you've never had it. And I mean a real chance." Her other hand gives his leg an affectionate squeeze just above the knee.

Her words are choking him. Would he have a chance to have a life, and one with someone like her?

The time he's been with her is a taste of what life could be. Enjoying conversation, playfully teasing, sharing interests, even doing the everyday mundane activities like cooking and laundry. Sharing your vulnerability with another person who sees the pain you carry and doesn't run from those ugly parts of you.

"With you?" *Dare he hope?*

She lets out a slow breath. "I know this isn't one of my stories. I'm too broken for anyone to want me, and guys aren't into me. I accepted the fact a long time ago I'm not going to have a happy romance book ending." Her words carry sadness.

"I've enjoyed my time with you. You're the only one I've felt safe enough with to let out the pain I kept buried. Hell, you've been the only one, other than Sammy, I felt safe to be myself with."

"Life flows with change, and our time together will end. After this, I'll go back to my life, and you will yours." A shadow crosses her face, which causes his hold on her to tighten. "I'm grateful our worlds met. You're the only one I've told about my father's inspections. It was humiliating. Somehow, sharing it with you took away some of the pain. Thank you for being here with me."

She rests her head back on his chest, their fingers lazily playing with each other. "About your question, I don't have an answer. It can be with anyone, or even just yourself. Don't be afraid to explore what life has to offer. It's all about choice, and you have to choose to live."

He doesn't know what he expected. It's not like she was going to confess to anything or agree to be with him. She's only known him a few days. He cradles her in his arms protectively and intimately, wishing he could have the ultimate closeness with her. He chances pulling his mask up and uncovering his nose enough to bury it in her hair and neck. He wants her more than he's ever wanted anything in his life. He wants every goddamn part of her — the good and the broken. Her tenderness reminds him he's human and not irredeemable.

"You're going to help so many kids." He's inhaling her scent to the point she's permeating his lungs. "If I'm to pursue a chance at life, then you have to stop saying you don't get a happy ending. If our circumstances were different—"

He'd what? Make her his girl? He can't lead her on when he doesn't know how long it will take him to hunt her father, or if he'll live. The cold, hard truth is, he has a dangerous job. She deserves a chance to find happiness, and he'll do whatever he can to protect her, even if it breaks him.

She lifts her head, and what meets her is longing in his dark amber eyes; it reflects her own longing. For the first time, she's found someone she wants to be closer with. This will probably be a mistake, but she'll bear the pain. She'll worry about tomorrow when it comes.

Chapter Twenty-Five
Don't be a Chicken

Some would call her stupid for throwing herself at a guy who's kept his face hidden and she barely knows. Is she being reckless? Absolutely. But this is the first time she's felt this type of connection with someone. With the compassion he's shown her, she knows he'll be gentle with her in intimacy.

In the books, they glorify rough sex when it's a woman's first time, but in real life, it's painful. She's been too scared to do it with anyone because she's endured enough pain in her life, and she wants her first time to not be tainted with more.

He's mostly been respectful; the ass slap and kiss were times when he pushed personal boundaries. He didn't take it any further when he easily could have, especially when she passed out drunk.

Interrupting her attempt to summon her courage, he moves her away and scoots closer to the couch, leaning against it for support.

"Come here." He spreads his legs and opens his arms, inviting her back into his embrace.

She accepts, awkwardly crawling toward him because the blanket is wrapped around her. She cuddles close, sinking into him, and his arms wrap around her. Once settled, he runs his hand over her back.

He's thinking about anything else other than her being naked under the blanket. She needs to be held, not fucked. It's painfully obvious she rarely, if ever, has felt safe, and he's going to be a secure place for her.

At the same time, Yasmine is psyching herself out. And if she thinks about it any longer, she's going to chicken out. Pushing off his chest, she allows the blanket to fall from her shoulders. Her breasts are on full display before him.

Like men do, his gaze takes in the curves of her breasts and then focuses on the supple pink centers. She's not busty, but her womanly features are beautifully feminine. He stares with a lascivious glint in his eyes. He lets loose a low groan; at the same time, he clamps down on his lip as a reminder to keep his hands to himself.

Safe space, safe space. He continues to repeat the mantra.

The intense ogling turns her nipples hard because no one has ever looked at her like this. The longer he stares without touching, the anticipation causes liquid heat to flood into her core.

When he lifts his gaze, she sees his amber eyes are wild. Her bashfulness causes her to look away. Then he's there, grasping her chin and making her look at him. His expression is one of questioning.

The disbelief of seeing her naked in front of him sends blood rushing to his cock, causing him to painfully strain against his pants. He doesn't care if she sees.

"You-you can touch me," she whispers, but it's awkward as hell since he's preventing her from looking away. Her inexperience is showing, and he must see it.

Ghoul is playing with fire, and he's fine if she burns his world to the ground. He's selfishly going to touch her because she's given him consent to do so. He brushes the back of his hand across the fading bruise on her cheek, trailing it down the length of her neck. He moves to her shoulder, down her arm, and back up.

His touch causes a shiver to run up her spine. It moves outward, making her skin prickle. Succumbing to how his hands feel moving over her body, she closes her eyes and sinks further into the sensations he's causing. She moans quietly in the back of her throat.

All his desire channels into razor-sharp focus. He's going to enjoy every moment of her, until she tells him to stop. The back of his hand brushes the swell of her breast gently, making slow passes over her erect nipples. His fingertips brush across them, and then he's squeezing until he coaxes a gasp from her, making his cock twitch in response. He starts massaging the fatty flesh and her nipples between his fingers. Her body is responding like he hoped it would. Except, she's too silent. He wants to hear all the sounds she can make.

He leans down and pulls his mask away quickly before suckling her. He feels how her body startles from him. She tries to move away, but he's not going to let her escape. His free hand fingers her other nipple while he alternates between licking and sucking the first one. He moans, filling his mouth with her breast. She finally relaxes into him, cradling his head in her arms.

He bites down, pulling her along with him, and her body has no choice but to follow. Just when the pleasure turns to the first twinge of pain, he lets go, pulling his mask into place. He's cupping both of her ass cheeks and looking up at her with a longing to dive into her entire being.

"Come here, angel. Put your back to my chest."

Before she can move, he's putting her right where he wants her.

"Angel?" she questions.

He crushes her to his chest, still fondling her flesh, and just like that, her question is gone. Especially when he pushes her against his hardness, which presses into her backside and makes her quiver in anticipation. She wants to feel more of him.

He misinterprets her shivers for being cold, so he pulls the blanket around her. Now he's under the blanket with her, running a calloused hand on the outside of her thigh and then bringing it up on the inside. He stops mid-thigh, hooks his hand into her flesh, and pulls her legs apart at the same time he's pinching her tit. She finally lets out a whimpering breath and leans harder against him, allowing him to open her legs wider.

"I like the sounds you make. I wanna hear more," he tells her after pulling his mask down. His hot breath tickles her ear, and his lips are brushing along her earlobe. He bites, pulling a startled whimper from her. Her fingers are like talons gripping into his thighs.

He brushes away some loose hairs from her braid, and then he's rolling his tongue down her neck. She tilts her head to the side, and something primal in him is summoned. The arm draped across her stomach holds her so she can't move while he sucks her neck. Her grip on him tightens, and she's groaning, biting on her lip. He pulls away, admiring his handiwork, a purple mark, with a boyish grin. He clamps down again because it's not big enough.

When she's marked, his fingers wrap around her throat. She instantly tries to pull away, haunted by all the times her father choked her. Before she can say anything, he's there, ready to catch her.

"Relax," he breathes into her ear, lightening his grip. "Enjoy how it feels to have a real man choke you in pleasure." He's caressing her tummy, and his voice turns teasing. "Besides, weren't you the one who mentioned hand necklaces? Don't be afraid to be as loud as you want. The nearest neighbor is miles away. So, be a good girl, and let me hear you."

Yeah, she never should have taught him about hand necklaces because he's using it against her. She nods, willing herself to relax into him. He's grabbed her neck before and didn't hurt her.

"Can I keep going?" He breathes into her ear.

When she nods, he places his hand on her neck again; the other is sliding up her inner thigh, and she instinctively opens her legs more. He stops at her tuft of hair.

He grasps her leg and pulls her wider to make more room for him before twisting and twirling the hair around his finger.

This man makes her brain switch off, and all she can feel is the heat they are generating. She reaches behind, hooking her arm around his neck. Her fingers are blocked on their way to his hair because of the mask.

"I want to touch your hair. Take the mask off, and your shirt while you're at it." She states her demands.

"Be good, and keep your eyes closed." He whispers into her ear.

"I will." She nods emphatically, scooting forward to give him room.

He rips the mask off, tossing it to the side, along with his shirt, and then guides her back into his chest. The electricity flows between them when their skin touches.

Her hands begin exploring the bottom part of his buzz cut and move up until they find the longer silky hair on top. Her fingers curl, grabbing a fistful when he goes back to twirling his fingers through the patch of hair between her legs.

Their minds are in sync as they twist toward each other, kissing over her shoulder. His tongue shoves into her waiting mouth, and at the same time, he finds her nub of sensitive skin and falls into a steady rhythm of rubbing and stroking. He doesn't need to dip inside her because she's already soaked. Her sharp, exhaling moan intensifies the throbbing in his balls.

"Do you like that?" He breathes into her mouth.

"Uh huh." She sighs, fisting his hair again and bringing their mouths together.

It's different with someone else touching her, and she's relishing in the pleasure building under his gentle touch. Another finger joins in circling her nub. He shoves his tongue further into her mouth, and his fingers move to do the same.

This makes her panic. She clamps down on his hand and then pushes him away. Her knees snap close.

Moving his hand back to a safe zone on her thigh, he takes a few breaths to calm himself. He was so close to feeling her wet insides. He shoves his confusion aside, reaches for the mask, and puts it on, then adjusts himself in his pants.

"Look at me," he says in his deep commanding voice.

She twists around at first and can't look at him because of the shame in pushing him away. It was an unintended reflex. She chances a glance and the damn look in his eyes makes her embarrassment deepen, but there's no reason to feel this way, not with him.

"Talk to me. What's wrong?" he asks.

She shakes her head, struggling for the words. "It's just..."

He's caressing her cheek with the back of his fingers, reassuring her, but she's shutting down. Then an idea comes to him.

"If you're concerned about pregnancy, I had a vasectomy years ago."

She shakes her head, wanting to crawl under a rock rather than admit this. It's not like there's anything wrong with her. He's not going to laugh or make fun of her.

"It's not that," she whines.

"The only girlfriend I've had for the past three years is my right hand. I'm clean." *Sometimes my left, if I'm feeling frisky.*

She groans, burying her face into her hands, even more mortified, and he pulls the blanket tighter around her so she doesn't feel so exposed in her nakedness.

"Take your time." He rests a hand on her knee. He has no choice but to wait.

"It's-it's just … I'm still a virgin." She whimpers and hides behind her hands.

Understanding dawns on him, and he recalls the way she blushes so easily, how she freezes in his presence when he gets too close, and he makes her nervous. She's all talk when she teases him and speaks about her books, but she's never been with anyone.

"You're still a virgin," he echoes.

This changes things. His mind snaps in a different direction, now planning how to proceed. If she wants to continue, that is. He's going to have to take this slower than he thought.

She nods, still hiding her face from him.

"Not even with hands or oral?" he inquires.

"Oh God," she roars, throwing her hands up. "No! Only my hand and a toy. I've never even used an internal toy." She wants the earth to open and swallow her. "You're the only one I've ever let touch me there."

No wonder she's not touching him back. She's never done it. Any of it. He pulls her into a hug and squeezes her through the blanket.

"We can stop." The last thing he's going to do is be *that* guy and force her.

"No." Her voice shakes. "It's just … I don't know what to do."

"You're telling me you read all your smutty romance stories with and let me quote, 'lots of fucking,' and you don't know how it works?" He gives her a throaty chuckle. "Do I need to have a birds and bees talk with you?"

"Oh, shut up!" She punches his shoulder.

He is surprisingly enjoying this moment and seeing the redness creep from her chest on its journey to her ears.

"Look at me."

She does, and he brushes his thumb across her cheek. He stares into her bashfulness, making it slowly melt away until he sees the beautiful soul inside staring back at him.

"I'll be gentle, and we can take our time. You'd be in control the whole way."

An old memory, long forgotten, comes back to Ghoul. The last time he saw his grandfather before he passed. He quickly tries to push the memory from his mind because this is NOT the right time to be thinking of his grandfather, but it refuses to go away.

They were sitting on the front porch drinking pop. His grandfather had just given him the knife, the same one he used to kill Yasmine's attackers.

"Listen, Johnny." His grandfather used his nickname. "I'm not going to be around much longer, so I'm going to pass on the secret of finding happiness." His grandfather tussled his dirty blond hair. "If you want to be happy in this life, find yourself a good woman who's not afraid to keep you in line, and one who will put up with your shit." He cackles.

"A good woman sees all your flaws and still loves you. If you find yourself a woman like that, put a ring on her and don't let her go. Do everything in your power to protect her and keep her safe. You'll know it when you feel it."

As Ghoul stares at Yasmine now, all he sees is a good woman who is sparkling with life. He feels it. *This is what Gramps meant. Thanks, old man, for the intrusive interruption.*

He smirks to himself and returns his focus to her.

"Do you want it to be me?" He holds his breath, waiting.

She looks away, unable to meet his piercing, hungry gaze.

She gives him a tiny nod.

Chapter Twenty-Six
Spicy Romance Has Nothing on Real Life

After getting to her knees in front of him, she pushes the blanket fully off her again. His hand goes to her side with the phoenix tattoo, and he takes in the vibrant colors.

"I wanted to see this." He brushes his fingers over the mythical bird. His light touch causes a shiver to run up her spine.

Ghoul's not a religious man by any means, but the woman before him must be a goddess in human form. He's peered into her pain and trauma, but she's remained untainted by the world's ugliness.

His eyes land on the white splotchy scar on her tummy. It doesn't bother him because he has enough of his own, and each has a story. His calloused hand runs over the scar, and her breath hitches. He wants to ask about it, but this isn't the time. Scars have painful reminders tied to them, and she's had enough for one night. He wants her to feel good.

Emotion wells up, stinging his eyes. The woman staring at him is making his heart feel things he's never experienced.

"God, you're so beautiful," he whispers before offering his hand. She's a treasure to be handled with care.

A timid smile forms at his compliment, but it's the way he's taking in every curve of her body that makes her self-conscious. She scoots closer to him, taking his hand.

With his shirt off, she can see his body is littered with his own scars and tattoos. She runs a hand through his dirty blond chest hair; it's the perfect amount of thickness for her. He's muscular like she thought, but not like the gym rats. His muscles developed from hard work and carrying equipment. She's taking in the tattoos, tracing each one, while he caresses her curves, giving her the time to explore his body. His left shoulder has a large skull with a rose that extends to his pec, where it connects to a bloodied raven facing off against a dragon. The dragon winds around his arm and ends at his forearm, where there's a Marine tattoo of an eagle atop the world with an anchor.

Her finger starts tracing each letter of the large Semper Fi tattoo in elegant letters above his navel. She only gets to the 'M' when he grabs her finger, holding back the shiver threatening to wreck his body.

"What?" she asks, confused. When he stays silent, she glances up, smirking. "Don't tell me you're ticklish?"

He rolls his eyes, releasing his hold.

"I guessed right, Marine. You do have the vibe."

He doesn't answer because that adorable, bratty, and knowing smirk of hers is distracting him.

The smirk turns into a shy smile when she leans back to soak in his body. He's shirtless, and she loves the feeling of his skin touching hers and the sight of his cock straining against his pants. He's wearing the mask with the bloodstains from the men he killed for her.

This man is something else. She might not ever see his face, but there are no words to describe him. He's clearly been through so much, yet he remains kind.

When their eyes meet next, his desire for her slams straight into her pussy like he's already inside. Her fingers curl into his waistband and begin fumbling with his belt. She's at the point of no return, but she bites her lip in frustration at the damn belt!

"No need to rush." He cups over her hands and then opens one up, pressing the palm on his cock while holding the other to his chest.

"Since this is your first time—"

But she's already taking control, squeezing him through his pants. He thought she'd need more coaxing ... Apparently not.

He lets out a groan, and tilts his head back, unable to keep his eyes open. She barely touches him, and he's already at the point he can't take it anymore. He pushes his legs together and grabs ahold of her waist, making her straddle him. He brings their chests together. Her soft breasts press into his flesh as he holds her tightly while allowing his hands to continue their exploration of her body.

"You're still in control here." He breathes into her ear. The mask is getting in the way, but something is telling him to keep it on and not to let her see his face.

Her head nestles into the crook of his neck, and she nods. Then her lips brush along his shoulder up to his neck. He sucks in a sharp breath when she bites; it causes him to groan and dig his fingers into her ass. Blood rushes to his cock, making him engorged. She's leaving her mark on him.

He holds onto a fistful of her braid and pulls her head back. "You should see yourself right now." His desire breathes out like dragon fire. "I can smell how turned on you are. Can you be good and close your eyes?"

She gives him a knowing look and then does as he says, snapping her eyes closed.

His lips slam into her, pressing their mouths together. The kiss is wild, filled with the built-up longing he's had to be with her. He keeps his hold of her hair in one hand, pulling her head back and making her arch. The other is waiting at her entrance.

"Can I?"

He can ask anything of her at this point, and it's his. "Touch me wherever you want." Her lips pucker, demanding his lips to return to hers.

He chuckles because she looks adorable. He accepts the silent demand and rubs her clit when their mouths come together. She inhales when he hits the spot with perfect rhythm. Her moans turn into whimpers. She thought the first time he touched her clit was amazing, but now her mind can only focus on one thing: his hand between her legs, which is making her body build to the point she's going to orgasm.

"I'm going inside." He breathes into her neck in warning.

He's careful and slow. Her wet walls pulsate around his finger, making him groan and wish it were his cock. He releases her hair, and his fingers find and hit her G-spot. As they work her insides, his thumb is rubbing her clit.

She's holding on to him for dear life, hoping he can hold her together. She never knew it could be like this. She groans, her grip becoming like iron when he causes her to shatter. The scream wants to come, but instead she bites into his shoulder to stifle it, clutching onto him so she doesn't leave her body. He's the only thing keeping her grounded to earth.

"That's a good girl," he praises, continuing to take her through her orgasm.

He'd rather hear her scream in pleasure, but the biting is equally arousing for him. He's enjoying the feel of her teeth sinking into his flesh. No one's bitten him before. He stops only when her body starts twitching and her muffled whimpers turn to gasps. He withdraws his fingers from her, and she collapses into his arms, breathless.

"Tha-that. Was. Wow." Her forehead rests on his shoulder as she catches her breath.

Holding her tightly until she comes down from her ecstasy, he brings his fingers to his nose to inhale her scent and then licks his fingers clean in anticipation of it being her pussy next.

He pulls the mask on. "Open your eyes."

Ghoul helps her slide between his legs in front of him. She tucks a loose strand from her braid behind her ear, a self-aware smile radiating from her.

He cups the side of her face. "You were perfect." His fingertips brush along her bottom lip. "You wanna stop?"

"Do you?" She puts it back on him in a somewhat snarky tone and reaches for his belt.

He grabs her chin between his thumb and pulls open her mouth; the fire in his eyes rekindles the heat in her core.

"Yasmine, I've wanted to fuck you since the first day I saw you. I'm not stopping unless you tell me to. So, check your bratty tone."

The voice he uses comes deep within his chest, almost like a feral growl, and it sends her pussy into shock. It wants to fall in line and stand at attention for him. That commanding voice of his will be her undoing if he pairs it with a "good girl."

"No, I don't want to stop," she answers, refocusing on his belt.

It's a lot harder to undo one when it's not yours. Her face is contorting as her frustration grows. He stops her flustered movements, covering her hands with his.

"Let me." He pushes her aside to unfasten his belt and pants.

His insecurities flare at this juncture because his fiancé claimed she cheated on him because of his "average size." He looks at Yasmine waiting patiently on her knees. She trusted him, and he can trust her.

He pulls himself free, pushing the waistband out of the way for her. The color rises to her cheeks as she stares at his cock with wide eyes. Then she bites her lip. The pube hair around his cock is the same color as his chest hair, so she can at least imagine his military haircut in the right color.

He moves closer, guiding her to the base of his dick.

She's seen her fair share of dick pics from creeps online, but this is the first time she's touching one. Especially one so ... engorged. She's wondering if he can even fit inside her.

He groans in the back of his throat when her fingers wrap around his length and take over the movement after he barely showed her how. It's been so long he's forgotten what a woman's touch feels like.

Hearing him groan in pleasure at her touch makes her ... happy? She might not have another chance like this, and he's been patient with her, helping her feel safe. What she wants is for him to feel good in return. She stops working him and repositions herself lower.

When she stops stroking, his eyes open, and it's at the same instant she goes down on him. Her tongue is swirling around his tip, tasting him, then exploring the length of his cock.

"Eyes on me." He lifts her chin.

She blushes deeper with their eye contact and him still in her mouth. She smiles shyly, and he pops out, which makes her giggle.

"Was that, okay?"

He runs the back of his hand slowly along her jawline and then down her neck, outlining the hickey he left on her.

"You're doing just fine, beautiful," he assures her.

Her body responds to the praise with a quiver.

"I'd like to try something ..." She hesitates.

"Anything you want. Just no biting."

Her eyes widen in horror.

"Is that even a thing? I think it'd hurt." She continues to fondle him while they speak. She's rather enjoying the new sensation of touching a man's penis.

"It's a thing, but I'm not into it." He can't stop touching her face and is now brushing his fingertips all over her. "What do you wanna try?"

She has no reason to be bashful at this point; he already saw her orgasm. Yet, she can't help it because everything about him is so ... delicious. His confidence and his strong protective side. He can be an alpha but also knows how to be gentle and caring. This is a deadly combination for a man.

"Can you pull my hair and feed me your—?" She stops because saying the words out loud is too cringey. "Never mind."

He tilts his head and smirks at her, enjoying this more than he should. "Feed you my what? I'm not a mind reader, Yasmine. You need to tell me what you want."

She's gnawing her lip. "Your cock," she whispers.

"You read that in a book, didn't you?"

Her face scrunches together, and then she's nodding.

He grabs a fistful of her hair, holding her in place. "Tap my leg if you need a break."

He forces her into his crotch and makes her watch while he takes over stroking himself in front of her. He brushes the tip along her lips, and her mouth opens, waiting, but he stays just out of reach.

He's basking in the moment since this is the first time a woman has asked him for this, and he's her first, which makes it that much hotter. When his tip touches her lips again, she tries to take him, but he denies her. She looks up at him with a huffy expression.

"You're a tease, aren't you?" She scowls.

"I did tell you I'm skilled with torture." He laughs at the dirty look she gives him.

In response, he stops denying her and shoves his cock in her mouth. She takes him without hesitating. Her scowl relaxes, and he slowly starts thrusting, letting her get a feel for him.

She melts with the new sensations coursing through her, wanting to feel all of him. With each thrust, her tongue rubs the underside of his cock. She's searing this moment into her memories, never wanting to forget how his dick feels inside her mouth.

She's always wondered why a dick in the mouth is a turn-on. A few times she used a banana to "practice," but she never felt anything from it. She gets it now. What she needed was a person. Hearing his moans and heavy breathing in response to what she's doing is making her drip down her thighs.

"Your mouth feels amazing."

And the praise, the reassurance he's speaking to her ...

"I'm going deeper."

Deeper?

He pushes to the back of her throat to the point she can't breathe, which causes a moment of panic, but then he pulls out enough, and she takes a quick breath before he thrusts again. He goes to the back of her throat until he coaxes a gag from her, and then he backs off.

The gagging and how her throat constricts around him sends more blood rushing to his dick until his pleasure is winding too tightly. He wants to keep going until he releases, but instead, he pulls himself free of her mouth to calm down — he's not ready to blow just yet.

He waits until her gaze is on him. "Are you doing alright?"

She blinks to clear the moisture from her eyes. A coy smile parts her lips once her brain can remember how to speak.

"I take it you like gagging? You got harder."

Without waiting for his reply, she's going down on him. This time, she takes him all the way to the back of her throat, bobbing on his hard cock and running her tongue up his length until she triggers her gag reflex.

She rests her head on the top part of his thigh and gasps for air, her eyes watering. Her fingers curl around him, pumping while she catches her breath. She never expected gagging on dick could be such a huge turn-on. When she gags, her pussy wildly demands attention and is jealous of her mouth.

"Are you trying to make me cum?" he growls, restraining her hands to stop her.

Her head raises and turns toward him with an innocent expression. "That's the point, right?"

"Not yet. Stop trying to rush this," he tells her before pushing her off and getting to his feet.

She stares up in confusion, wondering if she did something wrong.

He offers her a hand, which she accepts. The blanket fully slips away, and he takes a long, appraising look at her. Then he swoops down, wraps his arms tightly under her ass, and lifts her in his arms.

"What are you doing?" she asks nervously. How he's carrying her, she can't bring her legs around his waist. All she can do is wrap her arms around his neck and hold on tightly.

"You don't think you get to have all the fun, do you?" He turns. "We're taking this to the bed."

Chapter Twenty-Seven
Assault With a Deadly Weapon

Pulling the mask away slightly, she clamps onto the soft spot where his neck meets his shoulder, sucking his skin into her mouth and flicking her tongue over the lump of flesh. She then bites which makes it difficult to carry her, and he nearly drops her.

Positioning them on the bed, Ghoul guides her legs to straddle him. He crushes their bodies together so her breasts are pressing into his chest and stares up into her self-aware, smiling face, trying to decide what he wants to do with her first.

"Sit up for a sec," he says with a tap to her ass.

She stands, and he fully strips his clothing off in record time. Then he's dragging her back to his lap. He refuses to break physical contact for long. He only gets this one chance with her, so he explores every curve and line of her body, which responds to him like a musical instrument under his touch.

He wants to do everything with her, but it'd be impossible in one night. She's waiting and depending on him to take the lead because only now are her tiny hands tentatively touching him. He hugs her firmly to his chest, and she responds, returning the embrace and running her hands along his back. He squeezes her ass and then is moving her off him. He's decided what they're going to do first.

Ghoul turns his whole body to face the headboard and lies down on his back. He pats the space above his head, and she moves there. She's looking upside down at him with an unsure expression.

"Sit on my face."

"Huh?" She understands the words but hesitates.

He grabs ahold of her hips and pulls her to his face. "Be the good little Angel you are, and sit. On. My. Face."

He rubs the sides of her thigh when her knees cage in around his head. His calloused hands are rubbing over the curves of her hips and ass, guiding her into position over him.

She gnaws on her lip as she waits for him, but her eyes are drawn to his cock.

Once he pulls the mask off, there's no warm-up or going slow. He dives in, spreading her open. His tongue is on her clit, sucking it between his lips and licking.

The explosion of pleasure is instantaneous. She lets out a loud roar, collapsing forward straight for his cock.

He wraps his arms around her thighs, pulling her legs further apart.

"God, you're so wet." He chuckles as he inhales her scent so it permeates his entire being.

His cock is right in front of her, standing tall and waiting. Her lips wrap around him, and she's bobbing on his head. The deep throaty groan from him vibrates straight to her pussy.

"You feel good," she shakily moans, coming off his cock for air.

"And you're too damn hot." He's massaging her thighs.

His tongue's assault makes it to where he has to hold her in place so she doesn't vibrate off his face.

"You enjoying this?" he asks, his voice muffled.

"Yes." She breathes coming off him.

"Good answer." He follows up with a playful ass slap, making her inhale sharply, and then he's rubbing the sting away.

Both of their releases are building. They take turns moaning as the other responds with more feverous stimulation. They're both posed at the edge of the cliff, hand in hand, ready to jump together.

He lashes out, grabbing her braid to pull her off him, as his tongue continues to lap at her. She almost made him explode down her throat, and he would have if he hadn't restrained her. Her ragged breathing and how he's taken charge make her climax build for the second time. All she can do is take what he's giving her.

"Can you be a good girl and cum for me?"

He used his deep commanding voice paired with the "good girl," and it shatters every wall she's ever hid behind. Her entire body is thrown into convulsing tremors in time with her pussy pulsating. She cries out, digging her short nails into his thighs to hold on for dear life, while his tongue continues to ride out her orgasm. She tries to pull away from his onslaught, but his hold on her is too tight. She can't escape. When her body starts spasming and she stops breathing, only then is he satisfied and finally stops his onslaught.

She collapses on top of him, out of breath. Even after he stops and releases his hold of her, her body continues twitching on its way back to earth.

To be her first makes this time with her precious. If only they had more of it. He'd learn all the ways he can make her body respond to him. He'd use his torture skills and techniques to pleasure her senseless. That's what she deserves.

Leaving a trail of kisses on the inside of her thigh, he bites, making her gasp. He could listen to her make these noises the rest of his life, and it'd never be enough.

"How was that?" He's caressing her because she did so good.

"I don't know." She giggles breathlessly. Her body finally stops convulsing. "My brain shut off at some point."

She weakly pushes herself up.

"That's what I like to hear." He slaps her ass a little harder, pushing her hips away from him and reaching for the mask to put it on.

They untangle themselves, and she rolls off him, collapsing onto the bed on her back with great effort. He's instantly on top of her, pressing his cock into her pelvis.

Interlacing their fingers together, he pins her arms above her head, and her legs open for him. Her body tenses in anticipation of the coming pain. She's been pushed to the limit, and her body feels spent after those two mind-blowing orgasms, yet she's not satisfied. She greedily wants more and needs him inside her.

"Do you smell that?" he asks, holding her attention.

She nods, breathing in her scent on his mask.

"That's how intoxicating you are. You ready for me now?"

She consents with a small dip of her head.

Tucking his arm under her, he rolls them so he's on his back and she's on top with her legs straddling his waist. Her fingertips run through his chest hair while she looks into his eyes. The only clothing he has on is the mask. She wishes she could see his face, but it doesn't take away from the man under it.

"When you're ready, you mount me."

His words send shivers of renewed desire crashing through her. She never thought her first time would be with someone so considerate, and someone who would let her be in charge of her own body.

Sliding her hips toward his waiting cock, he refuses to let her go and helps guide her. He has a normal-sized dick, maybe a little above average, so she doesn't need to be worried about being assaulted with a deadly weapon, but her anxiety is rising at the coming pain. She positions herself over him and hesitates, her body tensing. He's right there, supporting her with a nice ass rub.

"Take your time," he encourages. "Don't tense up. Relax."

He continues massaging her ass and wherever else his hands wander to help her relax, but it's the tip of his dick, teasing her hole, that makes her tense.

The heat coming from her causes him to want to push into her, seeking her softness, but he has to hold back. It's a curse and a blessing because his hunger for her is insatiable, especially right at the precipice of joining with her.

Slow circles run the length of her back. "We don't have to do this."

"We're doing this," she counters immediately.

He pitches her ass, making her arch into him.

"So much sass," he chides.

She lowers herself down, the tip of his cock pushing inside, stretching her open.

A twinge of pain makes her tense up and pull away. He's there waiting with caresses, coaxing her to relax.

"It's alright. Go slow."

She takes a deep breath and pushes down a little further until she feels the sharp tear of skin. She hisses through her teeth and raises herself back up, taking some deep breaths.

"I'm right here." He's going to have the worst case of blue balls in the history of mankind if she decides to stop now.

The third time is easier, and she finds she can sit on him. She did it. He's inside, and their flesh is molding together.

"You're so hot and wet. You're going to melt me if I'm not careful." He moans when her wet heat envelops him. "Start moving. Get used to how it feels." He's breathing heavily with the great effort it's taking him to restrain himself from thrusting.

She nods and rocks her hips, getting a feel for the sensations coursing through her body as his dick stretches her wider. The pain is turning into pleasure the more his cock is rubbing against her inner walls. She finds a rhythm, sinking further on him.

He's not used to relinquishing control like this with anyone, ever. Like how he shut her brain off, she's doing the same thing to him. The only thing he can do is moan against her fire and focus on not losing himself too soon. But, her slow movements are building him toward release too quickly. The view of her on top of him, biting down on her lip, her breasts bouncing with her movement — she truly is magnificent. It's not the physical part, it's her. He chokes on the emotion building in the back of his throat.

It took her a bit, but she finds the part deep inside that has been demanding him. She loves how his hands are eagerly touching and encouraging her the more her hips rock into him. The pressure is building once more.

Fingertips brush along her lips, spreading them apart. She sucks his finger, and flicks her tongue like she did to his cock. She lightly bites, holding his finger between her teeth with an impish grin.

"If you keep doing that, I'm going to cum." The warning comes out in a deep rumble.

She teasingly pulls his finger from her mouth.

"It's not fair. I've gone twice, and you haven't." She stops rocking to speak and catch her breath. It's a lot more work to have sex than she realized.

His face softens. This woman is too much. He needs to be deeper, and he can't stay still anymore. They need to move together.

"You tell me if anything hurts. There shouldn't be pain, but I'm tired of lying here." His thumb brushes her lip. "Let's enjoy each other."

The smile she gives him is meant only for him, and this is the first time he has seen it. He pulls back and then slams into her, making her gasp when his tip hits her cervix. He keeps the movements going because the startled inhales and moans are the sweetest music to his ears. He falls into his own rhythm of thrusting, and he's going deeper than she took him. His release is building too quickly to the point he's forced to stop. She truly is going to melt him if he's not careful.

"How'd you like that?" His voice is graveled. He fondles her tits while they each catch their breath.

"I never imagined it could be like this." She pants in ecstasy. It's so much better than the books. Her fingers brush through his chest hair then trace the lines of his muscles and tattoos.

"On your back." He uses his commanding tone as he pulls out, and it's impossible for her to say no.

His gaze is hungrily devouring her, holding her captive from where he hovers. Her body trembles in anticipation.

"Open those legs wide for me." His voice turns dark.

She drops her knees, and he's pushing her wider to make room.

"I'm not going to be able to last long," he informs her as he easily slips back inside like she was made only for him.

He starts pumping slowly into her. Her eyes roll to the back of her head.

"Move with me," he instructs.

Her grip around his neck tightens, and her legs wrap around him. She's rocking in time with his movements, trying to push him deeper. If he keeps up with this movement, she's going to shatter for a third time. It makes her cling tighter to him, desperately trying to meld their bodies together. Where he's hitting inside, another climax is roaring to release, but her strength is giving out. The night has taken a toll on her body, not to mention she is still sore from before.

"I'm sorry," she laments, her legs falling away. "I can't. My legs are too sore to hold onto you and move."

The way her tone turns whiny has him leaning their foreheads together while he continues moving for both of them.

"Eyes on me, baby girl. I'll make you feel good. Hold onto me the best you can."

He throws her legs over his shoulder, bending her so he can thrust deeper. Her fingers curl into his skin to hold on until her nails dig in, leaving crescent marks in his skin.

Her third release is building, but it quickly fades because her legs are begging "no more;" they are tapping out.

"I can't ... my legs." She gasps.

He brings her legs down. He's not as deep, but it's okay. He resumes his thrusting.

She claws her way up to hook her arms around his neck. She needs to feel him crushing her with his weight. While her third climax is dissipating, she's still clinging to him because of this insatiable need to have him merge with her body. She senses their moment of intimacy is coming to an end, and she doesn't want to let go.

"Yasmine." He growls deep in his chest when he explodes.

He tries to keep moving, but his strength is gone from spilling into her with each pulse of his cock. Her legs wrap around him, and she resumes rocking her hips into him. His pleasure ramps up, coaxing more cum to pump out of him. He's clinging to her, burying his head into her shoulder, while she rides out his orgasm like he did with her. She stops once his body starts twitching from cumming the hardest he ever has.

"God. Damn. It." He breathes into her neck. "You fucking brat."

He lets out a breathy chuckle. She really is too clever. His arms cage around her, and her arms move to cradle his head. She did something to him in their lovemaking; he's not exactly sure what, but he feels shattered.

They stare at each other, breathless, both coming down from their highs. There are no words for what either of them is feeling, and they remain joined, unwilling to uncouple. He notices the tears welling up, and with his body pinning her in place, she has nowhere to hide when they escape from the corner of her eyes.

"Hey, what's wrong? Did I hurt you?" That's his first thought as he brushes the tears away.

She shakes her head. "No, it's not that."

She can't bring herself to tell him her body is physically, emotionally, and spiritually spent. She never knew anyone could make her feel complete after a life of feeling so empty. What's really shattering her heart is that when they leave the cabin, they'll never see each other again. She understands this is reality, but it doesn't make the crushing ache in her chest lessen.

The tears flow freely, and he pulls out, sending one last sensation of pleasure coursing through her with an escaping groan. He lies next to her, pulling her into his arms.

"I guess I'm just one of those who cries after sex." She whimpers, letting him hold her.

He cradles her close, pulling the mask up to kiss her forehead.

"Cry as much as you need to." He strokes her hair. "You were amazing."

Like her, he's lost to his emotions and thoughts, knowing this is their last night.

"I hope I made your first time special."

"You did." She hugs him tighter, nodding.

She nestles her head into his chest, letting his protective warmth cover over her.

Ghoul imprinted himself into her very soul, and she's pretty sure she's ruined for anyone else after tonight.

Chapter Twenty-Eight
Back to Reality

They lie tangled together while she experiences a different kind of emotional release than her earlier one. He's holding her securely to his chest and tracing lazy circles on her back while she cries.

"Are you alright?" he asks, not being able to stand her silence.

"I was just thinking I wish we could have more time together." It's not a complete lie; she just doesn't tell him the whole truth. "But, I know that's impossible," she quickly adds before he can speak.

Is it truly impossible? His errant thought demands. For the first time, he can see a life laid out before him. One with her?

His mind starts playing out a scene where they sit quietly next to each other while they read. She's in one of her romances, and him a military thriller. They take care of mundane household chores together. They come home after work knowing someone is waiting there with a hot meal. They play and have fun together. Nights of cuddling, watching movies, and endless moments of getting lost inside the one you love. In all the quick flashes of a life he could have with someone, it's her he sees.

Maybe, when he kills her father and survives, he can get out? He can take a desk job until his twenty years of service are done and then retire.

Would she wait until he finished his current op? His fiancé didn't wait, so he can't expect Yasmine to. She needs to have a chance at a life regardless of what he wants.

"I know." He runs the back of his fingers across her cheek. He steels himself for his next words. "But we knew this wouldn't lead anywhere."

Fuuuuck that hurts. He's never spoken words to cut himself so deeply.

She purses her lips together and sits up, turning away from him. She needs some space for a few moments so her heart can break alone.

"I know this is a one-night stand. I just wish we had more time is all." She slides off the bed. She needs to clean up.

"Do you need help?" he asks before she walks out of the bedroom.

She shakes her head and waves him off. "No. I got it."

There's an overwhelming pressure on his chest. He saw how his words crushed her, and he's a real piece of shit for saying it. He hurt her because he couldn't keep his goddamn hands off her.

After cleaning up, Yasmine returns to the bedroom with her blissfully dry clothes back on. She throws his shirt at him; it lands perfectly on his shoulder. He sits up on the edge of the bed with his clothing back on, and she smooths the quilt out since he didn't after changing the sheets.

He comes out of his daze when she sits next to him and leans against his shoulder.

Her eyes rove over his back tattoo. She can now get a better look at the cloaked angel of death, with its wings spread wide and a scythe in hand, standing atop a pile of skulls. Her fingers trace the lines.

"Your tattoos are beautiful."

He pulls his shirt on, covering them, and then rests a hand in the sweet spot between her thighs. He gives her a squeeze before standing up.

Her hand hurriedly grasps at his arm before he moves too far away.

"Where are you going?" She internally winces at how desperate she sounds.

"I'm going to bed." He points through the open doorway. "You need your rest after all you've been through tonight."

He brushes his fingertips over her hair. He tries to walk away, but she keeps a firm hold of him. She's not sure she can sleep without the feeling of his arms around her, and especially with the image of him moving on top of her still fresh in her mind. In fact, through her soreness, there's an echo of him moving inside like he's still there.

"You rest." He tries to let go of her for a third time, but she's stubbornly holding on.

"Stay. There's no point in you sleeping on the couch anymore. The bed is big enough for the both of us."

"Are you sure?" He's dealing with his remorse in how his words of dismissal from before hurt her.

She's on her feet, wrapping her arms around his torso and leaning her head on his chest. They may not have a future together, but they've developed a connection, and she needs his strength now more than ever. She's become addicted to it. Mostly, she doesn't want to be alone anymore. It might be temporary, but she can at least pretend someone cares for her.

She tilts her head up to plead with him. "Please. Stay?"

He holds her against him. There's no way he can say no to her. Not with the face she's making. It's another one he hasn't seen before.

"Okay."

He goes to the bedside table and clicks off the light, then removes his shirt and pants again, stripping down to his boxers.

She stiffly crawls into bed under the blanket and slides to the other side to make room for him. He follows and lies next to her.

"Get over here." He grabs her without permission, spooning her ass into his hips. "Time for aggressive cuddling."

He pulls her shirt up enough to place his hand on her stomach, right where he knows the scar is.

She sighs in content, quickly losing consciousness from her emotionally taxing evening and the physical activity. His eyes close as he breathes in the scent of her hair and the remaining smell of her pussy through the mask.

After this night, the mask is retired. He can't use it anymore to invoke fear, and he's never going to wash it because he doesn't want to wash her away. His body relaxes, and he falls asleep with her in his arms.

Chapter Twenty-Nine
In Terrible Danger

Yasmine wakes the next morning to find herself protectively nested in Ghoul's arms while he snores in her ear. She wonders if either of them moved in their sleep because she's still the little spoon to his big spoon.

She rolls over with great effort because of how sore, and thoroughly ravaged, her body is. She brings herself around to stare at his sleeping, masked face. Part of her wants to peek, but the other part of her is saying, "Don't do it." If she doesn't have a face to go with the man, then it might be easier to let him go when they part ways.

The previous night comes flooding back. Her eyes close as she remembers how amazing they felt together. The memories send renewed heat straight to her core where she still feels their bodies moving together. Yasmine hopes the feeling of him inside never goes away and is forever seared into her. She's glad she waited to give herself to someone she felt safe with, to someone she made a connection with.

Stupid situation. If only things were different ... She can't let her mind go down that road. They have no future together, she reminds herself, and he said the same thing last night.

Watching him sleep, she trails a finger down the center of his chest until she's slowly pulling his boxers down. She's sore and not sure if she can even walk, but she wants another go with him. The night before wasn't enough.

His snores continue, her fingers find his cock, which is erect. She pulls him free and gently strokes, which pulls a whimpering moan from him in his sleep. His hand snakes to her ass, squeezing into her flesh and pinning her against him, so she can't move. But, she still can squeeze, which she does, feeling him growing harder under her touch.

"Don't you know it's dangerous to wake a sleeping man?" he asks but keeps his eyes shut. He nestles the two of them closer together.

"Yeah, I'm in terrible danger," she agrees flatly.

He grabs her wrist, pulling her away from his dick. He pins her hands above her head and rolls on top of her, pressing his weight into her pelvis. She has that mind-numbing, adorable look on her face and is biting her bottom lip. If the mask were off, he'd be kissing her with how close his face is hovering over hers.

"Do you want me?" His voice is thick with desire.

The blush creeps to her cheeks, and she tries to turn away, but he stops her by grabbing her chin and forcing her to look at him.

"Oh no, you look at me when you give me your answer." He pushes against her to make his point. "Do you want me?"

Her eyes search his, and then she gives him a shy nod.

"Good." His thumb goes to her chin, caressing it, then it pushes down and parts her lips. "Because I want you. Now, be good and close your eyes for me."

This time, the sex is hot and primal. He's giving her everything he can, and she takes everything he's giving. The night before was about her and taking it slow. This time, the urgency and desire are burning between them since this is their last joining.

Yasmine doesn't care how sore she is. She tries to claw her way into him, into his skin, and he's trying to leave any piece of himself with her. He plunges into her like a man on a mission, and she's spurring him on with the feeling of her nails biting into his flesh. They're desperate for each other in these last few moments. He wants to feel her cum while he's inside.

His release builds. His fingers move to her mouth, and she instantly clamps on with her teeth, her tongue flicking his finger, and it's too much for him. He loses all control, spilling into her. His entire body is twitching along with each roll of her hips, riding out his orgasm.

Arms snake around his neck, then her fingers are running through his hair. She brings their mouths together through feel, her tongue brushing his lips, asking for entry. He opens for her, and her tongue dances around his. Once he can move again, he's thrusting into her because she's not done.

She tries to break away from their kiss, but he won't allow it. She moans in the back of her throat and into his mouth with each thrust.

Ghoul plunges without stopping, but his strength is slipping. He wants her to feel every inch of him. Her fingers become talons in his hair. This time, she's not careful and pulls, making him grunt, all while pulling him deeper as she clings to him. He responds to her by quickening his pace. No matter how they move together, it's not enough for either of them.

He brings her palm to his lips and bites into her. She yelps, and then his tongue is licking the pain away. His second release comes harder than the first. His body convulses, and he gives a deep growl. She bites down on the bicep caging her in, which only makes him spill into her harder.

He gave her everything he had. Yet, she didn't finish. He hates leaving things like this, but he can't go on. She cups his face, keeping her eyes closed while they lie there breathless, unable to move and unwilling to separate.

He turns her palm to him, kissing where he bit her. "Did I hurt you?"

He realizes only now how much she takes his breath away.

"No." She giggles. "This must be what it means when they say, 'fuck your brains out.'"

He pulls his mask down then collapses on the bed next to her, laughing at her comment.

"Does it feel like I fucked your brains out?" He brings her hand over his heart. "You can open your eyes now."

"My brain doesn't want to work at the moment, so I say yes." She makes a breathy laugh that turns into a groan as she opens her eyes and tries to move. Instead, she collapses onto the bed. "Oh God. I'm not sure if I'll ever be able to walk again."

"I don't know whether to say I'm sorry or you're welcome." He feels like she melted away everything weighing him down.

"Your heart is pounding." She rolls herself to rest her head on his chest and listen to his racing heartbeat. "I thought as a Marine you had to be in shape?"

He slips his arm under her, pulling her to his side, and pinches her.

"You're such a brat." He closes his eyes, allowing himself to bask in a few more moments with her in his arms before returning to reality.

"Seriously, why did no one warn me about this?" she complains loudly while dipping under the stream of water to rinse the soap off.

"Warn you about what?" He leans into her, putting the soap back on the little shelf.

"The soreness after sex." They're chest to chest in the small shower enclosure.

She looks up at him with a pout and then rolls her eyes.

"And you look ridiculous with the mask on. Really? Even in the shower? I've seen all of you, except for your face," she whispers, almost to the point of having a pleading tone. "You still won't let me see?"

"It's for your protection."

He knows it's a lame response, and it's also a lie, but at this juncture, he'll be easier to forget if she doesn't have a face to remember. He can fade from her memories, and she can move on with her life, even if he'll never be able to move on from her. But he's used to living with disappointment.

"Protection from what?" she demands. "Considering what my father's involved in, I'm not convinced I've ever been truly safe, or ever will be."

He brushes the wet hair away from her face. His gaze softens the longer he stares at her. It's hard to breathe through the wet mask, but it's mostly her that makes it difficult.

"It'll be easier on you if you don't have a face to remember." He decides to tell her the truth.

She shoves against his chest. "That's lame, and you know it. Fine, no need to show me. You're probably hideously deformed under the mask, like a pineapple fucked an older pineapple."

His eyes widen in disbelief. "Where do you come up with this shit?"

"I heard it in a movie." She shrugs, turning her back to him, but then her tone becomes serious. "I have a theory. The real reason is you want to come off as this big badass scary guy, but you don't want anyone to see you. The real you. Maybe you're not protecting me, but yourself?"

Goddamn it, how can she see right through him? Clever and now add perceptive too.

He pushes her into the wall, caging her between his arms. He does feel safer hiding behind the physical mask. Even among his team, he rarely lets anyone see who he truly is under the figurative one he wears.

If they had more time, even just one more day, he'd take the mask off. But he's out of time, and he has to keep his face covered to protect himself and the last remaining bits of his heart. He needs to let her go because he has a job to do, and a promise to fulfill.

She awkwardly slides down the length of his body to her knees, which brings his attention back.

"Goddamn it, woman," he hisses at her as she sucks his limp dick in her mouth like a spaghetti noodle.

"What?" she asks, looking up at him with innocent eyes after bobbing on him a bit. "Am I too much for you?"

She just might be.

Chapter Thirty
The Guy's a Dick!

Yasmine is nestled between Ghoul's legs on the couch with a new and depressing spy thriller, while he finishes the last chapters of his book. His arm is lazily draped over her shoulder. If he hadn't brought her to the point of barely being able to walk, and if she didn't break his dick, they'd still be going at it. Instead, their fingers lazily intertwine while they sit in silence reading because they are not ready to physically part.

"Was that a car door?" She startles. The concern is evident in her tone.

Yasmine sits up, closing her book and eying the door like it's going to attack her. This is the first time since he brought her here that she's felt any prickles of dread.

Ghoul sighs and closes his book. They're here — to take her away from him. He selfishly didn't tell her because he wanted to spend their last hours together without her worrying or being upset. He senses her growing unease, and he's glad he kept it from her.

"It's alright. They're from my unit." He squeezes her shoulder before getting to his feet.

The casual way he speaks sends her stomach into freefall. He knew they were coming and didn't tell her.

He peers out the window to check and sees two faces he recognizes, but the blond following behind the commanding officer causes worry lines to form under his mask. He's going to complicate things.

He casts a glance at her before he opens the door. Her braid is hanging over her shoulder, her leg is bouncing, and she's chewing on her lip. It's the haunted sadness and apprehension on her face that stabs him. He turns his back to her and opens the door for a tall, muscular man who leaves a trail of snow from his boots when he steps into the cabin. He stands taller than Ghoul by a good five inches and is dressed in civilian clothing. His honey eyes glance quickly at Yasmine, examining her before turning back to face Ghoul.

The handsome man with the dark umber skin tone carries himself with authority. She notes Ghoul's posture turns more rigid in this man's presence. She's seen enough service members cowering before a ranking officer to know this guy outranks him.

A shorter man comes through the doorway next. His blond hair is sticking out of his winter knit hat, and he's got a five o'clock shadow. Striking blue eyes land on Yasmine, and he's instantly scowling at her.

She stands, her book forgotten, while Ghoul allows the newcomers in. She moves instinctively closer and behind him for protection.

"Yasmine, this is Chad Hill." He motions to the scowling guy who is closer to her height than the two other men. He points to the tallest of the group. "And this is Henry Calvin."

He motions to her. "This is Yasmine Pennington."

She awkwardly waves.

"So, you'll tell me their names but not your own?" She huffs.

"Let me guess, he's kept the mask on?" Calvin asks while walking toward her with a warm smile and handshake.

Her neck cranes to look up at him. She's a few inches taller than the average woman at five foot seven, but this guy makes her neck hurt just to look at him.

"Wow, you're really big." She feels like a child having to stare up at an adult.

"That's what she said." He cracks a grin.

She can't stop the giggle as she takes his offered hand. Her previous worry directed at the newcomers relaxes somewhat. She can tell he's a good guy. The shorter blond guy, on the other hand, is a different story.

The one called Hill gives no indication that he cares to shake her hand. The way he's throwing daggers at her makes her think he'd leave her to die if given the chance.

"Being stuck in here for almost a week with this one" — Calvin jerks his thumb in Ghoul's direction — "I'm sure you're ready to get out of here."

That answers the lingering question plaguing her memory. It's been almost a week with him. She nods at Calvin and then shifts her gaze to Ghoul. For once, he looks away from her, unable to meet her accusatory frown.

"I guess you're here to take me?" She forces the growing emotion behind a blank expression.

"You have a little time," Calvin tells her with a wink.

He hooks his arm around Ghoul's shoulders, dragging him to the basement door for a private conversation. "Ghoul and I need to talk business, and I'm raiding his fridge for chow before we head out."

Hill glares at her in passing as he follows behind the other two men.

Yasmine seats herself on the couch and hugs herself, trying to hold it together. This is happening. She's going home, and she'll never see him again. The anxiety crushes her chest like a heavy weight, and fear engulfs her lower core with the unknowns she'll be facing.

Since he brought her to the cabin, she's been safe. She didn't have to worry about her father making surprise visits or inspections. She didn't have to live in fear of someone breaking in and kidnapping her in her sleep. She could relax, maybe for the first time in her life, and be herself without worry. Going back? She's not sure if she'll ever feel safe again.

What really causes her heart to sink into the depths of despair is the thought of never seeing Ghoul again. She might not know what he looks like, but she knows him. She knows the kind of man he is under the mask. They easily banter and tease; they have conversations without effort. They relax in the silence while they read. The sex and intimacy they shared formed a deeper connection with him, and it was definitely hotter than anything she's read in a book.

She knew this was coming, but it still hurts. The emotion threatens to drown her. She can't hold the tears back and needs to hide. She bolts for the bedroom, closing the door behind her. She's going to cry, and she'll be damned if these new men see it.

On the edge of the bed, her head drops to her hands. She knows how to cry in silence; she learned how to as a child.

"Absolutely the fuck not!"

This is the first time in Ghoul's military career he's spoken out against anything. But the thought of using Yasmine as bait makes him want to kill someone, ranking officer be damned!

"You don't have a choice," Hill shoots back. "And since when do you care about anything? Don't tell me a few days with the General's slutty daughter, and she's managed to wrap you around her finger?"

"Woah," Calvin interjects, holding a hand to Ghoul's chest and stopping him from tearing into Hill. They usually can't stand each other, but this is the first time a true fight is brewing.

"You keep your fucking mouth shut, Hill." Ghoul locks him with a death stare. "You have no idea what she's gone through at the hands of her father. I don't give a shit about your vendetta against the General, but if you carry that over to her, I will make you bleed and drown you in a vat of apple cider vinegar."

"That's enough." Calvin uses his commanding tone. "We have our orders, and we're going to take every precaution available to ensure she stays safe."

Hill folds his arms across his chest, but his eyebrows are raised in surprise. The absurd threat took him off guard. Hill hates General Pennington and dislikes Ghoul almost as much, but he knows not to push Ghoul. So, he wisely keeps his mouth shut, not wanting to tempt the man. Sure, the threat is ridiculous, but he knows without a doubt Ghoul would follow through.

Calvin pulls an envelope out of his pocket and hands it to Ghoul. "Your orders. Read them after we leave."

Ghoul takes the offered envelope and tosses it on the table before storming upstairs to get some distance from them. He's tempted to kill them, take her, and run.

The three men find the small living space empty. Calvin heads to the kitchen on the hunt for food, and Hill plops himself in the orange chair. He stares at the fire, a permanent frown etched across his face.

Ghoul heads for the bedroom where he knows she'll be. He doesn't bother knocking and barges in.

She jumps at his intrusion. She brings up her shirt to cover herself since she's only in her bra and panties. At the sight of the familiar black mask, she relaxes and slowly pulls the shirt over her head. Her eyes are red and puffy from crying.

Ghoul leans his back against the door and crosses one ankle over the other. He stares at the floor and jams his hands in his pockets.

"You knew I was leaving today?" she accuses, making sure to keep her tone low so the two in the living room don't hear.

He can only nod. He looks at her red eyes again and feels like a real piece of shit.

"How long have you known?" she demands.

"Since yesterday afternoon." He's back to staring at the floor. "I planned to tell you last night, but ..." He shrugs. "A lot happened, and then I didn't want to taint our time together."

The anger bubbles up quickly. Yasmine moves across the room in a flurry, not sure what she's going to do. She might shove him or deck him — she's undecided. He doesn't move to stop her. He deserves whatever she's going to throw at him. But she can't do it. She stops in front of him as new tears form, and then he's reaching to pull her to his chest. She melts into his embrace, and her anger slowly slips away.

"I'm fine." She speaks so low he can barely hear. "But you should have told me. I thought we could have a little more time together."

She tries to pull away, but he refuses to let her go. She can't look at him, so her eyes slam shut. He pulls the mask down, exposing his lips. Then they both are holding the other's face and kissing tenderly. Her tears mix with their saliva in their last kiss.

A dangerous situation brought two people together, and in the process, they formed a deep emotional connection. They give each other all the feeling and longing they can in their final kiss, wanting to leave the other with a piece of themselves to remember.

The moment comes to an end, but they're unwilling to let go. She clings to him. Her eyes sting when he gives her one last squeeze and then pushes her away, putting space between them. He covers his face with the mask. He wishes he could tell her how he feels, but he's not sure WHAT he's feeling because he's mostly numb. She's going to be placed in danger, and he can't do anything to stop it or protect her. The wheels are already in motion.

"You keep your head down, and you do whatever you have to do to keep yourself alive." His tone is commanding. He's back to leaning against the door. "You hear me?"

She nods, unable to speak from her seat on the edge of the bed.

"Yasmine, promise me you will do whatever you need to stay safe."

"I will," she croaks out. "I'm tougher than I look." After putting her socks on, she stands, squares her shoulders, and faces him. "I am a Pennington, and if I can survive my father, I can survive anything. Even if I have to, I'll beg on hands and knees to convince them to let me make up my finals."

She has no idea what's coming. He can't tell her, and it's cutting him in two. Protect her, or do his duty? He moves to her and grabs hold of her arm tightly. In a frantic whisper, he warns her about one thing.

"Be careful around Hill. He hates your father. He might try to take it out on you."

She squeezes his hand and brushes him away. "He's going to have to take a number and stand at the back of the line."

"If you two are done fucking, I'd like to go." Everything about Hill's presence screams hostility.

"Knock that shit off," Calvin barks from the stove. He's cooking whatever he found in the fridge. "We're not leaving until I eat. If they want to fuck, let them."

The hickey on her neck didn't go unnoticed by the newcomers.

Yasmine's head turns toward Hill when she steps into the living room. She slowly eyes him with an unimpressed glare, the kind you give a cockroach right before you step on it.

Ghoul's about to rip Hill's head off at the snide, disrespectful comment. They can get along well enough to work together, having mutual trust to have each other's backs when shit gets rough, but Ghoul never cared for the guy's attitude. Now it's directed at Yasmine, and he can feel his composure slipping.

"I bet you're a hit with the ladies, Chad. You're so charming," she says in mock excitement.

Hill's face reddens. "At least I'm not Pennington's slut."

Yasmine bursts out laughing, but her eyes remain mocking.

"Oh, is that all you got? Calling me a slut?"

Just as quickly as her laughter rings out, it stops. She appraises him thoroughly, looking for where to take the first bite.

"You don't look like the type to be a woman hater. Not with that pretty boy face."

Hill's eyes widen in surprised fury.

"I'm thinking Mommy issues? Or you were really into your last girlfriend, but she ended up cheating on you because you're emotionally unavailable. And now, the only action you see is your right hand and the occasional cheating you do with your left. Sometimes, a threesome?"

"You fucking bitch!" Hill shoots out of the chair.

Ghoul pushes her out of the way and puts himself between them. He warned her about Hill, and did she listen? NO!

Yasmine shoves past Ghoul, not backing down, and he tries grabbing her to get her behind him, but she shrugs him off. She's toe to toe with Hill and his boiling anger. She smiles up at him sweetly.

"I didn't take you for the type to beat women. But I guess it's you military types, like my father, who get off on it. Whatever floats your boat." She shrugs.

"Yasmine," Ghoul growls in warning behind her. He's positive she's causing him to have a heart attack.

Hill's breathing hard and trying to control his temper, but she ignores Ghoul's warning.

"I get it, you hate my father. Get in line. You don't think I know who my father is? As far as I'm concerned, you can eat a bag of dicks." Putting all her strength into it, she shoves Hill out of her space.

She's willing to take the hit. It's not her first, but she's confident she can do her best to dodge it. Even if Hill hits her, Ghoul will step in, and probably Calvin, to stop Hill before any serious damage befalls her.

"Hill. Stand down. That IS an order," Calvin barks from the kitchen.

Hill takes a few steps back, his fists clenching at his side. Once Hill plants his ass back into the orange chair, Calvin bursts into laughter.

"Man, she's got a mouth on her."

Ghoul shakes his head but doesn't take his eyes off Hill. "Tell me about it. I've been stuck listening to it."

"Aw, poor baby," she taunts.

Calvin roars louder with his laughter. "I like her. I guess having an Army General for a father, you had to learn to be tough, huh?"

Casting a wary eye on Hill, Calvin makes sure the man is standing down. He's sitting there frowning, so he's back in his normal state.

Without letting on her relief at Hill sitting, Yasmine checks on Ghoul. His wild eyes bore into her, and she can tell he's scowling under the mask.

She then takes a step toward Hill.

"You don't have to like me. What I care about is you doing your job and bringing down my father. From what the grumpy Ghoul here" — Calvin cackles but quickly tries to stifle it — "showed me last night about my father's side hustles, he deserves what's coming to him. You can insult me or call me whatever you want, just do it behind my back."

Hill's piercing blue eyes remain locked in a battle of wills with her. He finally blinks, and his face relaxes slightly.

"I can agree to that," he acquiesces.

"Perfect." She moves to sit on the couch, but Ghoul blocks her path.

"And you, get rid of that hideous orange chair. It's ugly, and it smells," she adds for good measure.

He folds his arms over his chest and ignores the comment about the chair.

"What did I say about keeping your head down and yourself safe?" He shoots daggers at her. "What do you do? You immediately try to pick a fight."

She shrugs, shoving past him. "If he went for me, you would've stopped him."

All Ghoul does is shake his head and let out an exasperated sigh.

To distract herself from the crushing weight in her chest, she turns to face Calvin, who's eating at the island.

"Sir," she calls respectfully. "Does Ghoul always wear this stupid mask?"

He looks up from his plate. "Not all the time. We unfortunately know what he looks like. He's really kept it on the entire time?"

She nods and then throws a dirty look at Ghoul.

"I was beginning to think he's hideously disfigured under there, like a pineapple fucked an older pineapple."

Ghoul's eyeroll makes her smirk.

Calvin bursts out laughing. "I do believe she just compared you to Deadpool."

"He's pretty ugly under the mask," Hill grumbles from the orange chair.

Ghoul groans and glares at Yasmine. She's such a brat! Yet, he finds his jaw clenching and the tightness in his shoulder returning. She's in the line of fire, and he knows he can't stop the cogs already spinning.

Chapter Thirty-One
Third Time's the Charm

Yasmine's the last one in the cabin when she pulls her boots on; it's taking longer because of the soreness in her lower half. The early afternoon sunlight is reflecting off the most recent freshly fallen snow, making it look like diamonds sparkling along the ground — it's blinding. The last of the storms has passed. Yasmine pulls her coat tighter around her and follows the three men. She falls in line, keeping her eyes trained on her feet. She finds it difficult to take a full breath from the building panic of the unknown. No one has mentioned if the danger has passed or not, and she really doesn't want to ask.

A black lifted four-door Ford truck sits parked next to Ghoul's 4Runner. She eyes it suspiciously. She's pretty sure she'll need a step stool to climb inside.

"Well, if someone isn't overcompensating," she grumbles under her breath.

Calvin hears the quip and flashes his perfect grin at her as he slaps the hood of the Ford.

"Oh darling, it's not compensating for anything; it's broadcasting the power under the hood." He winks.

She gives him a deadpan look. "And has that line ever worked for you?"

He leans on his truck and wiggles his eyebrows. "Is it working on you?"

"No." She'd laugh if she wasn't on the verge of screaming.

Calvin hangs his head in defeat. "Alas, then no, it's never worked."

Hill grumbles something under his breath and jumps into the front passenger seat.

Yasmine snorts air through her nose.

"Well, we have a long drive ahead of us. I guess I can educate you on how to properly woo a woman." She gestures to the truck. "This, is not it."

Then she jerks her thumb at Ghoul. "I gave him pointers, so I guess I can give you a few."

Yasmine's doing anything she can to distract herself from the overwhelming sorrow eating away at her.

Hill groans from inside the cab. "Please don't. He's insufferable enough as it is."

"You're just jealous, Hill. You've seen what I'm packing." Calvin climbs in and starts the engine.

"This will be a fun family car ride. One guy wants to kill me, and the other has big dick energy," Yasmine says, shaking her head.

Ghoul grunts something under his breath while he opens the door for her, but she doesn't catch it.

"Jesus, Calvin," she complains. "First point, if you take a girl out on a date in this thing, you need a step stool to help her get in."

Her fingers wrap around the handle on the doorframe. She pulls herself up and jumps at the same time. Her first attempt lands her back on the ground. After sex the night before and twice that morning, she hardly has the strength to support her weight.

"Don't encourage him. His ego is already too big for the world to handle." Ghoul bends down and wraps his arms around her legs. "Here, allow me."

He gives her the boost she needs to get into the obnoxiously large truck.

"Thanks," she mutters before swallowing the lump in her throat. "Thanks for everything. You know, saving me and all." She's not sure what else to tell him at this juncture.

He stands there, looking up at her. He sees how she's trying to hide behind a brave face. She's doing her best to not look at him and then reaches for the armrest to pull the door closed.

She pauses, remembering something. "Oh yeah, don't forget. Mavis Kemo. Read one of her books."

"I'll read one of your smutty books." The crooked smile reaches his eyes, and he pats her knee quickly before closing the truck door.

She gives him a tiny wave through the window as Calvin backs out of the driveway.

Ghoul stands in the cold and stares at the tire tracks the Ford left in the snow. She's gone, and he's left with a desolate feeling inside.

He shoves his hands in his pockets and turns back to the cabin to read his new orders.

When they reach the interstate, Yasmine realizes Ghoul's cabin is in South Carolina, somewhere in the Appalachian Mountains. They drive most of the afternoon and into the evening. The sun sets an hour before Calvin parks the Ford in front of room twelve after getting its key.

The motel looks the same as any roadside motel across the U.S. The bright neon sign with an arrow advertises the Sea Breeze Motel, even though they are nowhere near the ocean or a lake. The baby blue paint is cracked and peeling, showing visitors the motel is in desperate need of a facelift. Other than that, the motel looks pretty clean and somewhat maintained.

At least it doesn't give off too many *Psycho* serial killer vibes.

Yasmine's in desperate need of a shower and to lie down on something cushy. Being sore and stiff in a vehicle doesn't leave her in a comfortable state. More than anything, she wants to be alone with her broken heart.

She refuses to cry in front of the two men, so she kept her eyes trained out the window most of the drive. Calvin and Hill rarely spoke, and she didn't have the energy to give Calvin any tips on attracting women. The only time any of them spoke was if they requested a stop. She appreciated the silence; she already had too many overwhelming thoughts to worry about mindless chitchat.

"I guess we better get you something to eat." Calvin reaches over the seat and hands her the key to her room.

She takes it from him at the same time she opens the truck door, trying not to fall to the ground because of the height.

"I'm good." The last thing she feels like is food.

She shuts the door before he can say anything and goes straight to her ground-floor room.

He rolls his window down and leans his head out. "You haven't eaten all day. I'll go get something."

"I'm not hungry." She gives him a dismissive wave and closes the door behind her.

Yasmine steps into the old motel room and exhales. She won't have to see those two until morning, and then maybe she can force herself to eat breakfast. She's already breaking her promise to Ghoul to eat properly, but she can't think about food when her stomach is all tied in knots.

Surveying the room after flicking the light on and locking the door, she takes in the strange mix of furniture and décor. There's a small kitchenette in the corner with a single burner and a tiny sink. An old round fake wood table is next to the kitchenette. The two metal chairs with faded yellow and brown striped seat cushions look to be from the seventies. The one queen-size bedspread looks like it's from the nineties with its large mauve and pink flowers. The wallpaper and décor are from the eighties. The brown carpet is modern.

In the bathroom, the entire space is tiled in yellow; the shower drain is in the middle of the floor. There's no tub, just a round metal curtain rod and dingy white shower curtain.

"This isn't the Bates Motel, but it sure has the vibe." Moving to the toilet, she undoes her pants and sighs. "At least it's clean."

When she finishes relieving herself, she searches through the basket of toiletries, finding a toothbrush and toothpaste. After freshening up, she clicks the light off, collapsing onto the bed, and kicks her boots off. The shower she wanted is forgotten.

Light from the neon Sea Breeze sign shines through the thin curtains. She rolls to her back, sprawling out on the bed and staring up at the popcorn-textured ceiling.

Emotion swells in her chest, and the tears leak from the corner of her eyes and fall to the bedspread under her. She's alone, again. For almost a week, she had someone to talk to and keep her company. Even if they didn't talk, it was nice having someone in the room with her, so she wouldn't feel lonely.

Yasmine doesn't love Ghoul. How can she when they've only known each other a short time? Being honest with herself, she knows she has a strong attraction to him, but mostly it's because they created a bond with each other, and she could be herself with him. She showed him her unfiltered, authentic self. Not once did he tell her to shut up. Even when she punched him in the middle of her breakdown, he took it without retaliating. Instead, he carried her inside and cared for her. And he was so gentle with her during their lovemaking.

A small smile forms, though her heart is falling to pieces. At least she chose someone special to be her first. She never imagined it would be someone whose face she's never seen. That doesn't matter because she was drawn to the man under the mask.

Wiggling herself between the sheets, she pulls the covers over her head. Hiding under the blankets, she can at least pretend she's safe. The weight of reality is making it hard for her to breathe. She will have to face her father with the new knowledge of his secret life, and she doesn't know what to do with it. And the only person who made her feel truly safe won't be there to protect her.

Exhaustion finally overtakes her, and she drifts into a restless sleep.

She startles awake when four men, dressed in all black and ski masks, rush into the room. She tries to fight, but they quickly overpower her. She screams, kicks, and punches. She throws all she has into fighting the men off, but a half-starved, physically spent woman against four burly giants can only do so much.

One of the men gets Yasmine on her stomach and pins her to the bed, using his legs to secure her arms. She struggles to breathe under the man's weight and continues to kick out, but another man is pinning her legs.

A deep commanding voice speaks in French. The next thing she knows, she feels the sting of a needle being pushed into her arm. Her mind loses all control of her body; her vision blurs when hands pull her to her feet. She sees the emerald green eyes of the man in charge. He's taller and broader than all the other men.

Those green eyes are the last thing on her mind before her entire world goes black.

Across the road, in the parking lot of a small grocery store, the lifted black Ford sits with its lights off. Calvin and Hill watch the scene unfold.

A black van with all identifying information removed or covered is parked along the side of the road. One guy dressed in black gets out and breaks into the office. He returns a moment later. The van backs into an empty parking space in front of room twelve. Four men get out; the driver stays in the van with the engine running.

The four men rush inside. They come out a few moments later, two of them carrying Yasmine's limp body between them. One holds her feet, and the other has his arms hooked under her shoulders. They unceremoniously dump her in the back of the van when the motel's old manager comes out in a flannel bathrobe and slippers to see what the commotion is all about.

It's already too late. The van pulls out and disappears down the road.

Calvin starts the truck without a word. At the same time, Hill pulls out his cell phone.

The person on the other end picks up instantly.

"They took the bait," Hill says.

"You have your orders." General Forrester's voice is strained.

"Yes sir," Hill responds and gives a curt nod to Calvin before ending the call.

Calvin's usual jovial self has disappeared, and in its place is a permanent frown.

"This is the part of the job I hate," he mutters under his breath as he pulls out of the parking lot to follow the van.

"Even though I don't like her because she's a Pennington, I have to agree." Hill stares forward gloomily from the passenger seat. "She's being forced into a dangerous game as a pawn. It's wrong."

Chapter Thirty-Two
Screwed, And Not the Good Kind

The familiar sound of a crackling fire is the first sensation to break through Yasmine's unconscious state. With her awareness slowly returning, she wonders how she made it back to Ghoul's cabin. Then her body begins quaking from a chill that penetrated clear to the bone, and she realizes there's none of the familiar warmth surrounding her. The next sensation is the splitting headache and dry chemical aftertaste in her mouth. She tries to open her eyes, but only a groan escapes.

After great effort, she finally pries them open, hoping to be back at the cabin with Ghoul sitting next to her, with his hand on her thigh and his book in the other.

No such luck. She finds herself on a plush, dark leather couch with a thin blanket that's doing nothing to warm her. She blinks away the blackness still dancing around her vision in hopes the scene before her will change. She forces herself to sit up, willing her arms to work correctly, but the movement is sluggish, like she's underwater. It also doesn't help that her whole body is sore from her time between the sheets with Ghoul.

Her gaze lands on the matching couch across from her, and then she takes in the study's dark mahogany paneling. There's a large flat screen TV mounted on the wall; a crackling fireplace is on the screen.

Lame. The thought breaks through her throbbing headache.

She swings her legs off the couch, and her feet sink into thick plush carpet. It matches the dark rich theme of the office. She briefly wonders where her boots are when someone clears their throat.

"Ah. I see you are finally awake, mademoiselle." An apathetic, heavily accented male voice breaks through the stillness of the study.

She finds herself in the presence of a tall lean man dressed in a perfectly tailored three-piece grey pinstriped suit. He's staring at her from where he stands behind a large ornate mahogany desk. Behind him is a window, which takes up the entirety of the outside wall. The night-time view is a city skyline; the sun is either rising or setting — she can't tell.

The more her vision focuses on the man, the more he looks familiar. He has a strong jawline and European features. It's his hooked nose and cold, lifeless eyes she remembers the most. They're the same kind of eyes as her father's.

"You have been unconscious for quite some time. I was beginning to worry. It seems — what is the expression? — good help is hard to find. The man who gave you the Sleeping Jasmin, a sleeping drug of my own design, did not know how to properly dose you. I apologize for the inconvenience." He smiles, gloating over his creation. "But the overdose did provide some valuable data, and for that, I thank you."

If she wasn't so groggy, she'd groan internally at this arrogant asshole's bragging and fake apology. Her body is wrecked with shudders, and she doesn't know if it's from the cold, the drugs, or the fact that she knows she's in the presence of a dangerous man.

The man sets the papers in his hands on the desk. He smoothly takes his suit jacket off and lays it over the top of his ritzy dark brown leather chair. He slides casually around the desk toward her. He moves with an air of arrogance and radiates power.

"We—" She erupts in a coughing fit. Her mouth and throat are too dry.

"Shh, shh, shh." He holds up a hand. "No need to talk just yet."

He goes to a round table in the corner made from the same wood as his desk. There's a crystal pitcher with strawberries and ice in it. He pours the slightly pinkish liquid into a matching crystal glass and holds it out to her with a disarming smile, but even that doesn't break through his vacant gaze.

"Here. Drink."

Yasmine doesn't move and stares at the offered glass before she looks up at him.

His smile of perfectly lined teeth never wavers. His dark brown hair is meticulously combed and slicked back with way too much gel. His cologne is overpowering, even at the distance between them. Some might consider him "good-looking," but he's not fooling her. The man's a mosquito — a bloodsucker carrying disease.

"It is water infused with strawberries. Take it." He presses it closer to her. "I'm sure you are parched."

Yasmine licks her cotton tongue over her dry, cracked lips before accepting the glass with a nod. She knows men like this don't understand the concept of no. She tries to smile, but nothing is working right because of the drugs they pumped her with. Greedily downing the entire cup in one go, the cool, slightly strawberry-flavored water begins to rehydrate her, but does nothing to quench the headache or thirst.

Once she pulls the glass away from her lips, he takes it back to refill it. His fingers brush over hers.

She clears her throat, hoping to find her voice. "We've met before. You're the one from the restaurant, right?"

The French man holds the refilled glass out to her with an amused expression. "You remember me?"

How could I forget? You made my father lose his composure. But she's not going to say anything.

He takes a seat across from her on the other couch, pulls his cell phone out, and types a quick message. Then he returns his attention to her. His eyes rove over the expanse of her body, and he does nothing to hide his leering at her tits.

When Ghoul did the same, her stomach did backflips, but this guy makes her stomach drop in disgust and triggers the sensation of something crawling on her skin.

"I am sorry for the unpleasantness of that night and interrupting your birthday. Your father makes it very difficult to meet." He continues to stare at her chest, and then his mouth opens slightly brushing his bottom lip with his thumb.

"You have given me quite the trouble, mademoiselle." He crosses his leg over the other and laces his fingers together, resting them on his lap. He finally lifts his gaze from her tits. "You somehow escaped from my men. Then you disappear. Please, enlighten me as to what happened."

She takes another sip of water to buy herself a few seconds to think. She needs to be careful what she tells him, and how much. The danger oozing from this man could fill the room, and then some.

"You clearly know who I am. Do you have a name? Or should I just call you handsome?"

She hopes she hides the cringe from her expression. He's not handsome at all; he's vile, but a man like him has an inflated ego, so it can't hurt to stroke it a bit. If she does her best to remain respectful, then maybe she'll have enough time to figure out something and escape. She's completely on her own, and the thought causes bile to rise. The reality is, there is no masked man this time coming to save her.

The corner of his mouth curls upwards in amusement at her calling him handsome. "You may call me Jean."

"Jean," she repeats, mimicking his French accent. "Where do you want me to begin?"

"I'm glad to see you are willing to cooperate." He uncrosses his leg and recrosses the other one before leaning casually on the armrest. "Begin from when you were taken from the dance studio."

She takes a deep breath and lets it out slowly. Her first kidnapping seems like it happened to someone else a lifetime ago. So much occurred in the week she spent with Ghoul.

"Well, let's see." She feigns remembering to buy time, deciding it'll be better to stick closer to the truth. "One of your men kept threatening to rape me, and he came in to do just that, but some guy in a mask showed up and slit his throat. The man blindfolded me and took me somewhere. Next thing I knew, I was in some creepy basement with torture devices on the wall."

He eyes her suspiciously. "What did the man look like?"

She shakes her head. "I don't know. He wore a ski mask the whole time, but he did have an American accent."

"What did this man want?"

"He asked a lot of questions about my father, but I didn't know anything." Her voice takes on the tone of a whimpering child. "I don't know what's going on, to be honest."

He looks her over, his eyes once more lingering around her breast. "It appears you are unharmed, so he did not torture or hit you? Or perhaps violate you?"

"He did get a little rough with me, but I cooperated." She purposely keeps her eyes averted from Jean because men like him want submission.

"Is it alright if I ask you a question?" she stutters, keeping her head down.

"You may." His hands open in agreement.

"Are you going to kill me?" She can't hide the fear, so she lets it show.

"I do not make it a habit of harming innocent women. As of right now, no. But it also depends on you," he tells her truthfully, "and how cooperative you are. If you assist me in my endeavors, I do not see any reason as to why I cannot return you to your life."

She gives a tiny nod, her eyes pleading for her safety.

"How did you escape from this man?"

"He dropped me off at the motel and left. He told me not to talk about what happened or else he'd find and kill me."

"You poor thing. That is quite the ordeal to go through." His words are smooth, but she sees through the false sincerity. "As for my men who brought you to the studio, they were under strict orders to not harm you. I apologize for that." He places both feet on the plush carpet. "We can continue this later. You need to be cleaned up, and I am finding it difficult to concentrate with the grumbling sounds coming from your belly."

He claps loudly twice, and the wooden double doors open.

Two drop-dead gorgeous women, who look like models, enter in long, tight-fitting satin dresses. Everything about them is perfect. The blonde with the red lipstick looks at Jean seductively. The brunette with the cool shade of lipstick moves with a refinement that even makes Yasmine blink in awe.

The women carry themselves with confidence and elegance, something Yasmine lacks. They move with swaying hips to stand behind Jean, each running a hand over his face, shoulder, and chest like they both are his lovers. She guesses they probably are.

Keeping his gaze fixed on Yasmine, he speaks to them in French. From the way he speaks and his gestures, she knows he's telling them what to do with her.

He switches to English. "Evette and Marie will take good care of you. Please go with them and do as they say." But then his tone turns deadly. "Do not think of trying to escape. You cannot. The door locks will not open for you."

She awkwardly and stiffly tries to get to her feet, but her shaky legs give out and she falls back to the couch. The drugs and sex have taken their toll on her.

This is why they warn you of the dangers of sex, drugs, and rock and roll. The intrusive thought invades at the worst possible time. At least she's not regretting the sex with Ghoul; that part was one of the best things to come out of all this.

"I'm s-sorry," she says in embarrassment.

He speaks in French to Evette and Marie, and they leave his side, moving toward her.

"Please, allow us to help you?" The brunette says in perfect English with the slightest trace of a French accent. She offers her a hand.

The blonde moves to her other side, and together they get her standing. The two women support her as they walk her out of the room.

Chapter Thirty-Three
Coffee is Lifeblood

Two blocks away on the rooftop, three men sit huddled together. A light snow begins to fall on them and the city. Wearing winter gear and masks to stay warm, they observe the exchange between Yasmine and the bioweapons dealer. Their equipment and gear are spread out before them.

"Damn. She's good," Calvin comments when the two women lead Yasmine from Auclair's penthouse office. He lowers the binoculars and gives Ghoul an approving nod. "She's laying the helpless act on thick."

Ghoul frowns under the black mask. He lowers the binoculars, pulls off the headphones, and sits up, reaching for the thermos of coffee. He isn't so sure if she's acting or if she really is that scared. He was tempted to pull his sniper rifle out and put a bullet between Auclair's eyes for his leering.

He's been in a foul mood since he read his orders back at the cabin, and now this primal need to protect Yasmine is taking hold of his mental state. It was there when he rushed in to save her at the dance studio, but it's on a whole new level. He wants to kill any man who looks at her. No matter WHAT he wants, though, he can't storm in there and take on all of Auclair's goons on his own, not unless he has a squad, and then that'd be a different story. They'd tear into his men, leaving a trail of bodies in their wake.

Adding to his boiling rage is the fact that he hates being in one of the most crowded cities in the U.S. The constant buzz of traffic and people grates on his nerves. The sun has set, but the city lights make it seem like there is a constant state of twilight. He often uses the stars to help calm and clear his head when he's out in the field, but these lights snuff them out. Instead, he does the only thing he can and pours more coffee from the thermos into the cup.

Calvin and Hill easily figure something happened between Ghoul and Yasmine at the cabin because of how uncharacteristically antsy Ghoul is. But, in his current state, they dare not ask him for details and wisely keep distant with their silence.

Hill stands and stretches his cold, stiff muscles, the insulated blanket falling from his shoulders. He checks his watch. "I'm going to take this opportunity to run and grab us some chow."

When Hill disappears through the metal roof door, Calvin turns to Ghoul. "Take a break. I'll keep watch for now. I'll let you know if anything noteworthy happens."

He slips the headphones on and settles in to listen to the conversations inside the penthouse apartment.

Taking cover behind ductwork, Ghoul grabs his book from his combat vest and the small reading light. He needs something to distract himself. He doesn't trust Jean "Fingers" Auclair with her. Internationally known as Fingers, he likes to collect his victims' fingers, so the man is on par with her father. He's a French businessman on paper, but off the books, his business is in biotech and chemical weapons. Thanks to Yasmine, they now have a solid connection to tie her father to the man, along with the stolen U.S. missiles that keep getting sold.

Their black ops team has been working for the past two years to take down these terrorists. Eventually, they discovered there were people in the government involved. So they sent some of their top men undercover to gather intel to put a stop to this ring of warmongers. It was one of their men on the inside working for Auclair who leaked the news about Yasmine's kidnapping.

This connection only adds to General Pennington's list of treasonous crimes. It's bad enough dealing with terrorists, but when one of the terrorists is one of your own using their respected position to deal in weapons, there's no excuse. Pennington will be executed without facing a court-martial.

After reading the same paragraph three times and not retaining any of the story, Ghoul slams the book shut and stuffs it in his pocket.

Fuck. He hangs his head in his hands. *This is why you avoid any kind of personal connections on the job.*

His mind runs rampant with all the horrible ways "Fingers" could torture her.

God, if for once in your omnipotent life you listen to a prayer, please keep her safe until I can get her out. He prays to any of the thousands of gods who might be listening.

He pulls the bottom of his mask up to take a sip of coffee then shakes his head. He never prays. He gave up on the idea of a higher power a long time ago. How can he believe in any God when he has seen the horrible things that take place in the shadows of the world, and God has done nothing to end the suffering and violence? Why would any God step in now to keep her safe?

Chapter Thirty-Four
The Puppet Dons The Mask

Yasmine strips out of her tattered clothing. They need to be thrown in the trash at this point. She tosses her shirt on top of the pile, not caring that Evette and Marie are in her personal space taking her measurements, examining her shape, and speaking hurriedly in French.

When their assessment is complete, the blonde leaves without a word, while the brunette, Marie, stays behind.

"Clean yourself up. You have fifteen minutes to bathe. Dinner will be ready shortly, and Jean does not like to be kept waiting," Marie instructs before leaving her in solitude.

Yasmine lets out a long exasperated breath. She sticks her toe in the sunken and beautifully white marbled bathtub. The bathroom is larger than her studio apartment, and a helluva lot more pretentious. Everything she's seen since waking up in Jean's office, and while the two hotties led her to the bathroom, is to broadcast wealth and power. Everything is obnoxiously over the top and lavish.

The hot, steaming water envelopes her aching body. Someone added fragrant oils to the bath, so she breathes in deeply and sinks her shoulders under the water. Then she closes her eyes and leans her head back. She can't fully relax, but at least for the time being, she's safe.

Lying there, fully submerged except for her head, she longs to be back at the little cabin. Her heart lurches when her thoughts turn to Ghoul. She wishes he were here. He'd know what to do, and he'd keep her safe. She finds it funny how quickly her thoughts turn to him.

She trails her fingers through the bathwater, feeling the water move past her hands and arms. Alone now with her thoughts, she can't shake the feeling she was set up. How did the kidnappers know where to find her, and so quickly? Suspicions develop the more she questions who Ghoul works for in the government and their secret black ops military group. Calvin and Hill should have been at the motel with her, yet they couldn't stop those men from taking her? Meaning, they let the bad guys take her. She sinks lower in the tub, wishing she could become the water and escape through the drain.

They must have used her, and she figures the Frenchman will do the same to get to her father. While she sorts through the information, there is one burning question that leaves a bitter sting in her mouth. Did Ghoul know?

"You keep your head down and do whatever you have to do to keep yourself alive." His words echo through her mind, and anger wells up. To her, it sounds like he knew. A deep frown sets in.

Her eyes slam closed to hold back the vat of acid threatening to spill from them. She sits up so quickly the water sloshes to the marble floor, but she doesn't care about making a mess. He knew, and he used her. However unlikely it is, if she ever sees Ghoul again, she's going to give him a piece of her mind.

Pulling the bottle of fancy shampoo from the edge of the tub, she flicks the cap open and inhales. She hates how it smells of pretentious, fake flowers. Just like everything in this fucking place, it's a façade. It might look nice, but underneath it's something grotesque and rotten, just like Jean and her father. It's a good thing she has experience with men like this.

While she washes her hair, Yasmine resigns herself to do whatever she needs to survive. She's on her own. There's no masked man coming this time.

"They moved a table in his bedroom," Hill announces from his spot on the roof, the binoculars pressed to his face. "It looks like they're setting up for a meal."

Ghoul's head snaps up from the cold deli sandwich Hill got him. He shoves the last bite into his mouth and reaches for his binoculars and headphones.

"Anything on the audio?" Calvin asks, taking a bite of his cold sandwich.

"Just typical chatter. Nothing worthwhile from what I can hear," Hill reports.

From their position on the roof, they can see several of the main rooms of the penthouse apartment and the henchmen's quarters on the floor below. With their surveillance equipment, the audio is clear, almost like they are in the room with the bad guys.

Ghoul surveys the bedroom through the binoculars, and sure enough, a table has been moved in, the lights have been dimmed, and candles have been lit. He tightens his grip on the binoculars to the point his fingers turn white under his gloves. He's involuntarily grinding his teeth.

This isn't right. The thought has been lingering in his mind on repeat.

Auclair enters first and takes his jacket and tie off. He loosens the top buttons of his shirt and rolls the sleeves up. He checks his appearance in the mirror like a pretentious prick. When satisfied with his preening, he takes a seat at the table with his back to the window.

Good. I can put a bullet through his skull if he hurts her.

Ghoul doesn't voice this to the other two on the roof. Their orders are to observe and gather intel, but he doesn't give a fuck. He'll take a court-martial if it means she isn't harmed.

A servant brings in a bucket of ice; a bottle of wine is chilling inside it. Auclair uncorks the bottle, inhaling the aroma, and pours himself a glass. Then pours a glass for the empty seat across from him.

Ghoul grits his teeth. *Please let her not drink.*

"Jesus. I can hear your teeth grinding from over here," Hill complains as he finishes his deli sandwich.

"Mind your own fucking business. This is why your mom should have swallowed," Ghoul bites.

There's the sound of a door opening, and movement comes through the audio. The blonde enters and nods to Auclair with a seductive smile, and then leaves, closing the door behind her.

"I apologize for keeping you waiting," Yasmine voices from the doorway. She doesn't step into the view of the men on the roof. "Your lady friends insisted on dressing me up."

Ghoul wants to throw up his sandwich. He can't see her, but he knows Auclair has to be enjoying her with his eyes. He quickly glances at his rifle case and thinks about going for it now, but instead, he focuses on the two in the bedroom. If Auclair tries to hurt her like the other guy, he's going for the rifle — orders be damned.

"You look radiant, ma chère." Auclair moves to the chair across from him and pulls it out like a gentleman, motioning for her to sit. "Would you do me the honor of dining with me tonight?"

She steps into view for the men on the roof, and Ghoul sees her screwed on fake smile.

"Of course, but I've never been to New York City. Would it be okay if I take a moment to view the beautiful skyline?" she asks shyly.

Auclair's sleazy grin causes Ghoul's blood to boil.

"It's hard to believe this prick is one of the most dangerous men in the world with the way he's carrying on with her," Calvin mutters from his seat next to Ghoul.

"Auclair? He should change his name to éclair. He's thin, soft, and full of white shit, waiting to melt in a man's mouth," Hill grumbles from Ghoul's other side.

He really could do without those two and their commentary, but this is to be expected with how the Marine mind works. He'd add in his own quips if he wasn't planning all the ways he's going to gut Éclair.

Yasmine walks to the window and looks out over the skyline. She's wearing a long flowing silver gown with a high slit up one side. The silver fabric of the bodice has black floral embroidery woven throughout to accentuate her feminine features. The plunging neckline goes past her diaphragm, displaying the skin between her breasts. The back of the dress is open, and revealing. Her long hair is down and draping down her back. Her makeup is expertly done, and her lips are painted a light shade of pink.

Ghoul takes in her appearance. He enjoys seeing the dress revealing all the skin, but he wants to rip it off and mess up her hair and makeup. Not because his sexual desire for her is rising, but because the woman standing at the window is a fake doll compared to the real person he spent a week alone with. She'd rather wear baggy clothes instead of something sexy and talk about smutty romance books than be ogled. He ignores the fact he ogled her ... a lot. Who he sees standing at the window is not her.

Calvin whistles under his breath at seeing her sex appeal. "And you spent all that time alone with her. No wonder you couldn't keep your hands off her. I wouldn't be able to either."

This is the first time either of them has voiced their suspicions about them getting busy. Ghoul doesn't bother to respond. It's none of their goddamn business what they did.

Hill picks up his headphones, securing them to his head, and then picks up his binoculars.

"Hot damn. She cleans up nice." He whistles quietly.

Ghoul would have ripped out both their tongues right then and there if Auclair didn't start speaking, drawing his attention back to the bedroom with the romantic dining setup.

"I can't believe you have never been to this glorious city before," Auclair says, running his calloused hand up her arm and making her shudder.

She expected him to have soft hands with the "hands-off approach" and "let others do your dirty work" vibe he has going for him. You only get callouses like that if you work.

He lifts a lock of her hair, inhaling deeply. He then begins twirling his index finger around the strands, pushing into her personal space. To her credit, she remains calm and still. Even with the distance, Ghoul can see how lifeless her eyes are. It's the same look she wore when he saved her. She's mentally detached.

"I'm not really much of a traveler, I guess." She turns her face to him with a fake smile and a simple curl of her shoulder.

His fingers brush the bruise on her neck. "What is this?"

Her face drops, and she looks away. "I'm not sure. I have bruises all over my body. I don't know where they all came from."

No way in hell is she going to speak the truth and say Ghoul left a hickey.

She turns away from the window, but with him pressing into her space, she's forced to brush against him. Marie insisted she wear high heels, and she insisted she only wears flats because she doesn't know how to walk in them. In the end, she lost the argument and is now strapped into torturous three-inch heels that are making her feet hurt.

With her first step toward the table, her ankle twerks, and she loses her balance. Auclair is there, wrapping an arm around her waist to prevent her from falling. Her hands grasp onto him reflexively to steady herself; she's bending into him.

"I'm so ... sorry." She stutters, righting herself.

She holds onto him longer than she needs to because her balance is terrible with the heels. He looks lean, but she can feel how rock hard his body is under the expensive clothing. She realizes he's not so hands-off as she thought.

"I only ever wear flats, and I'm afraid I don't know how to walk in these." She chuckles anxiously. "Would it be okay if I take them off?"

His hand caresses down her back, and he notes the gooseflesh forming on her skin at his touch. His hand comes to rest dangerously low on her hip. Another two inches, and he'd be on her ass.

"Whatever you need to do to make yourself more comfortable," he assures her.

"Do you mind?" she asks before using him to steady herself.

He gives her a wolfish grin and puts his arm around her, pressing their bodies together in a familiar way. "Go ahead."

Yasmine places a hand on his shoulder, brings her leg up behind her, and fumbles with the strap. She gets the first shoe off and then switches to the other strap.

On the rooftop, the snow is beginning to stick around the three men and their surveillance equipment. Calvin and Hill keep glaring at

Ghoul because he's grinding his teeth together and muttering curses under his breath; it's grating on their nerves.

What's getting to Ghoul is the weak, helpless act she's putting on. He knows she has more fire in her than this. He's questioning if she put on an act with him at the cabin? He shakes the thought away. He saw the real her: the bratty hellcat. This is all an elaborate act, or she's reverting to the survival instinct she developed while living with her father.

He's experienced life-threatening torture once before in his younger days when he was still in the gang, but this scene playing out before him is worse than any physical torture. Auclair, the same man who can easily snap her neck at any moment, is escorting her to the table like a gentleman. She was a giggling, bashful virgin a couple of days ago with him, but now she's throwing her body at this pastry? He can't watch much longer. This whole thing is messing with his head.

"Calm down, Ghoul," Calvin hisses. "You look like you're about ready to leap across these rooftops and rip his throat out."

Ghoul glares but says nothing. Calvin's not wrong. He refocuses on the scene in the bedroom the moment Auclair pushes Yasmine's chair in.

"Would you care for some wine?" Jean motions to the glass he poured earlier.

She holds her hand up with a headshake. "Thank you, but no. I'm afraid alcohol makes me sick, and I don't want to ruin dinner."

"We certainly do not want you to be sick, do we?"

He refills his wine glass then spins the dark burgundy liquid around, inspecting the lines on the glass. When satisfied, he takes a sip.

"Tell me about yourself."

She stares at him for a few breaths. When her mouth opens to speak, she stops herself and turns her head to the side. Then tries to start again.

"I ..." She hedges, her eyebrows turning downward in a childish frown. "Uh ..."

She finally looks at Jean and gives him a tense smile. "I'm afraid you would find me incredibly boring."

She gestures a hand around her at the luxury and the elaborate display on the table of dishware and candles before ending on him.

"Compared to all this, and whatever it is you do, I'm a boring nobody."

He slowly rests his elbows on the table, interlacing his fingers. All the while, his gaze remains fixed on her and dips to the exposed skin between her breasts.

"You are General Pennington's daughter, though, are you not?"

She nods.

"That alone makes you somebody." He pushes himself back and sips from the wine glass. "Tell me what you do for work."

"I work part time as a substitute teacher, and I'm working on getting my endorsements and board certifications. But my focus has been on finishing grad school, and then I'm going to teach full time."

He fakes surprise because he already knows what she does. "You are a teacher?"

She nods and looks down at her hands. "I'd like to be, but the current situation has put everything on hold."

A light knock raps on the door, interrupting the conversation. The servant carries in a tray with their dinner and sets a bowl of stew in front of Jean first and then her.

He motions to the bowl. "Please, enjoy."

Yasmine doesn't need further prompting. She's so famished, she's going to eat even if her anxious stomach is telling her not to.

He stares intently at her until she takes the first bite.

"It's good. It's rich and hearty."

"It is called Coq au Vin. It is a traditional French meal." He turns his attention to his own bowl. "What do you plan to teach?"

"I did my first student teaching semester in a blended classroom with mainstream and special education students. I found working with the special education students to be enjoyable. Working with students with different abilities is what made me decide to continue to grad school to get more training under my belt to teach special ed. I'm focusing on teaching students who are deaf."

He sets his spoon inside the bowl and brings the napkin to his lips. "You know, I never would have imagined that of you. I'm curious, how did your father take your decision?"

She lets out a restrained chuckle. "Thankfully, by the time he found out I changed my major, it was too late. He threatened to take away his financial support for school, but I was already prepared to get student loans and figured it out on my own. But, in the end, he agreed to continue paying for college."

They eat in silence for some time. His eyes consume her every move, and when she looks up, he makes no attempt to hide his skin-crawling gaze. The only difference between this guy and his goon who tried to rape her is Jean at least is pretending to be nice. Even then, it's taking all her strength and focus to stay composed.

She struggles to enjoy the delicious French stew — each bite makes her stomach clench — but she needs to eat. So, she takes her time, and somehow, she manages to keep it down.

"Are you enjoying the meal?" He finally breaks the silence.

"I am. It's delicious." She smiles weakly. "May I ask for another bowl?"

She's forcing herself to eat until she's full, regardless of her protesting stomach. She needs the fuel to keep her strength up because she has no way of knowing what's going to happen or when she'll be able to eat again.

"I employ the best chef in all of Paris. I pay her very well to travel with me, so I always have the best food." He takes a sip of wine after his bragging session. "American food is not to my liking." He waves a hand in front of his face, swatting the thought away like a fly. "It is too greasy for my palate."

"I do agree with you on that." She pushes the empty bowl away.

He claps twice, and immediately the door opens to reveal the servant. He relays instructions in French, then she bows respectfully and leaves.

"Why do you not ask me questions? Is it not polite to have mutual dinner conversations?" Jean encourages.

She clears her throat. "You're right. But I'm afraid the questions I have for you would not make for proper dinner conversation."

She looks away, the color rising to her cheeks, and fidgets in her seat. She hopes he takes her reaction as being submissive and not loathing.

He covers her hand with his, in an intimate gesture, and begins to seductively caress it.

He leans in closer. "No need to be shy. I've never once gotten a complaint from a lover before." The grin conveys his intentions.

Fucking Ew. She screams in her mind.

His fingers continue making slow passes over the back of her hand, and it takes everything she has not to pull away from his revolting touch. Worst of all, the more he touches, the more it erases Ghoul's touch from her memories. She might be furious with him for using her, but damn if his touch wasn't nice.

She clamps down on her lip and closes her eyes, not able to meet his gaze. If she does, he'll see her hate.

He lets out a chuckle and brushes her cheek.

"You are blushing." The way his voice purrs with the accent almost makes her throw up in her mouth. "I'm curious, are you inexperienced in the ways of loving a man?"

Oh my God! This guy. She turns her face away slightly but then chances a darting glance. He's not reading the room at all. He's taking her nervous body language as something else, instead of disgust.

"That-that's a very pointed question." Her voice quivers. She keeps her gaze on anything other than him.

Leaning toward her, he catches her chin and roughly forces her to look at him. His desire to take ownership of her body is clearly on display. If he were a cartoon character, he'd be the wolf with his eyes popping out and tongue rolling on the floor. His thumb hooks around her bottom lip, pulling it down and exposing her teeth. He slides his thumb along the inside of her lip to the inside of her fleshy cheek.

A knock sounds on the door before it opens.

He reluctantly releases her and leans back in his seat with a scowl on his face. He's not happy with the interruption. It's a good thing it happened because she was about to bite his finger off. She grabs her glass and tries to wash away his salty taste, but with no success. She takes another shaky sip.

Jean sees her shaking, but, like before, he's misinterpreting the signs. The servant quickly switches out Yasmine's empty bowl with a new one, asks Jean something in French, and then disappears, closing the door behind her.

He leans back in his chair and watches her eat. "You did not answer my question."

She hoped he'd drop the subject, but luck is not on her side tonight.

"I don't have much experience with men," she mutters weakly, her focus still on the stew, though she hasn't tasted it.

There's just one man, she thinks. One who she wishes would storm into this room and slit this asshole's throat for good measure.

"I'm going to rip his fucking head off." Ghoul snarls deep in his chest and grips the binoculars so tightly he can't feel his fingers.

He saw how repulsed she was when Auclair shoved his finger in her mouth. The fear and disgust on her face ... and this motherfucker is getting off on it.

"Whoa, making it personal there?" Hill mocks.

Hill's never seen Ghoul lose his cool before. In fact, he's never seen him show any kind of emotion for that matter, and certainly not on an op. This is a new one on him. He wasn't even sure if Ghoul was capable of emotion. Most of the time, he keeps to himself and doesn't interact outside of work.

Ghoul pulls the binoculars away and fixes Hill with a violent glare but says nothing. Hill knows better than to push it right now with the comments. He wisely keeps his damn mouth shut, or he's liable to get his throat slit.

"For a beautiful woman such as yourself, I find that hard to believe," Auclair responds to her confession.

She takes a final bite, sets her spoon aside, and pushes the bowl away.

"I don't think I can eat another bite. It was delicious, but it's more filling than it looks."

He cocks his head to the side and inspects her with an intense stare. He claps his hands, and once more the servant enters. She might not know what he says, but with the commanding tone and the servant clearing the table, she gets the gist of it. He stands, moves toward her, and grabs her hand in his without asking.

"Shall we continue our conversation on the couch?" He motions to the window overlooking the city.

She has no say in this, and he's going to make her, even if she says no.

"Dessert will be here soon, so we can relax and enjoy the view until then." He picks up his wine glass with his free hand and pulls her along.

She only has a moment to grab her glass before he's dragging her to the couch. He's laying the charm on thick, as much as an alligator can before they kill.

She stiffly sits on the couch, overly aware of how high the slit rides up her thigh. His eyes linger at the exposed skin. Keeping a blank face, she sets her glass on the crystal coaster on the coffee table. Her attention focuses on the skyline. She's overcome with a brief wave of loneliness when she looks at the expanse of buildings, that is, until Jean presses against her.

He notes how she's sitting, and her innocence arouses him. Jean lays his arm across her shoulders. He brings his face close enough to take in the scent of her hair. His free hand grasps hers, and he brings her fingers to his lips and kisses them. He likes her dainty fingers and natural nails — her pretty little fingers would be a nice addition to his collection. The urge to take them stirs, and he shoves it aside because he'd much rather her fingers remain attached.

Taking her hand, he places her palm on his cheek. The wide eyes staring back at him bring forth another wolfish grin.

"Forgive me." He breathes into her ear. "You have beautiful hands. I wanted to feel them on my skin."

She stares in shock and snaps her jaw closed where it gaped open in reflex. The forced proximity and how he doesn't respect personal boundaries are causing her mask to slip. She tries to pull away from his hold, but he doesn't let her get away.

"I'm sorry. I'm just nervous." Yasmine can think of nothing else to say.

She's shutting down from the fear she's barely able to keep at bay. This man is dangerous, and his proximity is … This guy and her father are two faces of the same coin. The only difference is her father never violated her sexually and kept it to physical and mental abuse. But this guy will cross that line.

He grasps her chin and roughly pulls her gaze to him.

"You are so weak and timid." The corners of his mouth turn upward when he traces her jawline, noting the way her lip quivers. "Why is that?"

"Motherfucker," Ghoul hisses through clenched teeth. "She's anything but weak and timid."

He's not going to have any teeth left after this is done. She has the same look on her face as when she was about to be raped, and before she started to relax around him. A minuscule part of him briefly entertained the thought she was into Auclair, but with her current expression, he sees how wrong he is. She's not into Auclair. She's scared, and it's killing him inside.

Calvin places a calming hand on Ghoul's shoulder but has no words for his subordinate. This whole situation sucks. Each of them has done inhuman acts on others in the name of defending the country, but it doesn't mean they enjoy watching a woman being touched against her will.

Hill eyes Ghoul. His smart mouth turns down a notch in understanding. He once got too attached during a mission to a girl, and it cost him — she died. He turns back and looks through the binoculars.

"You did fuck her, didn't you?" Hill's tone is flat.

Ghoul's dark eyes lock Hill in a death glare. He's not in the mood to deal with any shit from him right now.

Hill, sensing the mood change and Ghoul's killer intent, continues looking through the binoculars. "I get it, man. Cuba became personal for me with Leona, remember?"

Ghoul nods. The image of Hill clinging to Leona's lifeless body flashes through his mind. Later, with their continued efforts to track down who was selling U.S. missiles, they discovered Pennington was the real reason for Leona's death, which is why Hill was so hostile toward Yasmine. Ghoul places a hand on Hill's shoulder, giving it an understanding pat.

"I get it," he tells him.

In this tense moment, both men share an understanding. It sucks when your girl is in danger.

Ghoul focuses his attention back on Yasmine. He's going to do everything in his power to make sure she doesn't end up like Leona.

Yasmine doesn't answer Jean's question right away. She swallows the lump of bile rising in her throat before meeting his piercing, soulless gaze. Jean and Ghoul are both killers, yet Ghoul's amber eyes still retained a soul and had life in them.

"Am I right to assume you're using me to get to my father?" She attempts to steer the conversation to literally anywhere else.

He tilts his head, deciding whether or not to tell her his intentions.

"Your father owes me quite a substantial sum of money, among other things, and he is being quite rude in ignoring my phone calls." He moves the hair away from her neck and brushes his fingers along her skin.

His touch is like being stabbed with thousands of needles. Her body wants to recoil from him, but her mind has taken over. She can't do anything to upset him.

"So, you want to use me to force a meeting with him?" she guesses.

"Yes, something like that. You are beautiful and smart." He begins playing with her hair enthusiastically and pressing closer into her space. "This is a dangerous and sexy combination for a woman."

He leans in, forcing their faces together so she can't turn away.

"You did not answer my question. Why are you so weak and timid?"

Basing her interactions with him on the truth has been working, so she decides to keep rolling with it. That is, until he slides his hand to her inner thigh in familiarity. This man is stealing all the lingering touches from her body that Ghoul left. Now all she feels is Jean, and his grubby hands.

"I have no affection for my father." Yasmine stares at her glass on the table to hide the tears. "What he did to me is the reason why I am the way I am. I'll help you however I can to get you the money he owes."

Taking a moment to compose herself, she faces him. She's startled to see murderous rage in his expression. It's the only real emotion she's seen reach his eyes since they've met. It's somehow more frightening.

"I'll cooperate, but I think you are putting too much faith in my father to care about me. He doesn't. He cares more about himself. But please, don't hurt me. I can't handle pain well, and I've been through so much."

She presses into him weakly. Her hand rests on his knee to appeal to whatever humanity he might have left. She hopes the rage she saw in him was directed at her father's abuse. Which she finds odd because Jean is a bad man, so why would he care?

Jean moves back, sizing her up. A renewed chill runs up her spine as she sees some plan forming in his mind.

"If you are willing to help, and if your performance is satisfactory" — he braces his hand on the back of her neck, holding her in place — "I promise not to harm you. And when I have my money, I will return you to your life. Deal?"

She nods.

The next thing she knows, his mouth is crushing on hers. His kiss is forceful and invasive. He shoves his way inside her mouth. She weakly kisses him back, but it's all wrong. She holds back the choking sob. His hand slips between her skin and the fabric of her dress and takes hold of her breast in his hand, pawing at her. Every fiber of her being screams in protest, wanting to shove him off, but if she does, he'll just hit her and take what he wants.

It's wrong — his touch, his feel, his taste.

She grasps his hand, covering it with her own, and places her other on his chest. She gently pulls his hand off her breast and pushes his chest at the same time, pulling away from his mouth.

"I'm sorry." She breathes, looking away. "I'm flattered. But, I'm not that kind of girl."

She prays the heat rising to her cheeks from her anger and disgust looks like a blush.

"We just met." Her giggle sounds so forced.

Jean brings her fingers to his lips, nibbling on them.

"Excusez-moi." He bites down on her index finger while touching her hair. "You are not that kind of girl. You are a woman who needs to be enjoyed like a rare vintage of fine wine." He kisses her cheek. "I will be taking my time with you."

Chapter Thirty-Five
He's a Real Bastard

"He's fucking dead," Ghoul bellows, making a grab for his sniper rifle case.

Auclair putting his hands all over Yasmine sends him into a spiraling, blinding rage. Not to mention, she was kissing him back. He's a dead man!

Calvin and Hill throw themselves on Ghoul, hooking their arms around him in restraint.

"No!" Calvin barks.

He's stupefied to see Ghoul so unhinged. He's their company's best tactician and strategist who always keeps his cool. Nothing ever gets to him.

"You cannot put our chance of getting to Judas in jeopardy. Do whatever it takes to calm down. But go. Calm. Down. We'll keep watch."

"Look." Hill draws their attention back to the room with Yasmine and Auclair.

The servant enters the room carrying a tray with two small plates of dessert and after-dinner tea, interrupting Auclair's assault. He removes his hand from her face, but he's still grasping her inner thigh like they're already lovers.

Ghoul doesn't want to calm down. He wants to stay right here, seeing how Auclair treats her. He needs to watch, so he has the fuel to kill Auclair and her father for putting her in this situation. She doesn't deserve any of this.

Somewhere through the rage, he realizes his reactions are the kind someone has if they have feelings for someone. He should be the only one who gets to touch her, but he doesn't have a claim to her. Ghoul shakes his head, trying to clear the thoughts. Still, when he turns his attention back to the scene playing out in the penthouse apartment, he can't help but compare how he'd do better.

She needs to be treated tenderly, until she's warmed up. Then she turns into a hellcat in the sheets. This French dickhead doesn't know the first thing about how to treat a woman like her, and he doesn't deserve to be in the same room, let alone breathe the same air, as her.

"You understand what needs to be done, ma chère?" Jean brushes his fingers across her face and moves her hair back over her shoulder.

"I do." The task is simple enough.

Two of Jean's goons, both dressed in black with matching masks covering their noses and mouths, are on either side of her. The one with green eyes is the biggest man in the room. He holds her phone out to her. She barely looks at him. His vivid green eyes and dark brown hair are the only things making him stand out, along with his hulking presence.

What is it with men and masks?

Regardless, she's taken aback. She doesn't remember where she lost her phone, but here it is. Using her thumbprint to unlock the screen, she sees all the notifications and missed calls. Ignoring them all, she pulls up her father's contact information and then holds the phone out to Jean.

"Here. I'm not convinced he'll agree to meet with you," she tells him truthfully.

"Merci." Jean taps the call icon on the screen with a wink. "You will find I can be persuasive."

General Pennington picks up on the second ring. The moment he does, Jean presses the icon requesting a video call.

"Yasmine, you stupid girl! Where have you been?" Her father's first words to her in weeks, and of course, he's blaming her in his condescending tone.

Yasmine frowns off camera and rolls her eyes. She's not surprised at all in the way he's speaking to her; it's his normal.

Nice to see you too, you fucking asshole.

Ghoul presses the headphones closer to his ears, his anger making him grip them tightly. Her father's a real piece of shit. She had to live with this man? He learned of the abuse she had to suffer through, but hearing the man talk to her triggers even more fury.

Jean waits to speak until Pennington accepts the video call and pops up on the screen. Then he turns his camera on.

"Greetings General," Jean says coolly. "I cannot help but feel you have been avoiding me."

Pennington sits in his home office. A large picture window behind him overlooks the grounds of his estate. He's dressed casually in a light blue polo shirt, like he just stepped off the golf course.

"Where's my daughter?" he demands.

Jean smiles and spins in his leather chair to show the giant green-eyed goon restraining her with her arms pinned behind her back.

"Father." Her tone and expression are flat.

The man makes her sick. She's not a hateful person, except when it has to do with him. There's no excuse for what he's done to her and others, especially the children. She hates this man with every fiber of her being. If she could go to the molecular level and rip the DNA she shares with him from her cells, she would.

"You got yourself captured?" His hand slams onto his desk, and his anger with her makes her flinch out of reflex. "You're pathetic. I raised you better."

Her anger rises, and for the moment, she forgets about the plan. This might be her only chance to say anything.

"Maybe next time you should ask better interview questions when you hire a bodyguard. That guy you sent, he was in on it." This is the first time she's dared to snap at him since her outburst years ago.

Her attitude toward him doesn't break through his glacier wall because he doesn't view her as a person, and certainly not his daughter. She's always been a pawn to him.

Jean spins around so Yasmine's no longer in the frame.

"I am sensing some animosity between father and daughter." He switches the video to the forward camera and points it at her. "Yasmine is correct, however. You need to screen your security better. It was so easy to slip my man in. We shall keep this simple. If you want to see your daughter again, with all her fingers, you will agree to meet with me. We can discuss how you will pay what you owe me and make good on our agreement."

"You do not call the shots here, Auclair," Pennington barks. The vein in his head is pulsating.

"It is simple, Charles. I only want what you promised, and then we go our separate ways. If you do not agree to meet with me, I'll make sure pieces of your daughter start showing up on the doorstep of the Department of Defense. I'm sure they will appreciate an anonymous tip on your side business."

Jean nods to the goon with the green eyes who's restraining Yasmine. At the same time, he zooms in on her.

The goon roughly shoves her face on top of Jean's desk. Her eyes widen in fear as she struggles against the big man. Jean speaks a command in French to the goon, and Green Eyes tightens his hold. Jean gives Pennington a front-row seat. The goon grabs a fistful of her hair, forcing her head up, and Jean caresses her cheek tenderly before he backhands her across the face.

Stars explode across her vision. This wasn't part of the plan! Jean promised he wouldn't harm her.

Slimy bastard! she roars in her head at the same time the tears start running.

Green Eyes forces her stinging cheek onto the chilly desktop. She's pleading, trying to break free from the goon's hold, but his grip is too strong. Her tears fall to the desk from the stinging pain and her utter hopelessness. Another masked lackey appears and takes over holding her down. Green Eyes presses her hand flat on the desk.

Jean trains the camera back on himself, grinning wickedly.

"I will send you her fingers as a keepsake before I dump her body at the DOD. After I have my fun with her, of course." He looks at the man pinning her hand on the desk and gives a nod.

Yasmine's terror is real. She's not faking now. Jean lied about not hurting her; she's about to lose her fingers, and more. Green Eyes pulls out a large wicked-looking knife, and she resumes her begging.

"Please, don't," she chokes out through her sobs.

She tries with all her might to break away from the other guy restraining her against the desk. The anticipation of the coming pain leaves her feeling suffocated.

"No." She whimpers, trying one more time, but Green Eyes' only response is to wink and slam the knife downward.

The General's face remains unmoved even at hearing his daughter screaming in agony off camera.

"I'd rather my business dealings not become known. I will meet with you, and I will have your money."

Her blood-curdling scream sends a pulse of pleasure down Auclair's spine, but he holds his wicked grin. He jerks his head, signaling his man to take her. Her sobs fade down the hallway, and Auclair can finish his conversation in peace.

"I'm glad you agree, General. Tomorrow night, New York City, dock six. The old McFlair warehouse." He gives the details once the room stills. "This will not be like when I gave your charming daughter your mistress's ring and finger for her birthday. This time, I will leave your daughter's mutilated body for your government to see what you have been involved in."

Auclair waves, dismissing the General. "See you tomorrow night. Do not be late. I already have another piece of her in mind to carve out if you fail to follow through with this arrangement."

Auclair signals his remaining man, who opens the door and gestures someone forward.

Yasmine, teary and red-faced, with a welt forming, returns to the office. Both goons silently exit without being told to, leaving them alone.

She plops herself on the leather couch, taking some deep breaths. She's exhausted and feels like crap. She's tired of being touched, tired of being manipulated, and most of all, used. She has nothing left to fight with.

Jean rubs his hands together in excitement. "Beautiful performance, ma chère."

She brushes her hair away from her tear-soaked face. She's a little surprised she still has all her fingers. For a moment, she thought Green Eyes was actually going to cut her pinky off. When he slammed the knife next to her hand, she screamed in frustrated relief. She sold the performance because the terror was real.

Jean goes to a bar hidden in the mahogany paneling and pulls out a bar towel, filling it with ice. He sits next to her on the couch, raises the same hand he used to strike her, and presses the towel where he hit. She flinches away from his touch, which only excites him further.

"Apologies." He smiles, but it brings no comfort.

She's broken, and the tears won't stop. She wishes Ghoul were here to take care of her face,

not this guy. She wishes she could be in his arms. The thoughts of him using her have vanished for now, and she'd give anything to feel his reassuring touch. Whatever fake care Jean is giving her makes her sick.

Jean wipes away the tears, holds the ice to her face where he backhanded her, and then he kisses her.

Ghoul has never felt this kind of weighted, crushing sensation. Not even when he found out his fiancé cheated while he was deployed or during the countless monstrous things he's done. There's nothing he can do, and once more, he's the helpless child he used to be. Her screams will haunt him for the rest of his life, and all he can do is close his eyes. If he goes for the sniper rifle, Calvin and Hill will just stop him because the mission comes first. They don't have a personal connection to her. Not like he does.

Her beautiful, loving hands are missing a finger now, or worse. He hangs his head, using the mask to wipe a lone tear away.

He allowed this. He could have taken her and run; he knows how to hide and disappear. So why didn't he?

Seeing Auclair with his slimy hands all over her and kissing her when it was just him a short time ago leaves Ghoul defeated. He can't bear to watch this anymore. He understands what Hill went through with his girl and why he turned into an even bigger asshole than he already was.

Calvin and Hill sit in stone-faced silence, both unsettled by what they are witnessing. The three men look on as Auclair continues kissing her; she's doing nothing to put up a fight.

"You've had quite the evening. Come. I will have Marie show you to a room."

Auclair offers her a hand up after finally pulling away from her mouth. She takes his offered hand without a word and the two of them leave.

"That was ... troubling to watch." Calvin lets out a long breath before daring to look at Ghoul.

His eyes are full of moisture, but he's holding it back somehow. Calvin sees the man's broken. This happens to the best of them if they're in the job long enough, and he's no stranger to being forced to pick between duty and caring for someone.

"She's fine." Hill places a reassuring hand on Ghoul's shoulder.

"No, she's not," he whispers. He *knows* she's not okay right now.

He knows what she lived with from her father, and Auclair's piled more on top of her. She's not fine; he saw it in her expression. She needs to be held, not pawed like a sex object.

A few moments later, Auclair enters his bedroom, undresses himself, and heads into the bathroom. His two playthings are waiting for him when he comes out of the shower with just a towel over his head.

When the three of them start having sex, Ghoul pulls the headphones off his head. The emotional exhaustion threatens to make him collapse on the spot. It's been a long month since all this started.

"Hill and I will set up the cameras and audio to send back to base camp. Take a walk. That is an order," Calvin commands. "Report to base camp by zero five hundred. You have an op to plan on that warehouse, and we need you at your best." Calvin places his large hand on Ghoul's shoulder. "Get your head on right, and be ready to go when you report in. We'll get your gear."

Ghoul nods without a word and leaves the roof. He opts to take the stairs instead of the elevator. His body moves on autopilot. He has no bearing on how long it takes him to get to the ground floor. His mind is elsewhere, focused on her.

Just before he slams into the door to exit, he pulls the mask off and stuffs it in his pocket. The streets are still crowded, even at this hour. Anyone who sees him doesn't give him a second glance. He's just some guy with a frown walking with his hands in his pockets — a nobody lost in the crowd.

Chapter Thirty-Six
The Green-Eyed Goon

"Ma chère." Jean runs his hand up the length of her inner thigh. "Your father is here."

Marie threw Yasmine's clothing in the trash, so she's having to wear the ones his girlfriends provided: black tailored slacks and a baby pink sweater. The whole outfit costs more than two months' rent. They caked on the makeup, to the point it's too heavy on her face, but at least the French braid they put her long hair in is something she can handle. This time, they let her wear black flats instead of heels.

She sits next to Jean on the tan leather seats in the back of the black Lexus SUV. She's so close. If she can survive a few more hours, she'll be free ... maybe. If Auclair keeps his promise to let her go, which she highly doubts will happen with all his comments about "spending time" with her. She even stopped trying to move his hands off her because they go right back on her immediately.

He brings her fingers to his lips, but instead of kissing them, he bites until she flinches. He started doing it earlier in the day, increasing the pain until she winces. He releases her before stepping out into the dimly lit warehouse. She thought he had fashion sense from the night before, but the Paisley blue suit he wears says otherwise. He left the tie off and the two top buttons undone on his white shirt.

When the door closes, she leans over to look out the front window, not caring about the dirty look from the driver. Two black Tahoes are parked in front of the one she's in. She cranes her neck but sees nothing past the SUVs. She places her ear to the window and can faintly hear her father's deep voice.

The driver is drumming his fingers on the steering wheel and seems bored with his elbow leaning on the door and his fist supporting his head. He's ignoring her, so she quickly takes in the warehouse, trying to see if there's a door she can escape through, even though she wouldn't get far with so many men with guns. She notes the stacks of crates and large metal containers off to the side.

She jumps nearly out of her skin when Green Eyes opens the door and beckons her forward. Once she's standing next to him, she cowers from his towering stature. He's been her handler, meaning he's never too far away. He doesn't say much, but at least his eyes still hold some life to them, and she's caught him looking at her with sympathy a few times before they turn cold. She's yet to see his face because, like many of Auclair's other minions, he's wearing a mask.

Green Eyes grasps her arm, but not aggressively, and leads her forward.

"You need to look more scared instead of pissed." Green Eyes leans down and speaks low in her ear.

He speaks French fluently, from what she can tell, but has an American accent. How any American can work for someone like Auclair is beyond her comprehension.

"I'm gonna have to get a little rough with you. Apologies, but we have to make it look real." He stands to his full height and wiggles his eyebrows slightly.

Who knew goons could be nice and considerate? Her inner sarcasm almost makes her laugh. Almost.

At least, this guy's been all right, other than scaring the shit out of her when she thought he was going to cut her finger off. Green Eyes pulls her forward, and it's her cue to start struggling to add to the charade. For a bad guy, there's something seemingly familiar about him, but for the life of her, she can't figure out what it is.

Green Eyes half pulls and half drags her to the front where Auclair stands in the center with his group of armed men. Her father's side is a mirror image, but from the looks of his men, they're military, and they seem scarier. The man who terrified and terrorized her, who caused so much pain, stands in the center of them.

General Charles Pennington's steel blue eyes lock onto his daughter when Green Eyes releases her with a shove. For added effect, she jerks away and stumbles. Then she levels her gaze with all the hate she can muster and throws it at her father.

"Father." It's not part of the plan for her to speak to him, but seeing the man she hates enrages her. "Interesting business partners you keep. I wonder if your superiors in Washington know of your little side hustle?"

Her father is dressed casually in his winter wear, and his face flushes crimson under his hat. The vein in his forehead is pulsing. If they were alone, or if she was closer, he'd hit her for talking back disrespectfully.

He turns to square off with Auclair, not bothering to give her any more of his attention.

"I'm here. Let's talk business." He jerks his head in Yasmine's direction. "I don't care what you do with her. You can keep her for all I care, but let's be smart and keep the government out of this. It would be bad for both of us if our business dealings were found out, and neither of us wants that. We have an opportunity here. Let's not waste it."

Hysterical laughter erupts from her chest; it echoes through the warehouse. Both men pause in their conversation to stare at her.

"Fuck you, you piece of shit." She spits. "Your business brought me into this and is going to get me killed. I'm ashamed to be your daughter."

Green Eyes grabs her arm from some unspoken signal from Auclair and starts pulling her back.

"Seems like you two need to see a family therapist," Auclair retorts calmly and with mock sincerity before dismissing her with a wave. "You owe me quite a substantial sum of money, and you did not follow through on our agreement. You give me what you owe, or I take your daughter as payment and expose you to your superiors."

He casually walks over to Yasmine and touches her face. She recoils. He picks up the fake bandage wrapped on her hand, making sure to hold it up for her father to see.

"Yasmine here is fascinating. She's so eager for a man's touch." She turns away when his hand goes to her neck. "As much as I would love to keep her around, I would prefer you honor our agreement. If not, I will leave her body on the steps of the Capitol. Between the two of us, you are the only one who would be at an inconvenience, considering your position, General."

Pennington looks his daughter over and shrugs. "I mean it. Keep her. She's no use to me. She's always been a useless child, and too emotional. It's the publicity I don't want. I have half your money now, and I will have the second half by next week."

Her father's thrown her to the wolves. She shouldn't be surprised or be feeling the sting of pain in her chest. She knew he didn't care about her, only himself and his image. Still, she can't believe she let herself hope he'd try to save her. Of course, he wouldn't. Hiring a bodyguard wasn't to protect her; it was so he wouldn't get found out. Bile rises to the back of her throat along with the sting of tears.

Auclair and the General's negotiations resume, and it quickly becomes heated. He doesn't want to wait for his money because Pennington's proven to be treacherous. Things escalate quickly with both men's narcissistic, inflated egos, and the warehouse is not big enough to contain this amount of toxic masculinity.

Green Eyes forcefully drags Yasmine back to the SUV because she's still recovering from the shock of her father throwing her completely away.

"I hope he rips your fucking throat out," she screams at her father, no longer bearing to look at him. "My only regret is that I won't be there to see it." She jerks herself free of the goon and storms back to the SUV.

She's dead! Auclair's going to use her, and then he's going to kill her — her fate's sealed. No way is a man like him going to let her go. How could she have been so stupid to think she could walk away from this? Her only hope now is if Green Eyes gets distracted, she's going to take her chances and make a break for it.

She wipes the anger away with the back of her hand. Green Eyes has followed her closely, escorting her. He holds onto her arm to steady her, but she's not paying attention to him. The only small comfort she takes is knowing Ghoul will keep his promise and kill her father.

Green Eyes leans into her space when he opens the door and positions her behind it but doesn't push her inside.

"When shit starts flying, keep your head down and stay alive. Get out of here or hide." He pulls back, and she can see he's smiling at her from under the mask.

Her brows furrow together, not fully comprehending his words or why now his green eyes bring an old familiar sense of calm.

"Huh?"

"Yazzie. There's a Ghoul on the prowl." He winks and walks away toward the heated argument until she loses sight of him.

His words take time to sink in, and then she gasps and covers her mouth. Understanding dawns on her.

There's only one person who ever called her Yazzie. A boy with green eyes, like those of that goon. The boy she shared her first childhood kiss with, who then gagged and she punched in the arm.

"Sammy?" she whispers in surprised disbelief.

How does he know Ghoul? Is he nearby? Renewed hope floods through her.

A choice stands before her. She can get in the back seat of the SUV, or she can take her chances and run. No one's watching her now. Even the driver is gone since he moved up to join the brewing fight. She takes a moment to take in her surroundings.

There are rows of old discarded crates and boxes, stacks of junk, and even a few shipping containers in the corner of the large warehouse. Not only is she taking in the physical environment, but she's looking for something. Rather, someone who might be hiding nearby in the shadows, stalking her.

Her eyes are probing the dark corners when Auclair and her father's voices echo around her. Some other voices start yelling threats and curses. Negotiations are at the breaking point.

She looks at the SUV and then the stack of crates, but before she can decide, the decision is made for her. Gunfire erupts, and she dives for the nearest hiding space behind a shipping container, moving as far away as she can from the shots and chaos.

"When shit starts flying, keep your head down and stay alive."

Yasmine wedges herself in a tight space between the crates and covers her ears against the gunfire.

Chapter Thirty-Seven
The Ghosts of Scythe Company

Ghoul's adrenaline courses through his veins. He's ready and has been ready to kill her father since he learned of the humiliation and abuse Yasmine suffered. Then there's Auclair. He's going to pay with his life for touching and hurting her. Either way, they both die tonight.

This is his element, so he finds himself calm and focused when he takes point, slipping into the warehouse from the side door. Calvin and Hill move silently in unison behind him without needing to be told what to do.

This is what he knows — killing — and that's exactly what he plans to do. The one and only guard they encounter at the back door is dead before his body hits the ground. Ghoul is the one to slit the man's throat using his serrated combat knife. His preferred knife, the one from his grandfather, is safely stowed with his personal effects.

Another fireteam of four is coming in from the other direction to surround and pin down Auclair and his men. Ghoul's fireteam will take Pennington and his men out. He had to make the call of who he'd take down, her father or Auclair. Both deserve a bullet between the eyes, but the promise he made to Yasmine took priority, so his sole focus is her father.

If he ends Pennington right here and now, then maybe he has a chance at a life with *her*. He quickly pushes the thought away before it distracts him from the task at hand.

The hours spent walking the streets of New York City helped him sort through some of his feelings toward her. In the end, he still couldn't figure out WHAT those feelings are. It'd be impossible to love her in this short amount of time, but he has an overwhelming sense of not wanting to let her go. He knew he had to shove his thoughts aside, though, to do his job and take out their Judas, her father.

When he reported to their makeshift HQ, a rundown old dump of an apartment, he was ready to start planning the assault on the warehouse after a hot shower and a meal. When the rest of the squad arrived, he already had most of the details worked out on their assault, which is why he was invited to join Scythe in the first place. He might be cold and detached, but he's the best tactician and strategist they've got.

He positions himself low, using a stack of discarded crates for cover. He peers through the cracks to get a read of the situation. Calvin and Hill take up positions on either side of him. He quickly starts marking targets and positions.

The unit is composed of the best men and women from various branches of the armed forces, each recruited for specific skill sets, to make this mission successful. There's a higher number of Marines serving with Scythe Company than any other branch. Marines like to blow shit up, and they have to blow up shit often.

He looks to his right at Hill, who nods, signaling he's ready. He shifts his gaze to the left to Calvin, who also nods. Yasmine's somewhere in the building, and he trusts her to stay down. She's smart, and a survivor. In their time together, she surprised him often, and he learned not to underestimate her. She will survive this.

He takes a deep breath to steady himself. He taps his throat mic three times to signal the other fireteam that his side is ready and in position. While they hold, he vows to make good on his promise to Yasmine, then maybe she'll be willing to put up with him.

He peers out, and this time he spots her. She's as far back as she can be and has good cover nearby. He makes a mental note of her position when the big guy from the night before leans in her ear.

The goon leaves Yasmine with a stunned expression, but then the man pulls his mask off and stands behind the man farthest from the encounter. Ghoul is startled at recognizing him. Puzzle pieces of information he wasn't privy to snap into place; it all makes sense. He makes a mental note, marking the new friendly on the gameboard.

Raised voices draw his attention at the same moment he hears the four clicks of static through his earpiece. The other team is ready. Then come the two clicks of static from the snipers who will be covering them from above.

The voices turn heated when the negotiations break down, and it's only a matter of moments before violence erupts between the two parties. Ghoul lines up his shot over Pennington's heart, starting his breathing cycle.

"Light 'em up," Calvin whispers over the radio.

Ghoul squeezes the trigger.

Scythe Company, a covert black ops unit, separates itself from the shadows of the warehouse. They move like ghostly apparitions seeking to consume the souls of anyone who dares to disturb them.

Each person is dressed in a black combat uniform and wearing black face paint to cover their appearance and to blend into the shadows, which makes the whites of their eyes more menacing. The only insignias on their uniforms are their unique call signs in place of their name tags, the backward American Flag, and their unit's emblem of a skull and scythe, all in a dark charcoal grey. The tactical vests are loaded with spare ammo clips for their M27 rifles and anything else they could need for this mission. Each one is armed and ready for a fight because Scythe Company is hunting one of their own, a traitorous Judas, and an equally dangerous bioweapon terrorist. Their goal? To end this ring of arms-dealing terrorists.

The moment the commotion begins, Auclair ducks low and his men race to cover him. All except for the one man in the back with

Green Eyes. He slices open the throat of the man in front of him, who falls at his feet. Then he ducks behind cover and pulls his firearm out, taking potshots at anyone other than his Company.

Luck is on Pennington's side because he shifted when Ghoul took the shot. Instead of the bullet going through his heart, it passes clean through his left shoulder. He and his men react instantly like the trained soldiers they are and make their way to the nearest car as bullets shoot around them. His men return fire but don't know where to aim because of the sheer chaos that's erupted inside the warehouse.

The snipers on the roof take out the two men covering Pennington when they reach the Mercedes, dropping them dead with a shot through the heart. When Pennington realizes there are snipers on the roof, he picks up his pace and dives inside the vehicle.

Once in the driver's seat, he slams the door shut and engages the door locks. He's bleeding all over the white leather seats. Two more of his men run up and claw at the door handle. They pound on the glass and yell to be let in, but he only cares about one thing: getting his ass out of there alive. If his daughter doesn't matter, then his men certainly don't.

Calvin lines up his sights on one man and Hill the other, and both men drop dead to the concrete. Ghoul creates a star in the bulletproof glass that's perfectly lined up with Pennington's head. He growls in frustration when the bullet doesn't pierce the window. For good measure, he empties the clip, hoping one will get through, but the glass holds. Pennington glares at Ghoul with a cocky sneer then turns away.

Pennington throws the car in drive, guns the engine, and weaves around Auclair's SUVs, running over one of the drivers who was scrambling to take cover. More bullets form stars in the back window as the red taillights of the Mercedes disappear into the night.

"Shit." Ghoul presses into his throat mic. "Judas got away. Focus on target two."

Swallowing his rage at Pennington escaping, Ghoul shifts his attention to Auclair. Thanks to their man on the inside, who he now knows was Levine, leaking intel for months, they have enough to track down the next link in the chain of this worldwide illegal weapon ring. This means Auclair's no longer needed. The world will be a little safer tonight when he dies. But Ghoul doesn't care about keeping the world safe right now. He's going to make Auclair pay for what he did to her.

The chaos of the fight continues around him. There are random shouts from his team telling the enemy to "surrender," but they don't listen.

The wrath clawing its way out of Ghoul transforms him into the creature rising from the pile of bodies his call sign is based on. She doesn't think he's a monster, but she never saw this side of him. The creature is out for blood, and it's Auclair's blood calling him now.

He moves quickly from cover to cover, all the while scanning the scene. All of Pennington's men are dead or dying. The only ones left putting up resistance are Auclair and his men. Ghoul spots the bioweapons dealer snaking his way to the SUV in the back, where he last spotted Yasmine. Auclair will never lay another hand on her again.

As Ghoul leapfrogs through cover, all her pained looks from the night before come to the forefront of his mind. Her screams, terror, and tears. When Auclair smacked her and then made her believe she'd lose a finger, Auclair became a monster in her reality, and Ghoul will rid the world of him so she can sleep better at night.

He circles around, not caring if Hill or Calvin aren't following behind. Gunfire continues to echo through the warehouse. He adds his own controlled bursts to the fray, taking out whatever men are dumb enough to step in his way and to provide cover fire as needed.

He rounds the back of the SUV as Auclair is reaching for the door handle on the driver's side. He lines up his sight and squeezes the trigger.

Auclair catches the movement from the corner of his eye and dives into the SUV for cover when Ghoul's shots ring out. He reaches for the extra handgun under the seat and chambers a round. He sticks the gun out the door and shoots wildly at Ghoul, missing the black ghost completely.

Ghoul misses when Auclair dives inside the SUV, and realizes he's used the last of his clip. He doesn't bother changing the magazine and instead drops the rifle. It now hangs loose from the strap on his shoulder. He reaches for his sidearm strapped to his thigh.

He can't see through the black tinted windows, and like Pennington's car, he guesses it is reinforced with bulletproofing. He tries the rear door of the SUV, and it pops open a crack. He ducks and pulls the rear door open before sprinting to the front because Auclair begins taking several wild shots out the back without having a target.

Ghoul trains his sidearm forward and rounds the driver's side door, keeping his head below the windows. He manages one shot at Auclair, which grazes him in the leg, but then he kicks out, knocking Ghoul's gun from his hand and sending it flying and skidding out of sight.

Auclair aims his weapon, but before he can get a shot off, Ghoul is manhandling him out of the SUV. He lands a hard punch to the bioweapon dealer's face, the same spot where he backhanded Yasmine the previous night. Ghoul punches again, feeling the satisfaction of cartilage crunching and breaking under his fist. Auclair is dazed and bleeding from his broken nose. He barely comprehends the words the masked man is yelling.

"This is for her, motherfucker!" He punches Auclair once more for good measure.

Through his daze, Auclair manages to land a blow to Ghoul's jaw, which causes him to stumble backward. Then he follows up with a kick to Ghoul's chest, sending him further away from the SUV.

Ghoul throws the pain aside. It's how he trained himself to fight when he was on the streets and heavily reinforced in the Corp. You keep going until you can't and ignore the pain, pushing through it. Which he does now because this fight is personal, and it causes the adrenaline to pump through his veins. Auclair is in for an ass beating. He draws his combat knife and dives back into the close quarters of the SUV where Auclair has recovered some of his senses.

Auclair levels his gun at Ghoul, but he knocks it out of Auclair's hand easily, sending it flying into the back seat. Ghoul brings up the knife to plunge into Auclair's heart, but he deflects the knife's trajectory and expertly knocks it from Ghoul's grasp.

Both unarmed, all they have now is their fists. Ghoul grabs hold of Auclair's bloodstained suit jacket and hauls his ass out of the SUV, tossing him to the ground. Instead of falling to the concrete, Auclair awkwardly stays on his feet and turns to face off against the man in the mask.

The two begin the dance of hand-to-hand combat. There's nothing elegant about it; it's a dirty street fight. Both are equally matched in skill and strength with real-life street experience.

Ghoul deflects Auclair's incoming punches and lands his own into the man's ribs, feeling his knuckles sinking into his chest cavity and forcing the air from Auclair's lungs. He follows up with another punch to Auclair's abdomen and finally a knee to his midsection.

Auclair, like Ghoul, shoves past the pain and lands a weak, grazing blow to Ghoul and then follows up with a kick to the groin. He misses and instead grazes Ghoul's thigh. When he saw Auclair's preference for kicking, Ghoul knew to move in closer to make it difficult to have his feet kicked out from under him. He knows from experience, if he goes to the ground, it's much harder to defend and attack. He needs to stay on his feet if he's going to win this fight.

Street fights are dirty and bloody. There are no rules. It's two men trying to beat the shit out of each other until one wins, or they're both knocked out. In this fight, it will end when one of them is dead. With the level of ferocity Auclair and Ghoul are putting into the fight, they are quickly losing stamina.

Auclair lands some lucky punches to Ghoul's stomach and side, causing the air to leave his lungs. He doesn't have time to pull in a full breath because he brings his knee into Auclair's face and quickly sends his elbow to the back of his neck. Instead of the elbow connecting, Auclair grabs his leg, and then Ghoul's on his back, the air fully knocked from his lungs. Stars explode across his vision. He's staring up at the cold metal ceiling; his body is desperately trying to pull in a breath. He can't with Auclair pinning him with his full body weight.

Through sheer will, and rage, Ghoul pushes past the pain and blackness threatening to take him. He claws his way back to the light. Auclair punches Ghoul's jaw, causing his vision to blacken further and pushing him back into the darkness.

He slams a weak fist in Auclair's sneering, bloody face above him. There was still enough force to split open the man's lip. Auclair rears back and lands the hardest blow yet to the side of Ghoul's head. The blackness almost takes him, but he somehow manages to remain conscious. His head rolls to the side. Through his nearly unconscious state, he sees a ghostly apparition. Tears are falling from her hazel eyes.

Why is my girl crying? The thought breaks through the blackness.

Ghoul's survival instinct kicks into overdrive, pumping more adrenaline into his system. He can't die here — he has a promise to keep.

Reaching for his pant leg, Auclair pulls it up at the same time he presses all his weight into the arm, cutting off Ghoul's air supply. The man under him tries, weakly, to break the hold. Auclair pulls the knife from the leg sheath with a sneer.

In one quick motion, he slashes the knife downward to the man's throat, but Ghoul, having a renewed will to live, catches Auclair's wrist, preventing the tip of the blade from making contact.

Ghoul doesn't have much strength left, and with the lack of oxygen, he's close to the brink. He has seconds before he loses consciousness completely. His body is desperately gasping for air that isn't there. His head feels like it wants to explode from the pressure, and the loud ringing in his ears deafens all other sounds around him.

Auclair leers down at Ghoul, bringing his face close. The twisted sneer makes him even more hideous than he is. He's overconfident in thinking he's about to add more fingers to his collection.

"I normally prefer to take my trophies while the person is alive, but I will make an exception for you. Your fingers will make a nice addition." He pushes, bringing the knife closer to Ghoul's throat to the point the tip draws blood.

Ghoul musters the last of his strength to get out of Auclair's hold, but it's futile. He curses his luck. He won't be able to fulfill his promise to her. He curses that he never got the chance to make things work with her or tell her how he feels about her. How much he wants to be in her life.

The last single shot of gunfire echoes through the warehouse before silence descends. The side of Auclair's head explodes in a shower of crimson, bone, and brain matter when the bullet exits the other side.

He sits frozen for one brief moment before his facial muscles turn flaccid in death. Ghoul takes control of the knife and pulls it away from his throat before roughly shoving the dead man off him.

He lies there, gasping for breath, which triggers him to cough. His vision slowly begins to clear with each breath he can pull into his aching lungs. Lying on his back, he stares at the metal ceiling, gasping and waiting for his vision to clear. His body throbs from the blows he took. He takes a quick inventory of his condition when his hearing returns. Voices are echoing through the warehouse, yelling "clear."

He turns toward the direction of the shot that took out Auclair, and his eyes once more meet hazel. Yasmine sits back on her haunches, white as a ghost.

"I told you I wasn't as weak as I look." She tries to joke, but her face scrunches together from the sobs taking over.

Chapter Thirty-Eight
It Never Goes as Planned

With great effort, Ghoul gets to his feet, swaying once he's up. He's going to feel that fight for weeks because he's not a young man anymore. He's getting too old for this shit, but at any rate, nothing seems to be broken. He's battered, bruised, and beaten to hell. It's been a while since he's been a participant in a street fight.

"Clear," Ghoul shouts because his radio got busted in the fight.

He tosses Auclair's knife on top of his lifeless corpse, not bothering to take it as a trophy. The knife is nothing special. He picks up his M27 rifle with shaking hands. The rifle came off during the fight because the strap broke. He quickly changes out the magazine and flips the safety lock.

Her wide-eyed and scared face looks up at him. Her gaze searches him to make sure it really is Ghoul and not someone else who's there to hurt her.

"You're injured." He's taking inventory of the wounds he can see.

She looks down at her bleeding arm and wonders when it happened. She didn't feel it, but now, seeing it, the sting of pain reaches her brain. Her senses are overwhelmed, but it seems like it's all happening to someone else.

From her hiding spot, she had heard the close gunfire but dared not peek out, except when she heard a familiar voice yelling *"That's for her, motherfucker!"* She risked looking out from her hiding spot to see Auclair and a masked man dressed in black fighting. She somehow knew it was him. Sitting on the sidelines watching him fight and get hurt was one of the hardest things she's ever had to do. Her anger toward him was quickly forgotten, but she couldn't do anything to help him. She'd just be in his way.

But, when Auclair pinned him to the concrete and she saw him starting to lose against the Frenchman, she found herself reaching for Ghoul's gun, which had landed somewhat near her. Her body moved on its own.

Now she sits, petrified, blood dripping from a gash at her temple and from the wound on her arm. She's in too much shock to move, so she sits paralyzed on the cold concrete. She might be looking up at Ghoul and feeling relief he's alive, but she also can't trust him. She hasn't forgotten he used her.

"Is-is he dead?" Her words come out shaky.

"Very," he confirms.

She pulls her knees to her chest, hugging them tightly to her. She's trying to breathe, but drawing a full breath from the throbbing pain now adds to her list of physical and emotional distress. She closes her eyes to the man she killed, who's lying in a pool of his blood, and the man she can no longer trust. If she looks at either of them, she'll vomit.

Auclair was a terrible man with ties to unspeakable crimes, and she's traumatized from him constantly touching her. But a life is a life, and she just took his, regardless of whether he deserved it or not. With what she's suffered at the hands of her father, she's become his opposite to the point that she hates killing spiders and relocates them outside.

Ghoul gently grasps her wrist, which makes her flinch, but he carefully pries the M17 from her hand. She puts up no fight and lets him take the gun. He turns the gun over to snap the safety on and is surprised to see she already did it. Even in her current state, she had the wherewithal to put the safety on after her shot.

He holsters his sidearm and then brings his rifle to his shoulder, taking a defensive position over her. As much as he wants to pull her into his arms, he needs to stand guard.

A few moments later, Calvin's deep voice booms through the warehouse. "All clear."

Ghoul relaxes immediately and gets to his knees in front of her, setting his rifle to the side.

"Yasmine." His fingerless gloved hand softly rests on her shoulder, the other on her head.

When he moves to touch the side of her face, she roughly shoves his hand away. She's been touched enough, and she's recoiling from him because he made love to her and then put her in danger, which hurts worse than the physical injuries.

"I'm going to help you up," he informs her, swallowing his hurt.

He pulls them both up, and thankfully, she lets him help, but her legs give out. She would have crumbled if he wasn't holding her tight to his side. His touch is reassuring and revolting at the same time, but she doesn't have the energy to do or say anything.

Once she is steady on her feet, he stiffly bends down to pick up his rifle before tucking her in close for support and using his body to shield her from the gore. She doesn't need to see Auclair's brains leaking from his head. He leads her to where his team is assembling. Calvin's barking orders and directing the team. As always, they move with efficiency and skill.

Two of Auclair's men surrendered and are now secured with zip ties and armed guards. They will be brought in for questioning, but it's not needed with what their undercover operative leaked to them. All of Pennington's men lie dead.

Yasmine barely registers any of this. Her mind shut off to protect itself and her emotions. The only reason she's still conscious is because of the man walking beside her. Even if she's mad at him, his presence still brings a familiar warmth, which she desperately needs.

Ghoul walks her closer to Calvin.

"Colonel, she needs the Doc, and my radio's busted," he calls out while motioning to Yasmine.

Colonel Henry Calvin gives her a once-over. She's ashen in color, and blood from her head drips down her cheek to her dirty sweater. He struggles to look at her. It was his idea to use her to lure out Auclair and her father. This is another thing he'll have to live with.

"We need doc in the warehouse," he says over the radio.

Then he jerks his head, motioning to the rust-colored boxes off to the side, away from the commotion of activity.

"Put her over there, then report. We have a situation and need your expertise."

"Yes, sir." Ghoul escorts Yasmine to the metal boxes.

Before he gives his report to Calvin and sees what they need him to do, he quickly inspects the wound on her arm to see how bad it is. It will more than likely need stitches. Other than that, she has some minor cuts and scrapes, but nothing too serious. He puts his hand on her head, tilting it back to inspect the wound. Her tear-soaked eyes stare up at him blankly. He swallows the lump in his throat that's trying to choke him and focuses on the gash on her forehead. It's probably going to need stitches too.

"The Doc's coming, and he'll patch you up," he tells her while trying to figure out how else he can reassure her. "You're safe now."

His words are falling flat, but she manages a slight dip of her head in acknowledgement.

He stays with her until the doc comes, refusing to leave her alone in the aftermath of what happened. He's finding it difficult to look at her through his guilt.

"Doc," or rather the Corpsman, comes trotting up with his bag. "She the one?"

Ghoul nods. "Patch her up, and look after her for me." He then addresses Yasmine by squeezing her hand. "I'll be back soon to check on you."

"I'm Beck," the corpsman tells her with a warm smile and large dimples. "I'm going to be checking you over."

He flashes the light in her eyes to check her responsiveness. "Do you feel cold?"

She nods, and her body shudders with a chill at the suggestion.

He rifles through his bag until he finds the emergency blanket. He rips the package open, unfolds it, and wraps it around her.

"This will help to warm you up."

She grasps the blanket tightly. She might be in shock, but she's still responsive.

Beck quickly checks her head wound, then her arm. "I'm going to flush the cut on your head. Can you lean forward for me?"

He works efficiently. He's used to patching up members of his team quickly in the field. After flushing the wound, he places a bandage over it. It wasn't very deep and looked worse than it was. Once done, he turns his attention to her arm.

"I'm going to have to cut your sleeve off." He pulls out his scissors and begins cutting her shirt above the wound on her arm. This one is much deeper.

He quickly flushes it. "Were you shot?"

"I don't think so." She whispers so low he barely catches it. "I think I got cut on some metal."

"When you get to the hospital, make sure they give you a tetanus shot." He purses his lips together. "You're going to need stitches on this. I can do it for you, or you can wait until you're at the hospital."

"You do it."

He reaches into his bag and pulls out a needle and small bottle of numbing agent.

"I'll numb you first." He cracks a grin. "Just don't tell anyone I have this. I never numb them up when I need to stitch them up in the field."

He has a great bedside manner, and with his boyish good looks, raven color hair, and ocean blue eyes, he hoped the dry joke would get a reaction. But her expression remains vacant.

Beck finishes sewing her arm up in under five minutes. He hands her a bottle of water and sits next to her, keeping a careful eye on her in case she passes out.

Sometime later, Green Eyes strolls over with some blood splattered on the side of his face and neck. His brown hair is plastered to his sweaty forehead.

"I'll keep an eye on her," he tells Beck. "Hill got a scratch and is crying about it. You better go check him out before he starts throwing a fit."

Beck rolls his eyes and, with a chuckle, gathers up his medic bag.

Green Eyes has the warmest smile, and it melts her from her frozen state. She might not be able to trust anyone around her, but this is her friend. She can trust him, even if she barely recognizes the boy she knew. He is now a very large full-grown man, complete with facial hair.

She manages an exhausted smile for him.

"Sam Levine. I never would have thought in a million years I would see you again, let alone like this."

Sam takes the seat Beck vacated and scoots closer to her before throwing his arms around her. It's been so long, and she's grown into a beautiful woman since he last saw her.

She twists at the waist and hugs him back. After a few silent moments, she breaks the reunion and stares up at her old friend. She runs her fingers through his facial hair and then cups his face.

"You certainly grew up. You were so scrawny in middle school." She squeezes his bicep.

She smiles, remembering the boy with the playful green eyes and dark brown hair. It's difficult, but she can still see glimpses of the boyish face between the hard lines of the rugged man in front of her. But it's the warm smile he always gave her when she went to him after one of her father's tirades; that smile is the same.

"Damn, you grew up to be quite the looker." She squeezes his arm once more and leans into him. "You even have muscles. I bet you break all the hearts."

Sam smiles. There's a slight blush to his cheeks as he runs a shaky hand through his oily hair, which is out of regulation. Not to mention, he desperately needs a shave.

"I'm a heartbreaker without even trying." The two friends pull each other into another hug, and he playfully pinches her side. "I see you're still not eating."

She ignores the comment. She's too tired, and she heard enough of that from Ghoul.

"I imagined you going to college, and I don't know, owning your own business." She leans into her friend. "You scared the shit out of me, you know. I thought you were going to take my finger."

"I'm sorry about that. I've been working undercover for too long to get where I needed to be for today to work smoothly. But, regardless, I wouldn't have let anything happen to you. I would have blown the whole op if it meant keeping you safe. Still, despite my best efforts, you got kidnapped and had to go through all this." The remorse is clear on his face. He brushes her cheek where she has the bruise. "You were hurt, and I don't know if I'll ever forgive myself for that."

"He was repulsive," she says with disgust. "So why do I feel so guilty for killing him?"

Her voice breaks, and the tears begin to fall freely. She buries her head in her friend's shoulder, prompting him to protectively wrap his arms over her, just like he did when they were kids.

"I know he deserved it, and it does the world a favor, but I still feel horrible." Her shoulders quiver from the sobbing.

Sam pulls her to his chest, protectively placing a hand on the back of her head and holding her to him.

"Taking a life is never easy, even when it's someone who deserves it. Even if you did it to save another. I wish I could tell you it gets easier, but it doesn't. I wish I could tell you, you'll forget about it, but you never will." Sam kills people. He knows all too well it never gets easier.

"All you can do is sit with the pain and let time do the healing. Because you feel remorse, it means you're human."

She's used to sitting with pain. What's one more thing to add to her therapy list?

Calvin is explaining the situation to Ghoul and how he needs to safely dismantle the canisters they found. Apparently, the canisters were rigged with a bioweapon agent to kill Pennington. Ghoul tries to pay attention, but he's only half listening because he keeps casting glances at

Yasmine and Levine, who are looking way too chummy in each other's arms.

Jealousy overtakes him, and he doesn't know how to manage it. Even when Jessica cheated on him, he was mad and felt betrayed, but he wasn't jealous. He shrugged it off and delved into work. Ghoul forces himself to look away from them and returns his focus to his task of safely disposing of the poisonous canisters.

At least Levine is there for her, and he's better suited to keep an eye on her anyway; Ghoul needs distance to start letting her go. With Pennington escaping, any chance of them being together is blown to hell. He still has a job to do and will be pursuing her father.

Like Yasmine said many times at the cabin, real life doesn't have happy endings. Real life is not a romance story where the two end up together at the end. This proves it, regardless of what he wants.

Chapter Thirty-Nine
The Truth Hurts

Yasmine pulls away from Sam's embrace, wiping her eyes with her one good sleeve.

She's cried enough and doesn't know how much time she'll have with her friend. What she needs right now is a distraction. She catches Ghoul walking out of sight as he follows Calvin. If she and Ghoul have a chance to talk before they move her, she has some questions for him. For now, she wants to turn away from the dark thoughts swirling around her.

"We have so much to catch up on, but my guess is we don't have much time." There is never enough damn time! "Can you tell me who you work for? Ghoul was tight-lipped, but I'm pretty sure it's for the government."

Sam laces his fingers through hers like they did when they were kids when they talked.

"I'm not surprised. Ghoul doesn't share much with anyone. Even though I've known the man for years now, I know very little about him." He shakes his head, removing the hair from his eyes. "I can't tell you much, but I do work for a special branch of the military along with joint members from all branches that take care of things like this."

He motions with his hands at the scene in the warehouse. "But for me, I joined the Marine Corps after I dropped out of high school and got my GED. I took classes while I worked on getting my degree, and then I became an officer. I moved up quickly because I had the brains." He taps his head and winks. "Not too long after that, I gained officer rank, and Ghoul showed up at my door to recruit me to this unit. Technically, and on paper, I'm still enlisted as an officer with the Corps."

He just dropped a ton of information she needs to sort through, so she sticks to the simple part first.

"Hold on. You dropped out of high school?"

"I did."

"What happened?"

He chuckles without humor. "When I came out to my family, it didn't go too well. They kicked me out. I still tried to do school, and some counselors and teachers tried to help, but I gave up and decided to enlist. It sucked, and life was hard, but it has been the best decision for me. I finally became someone who can protect others, and I know I make a difference, if only a few people know about it." He fixes his gaze on his old friend. "Even if I could do nothing to protect someone important to me."

She squeezes his hand at his implied meaning.

"I'm sorry I could do nothing to protect you back then. I know your father is a piece of shit, but I didn't realize how much until I took this commission. Imagine my surprise when I transferred to my current job and found out about him. He's a slimy bastard. He covers his tracks well, but he fucked up in working with Auclair." A frown forms on his handsome face. "I thought about reaching out to you many times, but I've been too ashamed to."

"I'm sorry, Sammy." She finally musters a response, not knowing what else to say about what he's gone through.

"You have nothing to be sorry about." He reaches into his pocket and produces her cell phone. "I kept it charged for you."

She takes her phone, surprised to have it back. The plastic case with the cute cartoon cats is damaged, and her screen protector is cracked.

He chuckles. "I can't believe you still use the same passcode to unlock it."

"You would be the only one who knows it since it is our birthdays combined, stupid."

"I took the liberty of adding my contact info, if you're interested. Understand, there'll be times when I can't respond for a while. It could be months at a time, or longer." His tone lowers as some of his old insecurities come back. "You are the closest thing I ever had to a family. I left you when you needed me the most. I regret that every day. It's up to you if you want to stay in touch or not. But if you want to tell me to fuck off … I'll respect your decision."

She holds his face between her hands and brings her lips to his sweaty forehead.

"Sammy, don't be dumb." She pulls back, still holding his cheeks to make him look at her. "I expect you to visit when you can. We're staying in touch. You hear me?"

His shoulders visibly drop in relief, and he playfully pinches her nose. "Yeah."

Her attention darts to Ghoul when he comes back into view, which doesn't go unnoticed by Sammy.

"You can't keep your eyes off him," he comments.

"Yeah, I guess," she grumbles. But she doesn't want to talk about HIM, so she deflects. "I'll always be here for you, so no more hiding from me. Understand?"

Sam gives a breathy laugh. "I won't. I remember how scary you are when you're angry. I missed you so much."

He hugs her close to his chest, and she nearly crushes him from how tightly she hugs him back.

"Life got darker when you left. I lost my best friend," she tells him.

Seeing them sit with their heads together and arms wrapped around each other, Ghoul is overcome with a wave of possessiveness. He knows Levine's not into women, but he moves toward them now that the canisters have been neutralized.

Whoever set them up was an amateur and had no finesse. It took him less than five minutes to neutralize the threat. Thankfully, they were rigged to only flood the immediate area around Pennington with the gas, and not the whole warehouse. Still, they took precautions and sealed the canisters with a biohazard tent, while Ghoul and another from the unit went to work.

"I'm glad to have you back," Yasmine tells Sam as Ghoul walks up.

Levine and Yasmine reluctantly pull apart when Ghoul stands in front of them. His eyes are blazing at Levine.

"Levine, Colonel's looking for you," Ghoul states in his deep commanding tone. "Go report."

Levine hops up from the rusted metal box and squeezes her hand. "Duty calls. Don't let them take you until I get a chance to say goodbye."

They hold hands, with her tightly clasping his until the last moment when the distance pulls them apart.

Ghoul watches Levine's back until he disappears and then turns to see the fiery wrath on Yasmine's face directed solely at him. He's never had anyone startle him like she is now, and he knows what "they" mean by "if looks could kill."

"You used me." She raises her voice, drawing stares from people nearby. "You used me as bait!"

Her words cut right through him.

"I didn't agree with it." He keeps his tone even, but he doesn't like where this conversation is going one bit.

She narrows her gaze, scowls, and turns away, folding her arms across her chest. Before she did, she checked his nametag. Of course, it's his call sign, and not his name. That pisses her off more, and the fact he's the only one wearing a goddamn mask. Everyone else is wearing face paint.

"Following orders. I know," she grumbles under her breath. Then her raised voice draws more attention from those around them. They stop to watch the drama unfold. "Did you know I'd be bait when you were fucking me? Was that all part of your plan, Ghoul? Just use me for sex and then hand me over to that perverted scumbag?"

Her anger and disgust are palpable. He glares at those listening in on her accusations, and they quickly walk away, disappointed at not being able to enjoy the entertainment. He's moving to touch her face like he did at the cabin, but she flinches, and he pulls back.

"I wasn't going to hit you," he tells her, his voice softening.

Right, she just had Auclair touching her with his grubby hands without consent.

The bruise on her cheek stands out more prominently than he realized. He's sorry he wasn't the one to kill Auclair, and now she has more trauma to deal with because he failed. He kneels in front of her and takes his gloves off, revealing how bruised and split his knuckles are. He slowly brings the back of his fingers to her bruised cheek, giving her the chance to slap him away, but she doesn't this time. He leans in close, dropping his voice so only she can hear.

"Please don't misunderstand our time together. What we shared was not just sex to me." He moves in closer still, his other hand lightly resting on her knee. "What we had ... I've never had with anyone else. I don't know what to do or how to make this, whatever *this* is, between us work."

Her anger drops a notch at the sincerity in his words. His gentle caress over the mark on her face makes her relax involuntarily. Damn him! She can see the raw truth of emotion in his dark ambered eyes and the hurt he's holding back.

"The sad reality is that with the work I do, I can't put the stress and worry on you. Not being able to contact you for months or even years at a time. It's not fair to you to have you wait, not knowing if I was alive or dead. It's better if we go our separate ways." He's cupping the side of her face now, and his voice breaks from emotion. "I will always cherish the time we spent together. You gave me a taste of what life could be like. I'm grateful for that."

No words come to her. She knew there was no chance of a life with him, but hearing him voice her own thoughts makes the last of her heart shatter. She wants nothing more than to curl into a ball and cry herself to sleep. She has nothing left inside except hurt.

Ghoul clenches his fists when he gets to his feet. Then he takes a deep breath, sealing the part of himself that wants to stay with her behind a thick iron wall. He can't be distracted from his mission.

"You're going to be taking a military transport back to Virginia tonight. You can go back to your life and become the best teacher ever and help those kids. I won't forget my promise. I'm going to hunt your father down and rid your world of that man. It takes a monster to hunt a monster."

Sometime later, Ghoul ushers her to a waiting Suburban. Before she gets in, she makes sure to hug Sam, both agreeing once more they'll not lose contact again, with him promising to call her as soon as he can. He can't go with her; he's staying behind to debrief. Despite everything she's been through, having her friend back is something good to come from this messed-up situation.

She doesn't have nearly enough time to say goodbye, but at least she has a way to stay in touch with Sammy, unlike Ghoul. She doesn't understand why she has the desire to, but she's not going to bother asking for his number. He made things perfectly clear where they stand. He might feel something for her, but the job comes first.

She slips in and out of consciousness, her head resting awkwardly on the doorframe as she and the other passengers make their way to an airfield with the waiting military transport. She's trying to put physical distance between herself and Ghoul, who is sitting next to her.

Calvin and Hill are also in the Suburban with her, along with a tall lanky guy who is driving and two other guys in the back. She falls asleep to keep her betraying eyes from glaring at Ghoul, who she swears is inching closer into her space.

Chapter Forty
What Now?

At the airfield, Ghoul opens her door, waking her from her short slumber. She almost falls out of the Suburban, and would have if Ghoul wasn't there to catch her, like he always seems to do. It makes her mad that he's still taking care of her. She'd rather he turns into a dick like Hill; it would make this easier. But, no! He has to be considerate. The dickhead!

Casting a stink eye at him, she yawns before stepping onto the tarmac and following behind the men who are loaded down with their packs and equipment to the waiting Blackhawk. Its rotors start spinning, warming up while the men store their gear like they have done countless times. Calvin, Hill, and the other guys jump in first. Ghoul goes last and turns to offer her his hand.

She's about ready to collapse from the exhaustion wreaking havoc on her body, and she is one large walking bundle of soreness, so she begrudgingly accepts it and awkwardly climbs in with his help. The men take seats closest to the cockpit. Yasmine, on the other hand, takes the farthest seat away from them, toward the tail section.

She awkwardly straps herself in with the complicated belts and turns in the seat to put her back to them all, which is the best she can do to get some distance. She wants space so she can wallow in self-misery. She doesn't want to be near Ghoul, but at the same time, she wants his warmth she grew accustomed to. Wiping a stray tear from her cheek, Yasmine's not sure how she's going to piece herself back together after this.

So much has happened, and in a relatively short amount of time. Pain, pleasure, happiness, more pain. Yet, like her childhood, she somehow survived. She'll be home soon and will have to figure out how to repair not only her life but also herself. She's already decided to start therapy again. Maybe this time she can tell the therapist about the things her father did.

Ghoul decided to sit with the others to give her space, but he can't stop glancing in her direction. He should stay away, so he does what he's been doing for weeks: watch her like a silent sentinel.

His resolve to stay back goes out the window when she brushes tears away and pulls her legs up on the seat, hugging them for support. He can't let her suffer alone; she's been secluded too much in her life. They have a little more time. He can try to give her some solace, even if she hates him.

Most of the other men are fast asleep in their seats within minutes of the helicopter lifting off as it makes its way through the darkened sky toward Virginia. He unbuckles himself and moves to the back of the helicopter.

From the loud rotor humming loudly in her head, she doesn't hear him approach or when he slides into the seat next to her. His leg brushes against hers to get her attention, and it makes her jump. She visibly relaxes when she sees the familiar concerned eyes under the mask. She shifts nervously, not entirely sure how to act with him now. Of course, he's staying true to character and keeping the mask on. She doesn't care anymore to see what he looks like. It doesn't matter.

He opens up his arms, inviting her in and leaving her with the choice. His body heat draws her in, and she curls against his side, laying her head on his chest, not seeming to mind the smell of sweat and blood on him. His arms fold around her, and he rests his chin on her head. Her eyes close, and she manages to drift off to sleep.

Hill's piercing eyes stare at the two of them, and Ghoul meets him head-on in challenge. Hill nods in understanding then leans his head back, dozing off.

Ghoul has never particularly cared for friendships. It's easier, considering the death sentence constantly hanging over all their heads, but Hill somehow became a friend during this mission. He wonders how the hell that happened?

He holds her tighter and closes his eyes. Maybe it's all right to form some bonds. He always hides behind the physical and figurative mask he wears. He rarely shows anyone his true face and even prefers they use his nickname over his real name. Maybe it wouldn't be a bad thing to change?

She shivers in her sleep, and he adjusts to wrap more of his body around her. Taking a deep breath, he enjoys her scent, which is the last thing he'll have of her, before he drifts off to sleep.

The Blackhawk touches down in Norfolk, Virginia, and immediately she's ushered into a waiting Buick for Ghoul to drive her to the hospital. She doesn't dare say anything to him on the drive to the hospital but gazes at the early morning city lights out the side window. He's likewise quiet, not knowing what to say, even though they're finally alone.

"I'm sorry. I can't take you back to Blacksburg." He breaks the uncomfortable silence. "Do you have someone who can come get you?"

She keeps her gaze out the window. Everything is happening too quickly. Her stomach has been tied in knots after she awoke to Ghoul gently shaking her.

"I'll be able to find my way home." She's not really sure what home she has waiting for her.

She's not convinced she'll be safe from her father. Knowing him, he'd come and kidnap her next, forcing her into his criminal world. That would be in character for the asshole. Or maybe some other business associate will come knocking on her door to use her like Auclair did. She has too many worrying questions and no answers.

She notices the large blue H sign with an arrow, meaning her time with him has almost run out, and then she'll be on her own again.

"I was surprised Sammy enlisted with the Marines." She tries to make small talk. "He said you recruited him."

He nods. "When I was a Lieutenant, he served under me. I saw his potential, and it was wasted where he was serving. When I took this job, I put in a recommendation for him to transfer."

Ghoul is deliberately driving under the speed limit, prolonging the little time he has left with her. He catches her nodding out of the corner of his eye.

"Thank you for saving me," he says. "I didn't get a chance to tell you before. If you hadn't taken the shot, Auclair would have killed me. I was close to losing consciousness." He grips the steering wheel tighter, his knuckles turning white. "That was a damned good shot."

"I think the world is a better place with you in it. At least you are trying to protect the world from guys like Jean and my father." She runs her tongue around her mouth, trying to coat the inside since it just went dry.

"He was a scumbag." He takes her hand from her lap, squeezing it. "His blood should be mine to carry. He was my target, and if I had done my job, you never would have been placed in the position to pull the trigger."

He brings her fingers gently to his lips through the mask, wishing to feel her supple skin on him one last time.

She doesn't jerk away, even though her body wants to. Auclair touched her more than enough to last a lifetime. She turns away quickly, not wanting him to see her cry. She wonders if she'll ever be able to stop because this is starting to annoy her.

She makes a huffing sound of a humorless laugh.

"Thanks, but I'm the one who pulled the trigger. I'll figure out a way to live with it." Sammy's words from earlier come back to mind.

He takes the turn in the hospital parking lot, following the signs directing people to the emergency room. He pulls up to the curb, and they sit in silence for a few moments, both thinking of ways to stall for time, but there's no time left. This is it.

He clears his throat. "You'll have a security detail watching you around the clock for a while until the higher-ups deem there's no longer a threat to you. You won't even know they're there ... But it won't be me."

"Awesome. More stalkers," she quips, opening the door.

He grabs her wrist, holding her in place before she can swing the other leg out of the car.

"I'll find your father and make him pay for what he's done to you." He repeats his promise.

"How scary." She gives him a weak, tired smile. "I wish you luck on your hunt, Ghoul."

She pulls away, gets out, and closes the car door. Then she makes her way through the double sliding doors of the emergency room, not daring to look back.

The male receptionist's overnight shift ends in another forty-five minutes, and he's grateful for a relatively uneventful night. Only a few people have come in with minor injuries. It's always a blessing to not have a bad night working the ER.

Movement catches his attention through the Plexiglas partition separating him from the waiting room. He looks up from his computer monitor and gasps. Working in the ER, you see your fair share of disturbing things, but the woman standing before him leaves him shaken.

Her baby pink sweater is filthy and covered in blood. The one sleeve has been cut away, and she has a row of stitches on her arm. Her black slacks are dirty and in tatters. A bandage covers a wound on her brow line, a bruise runs across the left side of her cheek, and she has bruising on her neck. Her brown hair is matted, and her eyes are glazed over. But it's the haunted expression in those hazel eyes of hers and the blood that causes the receptionist's stomach to drop.

"I'm wondering if I could get some help?" she asks timidly.

She's hugging her arms tightly around her middle, trying to hold herself together. She can barely keep herself upright and is swaying on her feet like she's about to pass out.

Chapter Forty-One
"This One Has a Happy Ending."

"Thank you, Miss Pennington. If I have any further questions, I will be in touch." The detective closes his laptop and tucks it under his arm. He looks tired. "If anything further should arise, please reach out to me."

The detective is an older balding man with glasses. He pulls a card from the inside pocket of his cheap, worn suit and hands it to her, leaving without further words. With the kidnapping and her injuries, the hospital called the police as part of their standard procedure.

Alone now, she sets his card on the growing stack of them on the rolling cart next to her hospital bed. Lying her head back, she stares at the sterile ceiling, lost in thought. Her phone buzzes, breaking through the thoughts. The text is from her classmate Kelly who is informing her she's on her way to pick her up.

Yasmine lays her head back once more after texting her friend. She's tired of being poked and prodded. Even though she informed the hospital staff she wasn't raped, they insisted on doing a rape kit, but she was too tired to protest.

She's grateful for the kind nurses fussing over her and making sure she's comfortable. Her physical wounds aren't serious, but it's the unseen emotional and mental wounds she's left with that will take the longest to heal.

The meeting with the social worker and counselor who came in to evaluate her mental state was especially draining because they asked questions she found difficult to answer. What can she tell them? Everything she experienced? She's finding it hard to believe it really happened.

She wants to hide under the blanket and be left alone to cry in peace until she passes out from exhaustion. She's only been able to catch quick catnaps in between the constant parade of people in and out of her room.

Which she's doing when someone else knocks on the door. Blinking the sleep from her eyes, she focuses on the older man standing in the doorway. He wears a service uniform with general stars on his collar.

His neatly cut jet-black hair is greying at the temples and is combed perfectly. Even after he removes his cover and tucks it under his arm, no strands are out of place. Every line of his masculine face is sharp and commanding. He looks at Yasmine in sympathy.

"General Forrester," she cries out in surprise. He's much older than the last time she saw him.

"Hello Yasmine." Forrester steps into her room and flashes her a warm smile.

He pulls the only chair in the room to the edge of the bed and sits without an invitation.

She sees the second star added to his rank. "I see you have two stars now."

Her mood lifts slightly at seeing an old family friend. Unlike her father, Forrester always treated her kindly, and his kids were her friends when their fathers served together on base many years ago before her mother left. She still occasionally keeps in touch with his kids through social media.

"Two years ago, I got my appointment." His expression remains somber despite the uptick of a grin wanting to form at the corner of his mouth. "I wish we could be meeting under better circumstances."

He gestures at the doorway to a man she didn't even notice. He is standing there stiffly and is dressed like Forrester in his service uniform.

"This is Major Cayde."

The Marine has the insignia of Major on his collar. He closes the door to ensure the conversation remains private and then stands at ease with his back to it. He barely acknowledges her with a nod before his eyes stare forward.

Despite everything she's been through, Yasmine still admires how utterly handsome the man is in his service uniform with the green trousers and matching jacket, his ribbons, the khaki blouse and matching tie. He's wearing those military-type sunglasses too.

She gives him a once-over, noting the dent where a dimple forms if he smiles. There's a large purple bruise on his jaw, and his lip is scabbed over. If she was in a better state of mind, she would want to take a good look at him. Like many women, she drools over a man in uniform, and the heat is already rising to her cheeks, so that's all the attention she gives him before turning back to Forrester.

"I take it this visit is about my father?" She wants to get right to the point.

"I'm afraid so." A deep frown forms across his rugged features. "We have been aware of his possible business ventures and have been keeping an eye on him while we conducted an internal investigation. Would you tell me what transpired over the past week?"

She takes a deep breath, closing her eyes, and hopes this will be the last time she has to tell the story. Since this is Forrester, she shares more of what occurred with him than she did the police detective, only leaving out details about the personal things transpiring between her and Ghoul.

Forrester's eyes narrow once she finishes. He's been fully briefed and read the reports, but he's hoping she might have something else to give them, like an idea of how to track her father.

"Anything else? You were gone for a week."

She frowns at the man. What else can she tell him? She's broken? Devastated? That her heart's in tatters over a stupid masked Marine?

"What more do you need? My father's a traitor, and I'm terrified he's going to show up." She shakes her head at how bitter her words sound. "Is this a conversation or an interrogation? I'm a civilian after all.

If you want details, then you can get a copy of the police report because I don't know anything else."

Forrester sits up straighter, but his body language relaxes, and he covers her hand with his. "I'm sorry, Yasmine. I know this must be a lot for you to process and handle. I'm going to call Sarah. You can come stay with us for as long as you need to."

She shakes her head. "Thank you, but no. I have a friend on the way. She'll be here later today to take me back to Blacksburg. I need to see if there's a way I can salvage my semester so I can get on with my life."

Forrester nods and pats her hand. He pulls away and stands.

"I'm still going to have Sarah keep in touch with you. There aren't too many who you can talk to or who can help you through this. Please, stay in touch, for your sake. I want to make sure you're safe." He gives her a reassuring smile. "I took the liberty of contacting your university and explained the extenuating circumstances as to why you missed your finals. They assured me they'll work with you to make up the work you missed so it doesn't impact your graduation."

"Thank you," she whispers, blinking back her relief.

At least one of her worries is gone. Forrester might not be her father, but he stepped in to take care of the school for her like a loving father would.

He reaches into his pocket and retrieves a card, which he hands to her.

"If they give you any hassle, call me, and I will speak on your behalf." He smiles as he looks down at the hurt woman before him, but then his tone becomes serious. "If your father should contact you, or if you hear anything about his whereabouts, please contact me immediately. My personal number's on the back. Call me any hour, day or night. Even if all you need is to talk."

He pats her foot under the blanket. "Find yourself a good therapist to help you work through this."

She nods, not knowing what else to say. She adds his card to the stack.

Just as he's about to reach the door, she calls out. "General. There is one thing I overheard Jean mention."

Forrester pauses, and Major Cayde stares at her in expectation.

"Jean was complaining about my father moving in on his territory and trying to push him out and take over, but take over what wasn't clear. And, well, he mentioned he thought my father was trying to create his own empire and bring certain criminal organizations under his control." She frowns at her wringing hands. "Knowing him, he's probably going to set himself up as the king of the criminal underworld. That'd be in line with his character."

"Thank you, dear. I'll be sure to pass this on to the correct people. Get some rest." Forrester gives her foot another pat under the thin hospital blanket.

She's once more staring at her hands and doesn't catch the knowing look Forrester shoots at the Major.

Cayde opens the door for Forrester and steps aside to allow the General to pass. Instead of following him out of the room, Cayde takes a step closer to the bed. He pulls his jacket from his chest, reaches in, takes a book out from the inside pocket, and drops it on the bed.

"A friend asked me to give this to you." His voice is familiar, but at the same time, not.

She glances at the book cover, recognizing it. Ghoul was reading it at the cabin. Her head snaps up to examine Cayde's features more closely, but he's already gone.

She cracks open the worn and dog-eared book. On the first page, instead of finding the book's publication information, there are six words hastily penned in chicken scratch.

THIS ONE HAS A HAPPY ENDING.

She crushes the book to her chest, clutching it tightly as the waves of sobs overtake her.

Major Cayde, aka Ghoul, holds the Buick door open for General Forrester. Once the General settles himself in the back seat, Cayde closes the door and then moves to the driver's seat. As the two speed down the interstate back to base, Forrester breaks the silence.

"I never would have expected Yasmine to be the one to get through that cold exterior of yours. Or she'd be the reason why one of my top operatives wants out."

"I may want out, sir, but I'll finish the mission. I have unfinished business with her father," Cayde responds, keeping his eyes on the road.

"You could have told her who you were," Forrester comments.

"I know, but with all due respect, it's better she goes on with life for now instead of waiting for me. And it's better if she doesn't have a face to remember." He keeps his tone even. "You know this isn't a safe job, and she's already been through enough."

"I respect that. What happens if she meets someone before you get out and you lose her?" He's being an old busybody at this point.

Ghoul shrugs. "Then I will wish her happiness."

Chapter Forty-Two
Always A Brat

MAY

"Yasmine Pennington, Master's in Education with a focus in special education." The dean of students calls her name.

She walks across the stage with a simple smile on her face and collects the maroon diploma cover before shaking hands with the line of people. Her classmates create a low buzz compared to the shouts of their family members when they walk across the stage. But there's a high-pitched whistle from someone in the back of the auditorium that stands out above everything. The whistle causes her to pause briefly, making the person behind her bump into her. No one's here for her, so who the hell is whistling?

With her diploma cover in hand, the handshakes, and the pictures flashing, everything happens in a blur, leaving her dazed. She follows the person in front back to their seats.

Even though she has no family or friends in the audience, other than her classmates, she still smiles widely. It had taken her longer to graduate than the regular college student because there were times she couldn't take classes full time, and not to mention, she was kidnapped and then had to deal with the aftermath. Through all the trials and hardships, she did it — she finally graduated.

The past five months have been the hardest. She had to deal with the trauma from the kidnapping, and the heartache. But she's still alive, and she awoke that morning to a text from Sam.

> Sammy: Congrats Yazzie. I wish I could be there to see you walk. I'm so proud of you. I have a gift for you, but I won't be able to send it for a bit. Imagine the loudest shouting, and that's me cheering you when you walk the stage. I want pictures.

Her world got brighter since reconnecting with him, even if their contact is sporadic. He rarely reveals much about his current location or what he's doing. All she knows is he's hunting down her father along with Ghoul. She decided when she returned to her normal life she wouldn't bring up Ghoul to Sammy unless he does first. She'd rather avoid the awkwardness and leave her friend out of it.

Once she returned to Blacksburg, she found herself a therapist who specializes in severe trauma. She started with therapy twice a week, then went down to once a week as she started regaining more of herself and processing the events of her kidnapping. Now she's down to twice a month.

Unlike her previous sessions with a therapist, this time she holds nothing back. She told the therapist everything about what happened to her, from her kidnapping to her father to her mother leaving. She is determined to not be held prisoner any longer.

She still wakes up at night sometimes, drenched in sweat from the nightmare of the warehouse playing out. What helps to calm her mind is to go back to a different cabin than the one she built in her mind to escape her father's "unpleasantness." Now she prefers to revisit THAT cabin, where she made a connection with someone who understood her — even if he left.

When she finally got around to Ghoul with her therapist, the focus of her therapy shifted to treating her for Stockholm syndrome and sexual abuse. She tried to explain there was a connection beyond Stockholm syndrome with him and it was consensual.

The therapist didn't listen, and instead dismissed the connection she felt during their time together, saying she thought of him as her savior. The explanation didn't sit well with Yasmine. Her feelings for him, while fucked up — they certainly didn't develop in a healthy way — are still valid, even if the therapist disagrees. There was something there between them, even if he's made no effort to reach out to her.

The more time she's had to work through what happened, the more she realizes he must have felt a connection too. She thinks of him often, wondering where he is, if he's with Sam, or if they have tracked down her father yet? Not knowing is the hardest part.

Her father's estate and assets were seized, but thanks to Forrester pulling some strings, he made sure she could access her college fund. He and his wife stayed in touch with her and even sent a graduation gift. They're probably going to give her an earful for not telling them about the ceremony, but she couldn't handle having to pretend to smile and be happy. Mrs. Forrester comes to visit Yasmine occasionally to check on her and bring her groceries. It's the closest thing Yasmine has ever experienced to a mother since hers disappeared.

Going through the motions, Yasmine follows along with her classmates and moves the tassel to the other side of her cap before zoning out again to her thoughts.

In two days, the movers will pick up her things, and she'll be driving herself across the country to start her job and new life in Flagstaff. She opted to take a job as far away from her old life as possible, even though there were no special ed positions open at the school. She needed to get away from the East Coast and wanted a smaller town.

Yasmine follows the procession out of the auditorium. Her new life is beginning. With everything she's survived, she's confident she can handle anything.

A handsome man with a dirty blond military buzz cut is leaning against the back wall with his hands in his pockets and his ankles crossed.

Several of the women passing by, even some of the married ones, check him out. Some even smile at him, which he acknowledges with a respectful nod. The women's eyes linger on him; they blush before hurrying off. He pays no attention to any of them. He's there for one purpose, and for one person, and he's still weighing his decision on whether or not to make his presence known. A quirk plays at the corner of his mouth when he thinks about what she would say. She'd definitely call him a stalker.

After Pennington escaped from the warehouse in New York, they only received sporadic updates on his location. In the four months Ghoul spent in the jungles of Indonesia, not only did they shut down a major supply chain for selling U.S. weaponry, but they also luckily discovered the location of an arms dealer bazaar. It doesn't fix the issue of U.S. weapons being sold illegally, but it helps to slow it down, and in the process, they shut down several other illegal operations.

His team received intel that Pennington has ties in the Middle East, and they are in hot pursuit, but he was granted permission to detour back through the States to attend Yasmine's ceremony before meeting up with Scythe Company.

Having Levine in touch with her is a blessing and a curse. Levine shares with him little tidbits about her, her messages, or the random selfies she sends. Levine showed him the selfie she sent him in the beginning of January, a few weeks after her kidnapping. It was a picture of herself sporting a pixie cut.

He quickly read the message tied to the picture.

> I can't deal with long hair and everything else right now, so off with it.

He loved her long hair, but she's still beautiful with it short. What really drew his attention was the haunted look in her eyes.

Ghoul stares at the picture of her on his phone daily. Levine sent it to him without asking, but he's not going to delete it. Whether he accepts it or not, he and Levine are getting closer on a personal level. Levine calls him a friend, but he's still in denial.

The final closing remarks of the ceremony bring his attention back to the present. He fingers the small gift box in his pocket.

He's going to introduce himself to her properly but doesn't really know how he should go about it. How do you officially introduce yourself to someone who bared her soul and body to you but never saw your face?

Hi Yasmine. I'm Ghoul. We fucked at my cabin.

Everything he thinks of to say sounds lame. She's going to laugh and have some smart-ass comeback. He knows it.

The graduates are led out of the arena, and the families are filing out of the stands to greet their loved ones. Apprehension is suddenly washing over him.

He can face the vilest of humans on the planet without losing his nerve. But this woman? This brave, sarcastic woman strikes fear into his very core. Will she recognize him? Did she figure out he was the one in the hospital with Forrester? He might be confident on the battlefield, but this coming encounter leaves him anxious.

He falls in line once most of the attendees file out of the auditorium. His new mission is to find her in the crowd.

Her priority, once free of the procession line of graduates, is to get water and unzip her graduation robe. Sweat has been dripping down her back since before the ceremony started. After that she's going to meet her fellow graduates for pictures in the atrium before going straight home. She's over the large crowds.

Downing the last of the water she got from the vending machine, she spots Kelly and her family walking to the front where the other classmates are gathering. Tossing the plastic bottle into the recycling bin, she hurries to her classmates to take their group picture before they go their separate ways and start their new lives.

Ghoul spots her standing alone in the corner drinking from a water bottle. Her eyes are roving around, taking in the scene of families together. He sees the pain and sadness in those eyes ... the loneliness.

When she throws the empty bottle into the trash, it's his cue to start walking toward her. He'll stop her, hand her the box, hug her, tell her congratulations, and then he'll leave. Easy.

She weaves her way through the crowd, sometimes stopping to wait for others to pass by. Now, with the crowd naturally thinning, they're walking toward each other.

His heart races like he just ran up the mountain fully loaded with gear from his bootcamp days. The closer he gets to her, the more he wants to take her and run.

When they are mere paces from each other, he realizes how dangerous this is. He can't tell her who he is. If she knows it's him, and she gives him any indication she still has any kind of feelings for him, he'll end up kidnapping her again and go AWOL. He wants more days with her at the cabin where they read together, she makes up crazy shit about him, and they have all the time in the world to make love. He can't do that, not right now when the lead they have on her father's whereabouts is solid.

A chance encounter, a brief touch — he can do that. He pulls the small decorative box from his pocket and has it ready in his hand. Quickly scanning her clothing, he identifies the pocket he'll slip the box into. It's a good thing she hasn't put her robe back on yet, and it remains draped over her arm.

He shifts quickly at the last second, shoulder checking her and making her lose her balance. He grabs her arm, spinning them to transfer the momentum so she doesn't fall. The moment he spins her, he slips the box into her pocket.

"Apologies, ma'am." He steadies her, relishing in his lingering touch on her skin.

He glances at her lips, remembering how they felt on his and how their bodies joined together perfectly. He breathes out his growing desire from finally being in her presence after five months. He averts his gaze quickly.

"I'm so sorry," she stutters in a daze, looking up at the man she ran into. Her eyes land on the large and jagged scar across his ear and part of his face.

When they collided, she instinctively reached out and grabbed his arm to keep herself on her feet instead of falling on her ass. Now she awkwardly removes her hands from the stranger once she finds her balance.

Her gaze locks on the man's face. Her stomach does the lurching *thing* at seeing how handsome he is with the light reflecting off his dirty blond hair; it leaves streaks of golden highlights. He's wearing khaki slacks with a black button-up shirt. But it's the way he's staring at her, like she's the only woman alive on the planet, that sends heat pooling into her core. His expression conveys insatiable desire, which makes her heart race. She blushes and looks down at her feet.

His hands drop to his sides and then go into his pockets. He has a crooked grin; he knows the thoughts behind the blush.

They stand in the middle of the crowd. The loud chatter of people is all around them, but to them, they are the only two people in the world. Her head tilts to the side once she looks up again, her brain sending signals of familiarity.

"Have we met?" Her brows furrow in question.

He pulls his hand from his pocket and starts moving to brush her cheek with the back of his fingers. He can't control himself, not with her. He has to touch her.

"Yasmine. Come on!" Kelly yells from somewhere behind her.

She hears Kelly's call, but she can't take her eyes off the man in front of her.

"Your friends are waiting." He nods, his eyes motioning behind her.

He's thankful to her friend for calling her because it broke through his thoughts and made him pull back his hand before he touched her. If he touched her, he'd be pressing his lips to hers.

She turns around quickly at the waist. "Just give me a second."

Turning back to try and place the man who ran into her, she finds he's gone. Like he was never even there. She searches the crowd, craning her neck on tippy-toes, but there's no sign of him anywhere.

"Yasmine!" Kelly yells again.

Yasmine purses her lips together. Turning, she joins her classmates for the pictures.

She returns to her mostly packed studio apartment. Except for a few stacked boxes, her bed, and sparse furniture consisting of a bean bag chair and bookshelves, she doesn't have much for the movers. All her important personal effects are already safely packed and ready to leave with her when she makes the drive to her new life.

Politely bowing out of dinner with Kelly and her family, she stopped on her way home to get takeout from her favorite Greek restaurant to treat herself. She's trying to be mindful and eat because it gives her something else to focus on. She is still a work in progress, but she is eating better and is slowly gaining weight.

Yasmine throws her graduation robe on the bed and starts undressing. She needs a shower and to get into her baggy pajamas. She hears a soft thud when her pants hit the floor.

She checks the pockets, and her fingertips brush over something. She pulls out a thin gold decorative gift box and shakes it. Something rattles inside.

"Where did you come from?"

Yasmine takes the lid off and pulls out a simple white gold chain bracelet. She holds it up to the light, focusing on the charm. Her other hand comes from behind to steady it.

The charm is a simple block letter design in white gold with an accent diamond spelling "BRAT."

Her mouth hangs open in shock. Her mind reels.

"How?" The guy who ran into her with the scar? "No. It couldn't have been? Could it?"

She quickly retraces her steps throughout the day, and there are no other encounters where someone could have slipped the thin box into her pocket.

She thinks back to the man, trying to pull the image of his face. All she can remember is how hard it was to make eye contact with him because of how handsome he was. She flings her back onto the bed and holds the bracelet above her, staring at it.

She sets the bracelet on her chest and then grasps her head. She forces herself to take deep breaths. She's become an expert in breathwork since she went back to therapy, and her therapist makes her start each session with it.

"What did he look like?"

Her fist is lightly pounding her forehead as she tries to jostle the image free. She remembers dirty blonde hair with golden streaks and a vague sense of familiarity. The only thing she clearly remembers about him is the scar. That's it. Nothing else.

No matter how hard she tries, all that comes to her are the feelings she had when they stood staring at each other. Giving up on recalling his appearance, she smiles and holds the bracelet above her again.

"He was there."

Emotion floods around her heart, threatening to drown her. She wasn't alone.

"That was probably him who whistled." She rolls to her side.

She never thought she would see him again. The expectation was he'd go back to his life, writing her down in his book as a brief hookup, and forget about her. It's been over five months, and yet, he came to her graduation.

Why didn't he tell her it was him?

"Stupid stalker!"

She lets out one of those laughing cries because she's pissed and happy at the same time.

Sam. Will he tell her anything if she asks?

She uses her pants to wipe her tears and snot away. Frantically searching for her phone, and not remembering where she set it, she finds it after several minutes. It's right where she threw it, on her bed under her robe and clothing. She unlocks the screen, pulls up Sam's messages, and quickly types.

> I think Ghoul came to my commencement today. I found this in my pocket.

She hits send and then takes a picture of the bracelet. She attaches the photo to her next message.

> He's the only one to ever call me "brat."

With nothing else to do but wait, she leaves her phone on the bed with the bracelet next to it.

Showering quickly because she still does it out of habit from her childhood, Yasmine puts on her baggy pajamas after securing the bracelet to her wrist. A tiny smile plays at the corners of her mouth. She can't stop staring at it. She might not remember what he looks like, but it was him.

She pulls open her nightstand drawer in a hurry. The book Ghoul gave her, which the Marine delivered at the hospital, rests on top of the stack of books she needs to read. School, therapy, and healing have kept her too busy and exhausted to read.

She pulls out the worn, tattered, and dog-eared book. She opens the cover and reads his short message to her for the second time since she got it. Her face softens.

THIS ONE HAS A HAPPY ENDING.

Closing the drawer, she throws the book on her oversized bean bag chair. Once settled with her dinner and a blanket over her legs, she cracks open the book.

She wants to see if this military thriller does, in fact, have a happy ending.

Follow Me on Social Media

Facebook Page: Mavis Kemo - Author
Instagram: @maviskemoauthor
Threads: @maviskemoauthor
Tiktok: @mavis.kemoauthor
Tome: maviskemoauthor
Youtube: @maviskemo777
Or sign up for my Newsletter on my website

Acknowledgments

It takes a community….

And without the help, love, and support of a community of family, friends, and fellow authors, this book would still be inside my head.

The inspiration for this story sparked one night when Kemo was being bullied by ten-year-olds in Call of Duty. When his match was done, I said… "Ghost's hot. I wonder what a romance would look like for him?" That turned into an entire evening of brainstorming.

The first scene I wrote was the snowball fight – but I realized this story started stewing in my mind long before that night. It really started when 15-year-old me finally got the alternative ending in Metal Gear Solid on the PS1 with Snake and Meryl riding off on a snowmobile. Apparently, my younger self decided this was a romance between Snake and me, heading to his cabin, – (Information Redacted) – and from there, the story of Ghoul and Yasmine was born.

The first person I need to acknowledge is Kemo. You've been here every step of the way — from the moment the idea sparked to the last line of the story — holding me while I cried. You were by my side through the tears, the frustration, the writer's block, the IMPOSTER SYNDROME, the random growls, and the countless other stories I tried to outline (while you shook your head at me saying I need to focus on one.) I can't forget the endless exhaustion either.

To Kemo, my friend and love: this book wouldn't be here without you. You made sure I ate and drank water when I got lost in the story. You pulled me away when I needed a break. I hope I've done this story justice — and that when you read it all the way through, you'll recognize the moments between Ghoul and Yasmine that are inspired from our love story. Our love is the heart of this story.

My dearest baby girl and sister, Kat: You graciously put up with, and listened to, all my chaotic brain dumps, soapboxes, and wild rantings. During my meltdown moments through the revisions and editing process, you were always there — talking me down, reading random parts of the story, completely lost and not knowing a thing that was going on. You were there, telling me you see where I was trying to go with it, and telling me to go with my feelings in telling this story. Hopefully now, all the random pieces make sense.

My dearest sister Diana: I never thought running into you on some random comment section on TikTok would have led us to develop such an amazing relationship. I'm so proud to call you my friend and sister. I'm honored, and it is such a privilege to have your artwork in my book! All your help, support, and guidance helped me realize my childhood dream. My book is published! Now I'm excited, and look forward to seeing what we'll create together.

To my alpha/beta reader and friend Raven: You came into my life at the exact moment that I needed you, and it feels like we've been friends for years. Your help across both books has been invaluable. Seeing your excitement over Ghoul, and how much you've been wanting to cosplay him... I hope you realize how your excitement pushed me to keep going when I wanted to give up. On the hardest days, when I wanted to delete the whole book, the one thought keeping me going was, "I have to finish this because Raven needs to see this polished, and not the crap I sent him." I get why Ghoul didn't beat out your top #10 book boyfriend... but him being #9, beating out Zade, no one will be able to take that place in my heart when you gave the first compliment on this story. You are my first fan and the first to threaten me with bodily harm if something happens to "Baby" because he must be protected! I'm grateful to call you my friend and chosen family. You're stuck with me now, like a facehugger!

Adia, girl: You've been here from beginning to end. The best part was seeing your expressions and reactions when I dropped little scenes to you. But the best reaction was when I told you how they reconnect in the book, and you nearly fell out of your chair! I'm so proud to have the chance to see you become an amazing human.

"Just one more."

"I promise... this is the last one."

"This is it guys, oh wait, this is the last one... I promise."

YOU KNOW!

To my friends and beta readers.

Jayme, you made me cry in front of children. But I'm happy the spicy scenes met with your approval because I was worried about that! Your friendship and guidance along my journey to this "author thing" means the world, and you're always there ready to talk me down when I need it, or there to tell me to keep going. You saw me on the good and bad days. You are the stable rock in my life that I know I can depend on.

Oh, Stephanie, where do I even begin? I guess it's going to be with the lessons in stranger danger that clearly did not work on Yasmine! Your suggestions added Easter Eggs for me, sprinkled throughout the story. I'm not sure if I'll ever be able to look at you when we pass in the halls, and you give me "that look."

Ashley, the snowball fight is one of my favorite scenes, and the first one I wrote, and when you told me how much you loved it, and you wished it was a little longer ... yeah, me too! I took your feedback to heart and made it longer. I appreciate you pointing out what needed work to make the story flow better. I loved seeing your reactions, and your comments in real time.

Ellie, I'm still mad at you! I think I will be until I get book two, I'm just saying! I'm not sure where to start. You've been here the whole way with this publishing thing, helping me.... All of it. The times that you patiently explained things to me because my brain was not working. You took a lot of the stress off my shoulders because you'd always say, "I got you." Through ALL my freakout meltdowns, you had my back. I don't know where I'd be without you at this point.

Sgt J.D. "Psycho" Garner. I'm honored to have met you. All the

Marine stories you shared — some of them made me cry, some made me laugh, and others left me terrified. You gave me a glimpse into the mind of a real Marine. My favorite story is the desert Yeti, and I'm never going to look at crayons the same way again. You have been so patient with all my questions and sending you random bits of scenes to make sure I'm portraying the Marine Corp correctly. I've enjoyed learning about you, your time serving, and the Marine Corp. I look forward to hearing more of your stories, because you know I'm a whore for them!

Cynical, girl... you're just awesome! I don't know what else to say. I'm glad we got to meet and have become friends. You've been here, patiently waiting for this book, and that is terrifying. No pressure at all here, nope, none at all. I hope the story didn't disappoint you, and you enjoyed it.

LazyHunnyBee, not only did you take my cover art and make it into an amazing book cover, but you've taken the time to teach me about the industry. You've answered my questions and explained things. You were the one to finally point out what was wrong with the first chapter and why I felt something was off, but I couldn't see it. You point blank told me what was wrong with it without mincing words. I respect you for that. I appreciate you, and I'm honored to be able to call you, my friend. Thank you, isn't enough!

Torrie, you made me cry — A LOT! In my mind, I envisioned you with devil horns tearing my book to shreds like a fiend. You made me bang my head against the wall with your feedback a few times. You taught me so much, and you made me become a better writer. You held nothing back with pointing out my weaknesses. I took them all to heart to make the story better. You saw this at its worst, and I hope when you read it, you can see how your brutal honesty made me want to do better. You might not be in the classroom anymore, but you're still a teacher at heart because you taught me to look at my own work objectively through the eyes of an editor.

Karlee, you took all my hard work in crafting this story and polished it into something I'm immensely proud to show the world. You are a joy to work with, and you took so much of the stress off my shoulders with this last push in getting this book ready to publish. I look forward to working with you again when it comes to the second book.

To everyone who has touched this book before publication, (the early arc readers, the ones who helped with the TW page, those who answered my questions, who looked at the first chapter to make sure I could hook readers, content creators on social media who I bugged asking for your opinions), there are too many of you to list individually, but your support helped me realize my dream. I'm now a published author. I don't say this just to be dramatic, but if it wasn't for your help, feedback, suggestions, critiques, and everything else in between, this book wouldn't be what it is.

To the Indie Author Revolution (IAR) discord group. I'm grateful to have been invited to join the group. The moment I joined, I knew it was a game changer. I was no longer floundering, alone, trying to figure out how to do this whole Indie author thing. It took me a hot minute to get myself grounded, but to the members of the IAR who have helped me with realizing my dream, y'all are equally important in getting this book in print. Who would have thought the ISBNs would nearly be my downfall, when it really is so simple, but my mind made it more complicated than it needed to me! IAR for the win!

Lastly, to the readers who gave this new indie author a chance and read my story. I don't care whether you loved it or hated it, I'm grateful you took the time to read it.

Mavis Kemo

I write gut wrenching, genre-bending stories with grit, heart, and enough heat to fog up your reading glasses. My debut novel is a dark military romance (yes, all of that) because who says I must stay in my genre lane?
I struggled to read as a child, and now I devour books like they're my favorite snacks. Romance with plot is my preference, but I will read anything if the story hooks me.
I try to live a quiet, cozy life with my husband, who is my brainstorming, plot-twisting, co-conspirator, and the reason several characters and spicy scenes exist. When we're not building fictional worlds together: we're either gaming, talking about everything and nothing, or being bossed around by our one dog and four cats.
This is the beginning of my writing journey, and I'm thrilled to have you along for the ride. Make sure to buckle up!